M000208029

Two nightmarish creatures exploded through the trees—demons with sharp black bodies and heads like shrieking skulls. They caught Kotaru's scent and screamed in hunger for their prey.

Kotaru fled through the woods, fronds ripping at his wings. He dived through a gully and plunged into a dripping world of ferns.

The demons lost sight of their victim and clattered to a halt. Mad eyes stared down into the green.

Kotaru flattened himself against a tree and prayed as he had never prayed before. He slipped down into the ferns and tried to glide for deeper cover.

They sensed the flaring of his aura. With a demented scream of fury, the demons were on his trail. . . .

Other Vision Books

Blood Memories
Barb Hendee
ISBN 1-887038-06-X

Sweet Treats
(A Dessert Cookbook)
Margaret Carspecken
ISBN 1-887038-02-7

The American Journal of Anthropomorphics
A Collection of Artists' Works
ISBN 1-887038-01-9

Coming Soon...

TALES OF THE MORNMIST
A New Shared-World Series
By Co-Creators
LYNN ABBEY & ED GREENWOOD

Book One
The Rats of Acomar
Paul Kidd
ISBN 1-887038-05-1

Book Two
Flying Colors
Jeff Grubb
ISBN 1-887038-08-6

Book Three
Those Who Hunt
Elaine Cunningham
ISBN 1-887038-07-8

Book Four
Unicorn's Gate
Mary Herbert
ISBN 1-887038-09-4

The Front and Back Cover Illustrations of this Book are available as
large, framed Prints! Contact the Publisher at the address on Page "iv" for a
Free Catalog of all of Vision's exciting products!

A Whisper of Wings

Paul Kidd

PROPERTY OF:
ANAHEIM PUBLIC LIBRARY
500 WEST BROADWAY
ANAHEIM, CALIFORNIA 92805

DISCARD

CENTRAL

A WHISPER OF WINGS
BOOK ONE OF THE KASHRAN CYCLE
Copyright © 2000 Paul Kidd

All characters in this book are fictitious. Any resemblance whatsoever to actual persons, living or dead, is purely coincidental.

This book is protected under the copyright laws of the United States of America. Any reproduction or other unauthorized use of the material or artwork contained herein or upon is prohibited without the express written permission of the publisher.

INGRAM and its affiliate companies have worldwide distribution rights in the adult book trade for English language products of Vision Novels. [Distributed to the book and hobby trade in the United Kingdom by INGRAM.] Distributed to the toy, comic and hobby trade by regional distributors.

Interior & Cover Illustrations by Terrie Smith.
Rear Cover Digitally Painted by Dawn Varner.

The VISION NOVELS logo is a trademark owned by Vision Novels, a division of Med Systems / Vision Entertainment, Ltd.

First Printing: October, 2000
Printed La Vergne, TN, in the United States of America.
Library of Congress Catalog Card Number: 99-65676

9   8   7   6   5   4   3   2   1

ISBN: 1-887038-04-3

Edited by J. Robert King

Vision Novels
Is an Imprint of

Med Systems / Vision Entertainment, Ltd.
Post Office Box No. 580009
Flushing, New York 11358-0009

PROPERTY OF
ANAHEIM PUBLIC LIBRARY
500 WEST BROADWAY
ANAHEIM, CALIFORNIA 92805

CENTRAL

**For Christine, who stood beside me as we first beheld
Shadarii-Zha.**

DISCARD

One

Deep within the sighing forest, high up in the cold air of the mountains, there lay a world of ancient, eerie beauty. It was a world of hushed, still shade and velvet light; a world of towering trees. Earth and forest, Wind and Rain were bound forever in their calm, unhurried harmony.

The forest blanketed the world in darkness. It was a place of sharp, clear water; of endless cool and soothing wet. Trunks of regal eucalyptus soared to the lofty canopy, and beneath them, lush tree ferns spread their fronds above the mold. Lorikeets drifted bright as flame, and bellbirds made the hollows echo with pure, clean peals of sound. In dark places, platypi crept into streams and echidnas snuffled long noses through fallen leaves.

Something soft and beautiful slid silently above the ferns, slowly banking through the mists beside a waterfall. Fur rippled as a supple figure sank down beside the stream, and the young Kashran female peered about herself in awe. Her wings— huge orange butterfly wings that sang and flashed with color—folded smoothly at her back. The girl sighed in wonder, lost in the hypnotic beauty of the trees.

Framed against the ferns, the Kashran girl had a strange, foxlike figure—round and full of body, with heavy breasts and solid hips. Tall, pointed ears framed a fox's face, and green eyes shone as she turned her muzzle toward the delicious scents of trees and mist.

The girl wore a simple skirt and halter made from tanned autumn leaves. Shadarii's fur glowed like orange flame in the subtle forest light, and a long, bushy tail waved gracefully behind her. Curling red hair spilled down Shadarii's shoulders like a rush of liquid fire, and delicate antennae quivered at her brow.

Shadarii drew closer to the waterfall, savoring the delicious kiss of mist across her fur. Her face craned toward the swirling trees, and she reached out to touch the presence in their depths, the life that lay behind the shadows. Her antennae shivered to the caress of unseen winds.

All about her, Shadarii sensed ïsha[1], the underlying soul that shaped the world. She merged into the flow. It radiated from the trees and from the water; it shone like brilliant jewels where the birds sang their songs. Shadarii sank into the currents and felt her spirit drink and heal.

She spread out her hands in joy as something vast and powerful stirred behind the falls. An ancient awareness slowly surfaced from the deeps, swelling out to surge

---

[1]**ïsha:** The background aura or magical field generated by **Ka** (spirits). Kashran antennae sense the subtle *ïsha* flow around them, interpreting the changing character of the fields. *ïsha* perception shall be rendered as seeing "colors" or reading "tastes," although the actual sensations are radically different. The Kashran sensitivity to *ïsha* is one of their most delicate, discriminating senses.

toward the enraptured Kashran[2] girl. The Ka spirit rose forth to caress her with its ghostly touch, filling Shadarii's mind with the precious gift of peace.

She was welcomed, treasured, and the cool peace of the waterfall opened out to enfold her. Held safe from prying eyes, Shadarii lost herself in her own private world. The sun was warm, the water sweet, and loneliness could sometimes be a soothing thing.

Shadarii let her garments drop and stood gloriously naked in the morning sun, poised upon the water's edge with a dancer's easy grace. She sprang out across the water, her wings flipping wide to swoop her though a lazy, twirling dive. There was a flash of fur, a splash of light. Plant souls streamed down to dance gleefully in Shadarii's wake as the unseen beings of the forest rejoiced around their gentle Kashran friend.

Shadarii: The silent one.

The girl who had no voice.

03 &0 80

Far off in the forest, a wallaby sat cropping sweet new grass. It was a neat, bright little creature with a handsome black-striped snout. The wallaby sat back on its great hind feet and scratched its fur, long ears twitching to a fly's persistent buzz—the only irritation marring a perfect springtime day.

Twelve spans away, a deadly shape lay silent beneath the ferns; a shape as cruelly beautiful as a polished blade. Black fur shone like liquid night, sending icy highlights rippling as the watcher stole toward its prey.

The girl's slim body was an instrument of taut perfection. Streaming hair of purest black spilled down her spine, half shading a sharp, thin face set with a pair of cruel blue eyes.

She lay in utter silence, her long spear firmly nestled in its woomera[3] as she watched her victim graze.

Something dark and wicked quivered in her spear. The Ka of a tiger had flowed into the weapon one dark night, and now the spirit chittered as it sensed the blood of living prey.

The wallaby peered in suspicion at a distant patch of shrub. The creature began to sink back down to graze, paused, and stood once more—

The huntress threw, and her spear flashed, jamming through the target's squealing flesh. The wallaby hurtled back its head, coughing in surprise as a second spear transfixed its chest. The beast fell kicking on its side, writhing out its life in agony across the forest floor.

"No!"

The huntress sprang to her feet, snatching her spears. She launched herself out across the clearing to crouch above the jerking corpse.

---

[2]**Kashra(n)::** Contracted from the words *Ka-shis Shatra Ramuuh*—'Children of the Wind and Rain."

[3]**Woomera:** A spear thrower. A length of hardwood held in the spear hand to increase the effective length of the thrower's arm.

"How dare you! This is my kill! Mine!" Her voice rang clear and magnificent in her fury. The girl's wings flashed iridescent blue as she posed defiantly across her prey. "Come out! Show yourself! Who's the fool who thinks he can steal from Zhukora?"

Something languidly stirred high in the trees. A huge, arrogantly handsome male emerged, sank to the ground, and gazed with bored, insolent eyes at the angry huntress. Zhukora's ears flattened as she recognized her foe; blue eyes glittering in her unforgiving face.

Zhukora wore her hunting clothes with rakish style. To the Katakanii tribe, elegant simplicity was the highest form of art. Zhukora's halter bared her throwing arm. Long leggings and supple moccasins clung lovingly to her legs. Great butterfly wings framed her body—jet black and splayed with patterns of magnificent royal blue. She was slender as a coiling snake, and fully twice as deadly.

By contrast, the intruder looked merely indolent and bored. Vast, corded muscles were sheathed in a coat of thick red fur. His face was cultured and refined, dominated by a pair of insolent brown eyes. Like Zhukora, he was from clan Swallowtail, his wings flaring out into florid, trailing fins.

Zhukora finally broke the silence. The girl's voice dripped with the venom of absolute dislike.

"Go away, Prakucha-Zho. My spear struck first; the kill is mine."

Prakucha was a noble[4] like herself, and so Zhukora addressed the intruder with his formal title. She fixed her glorious eyes upon him and speared him with her scorn.

Her enemy felt her power and gave a cool, delighted smile.

"Oh, Zhukora-Ki! Always so full of fight. Must you be so absurd? Anyone can see that the kill belongs to me."

Prakucha used the 'Ki' endearment reserved for little children. Zhukora remained utterly unmoved. Long hair spilled down across one eye, shading the dangerous glint of female fury.

"I say my spear took the beast."

Prakucha shook his head, as though explaining simplicities to a child.

"And I say that mine was the weapon that struck first."

"Then that is a lie."

The male hunter clucked his tongue. "But I cannot lie! I am your superior. Are you challenging me? Me, a hunter of the upper tier? Oh, Zhukora, do be reasonable."

A great flight of rainbow lorikeets came spilling through the canopy only to disappear back through the treetops as they caught the ïsha scent in the clearing below. Suffused by a cold, slow fury, Zhukora clenched her fist about her spear.

"I name you thief! The clan assembly shall be the judge of this!"

"Zhukora, you are but twenty-five summers old. No husband. Not even a lover! Who will the elders find in favor of, you or me?"

---

[4]**Chaki-Zho:** Literally "honored folk". The upper strata of clan society. The Kashran nobility are distinguished from commoners by their brightly colored wings.

Zhukora's face went blank with shock. Was the man insane? Her jaw dropped in astonishment.

"You dare? I am Zhukora! I am the eldest daughter of Nochorku-Zha![5] My father is the clan Lord!"

"Oh, Zhukora, the man is old! Already he can hardly cast his vote at council. When he has gone, who shall the Swallowtails choose to be their lord? Their finest hunter, or an arrogant virgin girl?"

The girl's antennae rose.

"I—I am his eldest! Mine is the right. Mine!"

Prakucha looked down at the girl and laughed as though the world shone bright and new.

"Ah, Zhukora! To be so young. So very, very young—"

Zhukora let her spear fall, and her enemy laughed at the expression on her face.

A cry came from above. Three figures swooped down onto the grass behind Zhukora, and a blonde female snapped into position at her side.

The new girl hovered near Zhukora with an avid, protective air. Daimïru. Her fur was a golden honey-brown—a mildly pleasing color that merged with her dull-brown wings. She had the watchful, predatory air of a hunting hawk, staring at Prakucha with a pair of wild black eyes.

"What is it, leader? What is he doing here?"

The group tightened defensively about Zhukora.

Prakucha sardonically raised a single eyebrow. "Your hunting companions are commoners? Oh, Zhukora, how terribly quaint your notions are. No wonder the council despairs of your behavior." The massive hunter bowed mockingly toward the new arrivals. "Your hunt leader and I have had an enlightening conversation. I believe her thinking has become much clearer." Prakucha clapped his hands together and approached the kill. "Well! This has been a pleasant interlude, but the day grows old. I really must be moving on."

Daimïru tensed and made to move. Zhukora made a tiny gesture with her hand, and the golden-furred girl reluctantly subsided.

The thief bent above the huddled corpse, a long dao ax/knife glittering in his hand. With an easy chop, he hacked into the corpse's skull, setting free the spirit of the prey. The little Ka wailed in disbelieving shock, drifting aimlessly about the ferns.

The hunters ignored it; no one made apologies to the spirit; no one gave the ritual gift of energy to soothe the creature's soul. Prakucha tore out Zhukora's spear and then reclaimed his own weapon before swinging the corpse across his shoulder by the tail. With an airy gesture of his hand, the thief flew on his way.

Zhukora stood completely still, her eyes ground shut in fury as she shivered, slowly drawing in her breath. The other hunters recognized the mood and wisely stayed silent. They retreated to the shadows, waiting for Zhukora to regain control.

Zhukora reeled with anger; a whole kill gone! A hunter's status depended on her generosity. The meat could have been given to the poor, winning Zhukora praise

---

[5]**Zha:** Literally "revered folk"—the suffix reserved for a clan chief or tribal king.

around the fires. Instead Prakucha would bask in stolen glory. Zhukora clutched her skull and felt the hate stab through her brain.

Prakucha! The old order crouched across the forest like a spider in its web. The rules choked her every way she tried to turn; a whole future trapped by scheming bureaucrats. The girl snarled, jerking as she dreamed of Prakucha's throat bursting between her jaws.

When Zhukora opened her eyes, she had rigidly regained control, and her voice shone falsely bright and brittle.

"Thank you, Daimïru. Thank you, gentlemen. Let's get on with hunting, shall we?"

From a tree above, a fat green cicada began to buzz, its music almost loud enough to stun the ear. The sound filled the sudden silence as Zhukora's hunters stared at the ground in shame.

The youngest male—an iron-smelter's son—gripped his dao in seething rage.

"Zhukora, how long do we have to stand for this? Is it a crime just to be young? That kill was yours, leader! He knew it just as well as we!"

"Then we shall find another! It's only a dead wallaby."

The second male dug his spear into the sod.

"It's more than that. It's an attitude! The whole tribe's stagnant. Nothing changes! Everything's choked by rules. It feels like—like slowly drowning under clay!"

"The game's drying up, too. There's more people than last year. Something has to change. The old ways just aren't enough anymore."

Daimïru silently cleaned Zhukora's bloody spear. She knelt and reverently placed the weapon back in her leader's hands.

Zhukora gave the males an icy stare. "The old ways are the only ways. There's nothing you or I can do to change them." She looked down at the patch of blood on the ground. "Nothing."

She suddenly hurtled herself into the air. With a hard glance at her companions, Daimïru snapped into place behind her leader's tail. The other hunters hastened to follow, their wings whirring in the gloom.

Far below, the wallaby Ka began to wail in fright. Fresh blood sparkled in the sunlight, glittering like jewels, and the Ka wept as the blowflies drifted down to feed.

CB ℗ ℘

Leaves rustled as a hand stole around a fallen log, a vile yellow slug dangling from its elegant black fingers. Mucus bubbled as the slug writhed in indignation.

A delicious tang of mischief quivered in the air, curling across the senses like an exquisite, wild perfume. Slowly, carefully, the hand dipped down toward a costume made of finest silk, and the fat slug dripped onto the clothes.

The hand paused a single, precious moment in delight, the silent flourish of a true artiste at work, before fading back into the ferns.

"Shadarii!"

The hand gave a guilty jerk, and Shadarii's head shot out of the bracken.

"Shadarii! Dozy wretch, now where have you gone?"

The imperious voice pealed out across the clearing. Shadarii swiftly flitted from the scene of her crime, her gorgeous wings sweeping open to carry her across the forest floor. She alighted daintily in the middle of the clearing, her eyes lowered to avoid Mistress Traveesha's baleful gaze.

The dance mistress stood glowering in a fog of dire humor , dismissing her with a quick sniff of her nose. The lean gray teacher turned back to address the other students.

"Since we are finally all together, we shall begin. First cycle, second movement, and I expect better timing from you this time around!" The woman's tail curled primly behind her. "Shadarii, no more of these flighty innovations. The dance is prescribed exactly thus and so! You must not presume to improve upon works crafted by your betters. If you wish to be a past-holder, you will have to learn the dances in their perfect forms. Would you change history because you want your tail to the left instead of the right? Fa, girl!"

A dozen maidens waited sourly around the clearing, all noblewomen training in the art of dance. Their carefully tended figures gleamed in svelte perfection, and Shadarii tugged her scruffy hair and slowly shied away. To seek friendship was to invite rejection, and it seemed best to keep well clear.

Shadarii rarely missed the company. Who could be sad when the trees were oh-so-green, when little tadpoles nosed along the streams? Shadarii felt at peace. She had known no loneliness; the forest world was hers to care for, and in return, it gave her love.

To Shadarii, the role of past-holder was a precious, holy thing, but to the other girls, it simply offered status in the clan. In a world that cried out for skillful artisans and hunters, a dancer was a rare and precious thing. Few families could afford to keep a daughter who provided no food for the lodge. A dancer never labored, she never fished or wove or spun; she became the ultimate status symbol, a creature devoted purely to the arts.

For untold ages the Katakanii had nurtured their ancient, subtle culture. Theirs was a civilization of pure refinement, of exacting forms and carefully delineated structures. Every word and deed was measured to ancient formulae. As the tree trunks held aloft the forest roof, so tradition elevated Katakanii life. Shadarii's people hunted the rain forests for their food. They dug the tubers from the dark old soil and reaped the wild grains from the riversides. They were the Kashra, the folk of Father Wind and Mother Rain, timeless and unchanging.

Tribal dancers preserved the stories of the past. Each tale had been recorded as a complex formal play. The centuries had refined the art into exquisite delicacy. To learn the Katakanii's repertoire of ritual dance was the love-task of a lifetime.

Shadarii burned with one shining, simple need. She sought to tap the wonder that she felt within her soul, and so she gave herself to the magic of her craft. When she danced, she was set free in a world of beauty, and her supple body spoke the tales that her tongue could never tell.

The dream of knowledge burned bright enough in Shadarii's heart that she was willing to suffer Mistress Traveesha's scorn. For the sake of knowledge, Shadarii would endure.

Mistress Traveesha paused in thought before sending her dancers scurrying off into the bushes.

"Shadarii, you shall lead the chorus dancers. Javïra, my dove, to your place! Everyone attend the cues and listen for the harmonies. Come along, the day is wasting!"

Shadarii's great orange wings flipped out to catch the ïsha, and she swirled high into the air, taking her place in the branches of a silver eucalyptus tree. Mistress Traveesha briskly flitted to the sidelines, and with a sharp clap of her hands, she signaled the rehearsal to begin.

It was a simple tale of creation; the meeting of First Mother with the spirits of the forest world. For the dancers of clan Swallowtail of the Katakanii tribe, the dance should be an easy task. One by one, the girls fell quiet—poised like graceful, precious flowers high above the forest floor.

From hidden players, music rose to brush across the air. Breath by breath, the rhythm grew. The trees stirred gently to the ebb and sway of sound.

A naked dancer preened herself at the center of the clearing. Javïra was a creature of perfect, pristine beauty—a beauty that could hurt with all the malice of a wild-cat's claws. The sun shone from her pure white fur, tracing icy highlights across her flanks. The painted mask[6] on her face merely emphasized the cool perfection of her form.

The music surged. Javïra swayed into the dance. The girl shamelessly indulged herself, stretching out her solo for more than it was worth. The music seemed to wilt and groan, dragged far past any memory of its initial charm.

High in the trees, Shadarii's ears flattened, her tail thrashing as she shared the dance's agony. Javïra was the darling of the clan; the first choice for any solo part. She had become the most sought-after woman in the tribe. The dance mistress doted on her, applauding the "perfection" of Javïra's talents.

Javïra also happened to be Mistress Traveesha's niece....

Far below, Javïra threw out her arms and turned yet another pirouette, tossing out her snow-white hair and dancing beneath a streaming shaft of sun. She paused, looked slowly into the treetops . . and whirled about to start her solo dance again.

Enough was enough! Shadarii set her jaw and dived headfirst toward the ground, great wings sweeping out to guide her fall. She banked and made a dizzy curve past Javïra's astonished face, then looped triumphantly into the sky.

Shadarii reached out to touch the ïsha flow, winging through the currents as she flipped over in another dive. All around her the other dancing girls came tumbling from their perches, laughing brightly as they hurtled through the air.

Javïra flapped her mouth open like a landed fish, then slowly swelled, her fur going stiff with anger. Finally she hurled her mask down to the ground and stamped in wanton fury.

---

[6]**Dance Masks:** By donning a mask, a dancer in effect becomes a housing for the Ka of the depicted deity. Nakedness is connected with the assumption of deific power—a deliberate abandonment of mere worldly things.

"NO!"

Far up in the air, the dancers dipped and whirred in delirious abandon.

"No, no, no! Stop it! I said stop it!"

Javïra shrieked in indignation. Dancers halted, tumbling in confusion as they broke apart their dance. Shadarii banked frantically to avoid a milling group of fliers.

"It's ruined! That scheming little skreg[7] has ruined everything!"

Javïra tore at her hair, prancing up and down in a magnificent tantrum. Mistress Traveesha swooped down from her perch, her jaw firmly set in disapproval.

"Javïra! Whatever is the matter with you?"

"That—that useless lump of lard!" One white hand pointed in accusation at Shadarii. "She deliberately destroyed my solo!"

"Now Javïra..."

"She jumped her cue! That little lardball jumped her cue!"

One by one, the dancing girls fluttered to the ground. Javïra became the center of a fussing cloud of sympathy. The girl swiftly wreathed herself with tears.

"Did you hear the cue? Did you? No! It was her. She's ruined it again!" The white-furred girl hissed in spite, and Shadarii quailed, feeling opinion firmly turn against her. She tried to back away, feeling torn to ribbons by the others' scorn.

It wasn't fair! She had been right! Javïra had been ruining everything. The others had seen it, felt it... why wouldn't they just come out and say it?

Butterflies scattered from the dark swirl of ïsha in the air. Mistress Traveesha coldly folded her arms, and Shadarii felt the displeasure of her regal gaze.

"Shadarii, come with me, if you please."

Her tail dragging, the little Kashra allowed herself to be led away. Shadarii's eyes burned with hidden tears as the dance mistress stood glaring at her from above.

"Shadarii, why did you disrupt the dance?"

Shadarii slowly closed her eyes. Her fingers flew in the formal symbols used in dancing as she pointed at Javïra, making the sign for ruin and catastrophe. The dance mistress barely bothered to pay the girl attention.

"Well yes! Of course you ruined it! Dear Mother Rain, Javïra's nerves are in tatters. Have you no shame?"

Shadarii furiously waved her hands, then flung her fingers and tried again. Traveesha lost patience with the whole wretched exercise.

"What's that? Ruining? Ruining what, girl? You mean Javïra was ruining the dance?"

Shadarii nodded, defeated by a simple sentence. Mistress Traveesha mulled her next words patiently before she spoke.

"Now Shadarii, I want you to listen very carefully to me. I am aware of your talents as a dancer. I am also aware of your antipathy for our poor Javïra. We are past-holders! Here, art utterly rules our lives. Talent, not ambition! Harmony and never conflict. Each of us has her proper place, each working as one small piece of a greater whole. This is how society must function. One sour note in the music can ruin the work of all."

---

[7]**Skreg:** Any unidentifiable, gluey mass found adhering to the sole of a foot or moccasin.

High overhead, a zephyr spirit drifted across the glade, sculpting elegant curls into the ïsha flow. Not caring to notice the passing Ka, the dance mistress gazed loftily down at Shadarii.

"Shadarii, jealousy does not become you. You are a fine dancer, one of my best, but your willfulness has pushed my patience to the limit. We have tried to work around your disability, but we cannot pity you forever! Now either learn to cooperate with the other girls, or find yourself another life path. Do I make myself absolutely clear?"

Shadarii nodded miserably; she was defeated, trapped by her need to belong—even to belong where she was unwanted.

They walked back into sunlight. The other girls swapped venomous whispers back and forth behind their hands, and Shadarii tried to close her ears, knowing full well that they meant her to overhear.

Mistress Traveesha strode between the girls and clapped her hands with brisk authority.

"Well now! A small disruption, but I think the breathing space has done us all a world of good! Shadarii, why don't you take station in the second flight of fliers. Javïra dear, do go and fetch some proper clothes. We'll not try your solo again today. You may take Shadarii's place as the leader of the aerial ballet."

With an insolent sneer, Javïra swooped over to the pile of her abandoned clothes. Traveesha's long hands rubbed together in satisfaction; discipline had once more been upheld.

"There, now! No more dramas for the day. We'll start afresh with gaiety and devotion, shall we? We have rightfully seen that personal initiatives have no place within an ordered set of forms...."

A shriek of horror ripped through the air, and Shadarii lowered her long lashes in exquisite pleasure. Javïra's squeals were pure balm to the soul; the girl hopped absurdly on one leg as she frantically plucked a slug from inside her loincloth, then slipped and fell on her backside in a handy pool of mud.

Girls swapped astonished glances, only to see Shadarii laughing silently behind them. Her face fell as she suddenly met Traveesha's gaze.

"Shadarii! Go tend the drums." Mistress Traveesha's wings spread wide in threat. Shadarii backed away, Traveesha coldly following her, anger in her eyes. "Now! Go on!"

Shadarii simply turned and fled.

The other women watched her with contempt, and a lean black dancer petulantly thumbed her snout. "Good riddance! P'raps she'll fly away and leave us be!"

"Hmph! With a build like that, I'm surprised the beast can even fly!"

"I don't care whose daughter she is, I still say she's no dancer!"

Javïra wandered back with her clothes clutched against her breast, glaring bitterly toward the forest.

"We can make her want to leave! I say we push her out. There's no place for cripples here!"

Traveesha wagged a finger in admonishment. "Now, now! She has a wild flair for shaping ïsha. Her ability is really quite entrancing."

"Well, I'm sick of her! Just keep the little skreg away from me!"

"We shall do as best we may, my sweet, but we must all be a little tolerant. Shadarii is slightly different from the rest of us. The poor girl deserves our pity."

Javïra made a spiteful face. "Oh, yes—pity. Let's pity poor dear Shadarii." She spoke so that her acid voice would carry clean across the clearing. "Poor, poor Shadarii!"

Nestled among the forest eaves, the springtime settlement of the Swallowtails spread like beehives off into the night. In the boughs high, high above, the tree houses shone with lamplight and candle fire. The houses gathered into clumps and drifts, stars high in the sky—hundreds of households ringing with the noise of any village. Children played. Women tended to the evening meals. Girls laid aside their work clothes and dressed themselves in painted skirts and shining beads. The whole forest flowed with life as a warm moon arose to spill its silver light across the trees.

Of all the houses in the settlement, none were as tall, as stark and perfect as the house of Nochorku-Zha. The family of Chief Nochorku was quite comfortably off. They owned a number of fruit orchards and groves of succulent yams, and like any other noble house, received a tithe from the common villagers. As ruler of clan Swallowtail, Nochorku-Zha had been given many gifts over the long years of his reign. Every day, fresh presents were brought by supplicants who sought his good opinion. Nochorku-Zha's two daughters had been well provided for.

There was metal enough to waste on sheer frivolities. A real iron pot bubbled on the stove, and an iron skillet hissed and spat above the coals. In the branches high above the sheltered hearth, the family tree lodge was wide and luxurious. It broadcast a statement of refined good taste and carefully preserved austerity;. Nochorku had created a unique expression of his own unsmiling personality.

Shadarii returned home with the lengthening of the shadows. She fluttered miserably down to tend the hearth, her heart still crying out with hurt from her disastrous day of dance. Javïra's taunts festered deep inside her like a set of poisoned barbs.

There were fruit balls and lily bulbs stacked beside the hearth, and honey cakes were arrayed in bowls for the taking. Shadarii fed the fire and unhappily began to eat.

Shadarii was plump. The very thought of it made her miserable. The other dancing students were slim and svelte—a fact they pointed out at every opportunity. The more unhappy Shadarii felt, the more she ate; the fatter she became the more miserable she felt. It was a cruel circle.

One of the village wives had come to tend the chieftain's fire. The woman sat by the iron skillet, her hands busy as she arranged meals into individual works of art. On the fire behind her, fat white wood grubs toasted. From time to time, she turned the crispy delicacies with her chopsticks, sending juices sizzling across the grill. Shadarii licked her lips and reached out for a crisp, fried grub—then jerked away in guilt as Zhukora stormed in through the door. With no catch in hand, the huntress seethed inside a dark, brooding cloud. She shot Shadarii a withering glance, then helped herself to a cup of lily tea.

Shadarii retreated outside of the hearth hut. The village bustled with the warm activity of evening, and the air swirled with the smoke of a hundred cooking fires. Beside the council lodge, the evening's dancing had begun. Mistress Traveesha had been quite firm. Tonight, Shadarii's services were definitely not required. The girl sighed and kicked her feet, stung by the sound of distant laughter.

A tiny creeping orchid clung to the gigantic house tree. The little plant seemed strangely tired and wan, and Shadarii made a silent *aaaaaw* of disappointment. She held the twisted, wilted leaves, and felt her heart fill with sorrow.

The girl closed her eyes and stilled her mind, reaching out to feel the flower's pain. A gentle, unseen wind stirred softly through Shadarii's fur as she bent down to kiss the bloom, stroking at the petals with her loving little hands.

For a tiny, fragile moment the forest seemed to hold its breath.

The orchid sighed beneath Shadarii's sweet caress, drawing strength from the dancer's glowing ïsha field. Bit by bit, the petals slowly straightened, and the tiny plant spirit stretched in joy. It crooned and danced in gratitude, patting Shadarii's soul with little tendrils of delight.

Shadarii smiled. For a moment her troubled mind lay quite at peace.

The curtain to the hearth hut crashed open. Shadarii gave a guilty jerk and swiftly hid the orchid behind her wings. Zhukora stormed out from the hut, a struggling long-necked tortoise dangling from her claws. With a scowl, she thrust the hapless creature into Shadarii's hands.

"You! Do something useful for once in your life! Kill the beast and clean it."

Shadarii looked unhappily at the tortoise, but Zhukora shoved the little dancer on her way.

"Well, go on! Father's waiting for his meal. What are you doing out here, anyway? Eating again, eh? Rain's Blood, girl, don't you ever stop?"

Zhukora raised her hand, and Shadarii flinched away in fright. Zhukora ground her fangs and gave a snort.

"Oh, stop cringing! Just go clean that tortoise!"

On a stump nearby, a broken branch slowly grew a pair of glowing yellow eyes. The frog-mouthed owl shed its motionless pose and gave a yawn, blinking as it contemplated a night spent on the wing.

Ignoring the creature, Zhukora gazed aloft and irritably tugged her hair.

"I'm going to see Father. There's a meeting of the clan elders tomorrow. If he's going to preside, I'd better make sure he understands the issues."

Zhukora brushed off her hands against her leggings. She looked around and seemed annoyed to find Shadarii still standing in the shadows. The red-haired girl held the tortoise, a horrified expression on her face, and Zhukora gave an irritable sigh.

"Oh, give it to the cook! Just go fetch water for the tea."

Shadarii silently surrendered the tortoise, then spread her wings and fluttered off into the gloom. Zhukora poured herself more tea from the iron pot. She glowered across one shoulder, cradling her pottery cup, and watched her sister's tail dwindle in the gloom. Zhukora sipped her tea, made a face, and then stood and hurtled the dregs into the ashes.

With a brisk flick of her feet, she sprang aloft, fading silently into the black, sharp shadows of the evening.

"Father?"

The inside of the lodge was always dark. Zhukora's tail lashed, her spine prickling with emotions she dared not recognize.

Here the regime of tradition lay enshrined in all its glory. The room was austere and restrained, with decoration kept to a minimum. Zhukora smoothly knelt at the edges of the shadow, her wings sweeping out to shade her impassive face.

"Honored father, it is almost time to eat. Councilor Kikori and his wife are joining us tonight. They bring news of the famines in the western tribal lands."

The room remained frozen in unmoving, aimless darkness. Zhukora kept her gaze firmly nailed to the floor.

"Sire, the elders of the clan will meet tomorrow to discuss the coming toteniha festival. We must review the topics they will raise. You must decide on your policies."

Something in the shadows stirred, and a deep, smooth voice whispered, "Yes... policies..."

Zhukora's wings quivered.

"Father—It's important."

"Yes... but no hurry. It will all still be there tomorrow. The young always place so much importance on haste...."

Zhukora rose and trimmed the lamp. The shadows swam and fled. There, beneath paired masks of Father Wind and Mother Rain, sat the high lord of the Katakanii clan Swallowtail.

Nochorku-Zha had bones that jutted hard like struts of steel. His fur glittered with a sheen of gray, and hair once as black and straight as his daughter's now shone pure white with age. Long antennae stirred as he sat in the shadows of his empty home.

His eldest daughter's face remained frozen in a cold, hard mask of duty.

"Father, I must talk to you. Something—something happened today. I was in the forest hunting. My kill! Prakucha stole from me!"

Her father smiled. "Prakucha cannot steal from you. He is a hunter of a higher tier. He would never act in such a way. To do so is unthinkable."

Zhukora clenched her fists, frustration piercing her voice. "My spear struck first! He stole from me!"

"His spear takes precedence. He is an older man. His rights must be upheld."

"Rights?" The girl's lithe body seethed with hate. "The kill was mine. Mine! It isn't fair. He is guilty of a crime!"

"He cannot commit a crime against you. He is higher in status than you. His own claim therefore must be correct." The old man's wings stirred softly in the gloom. "This is the forest, child! Nothing ever changes. All is as it must be. In the perfect order, all creatures have their place. This is the divine necessity of stasis."

"Father! Things are happening!"

"Nothing is happening. All troubles pass. We know this because our troubles have always passed. The forest is eternal; the Kashra are eternal. We bask beneath the Wind and Rain in the one world of the earth."

Zhukora felt a rising sense of panic. "Father, I am a huntress. The game is running out! The hunting zones empty more quickly every year!"

"We shall soon be moving to our summer villages. The game will be plentiful, and the garden groves shall all be full."

"Father..."

"Hush, child. You shall be present at the council tomorrow to help me to my place. You may stay and listen to the wise decisions of the elders."

Zhukora's ears flattened. "Yes sire. As you say."

At one hundred ten years of age, Nochorku was a pillar of clan society. Even so, his inner strength had faded; since the loss of his wife in childbirth, the spark within him had slowly died. Nochorku had slipped into a strange, vague world of self-involvement, and the only glories of his life were precedent and tradition.

Zhukora glared down at the ground, her eyes glittering with bitterness. Would he have ruled against the interests of his own eldest daughter? Would he have shamed her before the whole assembled clan?

Oh, yes. Oh, yes, indeed....

Time passed, but the old man felt no need to speak. He asked no questions about Zhukora's life. The silence inflicted a dull pain she had almost grown used to. Zhukora finally stood and smoothed her gleaming hair.

"I shall fetch your jewelry, Father. Someone might come visit us during dinner. It would be wise to be prepared."

"Yes. Well hurry on, then!"

Zhukora knelt dutifully behind her father, tying gleaming belts and headbands into place.

Suddenly the old man chose to speak. "I dreamed your mother's Ka again last night. She came just after midnight when the moon was full. She always did love the moon; it always brought the red out in her fur.... It was so nice to see her once again. I do love her so. Sometimes it's so hard to be without her. So very hard...."

One eye suddenly opened, suddenly gleaming, sharp and lucid. "How is Shadarii?"

Zhukora made a face, tugging grimly at a leather thong. "She's disgraced herself again! The dance mistress came to me with yet another complaint about her! She refuses to toe the line and work with other girls."

Her father seemed not even to have heard. His thin, long face nodded slowly up and down.

"Yes, a strange girl. So very strange. A certain beauty, though. So very like her mother..."

Zhukora's hands froze, and pain sparked deep inside her eyes. The girl stiffly stood and walked over to the lodgehouse door.

"We shall be waiting below, Father. Please come down when you are ready."

With that, she stepped out into space and plunged toward the ground. Dark wings flicked deftly out to slow her fall. The huntress landed silently, her face poisoned by a welling tide of bitterness.

Shadarii emerged from the hearth shelter, a bowl of water balanced in her hands. Zhukora gave the girl a vicious shove, sending Shadarii sprawling in the dirt.

"Get out of my way, you useless little cripple! You slew my mother with your cursed birth! You bring shame upon my mother's soul and shame upon our house!" Zhukora's voice cracked with hate. "Keep away from me! Take your fat arse and go eat where we won't have to look at you!"

Shadarii hunched beneath the onslaught, her antennae bowed. Pale ïsha fields of pain flailed brokenly about her. Zhukora stared down at her in fury, her chest heaving, then with a sudden lurch, the huntress stormed away.

Shadarii wept in silence, covering her face in shame.

Overhead, laughter rose to tear at her in spite. Javïra whirred past with a giggling stream of girls behind her. They were sneaking off into the night—off to meet their sweethearts in the forest bracken.

The laughter bubbled on. Shadarii crushed her ears between her hands and fled, launching herself out into the dark.

She flew in vain. No matter where she went, her pain followed close behind.

Two

Once upon a time, there was an Age of Poison.

The earth was sore abused. The trees were thin and sickly, slowly dying from toxins in the soil. The seas and rivers flowed thick as pus across a tortured world.

The Wind had been seduced. He had taken the spirit of Poison as his lover—Our Lady of the Withering Hand. She was beautiful, and she was wanton. Her evil spirit laughed and rolled in destruction while the Wind lay trapped within her spell, shivering beneath the ecstasy of her touch.

The Rain wept, her heart torn by unrequited love. Without the Wind, her powers dulled, for no one came to bear her into the skies. Rain languished on the ground and wept, trying to forget the love they once had shared. Finally the pain proved too much for Rain to bear, and she burrowed into hiding, far beneath the ground.

On the world above, the reign of Lady Poison raged unchecked. The forests dried and withered. The few remaining creatures wandered lost in a haze of pain. Still the Wind sighed and whimpered in his lover's arms, blind to the destruction he helped to cause.

The animals finally raised a wail of hopeless terror, their voices joined by a thousand Ka who still clung loyally to the earth. Their cry pierced the darkness where the Rain sat and shed her tears.

A world died while, far above it all, Poison squealed for joy.

Deep in the darkness, a strange light bloomed. The Fire spirit coiled hissing in the deeps, a thousand wicked plots glittering in its eyes. The creature stealthily crept closer to the Rain. "Oh, Rain, I have brought you a gift to serve your anger. Take it! Reach out and hold the precious thing I offer."

Rain stretched out a trembling hand. Fire's gift seemed to sigh and sing like a hungry animal crooning for blood.

"Lord Fire, I fear to touch it! What will it do to me?"

"Why, everything and nothing. It is only a tool; you will make of it whatever you wish. Only remember this: once your hand has touched it, the gift will never leave you. No matter how much you pretend, no matter how deep or far you hide it, the gift shall always be there when you secretly desire."

Mother Rain suddenly reached out to snatch the gift. The Fire Spirit hissed in glee, then scuttled back into the gloom. The Rain held aloft the shining gift and felt her mind spin bright and new.

"Wait! Fire, what is this gift called? What have you given to me?"

"I call it, 'blade'..."

"How shall I pay you? What do you desire from the Rain?"

The Fire only hissed and faded back into the dark.

Rain felt her spirits soar. She hurtled up from the darkness, stars streaming from her tail, and sought to do battle with her enemy.

Lady Poison had news of her coming, and as Rain stared at the withered world, her rival screamed into the attack. The two mighty Ka battled one against the other for the love of Father Wind. Clouds burned and earth trembled—wild energies boiled the waters of the rivers. Hour after hour, the combat raged. Piece by piece, the Rain began to weaken, driven to despair by Poison's strength.

Finally, the Rain was almost spent. Poison lunged in for the kill, but she had not counted on the strength of love. The Wind shouted out in fear, finally seeing how he had been deceived. He flung his power to the Rain, giving her the gift of his might.

The Rain lashed out, striking Poison a devastating blow, and the evil Ka reeled back, her blood smoking on the ground. Rain bound her, trussing the shrieking demon in her own foul hair. Rain banished the evil creature to the cold, dead moon, there to languish in eternal bitterness.

The Wind looked in dismay at the wreckage of the world. Slowly, painfully over many weary years he labored to set right the evils he had done. The Wind blew away the touch of Poison in the skies while Rain gently washed the burning venom from the earth. They labored long and hard to make the world as beautiful as it once had been.

When their work was done, the Wind came and begged forgiveness of the Rain, and she gave her love to him without regret; for the Rain knew that men can be foolish, and that the measure of true love is to forgive.

Rain and Wind softly wound together far above the forest heights and made love through a long and gentle evening, filling the world with joy. To mark their joining, the sun shone out to bathe them both in warmth; and so each sunset celebrates the blending of the lovers in the sky.

From the glory of their loving, Mother Rain grew great with child. The egg lay in the fertile soil, cradled by the Wind and washed lovingly by Mother Rain. When the egg hatched, they named their love child Zui-Kashra-Zha, the "first mother" of the Kashra. They took their child and nurtured her, teaching her how to care for the wide green growing world.

And so, the Kashra hold their sacred trust. They move within the forests, caring for the world. They dance eternally beneath the smiling Wind and Rain, the children of a perfect, timeless love.

So it is, so it was, and so it shall always be.

ೞ ೞ ೞ

To the great tribes of the alpine forest, the seasons were a never-changing round. The stately play of time was marked by many things. When cicadas sang in the willows, it was time to gather lily tubers. Fish swarmed up the rivers when the wattles were in flower. As rose hips appeared among the brambles, the time came for storing seeds to make winter's bread.

As the first bright days of summer bloomed, it grew time for the totenïha ceremony: the yearly shedding of the wings. From all across the mountains, the clans of the Katakanii gathered; the Swallowtails and Bird-Wings, the Lacewings, Triangles, and Sword-Tails. For one full month, the scattered clans became a single tribe.

The Katakanii were an alpine people. Theirs was a world of mighty forests—of cold, clear nights and summer dreams. Far below them lay an untouched world of plains and valleys; an unknown wasteland where the sky glared above the open earth. The ancient laws forbade the alpine people ever to leave the sacred forest eaves. The tribes of plains and forest must never meet. It was the law of peace—the One Great Rule.

The alpine peoples lived in harmony with their precious world. As food resources waxed and waned, each clan moved between a series of permanent villages. The families swept the cobwebs from their houses, made repairs and preened the gardens. The hunters, gardeners and gatherers reaped the bounty that each new season bore.

The Swallowtails' move into their new season's village was bothersome. In addition to the normal woes of moving house, the clan was to host the totenïha. The village had to be swept spotlessly clean; great pit ovens had to be dug and foods gathered to greet the new arrivals. The Swallowtails were charged with a great responsibility. When the tribe gathered for the rituals, their reception must be perfect. It was a matter of great "place." The reputation of the clan depended on it.

CₛЗ ᶓꙘ ᶓꙘ

Water roared along a frothing riverbed at the base of the summer village. Spray glittered like white points of fire in the morning sun. The river leapt in wild excitement, showering the world with sheets of icy cold.

Fishermen swarmed through the forest, the river shimmering with the reflection of their wings. Deep down in the current, net men plowed though the foam, while overhead a glorious feral figure swooped and dived.

"Up! Keep that side up! Team Two, stay set until my signal."

Zhukora had been soaked from head to foot, water making slick runnels through her fur as she flew through the icy spray to direct her fishing teams. Hundreds of hunters had converged on the river to obey the girl's commands.

Zhukora had laid a wickedly clever trap. The rapids would tire the fish enough to take the sharp edge from their fight. Nets would close off the escape routes while spearmen charged in from the banks. Rather than gathering fish in ones and twos, Zhukora would trap them in their thousands.

New faces swarmed through Zhukora's hunting group. Young hunters flocked to her, eager for a single glance of her approval. Association with Zhukora held high rewards; her rebellious charisma had a growing reputation.

Zhukora remained unaware of the opinion others held of her. She was a creature who utterly despised anyone less motivated than she. She saw no difference between male or female, nobleman or commoner. She valued only talent and determination. Her chosen ones were the elite: hunters, thinkers, rebels, poets—anyone who had found the courage to be angry.

Today's challenge seemed a simple one; the tribe screamed out for meat. Something strange was happening to the world. Ten years of wondrous bounty had suddenly come to an end, and the swollen population no longer had enough to eat. Children hungered and babies cried.

Year by year, fewer catfish came. The Kashra were predators; the young and old would sicken without fresh meat in their bellies. This year, there could be no failure. Zhukora would make sure not a single fish slipped past her claws.

The hunting teams were ready. Blonde, slim, and serious, Daimïru hung at her station once again, Zhukora's self-appointed bodyguard. Daimïru kept a squad of trusted net men close at hand to swiftly patch accidents before they became disasters.

"There! Coming around the second bend!"

The shout came from far downriver: the first fat catfish hurtled itself into the air, leaping skyward above the river rocks. With an almighty splash, the catfish struck the water and dived clean out of view.

There was another, and another. In the blinking of an eye, the river suddenly came alive. Hundreds of fish swarmed between the riverbanks.

"Keep back! Keep down. No one spread a wing shadow across the water!"

Zhukora pumped her fist and sent her teams into action. As the school of catfish thundered past the rapids, nets instantly snapped into place. With a whoop of joy, the spearmen wheeled into the air. The water exploded furiously as harpoons whirred and stuck, transfixing scaly shapes that writhed in torment. The catfish were exterminated with terrifying speed; pregnant females, breeding stock—Zhukora's henchmen swept the river clean.

Suddenly something exploded from the deeps. A nightmarish, monstrous fish blasted up across the rapids and charged toward the killing zone. A solid ton of horror rose into the sky, smacking down across the nets like a gigantic falling moon. Fishermen screamed and dived aside while pregnant catfish dashed frantically upstream to safety. Zhukora turned about in midair, bellowing across the chaos.

"Mother of... *seal that breach!*"

Snapping into action, Daimïru folded her wings and dived onto the monster's back, snarling in a frenzy and stabbing home with her knife. The titan bucked and thrashed. Daimïru spun off into the water, landing tangled in folds of net. The last of the catfish crop fled past her to safety, and with a sudden surge of foam, the monster catfish turned and dived. The net snapped tight around Daimïru's throat, dragging the shrieking girl beneath the foam.

"Daimïru!" Zhukora's scream ripped through the air. She folded her wings, dived, and smashed into the river at horrific speed, disappearing utterly from view.

Seconds stretched, but of Zhukora and Daimïru, there was no sign. Anxious figures wheeled back and forth above the surface. Eyes flicked from face to face as the watching hunters licked their lips in growing fear.

With a mighty roar, the water broke. Zhukora burst out into the light, a limp figure gripped beneath her arm. She sobbed with effort, hauling Daimïru toward the banks. Other hunters floundered forward, reaching out to drag the pair ashore. Knives flashed as they tore the net from Daimïru's bloody throat. The girl lay still, her chest unmoving.

"No!" With a roar of rage, Zhukora flung herself across her friend and crammed breath into Daimïru's lungs. Their auras merged, and ïsha flared and roared.

Zhukora's eyes were wild; one wing hung broken, shattered by her impact with the water. The huntress ignored the pain as she poured energy down into her patient.

"Come on, breathe, damn it! Breathe!" Water trickled from Daimïru's mouth. Zhukora listened for a heartbeat, her teeth set in a snarl. "Up! Get up! Don't you dare give out on me! Damn it, I need you!"

Zhukora furiously gathered power, and a searing bolt of ïsha rammed into Daimïru's heart. The patient bucked in agony, then dragged one awful, ragged breath, her eyes opening in wild astonishment. She clung against Zhukora's breast, spewing water through her mouth and nose. The girls clenched tight together, fighting off Daimïru's pain.

Zhukora panted, cradling her beloved hard against her breast. She crammed her face against Daimïru's golden hair and dragged the scent and feel of her deep into her heart.

"No you don't. There are things to do together yet! A dream to follow, eh? You're not leaving me. I won't ever let you leave me!"

Daimïru's chest heaved as the girl looked in adoration at Zhukora. They sat amid the soaking mess, unwilling to release each other.

A hunter glared out across the water, relief and disappointment mingling on his face.

"The catfish have gone. We've lost the school!"

Zhukora gently stroked the hair back from Daimïru's dripping face. Her voice pealed a note of triumph through the air. "There'll be other days—other catfish. There'll never be another Daimïru. We'll catch some fish tomorrow."

"Your wing! We have to fix your wing!"

"In time, in time. The pain can wait. Fetch all the equipment. Find the prey that floated off downstream. We still go home in triumph with our catch!"

Zhukora somehow lifted her friend into her arms and turned back toward the village. The hunters followed in Zhukora's footsteps, her power shining in their eyes.

Far downstream from the village, away from the teeming thousands and their inevitable noise, Shadarii floundered waist deep in rich brown river muck. She waded through the river shallows and tended the plants, healing any that seemed somehow tired or sick. The self-appointed task had kept her occupied for many hours. She squelched happily through the nice cool mud and planted lily shoots while two mating dragonflies cruised up to settle in her hair. Shadarii laughed her silent laugh and let them have their fun. The ïsha tickled to the pleasure of the little mating bugs.

Suddenly the girl's antennae twitched. She stood up and scowled, searching thoughtfully across the river as her wings waved in the breeze.

Shadarii waded swiftly upstream, water foaming around her fine strong legs, then rounded a corner in the river bank and stared in amazement at what she found.

The titanic catfish was more than four wingspans long.[8] It lay belly-up in the reeds, its huge mouth gulping air as its mind tore at Shadarii in pain. The girl thrashed clumsily to the fish's side, running hands across its bleeding wounds.

Shadarii planted her feet down in the mud and grabbed the creature by the fins, snarling in silence as she fought to turn the catfish over. Muscles bulged as she heaved against the terrifying weight. With an almighty splash, the fish toppled over on its side and came to rest with its head down in the drink, gratefully sucking water through its gills.

A mighty presence shimmered in the ïsha. The girl ignored it as she drove herself to save the poor beast's life. Shadarii cradled its repulsive head and took a mighty breath.

A wild torrent of ïsha punched down into the catfish and seared its wounds. Wind shook the reeds as Shadarii reached out for the river's power, and the great fish gave a heave of surprise, jerking beneath the Kashra's healing touch. Flesh smoothed and auras blazed until the effort of the spell burned Shadarii's mind like fire. With a final flash of energy, she tumbled back into the mud. Shadarii rolled across the ground and retched, her body crumpling in an agony of abuse.

Dear Rain, it hurt! The girl's aura screamed and bled. She soothed it, clenched it, held it tight, until slowly the pain began to ease. Shadarii peered out beneath her muddy locks and looked into a pair of yellow eyes.

The catfish hung beneath the water, its fins cruising slowly back and forth. The creature's wounds had healed. It would go about its strange, silent life in peace once more.

Great glazed eyes stared up at her like bottomless wells, and the fish's gigantic ïsha field swept up out of the river like a pair of mighty arms. Shadarii gave a weary smile, and the fish seemed to twitch its whiskers in reply. Slowly it faded back into the dark, sinking piece by piece into the cool and silent depths.

Shadarii rose unsteadily from the mud, her legs shaking with the strain of walking. The girl gave a bow toward the river and then tottered off toward a water hole, thinking only of the pleasure of a long, hot bath.

Behind her, something huge and powerful spread ripples through the deeps. The ïsha glowed, the river sighed, and all grew peaceful once again.

ೞ ಐ ೫

"Revered Ones, welcome to the shelter of our wings! Clan Swallowtail is enriched by your presence."

Nochorku-Zha bowed low before the dusty priests, his wings creaking as they swept out to shade his eyes. The commoners behind him pressed their faces to the dust, and then the nobles and the councilors followed, one by one. Rank after rank

---

[8]**Systems of Measure:** Kashran measurements are based on the handiest available marks. Measurements are standardized as the "tail" (circa 3 feet in length) and the "span" (one wingspan, or circa 7 feet). The typical hunting spear is three tails long (the longer-shafted weapons having greater range and striking power).

rippled far back into the fields and trees. All told, two thousand Kashra spread their wings in homage.

Nochorku-Zha sat at the head of his mighty clan, his belts of office wound tight about his narrow waist. His daughter Zhukora knelt behind him, her presence stark and beautiful as a knife. She silently shored up the old man's weakness, reaching out to help her father straighten from his painful bow.

The arrival of the tribal priests demanded high ceremony. The high priestess was a fat, serene old woman with a pelt of iron-gray. Sharp, calculating eyes swam deep behind her smile, and ïsha swirled around her with awesome pulses of power. The priestly party numbered twenty, males and females in equal portions. Unlike the other Kashra, they bore items made from butchered skin or bone.[9] The skulls of birds and animals dangled from their belts, repositories for allied spirits bound within the living world.

These tribal sorcerers tracked down evil spirits of disease and hunted lurking vampire Ka. They stood aloof from structured clans, wandering the villages at need. Though the priestly dancing girls were long and luscious, the Swallowtail males fearfully hid their eyes. There was something chilling about the sense of power lurking behind their eyes. In any case, the priesthood were sworn to celibacy. Sexual appraisal must remain purely academic.

The high priestess looked out across the clan assembly, her gaze lingering on Zhukora before she turned to face Nochorku-Zha. She spread her plump old hands and beamed in welcome.

"Greetings to Nochorku-Zha! Greetings to our children of clan Swallowtail. Nochorku-Zha does his office great honor. We are pleased to see clan Swallowtail so prosperous and plentiful."

"Though the game is scarce, our numbers grow ever greater." Nochorku-Zha gave a rheumy smile. "It is good to see so many young ones filling the woods with laughter."

"The tribe grows, or do we old folks shrink? Some days it's hard to tell." The fat priestess cocked her head, piercing Zhukora with her eyes. "And we take this to be your daughter?"

"My eldest, Zhukora-Ki. A most obedient girl."

Zhukora wore a hunter's loincloth, moccasins, and leggings—a sharp contrast to the festival dress of all the other girls. The priestess raised one brow, her eyes never leaving Zhukora's face.

"Indeed? We honor you, young huntress. There are no qualities more highly prized than blind obedience and humility."

Zhukora seethed in silence as she hid her eyes. "A hunter's honor is found in duty, Revered One."

---

[9]**Animal Products:** Remnants of a dead creature can be haunted by the creature's Ka. Kashra therefore make no use of leather, skin, or bone for fear of offending the previous owner. Sudden house fires, sickness, or unlucky hunts are serious threats well within the capabilities of a malicious Ka.

"So? Well the rumors of you must be quite untrue. It seems you lack spirit after all." The old woman smiled as Zhukora failed to react, and then turned toward the chief, slowly dusting off her hands.

"Nochorku-Zha, we thank you for the welcome of your clan. With your blessing, we should like to bathe and rest awhile. The journey was somewhat hard on these poor old bones! Eighty years weigh heavy when damp is in the air."

Nochorku-Zha signed for Zhukora and muttered absently in his daughter's pointed ear.

"Aaaaah, your sister, What's-Her-Name—the quiet one—she bathes enough to be a fish! Have her take the priests to a pool where they can bathe, and be quick about it!"

Zhukora kept her expression tight. "Father, someone else should accompany Shadarii in case Her Reverence has questions..."

"Eh? Oh, yes, yes of course. Attend to it yourself. Swiftly now!"

"Yes, Father. I shall return shortly."

Zhukora curtly signed for Shadarii to rise, and the little dancer glumly did. Followed by the fat shape of the priestess, Shadarii led the way toward her favorite bathing pool.

The priests bothered her; the ïsha swirled thick and heavy all around them, and Shadarii kept her distance. Moving from the village and up into a land of rocks and cliff-side winds, Shadarii passed through a golden spray of golden wattle trees. The blossoms overhung a tumbling nest of rocks where water leaked slowly down the moss to sparkle in a dozen tiny pools, and warm rays of sun filled the air with mellow light. Seeing so much quiet magnificence, Zhukora glared at Shadarii in disapproval.

"How long have you been keeping this place to yourself?" The huntress seared her little sister with a glare. "I'll deal with you later. Just go help the lower priests find their bathing places."

Zhukora knelt beside a pool and plunged her hand in, ïsha crackling as the water swiftly began to steam. The high priestess glanced up in surprise.

"Thank you, Zhukora-Zho. You are a most energetic host." She stirred the water with a pudgy toe and gazed thoughtfully toward Zhukora's back. The water had turned scalding hot, with nothing but one short, sharp blast.

"Yes. Very energetic, indeed...."

The other priests struggled in teams, dredging up the energy to heat the other pools. The weird dancing girls gaily doffed their clothes; men leapt and dived, women squealed. Shadarii peered around in dismay, hovered by the high priestess and wringing her hands in consternation.

Disrobed, the high priestess was not a pretty sight. She eased her fat old bulk into the pool, sighing gratefully at the caress of heat.

"Ooooh, lovely! Zhukora dear, your talents are wasted as a hunter. This water is superb! Did you ever think about the benefits of entering the healer's calling?"

"No, Reverence, I have not. There are too many important things for me to do."

"I quite understand. We must follow where our hearts lead." The high priestess opened one eye, peering blearily up toward Shadarii. "Oh, what is it child? Must you fidget so?"

Shadarii knelt beside the bathing pool and waved her hands, pointing urgently toward the stand of wattle trees. The priestess watched the girl in utter mystification.

"What on earth is she doing? Is it some silly dance?"

Zhukora flicked a glance toward Shadarii. "No, Reverence. The creature cannot speak. Pray, forgive her stupidity."

The old woman frowned as she watched Shadarii's hands.

"What's that girl? You want to leave us? Why, by all means..."

Shadarii sighed in frustration and tried again. She made the sign for insult and tried to mime a little dance, but the priestess cut her short.

"What's that? Rude? No my dear. You aren't being rude."

Shadarii shook her head and pointed toward a huge old tree where a Ka hovered in the roots, resentfully aware of the intrusion in the pools. Shadarii pantomimed the giving of a gift, ïsha sparkling from her hands as she tried to make her message clear. The priestess finally seemed to understand.

"Oh, that! Well if you insist. How very quaint." She called imperiously into the air. "Kanoohï, pay the Ka for granting us his home for our bath."

A male priest flicked a ball of energy before the Ka. The being grumbled, sucking in its payment with ill grace, and the priests went back to their baths without a second glance.

Shadarii knelt beside the tree and wrapped the Ka around her, pouring apology out into the ïsha. The spirit grudgingly forgave her, its ego stroked by Shadarii's promises; she would tend the plants and heal their wounds, chasing off the grubs that bored deep into the tree.

Her task completed, Shadarii bowed before the high priestess, and then pointed back toward the village, acting out her need to return. The old woman watched her closely.

"You may leave us, child. As the chief's daughter, you will dance for us tonight, yes? I shall so instruct your dance mistress; I'm sure it will be a performance worth remembering."

Shadarii whirred away, leaving Zhukora trapped beside the pool. The fat old priestess lounged back in the water, idly inspecting the back of her pudgy hand.

"You are not happy with your father, are you?"

Zhukora's back stiffened. She kept her face firmly turned away.

"He is my father. He is the clan lord. I shall do my duty."

"But the duty becomes harder, does it not?"

"He is my father."

Sprits emerged from the rocks to slide across the cliff face like iridescent butterflies. In their wake, ïsha sparkled, making trails that drifted slowly past the high priestess's eyes. The old woman kept her eyes upon Zhukora as she ran the strands of magic through her hands.

"Nochorku-Zha is dangerous. So devoted to his useless rules that he cares for nothing else. A blind old man who has not even thought to secure a future for his eldest daughter."

The words bit home. Zhukora whirled, only to be caught and held by the priestess's gaze.

"Tell me Zhukora, are the young folk happy? Do they laugh with joy to find that food is growing scarcer? Do the jiteng[10] games take away the anger? Have you never thought that someone else might make a better clan leader—a better tribal leader?"

"You—you speak treason!"

"I speak survival! Don't act the fool with me. I know you, girl. I know you better than any father ever has."

Zhukora stood and strode away through the bushes. Moments later, her angry wings could be heard whirring through the underbrush. Priest Kanoohï rose, one hand slowly stroking his dead, dry skull.

"Shall I send a Ka to follow her?"

"Don't be ridiculous! The girl would sense you in an instant!" The old woman waved her assistant down. "Powerful, young, angry! She might be the one we need. We shall watch and wait; our journey may have brought us interesting gifts."

Shadarii fussed with the last few straps of her dancing costume. Somewhere in the distance, dinner sizzled on the fire, and the delicious smell of roasted lizard made a cruel distraction. Shadarii's mouth watered as she thought of tender, hot white flesh between her teeth....

"Shadarii! Pay attention, girl, there's no time for a rehearsal. We must get this right the first time or not at all!"

Mistress Traveesha's voice speared through the air. Shadarii hurried over to her side, still fumbling with her halter straps. Most dancers lacked Shadarii's ample breasts, and so costumes from the dance school's stores were always a nightmare for the girl to try and wear.

Javïra had supposedly dressed herself to represent the sunlight. As usual, she had taken liberties with the design of her costume. Many dances were performed naked, and others were made while wearing complex ritual garb; Javïra had struck a compromise designed to show off her overvaunted charms. Shadarii simply rolled her eyes and snorted in disgust.

Javïra made comment after comment as Shadarii desperately struggled into her gear. As she bent over to swing her breasts into their restraints, she heard spiteful laughter from behind. Traveesha seemed oblivious to it all. The dance mistress gathered the girls beneath her wings and bubbled in delight.

"The plan is simple. You shall be doing a 'summer greeting' dance in three axes. Improvise a rhythm change to lead the musicians after that. Javïra, I'll trust you at that point. Try to tailor something suitable to the crowd."

The dance mistress closed her eyes and held aloft one elegant black hand.

"Now, no errors. No mistakes! Shadarii, this is a good chance for you to show your worth. I expect the two of you to shine!"

Javïra smiled like a well-fed cat, and then reached out to take her dancing mask within her supple claws. The dance mistress slapped Shadarii smartly on the rump.

---

[10]**Jiteng:** A formalized team sport designed to provide an outlet for competition and aggressive energies.

"Go, children, go! Good winds to you. Now hurry!"

The girls flitted off into the evening air, bells tinkling merrily behind them. Shadarii swam into the trees to perch in silence while butterflies of anticipation danced inside her. Her own performance! With her identity concealed, there would be no one to laugh at the village cripple; hidden safe behind her mask, Shadarii knew she could shine.

Far below, the clan shared a feast with their important visitors—teeming hundreds of nobles and commoners crowding around the council fire. A ground oven was opened, to the joyous shouts of revelers, and it gave a delicious scent of roasted kangaroo. For once, Shadarii felt too intoxicated to heed the call of food. Her senses quivered with delicious sensitivity. Tonight she felt more alive than she had ever felt before.

"Ahoooooooooo!"

Javïra's call shivered out across the night. Her slim figure posed against the skyline, her arms thrown out to catch the wind. She leapt through the air and fell into a graceful dive, ïsha erupting as the sacred circle suddenly blazed with light.

A cheer ran through the villagers as the dancers hurtled overhead. Ïsha roared beneath Shadarii's wings, and with an excited gasp, she plunged toward the ground and landed in the sacred circle, her head thrown back in joy.

The crowd shouted while the dancers leapt and kicked the air. Safe inside her gorgeous costume, Shadarii felt herself tingling to the thrill. Ïsha sparked and tribesmen cheered as Shadarii rode the waves of joy, laughter bubbling in her heart.

The two girls whirled their tails and cut the circle boundaries. According to tradition, dances held within a sacred circle were inviolate. By slashing through the circle, the dancers gave an invitation to their audience.

Flutes fluttered in a cue. It was time to change the rhythm. Javïra signaled, making Shadarii spring high into the sky, but to Shadarii's surprise the other girl stayed firmly on the ground. Javïra threw out her hands and stopped her dance, posing in grinning triumph for the audience.

Shadarii sailed into the air alone. The musicians had all acted on Javïra's cue, suddenly stopping short. Shadarii had been deliberately set up to be a fool.

Never!

Shadarii rolled and tumbled in the sky, firelight rippling through her orange fur. She landed in the center of the sacred circle, hurtling herself into a triumphant pirouette. She danced her heart out in a dizzy swirl of joy. Shadarii streamed with energy, the ïsha rising out to swirl in brilliant shapes about her and hold the crowd enthralled.

The high priestess stroked her chin while idly chewing on a leg of roast goanna.

"So, Nochorku-Zha! Your youngest daughter does not speak?"

"Quite so, Your Reverence. To our regret, the girl's tongue is accursed."

"It's no tragedy. I suspect she makes up for it in many other ways."

"If only it were so, Your Reverence. I fear the girl is utterly useless. Such a disappointment to her mother."

Nochorku-Zha went back to gazing at the dance. He scratched his hide and wondered who the fat little dancer in the ribbons might be.

Out beside the fires, Shadarii swam in a dizzy cloud of ïsha. A young priestess stiffened as an eerie shape came to settle like a whirling cloak about the dancer's wings.

"Reverence, look!"

The dancer threw back her hair, hurtling out her arms to greet the wandering Ka, and it danced with her in joyous harmony. One by one, more spirits came to join the revelry. They swooped and swished among the crowds, rattling the pots and tickling the children. One pretty girl squeaked in alarm as her skirts were lifted by a passing ghost. The high priestess watched the dance in growing fascination, then sank back into folds of fat and slowly stroked her chin.

"I must confess, your youngest daughter interests me, Nochorku-Zha. She seems to have long been kept in the shadows."

"She has little enough to recommend her, Reverence. A sharp pair of eyes and nothing more. Good hips! She'd spawn eggs like a fish if she had brains enough to snare a husband. Hmph! Small chance of that. A speechless girl is no use to anybody."

"Quite. Still, I should like to speak with her."

From her place nearby, Mistress Traveesha gave the priests a sideways glare. "The girl is a dancer. The past-holders have already claimed her!"

"But of course! I simply feel such skill should be complemented."

Out on the open ground, Javïra fumed in rage. Her trick had failed. Far from becoming a laughing stock, Shadarii had moved in to steal the show. The audience clapped to Shadarii's beat, yelling in encouragement as she whirled deliriously before them. Javïra furiously leapt into the light, snatching up her place beside Shadarii. The red-haired girl took Javïra's hand, forgiving her for having left her in the lurch.

Javïra snarled. As Shadarii skipped her way between the fires, Javïra jammed out her foot. With a jerk of terror Shadarii tripped and fell, her left hand plunging deep into the coals.

Shadarii hurtled back her head and gave a silent scream. The ïsha ripped with agony, and all laughter died. Tears streaming from her eyes, the dancer gazed in shock at Javïra's triumphant face.

Javïra laughed aloud, her cruel voice ringing in the hush. The girl pointed at Shadarii's hand and shrieked with mirth. The laugh went on and on, mocking Shadarii's pain. The gentle dancer staggered to her feet, her heart suddenly brimming with hate. The Ka gathered all around her soul.

Ïsha punched out like a giant's fist, smashing Javïra to the ground. Javïra croaked, her eyes standing out in shock, and Shadarii advanced a pace, her body trembling in rage. She clenched her blistered fist and slammed the ïsha hard into Javïra's guts.

Lightning blazed; Javïra screamed as something tore inside her. Power ripped up the ground like the lash of a gigantic whip, blasting fur from Javïra's hide and smashing her against a wattle tree. The girl writhed across the dust and howled in agony.

"Stop! Please! Someone help me! Shadarii, I didn't mean it. Please don't!" She crawled away in panic, cringing in the dirt. "Help me! For Rain's sake, someone do something!"

Shadarii moved in for the kill, a ball of lightning shaping in her fist, but suddenly the storm of ïsha died inside her claws. Shadarii snapped her head around to see the high priestess shielding Javïra's back.

Shadarii's anger died as she blinked in shock at her sniveling victim. The high priestess strode into the sacred circle, waving genially with her arms.

"Be calm! Be calm! 'Twas just a minor accident. It was merely angry spirits, nothing more."

Traveesha clutched her niece against her breast, her face a mask of hate.

"She tried to kill her! We all saw it! That monster tried to kill my precious dove!"

Shadarii helplessly shook her head, tears streaming down her face as she clutched her injured hand. She hadn't meant... She—she had never wanted to really hurt...

The old priestess smiled and tried to soothe the crowd.

"Peace! Peace, good people! An excited girl—a blaze of pain. The Ka merely lashed out in her defense. Possession, that is all. 'Tis best the episode ends here."

With all due dignity, Nochorku-Zha rose creakily to his feet, leaning on Zhukora's arm. "The feast is over. Disperse for the night. Finish your meals at home" The old man stiffly turned to go. Zhukora turned a despising glare upon her sister before stalking off into the darkness.

Shadarii stumbled over to Javïra's side, her face torn by anguish. She tried to reach out in apology, only to be met by Traveesha's snarling fangs.

"Out of my sight! Get out! You're dismissed from the dancers. You've danced your last, you vicious little animal!"

Shadarii sobbed in misery, trying to drag out the words to show her shame, but the dance mistress slashed out with her claws.

"I said, out of my sight!"

Shadarii stumbled back and fled.

Traveesha rocked her niece and softly murmured in her ear. "Shhhhh. Forget her. Oh, I'm so sorry! Oh, my precious, how could I have known? She's gone now. It's all over."

Javïra's eyes were red with agony, and her voice shook with the power of hate. "Sh-she'll pay for this! By Wind and Poison, that crippled bitch is going to pay!"

Shadarii wept in misery, as the healer murmured spells across her injured hand. The agony of the burn slowly faded as magic lit the forest gloom.

The healing came only slowly. Shadarii's mind had turned blank with shock; her world had shattered like a ball of ice. Better they should let her die. Never to dance? What was she to do? Rain help her, what was she to do?

Something dark and deadly burst in through the night. Zhukora stood over her, shivering with rage.

"Father may be done with you, but I'm not! You've shamed us before the high priestess and dragged our family's name through the dirt! Your one chance to be some use to us, and now look what you've done. Are you satisfied? Well?"

Shadarii utterly ignored her, her thoughts lost inside a nightmare. The girl rocked back and forth, back and forth.... Zhukora shrieked in anger.

"Listen to me! Did you hear what I just said?"

Zhukora lashed out with her fist, and Shadarii's head snapped back, blood spraying from her mouth. She made no move to defend herself, emitted no cry or squeal of pain; Shadarii simply lay where she fell. With a cry of hate, Zhukora flew into the family lodge and firmly slammed the door.

Shadarii let the healer quietly help her to her feet. The girl simply sat upon a log and felt her daydreams die.

C3 &0 &0

The burial ground lay waiting. Trees reached out with jagged claws to scrape against the cliffs and creak softly in the breeze. The branches whispered dreadful secrets in the dark, plucking at their shrouds of dying leaves.

A living creature broke the breathless quiet, reeling blindly through the dark. Grave markers[11] leered from the shadows, and dry raven's bones lay emptily scattered across the ground.

The burial grove of the summer village was a very special place, for it was here that Shadarii's mother lay... the mother she had never known, who had never held her newborn baby girl...

The mother she had slain.

The marker stood just as she had left it. The grave tree moldered in comfortable silence, covered with plates of cheerful orange fungus. Shadarii crammed herself against the rotten bark, bright tears staining the bark as the girl wept in torment.

Her grief sent ripples chasing through the ïsha fields. Far above her, the forest seemed to take a breath of wonder. Something marvelous began to happen; rising from the stillness of the woods, a shining Ka began to fill the air with light.

Mama!

Shadarii shed tears in grief and joy, gasping as the loving spirit spilled around her. The girl joined with her mother in an ecstasy of communion, drinking in the love that she had never known in waking life.

They had never needed words; the spirit had always been there whenever she was needed most. Shadarii's soul soared on wings of adoration.

Oh, Mama. Oh, Mama I love you so...

Far off in the darkness, two shadows gazed down at their prey. The high priestess stroked her hands together, her gaze locked on Shadarii's face.

"I want her. Raw—untrained! Did you ever see such power? We need only shape her mind, and we shall finally have our weapon to rule the tribes."

Kanoohï nodded slowly in agreement.

"The dancers have rejected her. Her family will want her gone. I shall ask Nochorku-Zha."

"Don't be a fool! Have you learned nothing? Go to the power in the family. Zhukora runs the lodge of Nochorku-Zha. 'Tis her we must convince."

Kanoohï 's ears flattened.

---

[11]**Cremation:** Kashran dead are cremated, thus paying the Fire spirit for its aid to Mother Rain. The remaining ashes are carefully buried.

"Zhukora will be difficult to bend to our will...."

"Oh, I think not. You see, we have something Zhukora needs. We need only awaken her desire for what we have to offer." The high priestess bared her yellow fangs. "Oh, yes, she will grasp the chance to please us. We shall show her how to become Zhukora-Zha."

Down in the lonely glade, Shadarii opened out her arms. The spirit flowed around her, lighting the night with song as the priests sheathed their claws and faded back into the darkness.

Three

Zhukora hung poised in the air like a malevolent black wasp, her tail swirling as she shifted her grip on her catching staff. Beside and below her, skull-faced helmets glittered in the ïsha-light as Zhukora's players quivered at their leash.

Zhukora's team arrayed themselves with geometrical precision. There were twelve players, one for each month of the Kashran year. Slatted wooden armor sheathed the players from head to toe. Zhukora's followers were clad in pure jet-black. Their masks were cruel white skulls that faced the world with a snarl of death. The team was fast and ruthless. Zhukora inspired an insane élan. Skull-Wings often played on with shattered limbs and broken wings, screaming home goals against impossible odds. The savagery of their attacks ripped lesser teams to shreds.

Their opponents' armor glowed with all the colors of a forest spring, each player seeking to outshine the others with his costume. Their name suited them—Splendid Orchids Flowering. The Orchids made a confusing contrast to their silent, stark opponents.

A second, more subtle difference could be drawn between the teams. Most of Zhukora's followers had the dull gray-brown wings of commoners. Out of all twelve players, only two were noble, one of which was a leader who valued ability over social rank.

Prakucha dipped and wove within the enemy's front rank. As captain of the clan's prime team, he drew enormous status, and the vast crowd of watching tribesmen yelled in approval. The huge hunter flexed his biceps for a pair of squealing girls, then blew a kiss toward Zhukora, flipping around to show the girl his tail.

In stony silence, Zhukora ignored the man. Her team flickered with energy like an extension of her own will, yearning for the signal to begin. Daimïru hovered at Zhukora's tail, where she belonged. Zhukora looked over to her beloved friend and gave a savage smile, bringing Daimïru a dizzy breath of life.

The game of jiteng was a sacred ritual. The rules were deceptively simple; hoops were placed on poles at either end of a clearing, and a sparse group of trees provided cover and terrain. The players battled for possession of an iridescent ball, which could be caught and handled only by the player's catching staves—sticks two tails long and tipped with cups of woven wicker. The butt end of each staff ended in a densely padded tip, and any player struck in the head or torso by the staff was disqualified until the next goal had been scored. At the scoring of a goal, "dead" team members were restored to play. Any players within ten spans of the ball were fair game for an attack. No player could leave the field without forfeiting their right to play.

The first team to score four goals was declared the winner; an arduous task that sometimes might take an hour to achieve. The rules were simple enough to be easily understood, and therefore widely open to interpretation. Like all things among the alpine Kashra, the game's simple form had become a thing of complex subtlety; each match was treated as a unique piece of art.

For a thousand years the tribes had set aside the art of war. The age of battles had been deliberately removed from Kashran history; fighting and conflict were utterly unknown. Even tales of the ancient wars had been forbidden.

Instead there was the game.

More than half the clan had come to watch the game. A hush fell across the audience as the umpire shook the ball out to be blessed by Father Wind. He muttered the obligatory prayer and whirled the ball inside his catching staff.

"Spread wings. Ball high!"

The umpire hurtled the ball into the air, and the two rovers crashed together with a roar. The Orchids' player snatched the ball and hurtled it safely back into his team, where Prakucha arrogantly claimed the prize and bellowed out in joy.

Zhukora clenched her fist and signaled the attack.

"Fork formation, rovers high! Go! Go!"

The sky exploded into frenzy as Skull-Wings shot off in all directions. The Orchids blinked. A clear path to the goals suddenly opened before them. They surged forward in a ragged phalanx, each desperate to outstrip the others in an all-out race toward the prize.

Players screamed as black shapes thundered down onto them from above. Zhukora's team blasted through the Orchids' ranks. Wings tore and armor cracked. Prakucha laughed and dived away, leaving his men to deal with the attack. The flight path to the goals lay open; he could score the point alone!

He never even saw the figure streak at him from below. A staff hurtled through the air to smack into Prakucha's chest, and then swooped smoothly back into Zhukora's hand.

The Skull-Wings snatched the falling ball and speared for the goal. One player caught and passed, then another and another. The Orchid guards whirled in confusion. Slim and lithe, with blonde hair spilling out beneath her sinister helmet mask, Daimïru snatched the ball, turned a somersault, and hurtled it with demonic speed. A triumphant howl rose from the Skull-Wing team as they scored the first goal of the game.

Young villagers hammered wildly on the trees while older watchers sniffed contemptuously. The umpire argued bitterly with Zhukora, and Prakucha stalked back onto the field. He shot a killing glance toward Zhukora and sullenly rejoined his team.

The argument with the umpire went on. While there was no rule against throwing a staff, the umpire pleaded with Zhukora to replay the point in the name of good sportsmanship. The Skull-Wings were hearing none of it. Zhukora gathered her players and clawed back into the air.

Zhukora massaged the root of her left fore-wing. The injury from yesterday's dive still bothered her. Down in the audience, the dancing girls had formed a cheer squad for the Skull-Wing team, and the women laughed and wheeled as the umpires shook the ball.

"Spread wings. Ball high!"

With a scream of rage, the Skull-Wings drove back their opponents. Zhukora snatched the ball, hurtling it back into her team. Daimïru deftly caught the throw and drove down into the enemy. Zhukora ripped out with her ïsha, making Orchids swerve and fall. She cleared the way for yet another wild charge for the goals.

Suddenly, a shadow cut the sky, and something smashed into Zhukora's back. The girl crashed to the ground, wrenching her left wing as she tumbled through the grass. With a hoot of laughter Prakucha jammed his foot into her rump, using his fallen enemy as a springboard back into the air. Zhukora snarled and clawed up from the dirt. She was out for the rest of the play.

Damn him!

The sky erupted in a furious melee. A shrieking Skull-Wing threw herself into a tackle, dragging an Orchid player to the ground. The Skull-Wing goal guards streaked forward, abandoning their posts to claim the ball, and with a wild bellow they stormed across the field. The ball lashed toward the hoop, only to recoil from the goalpost. Players collided as each one scrabbled for the prize.

Blonde Daimïru took the ball, wheeled through the air and made a perfect pass, only to be brutally tackled from behind. The girl struck a tree trunk and rebounded, and her enemy launched himself at her throat. The Orchid screamed and punched her face, hammering her skull against the dirt. With a roar of hate, a Skull-Wing smacked his helmet straight into the Orchid's face, dropping him unconscious in a shower of blood.

On the field, the play went on. A Skull-Wing tumbled in a barrel roll and dunked a goal amid the yelling of the crowd.

"Foul! Foul! No goal. Play awarded to the Orchids!"

"No goal?" Zhukora screamed in anger. She raced over to snatch the aged umpire by his uniform. "It was a goal! Fair and square, a goal!"

The umpire thrust Zhukora back.

"No goal! Skull-Wings are penalized for unlawful blows and fighting."

"What? You son of a numbat! That mincing flower boy struck her first!"

"This is a game of skill, not a brawl! I will not have you indulge your aggressions on the field."

"He struck her from behind! He hit her first!"

"No goal!" The umpire snatched the ball and thrust it into Prakucha's hands.

Zhukora ground her fangs and went to put an arm about Daimïru's shoulders. "All right?"

The other girl nodded, her hands wrapped about her chest. Soft blonde hair spilled out beneath her evil mask, hiding her eyes as she tried to hold back the pain. Zhukora reached out to enfold the other woman in a sizzling spray of healing ïsha.

The horn blew, signaling recommencement of the game; Zhukora cursed and drew away, the healing barely just begun. The other girl shivered, still trying to gulp for breath.

"Y-your wing looks funny. It's dragging."

Zhukora's face was hidden by her mask.

"It's nothing! Come on, let's play!"

Shadarii glumly finished healing a tiny wattle tree. With trembling hands, the girl tended the plants about her bathing hole just as she had promised. In her numb, blank state, an oath seemed a very precious thing; Shadarii slowly moved from tree to tree, her hands stroking ïsha though the leaves.

Even the slow, soothing sound of water failed to reach her. Her life lay in ruins. She sadly bowed her head and stared down into the rock pool, her eyes barely registering the soft gleam of the waters.

A shining presence slowly drifted down the rocks. The water Ka softly laid its ïsha field beside her, and the water in the pool began to steam. With anxious ripples, the spirit tried to coax her in, stirring the water with a hopeful little splash.

Shadarii gave a weary smile. Have a nice hot bath and try to forget your troubles? The Ka seemed like a doting aunt. It was really very sweet. Shadarii softly closed her eyes and sent her thoughts out into the air

Thank you. Thank you from the bottom of my heart.

Actually, the water did look good. It had been a long, tiring day, and a bath would be pure magic. Shadarii slowly plucked the laces on her halter. She closed her eyes to savor freedom's kiss across her fur.

Deep among the bushes, the grasses rustled, and a face peered from a grevillea bush and dropped its jaw in shock. A young hunter stared in rapture at the plump vision glimmering before him. Kotaru gulped, his heart hammering frantically in his breast.

The girl began to slip out of her skirt, leather slowly sliding across her orange fur. Kotaru gave a whimper, and the girl suddenly looked around. Kotaru jammed his fist into his mouth and froze.

Rain and Fire—how beautiful! Kotaru breathed out in wonder; he had never seen a noble girl so close, so beautiful, so... so... so unclad! The breeze carried just the faintest hint of the woman's spicy smell, and Kotaru breathed it in rapture, every fiber of his being drinking in her soft perfection.

There were dimples on her backside. Kotaru smiled, propped his cheek against his hand, and gave a sigh.

He was a tall, beautiful young hunter dressed in scraps of wooden armor. Kotaru's wings were plain brown, and his fur as gray as moon dust. He was tousled, travel stained, and weary, but his eyes were lit with shining dreams.

The girl turned her back to him and ran her fingers through her hair. With flowing grace, she bent her face toward the water, her exquisite backside lifted. With an almighty crash, Kotaru fell back into the grass.

Beside the bathing pool, Shadarii shot erect, and then searched the air with suspicious, twitching ears. No creature stirred, no furtive rustles sounded from the brush. With a shrug she turned back to her bath, wading out to lose herself beneath the steaming waters. Shadarii sighed in pure contentment, her thoughts drifting with the gentle flow of steam.

Kotaru smiled dreamily, a song already glowing in his soul as his hand crept toward the ocarina flute tucked into his sash.

"Pssst!" Bushes rustled furtively beside him as an angry snout thrust out between the wattle trees. "Hey, what the skreg are you doin' here man? The others are waitin' for you!"

More twigs crackled as a second burly figure joined the first. An angry whisper rattled through the air. "You dozy wretch! Get fell in before I take my spear to your arse! Move out, on the double!"

Kotaru reluctantly moved downhill to where a silent group of figures crouched in the watercourse. Sixty hunters of the Vakïdurii tribe[12] were ranged beneath the cliffs. Kotaru felt less and less happy about the expedition. The very thought of it left a foul taste in his mouth. If there had been any way to retreat without losing face before his peers...

The boy's companion eagerly nudged him in the ribs.

"The scouts are back. Prince Tekï'taa was right! Rack after rack of drying fish— enough to feed a tribe! The food's down there, and not a guard in sight. We'll swipe it and be home before they even know it's gone!"

The prince gave a languid signal from the column's front, and the raiders fanned out into the shadows.

Kotaru swallowed, looking helplessly back toward the bathing pool. With a heavy heart, the hunter trailed after his companions.

Beneath a grove of ancient trees, far from the pressing worries of the village, the elders of the Swallowtails met in solemn council. The twelve councilors sat and sipped their tea, listening to the distant cheering of the game crowds.

Nochorku-Zha breathed in the scent of his perfumed cup. Long whiskers twitched as he savored the delightful wisps of steam.

"Aaaah, always the best aspect of the summer village! The river wisset gives the tea such a mellowing aroma." The clan lord idly swirled his cup. "Well then, what pressing business for today, eh?"

A plump woman of middle years gave an easy shrug. "Nothing too important, Lord. A certain scarcity of food. Last night's revelries have exhausted all our current stocks. We might have problems finding sufficient food when the other clans arrive."

"No need to worry. The problem will heal itself. Problems always do." The old man smiled, serene in his infallible world. The elders quietly sipped their cups, their minds moving with the music of the woods.

A lean brown woman primly pulled her nose. "I wish to raise the subject of this painting that has been commissioned. Does the clan lord really think the final work is suitable for presentation before the king?"

Nochorku-Zha set down his cup and picked up the artist's working sketch, painted on a roll of paper bark.

"Does the honored councilor have any specific complaint?"

---

[12]**Mountain Tribes:** The alpine peoples consider themselves to be divided into four tribes, all of whom share a common culture and language. These are the Katakanii, the Vakïdurii, the Urïshii, and the Hohematii. Of these tribes, the Katakanii are the most wealthy, and the Vakïdurii by far the most populous. The Urïshii keep to the colder southern alps. The Hohematii confine themselves almost totally to the highest peaks, and are infamous for their jiteng rules—which require the sinking of 5 goals rather than the normal 4.

"Indeed! The foreground is overemphasized. The main figures are all but lost against the colors."

"Really?" Nochorku-Zha frowned across his crinkling snout. "I had thought it rather clever. Are you sure of this opinion?"

A distant wave of cheers drifted out across the trees. Totenïha was coming—and with it the tribal jiteng championships. Ears twitched as the elders caught the sounds of the jiteng game, and a wheezing ancient rubbed his leathery hands together. He was so skinny that he looked like a piece of knotted string.

"Another year, another win for the Swallowtails! Ohputa of the Bird-Wings will be good for another bet. Last year I won three whole sacks of sugar candy!"

The old man smacked his lips in anticipation, while Fotoki carefully peered inside the iron teapot on the fire.

"Her Reverence has passed on an offer from Ohputa-Zha. He wishes to wager a hundred fingers of prime iron[13] that his team will win."

"Ha, done!" The ancient cackled in glee. "The Orchids will pluck his mangy wings for sure!"

A Ka had rather nicely decided to inhabit the council's teapot, and the creature proved a great aid in keeping their brew fresh and warm. The tea was poured, bets were discussed, and the whole council turned slightly sleepy as the glade warmed in the sun.

More noise came across the trees, disturbing the peace, and Nochorku-Zha irritably twiddled his antennae.

"What on earth is all that noise? The game can't be done already? Surely what's-her-name's team put up some fight against the Orchids?"

"I doubt your daughter's team made much of a show, my lord. When it all comes down to it, style and experience are all that count. The young have so much to learn."

"Aye. Aye, yes, indeed."

Nochorku-Zha seemed greatly pleased by the sentiment. Quite at peace with his world, he smiled and swirled his steaming cup of tea.

"Skull! Skull! Skull! Skull! Skull! Skull! Skull! Skull... !"

The chant roared through the crowd as Skull-Wings hurtled down the field. Zhukora's eyes blazed with energy. Her team was two goals up on the most powerful team in all the tribe!

The Skull-Wings moved like a single savage entity; each curt signal from Zhukora brought immediate response. They dived and flickered with wicked malice, weaving tight formations about their dandified opponents.

The Orchids grew angry, and their fury swiftly unhinged their fragile teamwork. The ball sailed down left field, pursued by a churning cloud of players. Zhukora watched the melee pass and signaled with her fist. Her tight spearhead of players

---

[13]**Fingers of Iron:** Ingots approximately the length and width of a forefinger. Iron is less common than gold—which is quite plentiful in alluvial deposits in upland streams.

screamed out of the sun and stole the ball before the Orchids even realized it was gone. With her bodyguards beside her, Zhukora tore off down the field.

Speed blurred her to a streak of black. Orchid guards flapped after her, helpless to intercept. Zhukora lashed out with a whip of ïsha, hurtling her enemy aside. Crowing with shrill delight, she speared for the goals.

Pain ripped through Zhukora's wing, and Prakucha dived past, laughing savagely. Zhukora screamed and fell. He had smashed her wing, deliberately going for an injury. Daimïru snatched her leader's belt and desperately tried to slow Zhukora's fall.

Down on the ground, Zhukora rolled in agony. The wing muscle had been only barely healed from yesterday in the river, and her great soft wing spasmed as pain twisted through it. Somewhere in the distance the game went on. Skull-Wing guards clubbed Prakucha to the turf.

"Raiders!"

The wild cheer faltered as a terrified youngster erupted through the trees. He flew as though all Poison's demons were chasing him.

"Raiders! Raiders in the village!" The boy skidded to a halt, clawing frantically at friends and neighbors. "They're taking it! Taking it all!"

Villagers milled in confusion, and the two jiteng teams clattered to a halt. Zhukora rocked in Daimïru's arms, fangs gritted, as a Skull-Wing came racing to her side. "Zhukora, there's raiders in the village! Warriors with spears!"

"R-report! How-how many?"

"Fifty, maybe sixty!"

"Who—who says?" Speech was difficult; her wing hurt like Fire and Poison.

"A lad saw them. Says they're sacking all the lodges!"

Zhukora hissed and brutally straightened her wing, her fangs clenched against the dreadful pain. "Get the team! Get our hunt group! If they can't find spears, they can grab stones from the river." The skull mask snarled for blood. "Kill anything that stands in your way. Move!"

Daimïru rose and yelled out the hunt group's rallying cry. Zhukora's fangs flashed as thirty hunters stormed into the air at her command, and the huntress pumped her fist toward their prey.

"Double spearhead formation. My lead, wing guards high!"

Zhukora staggered into the air, ïsha sheeting all around her like a storm.

"Stop it! Put it down! That's someone else's property!"

Kotaru's voice cracked in horror. His fellow tribesmen—his old hunting mates and nest kin—screeched like animals... They had turned into something Kotaru couldn't understand.

Men whooped and tossed lacquered boxes through the air. Each box was a stunning work of art, carved and painted by an artist's caring hand. With splintering crashes, the masterpieces tumbled to the ground.

"Stop it! Stop it!"

Kotaru cried out in vain. It had all started going wrong. It should have been simple. The Katakanii tribe were wealthy, everybody knew that. When someone had suggested raiding the Katakanii larders, the idea had seemed good. Even when the raiders had first set out, it had all felt like a childish prank.

It was a Katakanii holy day, and that meant jiteng. A game of jiteng meant no screen of hunters roaming the woods. The idea to strike on such a day had been Kotaru's. It was all his fault! Plain armor—blank face masks. The Katakanii were never to have known who had even done the deed, but now they would search. By Fire and Poison, how they'd search! No forest would be wide enough to hide in....

A female shriek ripped through the air. Kotaru froze, and the scream came again, a jagged sound of mindless terror. The young hunter threw out his wings and raced across the forest floor, smashing through a grove of ferns to find a pair of raiders tearing at a weeping twelve-year-old girl. She flailed out with a huge burst of ïsha power, spilling one man from his feet as Kotaru burst though the fern fronds above.

"Leave her alone!"

Kotaru's spear butt cracked across a tribesman's face; his victim's head snapped back, blood spraying from shattered teeth. The girl cringed away, sobbing weakly as Kotaru's spear point jabbed the other man.

"You sickenin' filthy animal! Pick up your spear! Pick up your cursed spear and fight!"

The other raider licked his lips. Kotaru snarled with hate.

"Pick it up, y' skregin' coward. Pick it up and fight me!"

Men drew back as a suave figure cruised serenely from the ferns. Prince Tekï'taa slowly looked around the glade, and one eyebrow raised as he saw the warrior held at spearpoint.

"There is... a problem?"

The injured man moaned, blood spilling from his broken teeth. Kotaru stared in fascination, mesmerized by the violence he had done. The second raider panted, his eyes nervously measuring Kotaru's weaving spearpoint. "He-he hit Gotaiku! He—he was... he was goin' to..."

"Yes... so I see."

The little girl crammed her fist into her mouth and sobbed. The nobleman disdainfully ignored her, turning his gaze upon Kotaru.

"All this nonsense... so unnecessary. You are a foolish man, Kotaru. One wonders why you bothered to tag yourself along?"

"Lord! These-these animals were goin' to—to..."

"To rape her? Why of course they were," the prince explained himself patiently, as if speaking to a child. "And what of that? You are acting like a fool." Kotaru stared at his liege lord, amazement slowly dawning in his eyes as the nobleman wearily spoke on. "We came here for a raid, Kotaru. Did you think I'd led us here merely to fill the bellies of some squealing villagers? We came her for a set of reasons; reasons that you clearly are not capable of understanding."

"They were goin' to *rape* her!"

Prince Tekï'taa sighed. "Kotaru—I am most disappointed in you. There's no place for fools within my hunting group. And you, boy, are a fool."

Kotaru slowly drew himself erect.

"If I am a fool, my lord, then 'tis proud I am to be one."

Kotaru contemptuously turned away. The little girl cringed as Kotaru knelt to take her hand; he took her safely in his arms and bore her off into the forest

The alpine tribes virtually knew no violent crime. Now Kotaru found himself involved in theft, destruction, and anger. He swallowed hard, trying to hide from the horror that he felt, then squatted down to tenderly stroke the weeping girl. "Are you all right girlie?"

She was skinny as an insect, with silver fur, silver hair, and pearl-gray wings. The girl nodded, staring at him in fright until Kotaru stripped away his face mask and dropped his helmet to the ground. "Sssssh, it's all right, now. No one's going to hurt you anymore."

She wept against his chest, her whole body quivering in shock. Kotaru rocked her gently back and forth, murmured softly in her ear. Finally he drew away, holding the tearful child at arm's length.

"All right now, what's your name, eh?"

The child looked back at him with eerie silver eyes. She seemed to be remembering his face in every detail. "Kï-Kïtashii. My name's Kïtashii."

Kotaru smiled his fine lopsided smile. "Aaaaah, that's a fine name, now, so it is! A brave name, but I'll not have you fighting anymore hunters."

The girl combed aside her long white hair. Kotaru gently wiped her skinny cheeks and brushed away her tears.

"That's better, now! That's my bonny lass. Now, Kïtashii, do you know somewhere to hide?" His answer came as a wide-eyed nod. "Go quickly, then; hide there and be quiet. 'Twill all be over soon."

The girl backed away, her face still numb with shock. Then, suddenly, she spread her wings and darted through the brush.

Kotaru sighed and stood. The incident had left a vile taste in his mouth. He dusted off his hands and turned to face the Katakanii village... just as a spear impaled a sapling by Kotaru's head.

The hunter stared, then frantically dived aside as a second spear ripped past his fur. It rammed through a tree fern to hang thrumming in midair.

Two nightmarish creatures exploded through the trees—demons with sharp black bodies and heads like shrieking skulls. They caught the scent and screamed in hunger for their prey. Kotaru fled through the woods, fronds ripping at his wings. He dived through a gully and plunged into a dripping world of ferns.

The demons lost sight of their victim and clattered to a halt. Mad eyes stared down into the green. Kotaru flattened himself against a tree and prayed as he had never prayed before. He slipped down into the ferns and tried to glide for deeper cover.

They sensed the flaring of his aura. With a demented scream of fury, the demons were on his trail. Narrow female bodies twisting through the air. Kotaru spun and hurtled his spear, deliberately aiming to drive the creatures back. The demons ducked, and Kotaru took his chance to speed off through the ferns.

A spear ripped toward Kotaru's back, and a Ka inside the weapon gibbered for his blood. Kotaru desperately tried to warp the ïsha in its path, but the spirit flicked his bolt away. Kotaru rolled, and the spear swerved and stabbed into his wing. With a hideous crash, the hunter slammed into the ground.

"Kaaaaah!" Somewhere in the darkness, demons howled hungrily. Kotaru sobbed and desperately dragged himself to cover, fangs clenched against a scream of pain.

Suddenly the open air yawned before him. He had scrabbled to the edge of a precipice, and a cliff plunged a hundred spans below him toward a tangled mass of rocks.

"Kaaaaah!"

Kotaru tumbled across the brink, flailing out in panic. He plummeted until, at last, ïsha bit and caught beneath his wings. His descent slowed. With a sickening crash, Kotaru plunged through a stand of wattle trees and struck the earth. Reeling with triumph, the hunter crawled into the shade.

Lost them! Lost them at last!

"Kaaaaaaah!"

Kotaru gave a croak of horror, then clawed back to his feet as the shriek of the hunters echoed through the air. He staggered deeper into the gully, blood dripping thickly from his wounds.

Somewhere in the dark behind him, a demon screamed in hate.

Shadarii climbed from her bath as the Ka fluttered in warning around her. The creature swirled, tugging Shadarii down the slope, pleading that she find a deep hiding place. With no idea why she did so, Shadarii followed, a thrill of fear rippling through her heart.

Ïsha flashed as Shadarii dried her fur, brought her clothes whipping up around her, and fastened them in place. She made to hide among the rocks, but the Ka pushed her onward toward a bare, blank stretch of cliff.

The Ka's presence began to fade as it reached the limits of its domain. Shadarii stroked it with her mind and bid it hurry back where it belonged. The spirit reluctantly withdrew, speeding toward the waterfall.

Lizards scattered as Shadarii crouched above a sharp, deep gully. Without the slightest fear, she spread her wings and leapt far out into the air. She landed by the cliff base fifty spans below and ran swiftly along beside the rock, and hunting for the promised hiding place.

Found it!

A low cave had been hidden by the overhang. Shadarii folded back her wings and scrabbled swiftly into cover, and then pressed back against the old, cool rock. The cliff made a superb refuge. Only someone on the ground could guess the hiding place was there.

The girl's breathing rasped in the sudden quiet. Frightened eyes searched the outside world, and suddenly Shadarii held quite still.

Out in the gorge, spirits fled into hiding. Something moved among the rocks, a broken, staggering thing that slammed against the stones. It wove drunkenly, stumbling through the bush to sprawl on the ground.

It was a man—a beautiful, bright-eyed stranger with fur as gray as smoke. He reeled and fought for breath, clutching the rocks with long, artistic hands while a wing flapped in ruin at his back. Ïsha left a trail of pain behind him, swirling and twisting like blood spilling into a stream.

"Kaaaaaaah!"

A deadly scream ripped through the air. The stranger gave a croak of panic and fell, slamming hard against a rock

Without knowing why, Shadarii sprang from her hiding place to drag the man to safety. He jerked in shock, staring in amazement at her face. Shadarii swiftly hauled him beneath the cliff and clutched him against her. She made a smoothing motion with her hand across the cave mouth, and ïsha rippled into sudden stillness. She had masked the cave, and the stranger's ïsha trail had gone.

"Kaaaaaaah!"

Black demon shapes exploded from the trees, spear points thirsting in their hunt for prey. Shadarii gasped as a wild silhouette framed itself against the sky.

Zhukora! It could be only Zhukora. The lean, feral shape glittered like a wasp as her skull mask searched the rocks for signs of her bleeding quarry.

They wanted the stranger; to—to kill him! Shadarii clutched her trembling companion, and for the first time looked up at her sister and felt the twist of hate.

Blood spilled hot against Shadarii's side. She daren't heal the stranger's wounds. The ïsha flare would be seen. The girl's sharp eyes searched their little refuge, swiftly finding the gnarled root of a red gum tree. She stripped the bark and gnawed it between her fangs, then pressed the stinging poultice against the stranger's wound. Shadarii placed a finger on his lips, her eyes pleading him to stay silent.

The demon shapes drew nearer, and Shadarii pressed herself against the back of the cave. The stranger's heart hammered as Zhukora's voice drifted from above.

"He's down there! I can feel him!"

"We'll find him." Daimïru—Zhukora's devoted acolyte. "The weakling's almost spent."

Cruel wings clattered overhead while black armor gleamed. Zhukora's left wing faltered. She staggered to one side, and a hiss of hate escaped her.

"Kill him. No games with the council! We hand the fools a corpse!"

"Will the council stand for it?"

"Who cares? I want him dead."

Shadarii stared in shock at the ground. The stranger's blood trail glittered in the sun, covered by a shield of glittering flies.

Oh, sweet Mother! If Zhukora sees...

"How's the wing?" Daimïru's voice sounded anxious.

Zhukora resented the very question. "It's all right! It's nothing!"

"You're hurt. Rest. I'll take him."

"No! He's mine!" Zhukora's mask jerked in fury. "I want him! He's mine."

"Zhukora..."

"Leave me alone! There's nothing wrong!"

"You'll damage it more!" Daimïru's voice cracked with anxiety. "Your wing is bleeding."

"Leave it be!"

The evil figure dipped ever lower. Shadarii flicked her eyes between her sister and the gleaming blood. Rain! If she came so much as one span closer...

Daimïru snorted, staring down into the gully.

"They haven't flushed him. He's circled round behind us."

"No, he's down there. Get down to ground, we'll see if we can find his trail."

No!

Shadarii suddenly slashed out with her mind, ripping the ïsha from beneath her sister's injured wing. Zhukora screamed and tumbled from the air, slamming hard against a ridge of rock. Daimïru gave a cry and shot to Zhukora's side. With a piercing whistle, she called in the hunt.

"Leave me alone! I can fly! I can still fly!"

Zhukora raged and staggered, trying to fight away Daimïru's arms. The other girl grimly held Zhukora on the ground, hunching down beneath a rain of hysterical abuse. Two more Skull-Wings whirled out of the rocks and raced to Daimïru's aid.

Zhukora bucked insanely in their grasp.

"I can fly! You bastards, I can fly! He's down there! Kill him! Kill him!"

She lunged and kicked, slamming Daimïru back against a stone. Zhukora's wing hung crushed and broken, and the pain must have been incredible; Wind only knew how she kept standing. Daimïru staggered to her feet as the other hunters grabbed Zhukora's arms.

"C-calm her down. Get her out of here before she rips the muscle more. Get her to the village."

Zhukora howled in fury, lunging for Daimïru's throat. "You bitch! I'll get you for this! I can still fly! Let me go, I can still fly!"

The hunters dragged Zhukora backward. Daimïru ripped off her mask and wiped her face, tears trembling in her eyes. "Get her out of here! Quickly!"

The Skull-Wings bore their leader back toward the village. Daimïru bent to collect Zhukora's fallen weapons, her hands shaking. Shadarii held her breath and closed her eyes. She could feel Daimïru's gaze searing across the cave.

The silence stretched as Shadarii held the stranger in her arms. His breath rasped, her pulse pounded like a drum. With a sudden clatter of retreating wings, Daimïru made her way back toward the village. The gully echoed in the sudden quiet.

The stranger stirred against Shadarii's side, and then turned to stare up at his deliverer, his face shining with disbelief.

Shadarii stared into a pair of fine brown eyes. It felt like falling into an endless well....

The stranger glowed firm and solid in her arms. His mouth seemed made for laughter, and his eyes for watching dreams. Shadarii basked within the pure warmth of the stranger's face.

The stranger made to speak, but Shadarii pressed her finger to her lips. She closed her eyes, her ïsha spilling down to fold him in a haze of peace, and the stranger gasped as energy poured through him like fire. His bleeding ceased. He blinked, his marveling hands reaching out to touch his healed wounds. Looking up in astonishment, he stared into Shadarii's gaze.

They both knew that he should go before Zhukora's men returned. Even so, he stayed. He floated in Shadarii's spell, sharing the gentle touch of magic.

The stranger lifted his face and spoke. His voice had a gorgeous accent that floated like a song. "I thank you for my life, my lady."

Shadarii felt her heart take wing. The man reached out to take her hand. It was time to go—he must! And yet...

Shadarii leaned toward him, drawn helplessly into his warmth. The stranger moved as though in a dream. Gently, softly, he reached out to take her chin. Shadarii felt her eyes close tight, and her soul tingled to his touch. Ïsha flared around them as his lips softly brushed her own.

She trembled, leaning helplessly into the ecstasy of the kiss. Her whole world spun as the stranger nestled in her arms.

After an endless age, they drew apart. Reluctantly the stranger backed away, his eyes locked adoringly on her face. Shadarii let his fingers trail slowly free. Suddenly, he turned and ran; brown wings spread as he soared into the open sky.

Long minutes later, Shadarii rose. It seemed almost as though the stranger had never been. She felt only the warmth of him on her lips, the lingering feel of him against her fur. Shadarii touched her mouth and turned to gaze into the clouds.

No dream; he had been real! A kiss—a *real* kiss—and brown eyes to shine inside her dreams! Shadarii hugged her arms about her sides and felt a glorious blaze of life.

"Father!"

The silent crowds of villagers were brusquely pushed aside as Zhukora fought toward the council. Two skull-masked hunters followed on her tail.

"Father!" The crowd melted before her. Zhukora saw the council seated calmly on their mats. She tore a path toward them. "Father, we gave chase! We've wounded one. If we can get fresh hunters on the trail..."

Nochorku-Zha raised his hand to silence her, never once glancing in his daughter's direction. His attention remained wholly fixed on another hunter.

Prakucha!

Zhukora's ears went flat. The girl ignored the swaggering hunter and knelt before her father. Her injured wing hung limp, conspicuously incapable of sweeping out in formal homage.

"Father! Father, listen!"

The council scowled in disapproval, pointedly ignoring her as Prakucha gave his report. He coughed politely and smoothed back his whiskers with one hand.

"In any case, Honored Ones, there is small damage done. A house door broken, a few dried fish taken. My hunters have seen the raiders off the premises...."

"*Your* hunters?" Zhukora stared incredulously. "You puking offspring of a slug! You cowered in the ferns while real warriors fought your battles for you!"

"Daughter!"

"But Father, he lies! He lies! We saw them off! My hunting group and I have been sweeping through the river gullies for an hour. We found a straggler and wounded him. If we can get fresh hunters on his trail, we might still run the thief to ground!" She looked around in anguish. "Why won't anyone help me?"

"Zhukora, enough! You shame our champion with your stupid prattle."

Prakucha shook his head and smiled indulgently. "Honored elders, this poor girl is clearly wounded and hysterical. I take no offense. Perhaps it would be best simply to let her have her say...."

Zhukora gave a scream of anger, then whirled and smashed her armored fist against the ground.

"Don't you dare patronize me! Why if you were half the man you pretend to be, I'd..."

Nochorku-Zha hurtled out his hand.

"Zhukora, this has gone far enough. Have you forgotten the jiteng game? Have you no interest even in hearing of the final score?"

"What?" Zhukora wiped her face; she simply didn't understand. The world was going mad. "Father, it doesn't matter!"

"Why of course it matters! By leaving the field, you have lost the game. Prakucha and his Splendid Orchids have proved their skills once again."

The girl's brain hammered with a raging headache. The smoke of burning houses still hung above the trees, and yet the council chatted amiably about some foolish game!

Her father shook his head in wonder. "Zhukora, have you no congratulations to offer the winning captain of the game?"

Zhukora stared at the elders, then pressed a hand against her skull as a throbbing headache raged inside her head. "It doesn't matter! Can no one see? Our village lies in ruins! Our homes are violated, families will go hungry, and still you—you waffle on about some stupid, futile game!"

Young hunters stirred and muttered in agreement with Zhukora's words. Old Councilor Fotoki glared at the girl across his folded arms.

"One of the hardest lessons we must learn in youth is perseverance. The rules of jiteng are quite clear; any player who leaves the field forfeits her right to play."

Zhukora wept in sheer frustration. "Rules! Does nothing matter but your stupid, endless rules?"

"You must learn the value of submission. Rules embody a perfect, ordered harmony. The game should teach you...."

Zhukora hurtled her helmet to the ground. "The game doesn't matter! We have been robbed! Homes burned, goods destroyed...."

Fotoki smugly settled in his seat. "Of course the game matters! It has demonstrated the strict principles by which we live...."

The huntress found her self-control. Tears streaming down her face, she tried to speak with reason. "Father, give me a dozen hunters! Volunteers who wish to go. Just let us try to find the looters' trail...." She opened her eyes to see her father wearily waiting for her to cease. Zhukora's final whisper carried to the silent crowd. "Has Katakanii honor sunk so low?"

The answer dripped from Nochorku's pinnacle of righteousness. "You are a foolish, twisted creature. You have shamed my teachings with your wild, destructive ways. Honor and violence do not intermingle. If someone has stolen from us, we must only regret that they did not simply ask us to fill their needs. What is a house burned or a few possessions broken? A year from now, who will really care?"

Zhukora gave an incoherent scream of anguish, then whirled to face the villagers and opened her arms. Nochorku-Zha impatiently hurtled his cup aside.

"Zhukora! That will be enough! You are dismissed. Go to the lodge. You are in disgrace!"

Zhukora stood, her wing hanging like a broken banner, and every eye hung on her as she stalked proudly through the crowd. The young folk watched her go, and then turned away and lost themselves in bitterness.

Long blonde hair rippled in the night as Daimïru landed on the ground beneath the lodgehouse of Nochorku-Zha. The hearth hut lay within an inky pool of shadows. Daimïru hesitantly crept toward the door, her eyes blinking nervously and her pulse hammering in her throat.

"Z-Zhukora?" Daimïru's voice quavered as she fearfully dragged her hair back from her face. "Zhukora, please! Please let me speak with you. I did it for you! You were hurt—I couldn't bear to see you tear yourself apart."

Something black moved inside the doorway.

Daimïru's wings fluttered miserably. "Please, I only wanted to help you. I did it because I love you. Please don't hate me! Please?"

The silence stretched, leaving the golden huntress racked with agony. She almost spoke again, but seemed to lose all hope; Daimïru hung her head and softly turned to go.

A weary stir of motion came from deep inside the hut. A sick voice whispered in the darkness. "Come, enter. Come and laugh like all the rest of them."

Daimïru crept into the dark, her antennae quivering to the scent of pain. Zhukora sprawled despondently before the fire, her head propped upon her knees. Her spirits had plunged from their mighty heights to smash to pieces on the ground.

The smell of sickness hovered thickly in the air. Zhukora's hair hung unbound to hide the telltale tracks of tears.

"Sit awhile. Sit beside the 'warped and twisted thing'. Come see the mad creature who thinks life is more important than mindless rules."

Zhukora sighed and closed her eyes. Daimïru hung her head, unsure quite what to say. She had come prepared with speeches, expecting hate, expecting fury. But to find this? It felt like being struck full in the face.

The women sat together, staring down into the ashes. Daimïru reached out to touch Zhukora's back.

Zhukora hung as listless as a slowly dying bird. "How do I ever dare show myself again? Did you see how he mocked me? All the world has seen just what the great chief feels about his eldest daughter." The words trailed off in bitterness. "Poison! How they must all be laughing at me..."

"They didn't laugh at you. No one laughed; they all knew you were right! Just go and ask. Go outside to any campfire, and you'll be cheered as a hero!" Daimïru found her strength, and wild eyes flashed with power. "You were right. When the cowards fled, it was you who fought! You shamed them all!"

"My father..."

"He is nothing! What is he compared to you? Like a candle against the blazing sun!" Daimïru's words trembled with emotion. "You are the future. You are our strength. Go, and I will follow you! Stay, and I will serve you! Call, and I shall fight for you while life still burns in my body!

"There is a dream in you. Something wonderful, something fine. To touch you is to feel the burn of glory. It's like—like being awake for the first time in my life! We need you. If you surrender, we are beaten. Remember who you are! Remember what you mean to us!

"Remember the Dream!"

Daimïru clenched Zhukora's hand, and Zhukora slowly straightened as strength flooded back into her soul. She looked out across the darkened village, drawing a deep breath.

Daimïru had been right; the people had not laughed at her. Not one! She looked around to meet Daimïru's burning eyes, and the girl touched Zhukora's drooping wing.

"Your wound—may I help to heal you? I would be honored."

The black huntress hesitantly stretched out on her bed while Daimïru knelt quietly at her side, her hands reaching out to stroke Zhukora's fur with a quiet ïsha tide. Smooth fingers brushed across the injured wing, bringing in a blissful flood of cool.

Zhukora sighed, her muscles letting go as pain simply drained away. Daimïru murmured comfort in her ears, coaxing her down into the gentle sleep of healing. Zhukora whispered as Daimïru's ïsha folded her in sweet, protective arms.

"You... you are a very precious friend, Daimïru. You are very patient."

The last spark of fury left her; Zhukora's antennae slowly drooped.

"So very, very patient..."

Zhukora's breathing softened with the kiss of sleep. Daimïru gently ran her fingers through Zhukora's fur, her eyes hidden beneath sheets of golden hair.

"Whatever you need in life, that's all I want to be. Whatever dream you dream, whatever path you fly, I will be there at your side. Always..."

Daimïru's hair spilled down to fold Zhukora in a screen of silk, and the forest moon arose to sheen the world beneath a kiss of light.

Four

A tall tree glowed beneath a sheath of orchids while butterflies circled in erratic joy, their wings flickering like flames. They danced in peace and happiness, safe within the endless forest calm...

"YOU DID WHAT?"

Butterflies scattered. Flowers shook. Prince Teki'taa gulped and hunched beneath the storm.

"Well, I-I..."

"You idiotic cretin! You droolin' imbecile! Fire curse the day your useless egg was wished upon my lodge! Rain only knows why I didn't smash the shell! I'd rather have had an omelet than a useless, sniveling son!"

The prince flattened his ears, his pride smarting beneath his father's lash; half the tribe was witnessing his misery.

"Sire, there were reasons! The very best of reasons..."

The king of the Vakïdurii strode back and forth across the clearing. "Reasons? I'll give you reasons!" The king ground a finger into his son's scrawny breastbone. "You want to replace me, don't you, boy! Well you won't—and do you know why?" The old king ground his teeth in fury. "You'll fail because you've got the mental prowess of an oaken stump! I've seen brighter critters lying belly-up on the bottom of a pond!"

Prince Teki'taa's ears flushed red. He almost shook with anger, but swiftly lowered his gaze as his father swung around.

"Do you know what you have done? Do you?"

"I've saved the tribe! There's food for empty bellies! We've proved ourselves against the Katakanii."

"You've started a war, you fly-brained fool! A war, like what they have in the old, old stories!" The king clapped his hands against his skull. "Peace has reigned for nigh a thousand years, but oh, no—my idiot son decides to start the first killin' match in all recorded history!"

The prince slammed his spear against the ground. "We can beat them, Father! Let them come if they be fool enough."

"Arrogant idiot! Didn't you even stop to think? We don't want to fight them; there's trouble enough just keepin' food in all our bellies! So what will the Katakanii do now, eh? Did you consider that? They have enough iron to throw away! Even their wretched hatchlings have knives. You arrogant, thoughtless, connivin' little..."

The returned raiding party knelt unhappily in the dust as King Latikai pelted them with abuse. Well distant from the rest of them sat a single lonely figure. The young hunter had half-healed wounds across his chest and wings, but it was he who had arrived home first. The king looked down at the boy and gave a derisive snort.

"You there—the one with the dopey look! What've you got to say for yourself?"

The hunter smiled dreamily into empty air, seeming never to have heard. King Latikai gave a snort; they were all as useless as each other.

"Veterans, eh? Veteran hunters. Well I hope you're proud of yourselves! This'll take some fixin'. I thank Wind and Rain you were at least smart enough to think of wearin' masks. With luck they'll not know who you were or where you came from. I'll see what can be done to reaffirm our cordial relations!" He glared down at his son and suddenly felt sick. "Oh, get out, all of you! And you can stuff that dried fish up your arses for all the trouble it's caused. Go on, out of my sight before I'm pukin' ill!"

The hunters swiftly fled the scene—all except the dopey one, blissfully ignorant of the whole affair.

The king gave a snarl and stamped away to find his wife. These youngsters were more of a problem every day!

Latikai's wife sat beneath a flowering wattle tree. She jammed a needle through a complex knot of embroidery and gave a huff of disapproval.

"Damned fool boy! This is your fault. He needs a father's iron hand!"

"My fault? 'Twas you that let him become a dandy!"

"He's a bully! I'd never thought I'd see the day I'd be ashamed of my own son. He's dangerous, and I say he should be watched."

"Aaaaaah, he's too young! He'll not dare make a move on me for a dozen years or more. Who's going to follow a mere hatchling in his twenties?"

"He'll do for you one day! You just watch that little snake. He's not the fool ye take him for."

An unpleasant silence settled, and the Queen of the Vakïdurii sullenly went on with her sewing.

A sigh hung on the air behind them. Latikai turned and glared back toward the clearing. There, the dreamy-eyed young hunter wandered through the grass. A look of dawning disbelief lingered on his face.

Pah! Now, there was a strange one. An honest soul, but about as addled as they came. He was young, and therefore unimportant. He was a commoner, and therefore expendable. He was honorable, and therefore gullible...

And there lay the beginnings of a plan. King Latikai looked at the boy and rubbed his hands together.

"Torvara, my love, we need the makin's of a very special jiteng team; a team designed to lose! They must play their blessed little hearts out, never even suspecting that they haven't got a chance."

The king eyed the vapid youth who fluttered off into the trees.

"Aye, a brand new jiteng team—and I think we've just found ourselves a captain...."

Ꮸ ᏶ ᏸ

Rain spilled through the leaves, spattering the ground with countless stars of light, and the ïsha of the forest took a grateful breath. Shadarii looked out upon the holy Mother's face and gave a smile.

One week later, and still the stranger's kiss burned on her lips; a week of dreaming, and still his eyes shone in her mind. Had it really happened? Sometimes the memory seemed so unreal, and then she would see those eyes before her—feel the warmth of him against her tingling fur...

He had been real. He had to be!

How to find him? Where had he come from? The whole village buzzed with gossip about Zhukora and the raiders. Now Zhukora had taken her angry followers far off into the forest, and her absence had only made the days sweeter. Shadarii no longer cared about her ruined life path. Worry melted in the face of beautiful new dreams.

A voice droned somewhere in the background; young Kïtashii and a clutch of other prepubescent girls sat listening to Deportment Mistress Teenahu. The teacher smoothed her perfect hair and shot a dark glance at Shadarii.

"...The secret of the 'wandering brightness' school of flower arrangement is simple enough in principle. Like all true arts, it is the interpretation that adds depth to the meaning. The seemingly random combination of sharp edge and softer textures... Shadarii, are you paying attention?"

Shadarii idly rolled her head to view her teacher and blinked dreamily.

Teenahu wrinkled her muzzle with a snort. "Shadarii, this is for your benefit as much as anybody else's! Since you know so much, perhaps you can show us how it's done!"

Hmmmm? Shadarii reluctantly dragged herself back into the present, reaching out toward the pile of fresh-cut flowers. Unseen by the others, a blossom simply floated up into her hand. Shadarii buried her wet black nose within its fragrance and breathed in the sweet perfume.

Teenahu huffed impatiently. "Shadarii, wake up! What's the matter with you, girl? You've been acting like a dizzy fool all week!" Teenahu's long white hair glinted. "Now do you know how to make the flower arrangement, or don't you?"

Shadarii moved without any hurry; her hands dipped among the flowers, plucking out a strange array of blooms. Finally her slim black fingers fell away. The flowers were perfectly arrayed in simple, subtle patterns; it was an utter masterpiece.

The girls sighed in rapt appreciation.

Teenahu's ears fell down flat. "Hmph! Yes, well, innovation is all right in its place. In any case, I see you have grasped some of the basics."

Shadarii buried her nose deep in the bouquet and sighed. For once, the world of worries seemed so very far away. She rose and danced out into the rain, her face turned up toward the gentle sky. One by one, the deportment class came out into the mist to watch and marvel.

Kïtashii stared at Shadarii, adoration in her eyes. Teenahu gave an impatient snort and flipped her wings. "Go back inside girl, there's lessons to be learned. What can you be if you don't study?"

Kïtashii sighed in rapture, her eyes fixed upon Shadarii's flowing form. "I want to be a dancer! I want to be beautiful. I want to be like her!"

Teenahu merely tossed her head and turned away, leaving Shadarii to her own affairs.

Far off in the bushes, a pair of ice-blue eyes watched Shadarii in malicious silence. A white tail stirred, then slowly sank into the shadows and disappeared.

ᏣᏛ Ꮪ Ꮄ

The dawn burned cold and bitter in the forest mists. Zhukora breathed in its beauty and felt life flow through her veins. Her hunting group ranged the forest all around her. For a solid week, they had lived off the land, binding themselves together in a grim, determined fellowship.

One week. One week since her humiliation. The young folk of the clan had turned away from their elders, finally rejecting the ancient regime. They came to Zhukora's hearth fire in the evening just to bask within her glow, and a dozen folk had clamored to join the Skull-Wings. Zhukora thrilled as a strange power flooded into her hands.

The people needed her. When she smiled, the men walked taller, the women squared their shoulders and lifted their heads high. Zhukora had become their symbol of defiance.

The hunters made a strange, grim spectacle as they glided through the trees. Each man and woman wore tough leaf-leathers to protect them from forest thorns, while a pack across their chests held the few supplies they needed to survive. A dao ax, a wicked bunch of spears, and a woomera for throwing them made for a deadly armament. These were the elite—Zhukora's chosen few. The nobles could keep their traditions and their rules. The trust of one of these common hunters was worth more than all the jewels in the sky. Zhukora looked out across her chosen ones and felt a thrill of love.

It felt good to be far from the villages. Zhukora's headaches had driven her out into the dark. The councils had betrayed them all, and too few people had the eyes to see. They listened to the elders and believed the lies they told. A disaster was coming, the councils would do nothing, and the people were apathetic!

The hunt had led Zhukora high into the deserted peaks. The forest's food supplies were drying up, and all the game had gone. Zhukora meandered along forgotten ïsha trails as she led her teams in search.

A whistle trilled from somewhere in the ferns, calling for Zhukora's personal attention. The woman flicked out her wings and dived silently off into the fog.

Daimïru flew behind her; all was as it should be.

The women speared through the mist, their wings leaving swaths of phosphorescence in their wakes. Zhukora banked past a looming tree trunk and swirled down beside her forward scouts.

The man knelt beside a massive something that gleamed against the forest floor. Smooth green stone had been carved into shapes; there was something like a nose and eyes, the broken tips of wings—

It was a buried statue!

Zhukora knelt down and reached with marveling hands to touch the thing. A life-sized Kashra had been buried neck-deep in the mold. The artistic style seemed crude and barbarous—an object from uncultured ages past.

The other hunters gathered as Daimïru took her dao and dug into the dirt. She uncovered the statue's shoulders, chest, and breasts. The girl exhausted herself long before she reached the statue's waist.

Curious... still, it might look good outside the lodge. Zhukora stroked her muzzle and wondered whether it was too heavy to be carried home—

"Hunt leader! Another one!"

A second statue stood, facing the first. Hunters spread out and began scratching at the mold.

"Here's another!"

"And here! Another!

Someone had found a third, and a fourth, fifth, and sixth, dwindling off into the gloom. The mist held hundreds of shapes, ranked into a silent avenue.

Zhukora gazed along the lines of statues and signaled her followers aloft.

"Follow; we'll see where this leads."

Great wings stirred as the hunters drifted quietly in the mist. Beneath them the lines of statues led their way into the mountain peaks—up into a land of bitter winds and barren, folded rocks. Finally the trail led to a massive, broken cliff, and the Kashra drifted earthward one by one.

The ïsha stilled, and the birds stopped their singing. Leaves swirled and rattled through a dead, forgotten world. The hunters stood among a vast wilderness of crumbled walls. Huts? Lodges? Who could tell? The ruins lay like the green bones of an ancient corpse. Zhukora landed in a sea of brittle weeds, her nose twitching to the pungent, acrid scents of broken leaves.

A huge cave yawned before them; a strange, smooth tunnel with walls slick as a dripping tongue. The line of statues plunged straight into the cavern's heart.

Round, gray stones paved the ground before the cave. The hunters warily followed them inward. Daimïru knelt to run her hand across the surface, and a piece broke off beneath her touch. Puzzled, she took her knife, broke a lump of paving free, and turned it over in her grasp.

Empty eye sockets stared madly back at her.

The girl gave a croak and hurtled the thing away, while hunters scattered in superstitious dread. A skull was the seat of a being's Ka. No Kashra would touch the leavings of the dead.

Deep within the cavern, the ïsha slowly stirred. Zhukora seemed fascinated by the cave; step by step she drew closer, her footsteps crunched on the rotten skulls. Daimïru swallowed, her pulse pounding in her throat.

"Stay back, Zhukora! There—there might be spirits!"

Zhukora's voice whispered with a strange intensity. "Daimïru, don't you feel it? Can't you feel the power here?" Zhukora's fur stood all on end. "Sweet Rain, the air's alive!"

"Come back! The place reeks of evil! There might be an ïsha vampire."

"But why fear it? We could hunt it! Kill it!"

"Zhukora?"

The lean black huntress stared into the dark, her eyes strangely bright and hungry. "A challenge. To face it down alone! The ultimate test—power against power, soul against soul! The loser falling down into absolute oblivion..."

The leader drew a long, deep breath. Finally she turned back to her followers, and her face seemed animated with a strange new energy.

"We camp here for the night." She looked around with bright-blue eyes. "Yes, here among the ruins! Let us see what dreams the night stars bring."

The hunters looked unhappily about at the ruins, gloomy even in the early afternoon light. Zhukora reached out to fold her people in the power of her gaze.

"Don't be afraid. I am with you."

She walked into the weeds, her tail trailing out behind her, and without hesitation, the other hunters followed, exploring.

By nighttime the ruins had yielded many puzzles—here a lump of rusted iron, there a row of tiny figurines. Rocks had been fused and melted like long strips of ice. The hunters had searched all day, and still there were no answers for any of it. What had happened here, and why had even the faintest ïsha traces fled?

There were tales of the past that were never danced. Many fists of years[14] ago the Kashra had been more numerous. They had dug houses in the soil and had thronged the skies. And then—what was it now? Something bad had happened....

Shadarii would have known. The cripple sucked up stories like a toad hoarding water. For once, the little mute might actually have been useful. Zhukora found the thought strangely irritating.

The firelight stained the weeds a dreary, spectral gray, making hunters pull their sleeping robes about their shoulders. There were no possums creeping through the boughs. The bats and frog-mouthed owls seemed to shun the very air. The only animals worth eating were snakes and warty toads, but the stringy meat lacked any taste. For some reason, Zhukora ate her meal with avid speed. Finally she wiped her fingers on her leggings and reached out to find her weapons.

"We set a watch tonight. Two of us will be awake at any time. Each time the fire begins to fade, we change one sentry." With twenty to share the watch, the waiting would be easy. Zhukora threw away her sleeping robe and slung her spears. "I'll take the first watch."

Ever loyal, ever watchful, Daimïru silently followed Zhukora out into the dark. As the other hunters turned back to their food, Zhukora left the campfire far behind and walked into the empty lands of stone.

Black hair shimmered; blonde hair shone. Daimïru's quiet voice finally broke the silence. "You're going to the cave."

"Yes. Go back to the others. It's too dangerous to follow."

"No. I will stay where I belong."

The cavern seemed nothing but a patch of thicker darkness. Light flared as Zhukora spat the ïsha into life. A dry branch crackled, and flame caught in its crown. With a torch held firmly in her hand, the huntress led the way across the field of moldering skulls and down into the cave.

---

[14]**Fists of Years:** The alpine custom for counting numbers counts all five fingers on the right hand, and then the wrist, forearm, elbow, upper arm and shoulder, and so on in reverse down the other arm. This allows ten numbers to be tallied for each arm. A fist is made when the last finger is closed when reaching the number twenty.

Thus if a hunter touched her left forearm to indicate a number, she would be signaling the number fourteen. A touch of the right shoulder would be ten, and so forth. A fist of fists is equal to twenty times twenty.

Light died against a wall of liquid black. Isha snapped and sparked across Zhukora's metal weapons as she crouched with wings spread wide. Antennae quivering, she sniffed a presence. Zhukora hissed in challenge, fangs flashing in her cruelly perfect face.

The women stalked into the depths. Overhead, the ceiling opened out until it faded far from view, and walls glistened slick as eel skin in the torchlight. Daimïru and Zhukora reached the far end of the cave, only to find it blocked by rocks; their journey had come abruptly to an end.

Shattered Kashran skeletons were strewn across the floor. In the breathless air, the dead had withered into shrunken mummies. Daimïru kept her spear in its woomera, her eyes fixed upon the screaming faces of the dead. The huntress almost feared to speak within the oppressive silence.

"Th-the tribe. Nochorku-Zha will want to know. About the cave, I mean."

"The tribe!" Zhukora gave a snort, then kicked a withered corpse. "Nochorku-Zha and his heroic band of elders. Why waste time telling them?"

Zhukora tried to hide her disappointment. The cavern's promise of adventure had withered; there were no enemies to battle, no wild discoveries to thrill their eyes. Only broken corpses and an empty, useless hole.

"Nothing! No more life than my stupid father!" Zhukora stamped on an ancient skull. "Useless! All useless. We're wasting our damned time! Nothing ever goes the way it should!"

"Zhukora!"

The leader slammed her fist against the wall.

"Nochorku-Zha! That thief Prakucha! Rules and ties and regulations!" Zhukora reeled as the sickness twisted at her brain. "Fire's death! It makes me burn every time I think of them. There's no hope, no freedom. Just endless repetition, on and on and on..."

Stop sniveling, girl. If the world offends thee, go out and change it!

Zhukora jerked in shock. She leapt and snatched her spears, slamming her back against the wall. "Who's there! Come out and show yourself!"

Daimïru blinked. "Zhukora?" Her leader stared out into the dark, breasts heaving in alarm. Daimïru looked around in puzzlement. "Leader, what is it? Did you hear something?"

Zhukora stared into the dark, relaxing bit by bit. She finally released a long, slow breath.

"Nothing! It was nothing. The cave is empty."

Slowly relaxing from her battle stance, Daimïru sighed in gratitude. "Let's go back, then. There's nothing for us here. Just bones and stinking rags."

"You go and wake your relief. I'll join you shortly."

"I'll stay with you."

The torchlight flickered across Zhukora's face. "Go! I said go! I'll follow. It's... it's quiet here. I just need—I just need some time alone to think."

There was no arguing with her. Daimïru reluctantly spread her wings and flitted from the cavern.

Zhukora waited until the night grew still once more. She stood within a ring of skulls, her long hair spilling down to glitter in the dark. "Show yourself. Come out and face me! Or are you nothing but a coward skulking in the dust?" The words echoed in the empty cavern. Zhukora merely glared and waited.

The ïsha trembled as a titanic presence slowly split away from the dark. Its light spilled up from corpses, from rocks and ancient crevices, while unseen winds swirled and hammered through the cave.

I am here, girl. I have watched thee—felt thee—waited patiently for thy coming. It is rare to find a creature such as thou.

The girl confronted the shifting glimmer of the Ka. "What do you mean a creature such as I? What sort of creature?"

One who holds the world within her hand. Thou walk'st through the dream of power like an all-consuming star!

Zhukora slowly let her spear sink down and suspiciously eyed the huge presence hovering about her.

"You speak nonsense. How is it you can speak at all?"

I am not some pathetic nature spirit! I like the world, girl. I like the power of it.

"So why speak now? Why show yourself at all?"

I spoke because I am intrigued by thee. I spoke because I like what I have seen. I spoke because I can bear no more of thy pathetic, childish whining!

Zhukora's jaw dropped in indignation. "You dare!"

Dare? Yes, I dare! Zhukora. Zhukora the complainer. Zhukora the coward!

"I am Zhukora! Zhukora-kai-Nochorku-Zha. None dare call me coward!"

Prove it, then! What mighty deeds has Zhukora done? What great achievements can she boast? What powers has she gained? Is she happy with her pathetic little life of servitude?

Zhukora's power blazed; she gave a snarl and punched out with a bolt of light, and the spirit casually parried it aside.

Thou wouldst fight me, then? Good.... It seems courage has not died in these last thousand years. Come, daughter, still thy anger. We must speak together.

Zhukora hissed; the power still blazed within her hands. "Fight me! No one calls Zhukora coward!"

I will not fight thee, Zhukora the warrior. I shall not pluck this world's most priceless flower. Come! I have a gift to bring to thee.

"What do you mean. What sort of gift?"

I bring thee the gift of sight.

The spirit stirred, and corpses rolled and tumbled in the breeze.

This carrion—do you see the fallen? A monument to their own cowardice. Where courage called to them, they responded with terror. They lost the purity of their vision.

If thou fear to take the future in thy grasp, it will always escape thee.

Zhukora scowled as the Ka glowed and coiled sinuously around her.

Thou crave'st challenge? Then here is challenge for thee, Zhukora of the forest clans! Here is the test to prove thyself before the judgment of eternity! Thou say'st that thou wish changes? Then make the changes happen! Rise and take the future by the throat!

Zhukora's breath grew ragged as she stared into nothingness, her mind alive with furious energy. She felt power flowing through her—the dawning realization of a wild dream of destiny!

"I... I can do it!"

She blinked, looking up in wonder at the being hanging there before her.

"I can do it!"

The girl gaped at the whole new world revealed to her.

A thousand years of stasis—a race trapped inside its self-made cage. Corruption slowly bred in the stagnation. No challenges, no progression, like an animal pacing around and around again inside its pen until it drives its spirit mad.

They must break free. Everything—everything must be changed! Like a butterfly emerging from its chrysalis to soar into the sky, the people must be awakened.

"It will take time! I-I must make plans. I never...   I never really stopped to think..."

Thou art a hunter! Take the opportunities and strike with unrelenting fury. Thou art a thinker. Resolve thy obstacles into problems and deal with them one by one! Be ruthless. Be savage. Think only of the price of thy failure.

Zhukora looked up, her face lit by dawning joy. "Why? Why are you even interested in me? What does a spirit care about mere mortals?"

I care, Zhukora! This earth is dull—no fit place for brilliant creatures such as thou. I would see the world grow bright again. Find the dream! Light the fire sleeping in your soul and bring the glory back again!

Zhukora moved to the cavern mouth, her face still blazing with her revelation. The girl paused in the entrance, pulling her hair back from her face.

"What is your name, my lord Ka? What should I know you by?"

My name is not important. But if thou wish'st, thou may call me Serpent.

"I thank you for your words, Lord Serpent. I thank you for your gift." Zhukora moved out among the weeds, the spirit's words drifting softly on the wind behind her.

I wish thee well, sweet daughter. I wish thee joy....

"Up! Move out! Move out!"

Heads jerked as sleepy figures rose from the weeds. Zhukora streaked down beside the campfire and kicked the embers.

"On your feet! We're moving. Hurry!"

Hunters scrambled for their equipment.

Daimïru crawled out of bed, her eyes blinking wide in puzzlement. "Zhukora! Is it danger?"

"Danger? Yes, it's danger. Danger of growing old within this hell! Danger of letting ourselves fade beneath their rules. It's our world, our future! It's time, my love! It's time we flew out to ride the winds of destiny!"

Daimïru's face lit with joy. Zhukora grabbed her hand and drew her laughing into the air. "We can change the world! We have only to want to make it happen. We can take the nightmare and turn it all around into a glorious new dream!" Zhukora buried her face in Daimïru's shimmering blonde hair. "A future, Daimïru! It's ours if we choose to make it! We could sit and whimper, or fight to take what's ours!"

Daimïru clutched Zhukora's waist and was whirled by a dizzy rush of power as Zhukora cried out to her hunters, "Are you with me? Will you share the Dream?"

Her answer came as a blaze of adoration. The hunters raised a howl of fury. Wings swept out, and Zhukora's followers stormed into the nighttime sky.

Zhukora hung before them in the air, her soul ablaze with light.

"Back to the village! We're wasting no more time. Back—back to forge a future!"

Wings flashed. The band of hunters followed a dream into the dark, pulled behind Zhukora's burning wake.

മ ഇ ഇ

Shaded prettily beneath a pair of orange wings, Shadarii sat basking in the rosy glow of a rich, creative mood. She had perched herself on a rock in the middle of a waterfall, and clean white river foam surged past her in a wild, refreshing spray. She sat cross-legged on the rock, her soft tail curling in her lap and her wings flipping open and closed in silent thought.

A "music stick" lay in her lap. The long strip of wood had been notched with marks, each of which showed the position of the fingers when blowing a note upon a long reed flute. It was a simple trick that music students used to memorize their tunes.

The girl stared, her mind alive with tenuous thoughts. In a state of absolute absorption, she gazed out into nothingness and let the ideas take hold. She tapped a piece of charcoal against her fuzzy chin.

The name Shadarii was a melding of three other words: Shadii Dalu Rïkra—"Precious gift of love". A name honoring the mother that had borne her at the cost of her own life.

Shadarii; a message in three parts.

When an artist created a rock painting of a story, she made a simple representation of each object she depicted. Could an abstract word be shown in much the same way? What if words could be made into pictures? What if one day, Shadarii could paint her words for everyone to see? Finally she would have her voice!

So if one . . one simply tried to paint a sentence like a story is painted on a rock, what then?

An object seemed fairly simple to depict. If you needed to say "rock," a rock could be drawn on the bark. But what about an action? Running? Flying? Difficult, but possible...

What about something truly abstract and unseen? What about an emotion, or a name?

Shadii Dalu Rïkra. Precious gift of love. How do you draw a picture of love? Two partners joining in the bed? Surely not! Precious gift of sex? Hardly a name she wanted to be stuck with—although perhaps Javïra...

Bah! The problem still remained. How? How to show it? Shadarii scratched her pretty nose and frowned; there was an idea almost forming in her mind. Almost but not quite...

Bah!

It wasn't working. There were too many indefinable words. Just thinking through a list of peoples names made her brain whirl. Shadarii, Zhukora, Nochorku... Who could possibly find a way to turn them each into pictures? What use was a sentence made only of things and objects?

Damn!

Shadarii had a dream—a dream of knowledge being held and cherished like a treasure. Day by day, an untold wealth was lost! Each old man who died took with him a thousand stories. Every grumbling old woman owned a store of cranky wisdom. If it could only be captured. If there were some way other than ritual dancing, some way that could store and keep thoughts in a single form without endless reinterpretation....

"Shadarii!" Little Kïtashii stood on the banks, her silver fur covered by a patched and faded set of clothes. "Shadarii, the council says we must all help gather food in the gardens!"

Oh? Shadarii spread her wings and rode the smooth, soft ïsha currents of the river, swooping down to land beside the skinny little girl. Shadarii let herself be led into the trees to where the forest was being stripped back to the bone.

The Swallowtails were desperate for food. Guests were coming, and the garden groves had already been plundered bare. Even the seed stocks had been eaten; the trees were stripped of fruit, the yams were dug and the nuts all picked. Hundreds of women splashed in the river harvesting bulrush roots, while men hauled angrily at empty fish traps. Every last scrap of food had been combed out of the forest, and still it wouldn't be enough.

There were more people in the clan than ever before. Ten years of good weather had increased the forest's yield, and the population had expanded to match nature's bounty. Now, the price was being paid; this average year had triggered a famine.

For the moment, the forest was overrun with frantic furry shapes. All around Shadarii, teams of women labored in the undergrowth, grubbing in the mud for yams. Men split tree ferns to reach their tasty pith, making the forest ring to the sound of hundreds of blades. It was ugly and destructive, and Shadarii looked on their works with disquiet. Tree fern pith was tasty, but what of next year? It took seven years for a tree fern to grow. Every fern around the village would soon be gone! Surely the elders had a plan?

There was real hunger here; babies wailed while hard-faced women tore into the dirt with digging sticks. Shadarii's tail fell. While the nobles had dined off meat and honey, the commoners had made do with pounded seeds and stringy roots. No commoner would complain of the low fare.

But still, Shadarii saw...

Shadarii smiled as the women gave her welcome. She was often here, healing plants or sniffing out wild berries for the children. She had an uncanny talent for divining the location of hidden tubers and nests of tasty ants. Within minutes, she was swiftly burrowing through the soil, forming an impressive pile of roots behind her. A dozen other women followed her, trusting her antennae to find the food their eyes had missed.

Mistress Traveesha's dancing class came trooping down into the grove, the haughty faces of the girls soured by ill humor. They had clearly been dragooned into the workforce, and gardeners smirked and hooted as the dancers wandered past.

Shadarii wiped a muddy hand across her face and grinned as Javïra minced fastidiously through the ferns. Her fine white fur had been freshly preened and scented—her skimpy clothes were carefully arranged. Javïra watched in horror as laughing gardeners tossed each other freshly dug grubs and muddy roots.

Mistress Traveesha wore a painfully understanding expression. "All right girls! Now we must all pitch in if there's to be enough food for the ceremonies. We must show that in these hard times, we can cooperate, eh? Chins up! Everything will be all right as long as we keep smiling!"

With these stalwart words of wisdom, she left her students to their own devices, hurrying home to a hard-earned cup of tea.

The leader of the nearest digging group sniffed and wiped her hands, eyeing her new workforce with a professional gaze. "All right me precious lovelies! If your ladyships would be so kind as to step this way, I'm sure we can accommodate you. There's digging sticks down on the mat and baskets by the trees. I'd suggest you take your off your jewelry and dump it over there."

Srïhooni's elegant figure cringed back from the dirt. "How do we... I mean..."

The gardener gave a derisive snort as one huge hand curtly beckoned Shadarii. "Hey copper-locks! You're one of 'em! Take our precious ladyships and show 'em how it's done."

Shadarii had no wish to be anywhere near the other dancers. Since leaving their company, she had felt better every day. With a curt swish of her tail, she fluttered off among the tree trunks. One by one the other dancers followed, their wings daintily carrying them high above the grime.

Digging stick in hand, Shadarii demonstrated the heady skill of excavation. Like all things, collecting yams involved a ritual; a tiny piece of tuber was left attached to the root stalk of the plant, ensuring that there would be a new yam to collect next year. Shadarii soothed the angry little plant Ka with a caress of energy, thanking the little creature for its precious gift of food. She flipped the root into the basket and silently indicated other yam plants lurking in the brush.

The dancing girls fell to their work with ill grace.

"Ow! I broke a nail!"

"Get off my tail!"

"My nail! Skreg it-it's ruined!"

Slowly and painfully, yams were yanked out of the dirt. Most girls dug vast trenches to find a tiny bulb of root. Shadarii quietly dug up three yams to the other dancers' one. She diligently soothed the offended plants, taking the time to heal the few that seemed sick or old.

Javïra stared at her, and the look within her eyes seemed strangely disturbing. She jammed her stick into the dirt as though stabbing into someone's heart. Shadarii ignored her and let her mind wander off into her private dreams.

Eyes. Brown eyes that sang with wonder, and one, sweet, perfect kiss...

Srïhoonii tugged unhappily at a root and slung it in her basket. "What's up with fatso? What's she got to smile about?"

Javïra jerked a root and hissed in spite. "She thinks it's funny, don't you, Shadarii! You like laughing at us, eh?"

Shadarii never even heard; she stared serenely off into the air, her hands delving down to coax another tuber from the earth.

Javïra bared her fangs in hate and went back to her digging. She planted both feet in her hole and threw her weight against a stubborn piece of root. "Awk!" The plant pulled free in a rush of dirt, and Javïra hurtled back with a squawk. The other girls laughed as she struggled upright with a tiny yam held in one hand. Javïra threw the root into the bushes and shrieked. She saw Shadarii smiling quietly in one corner and slammed her fist against the ground. "Don't you smile at me, you freak! Don't you dare smile at me!"

Shadarii looked resentfully at Javïra and turned back to her digging.

Javïra hissed and threw a dirt clod at her foe, and the lump struck Shadarii on the shoulder with a cruel thump. "You think you can smile at me, eh? Well go on! Smile!"

Shadarii's ears went flat, but she kept on with her work.

Javïra groped for ammunition, suddenly the center of attention. "Hey, you! Hey, cripple! I'm talking to you!"

Another dirt clod flew; Shadarii winced as it crashed into her side. She ground her teeth and closed her eyes, refusing to react.

"Do you like it? Do you like the dirt?" More earth showered Shadarii's hair. "Go on! Here's some more! Grovel in the dirt!"

One of the other dancers scowled unhappily. "Uh, hey Javïra..."

Javïra was enjoying herself; her spiteful face sneered in triumph as another lump of dirt shot through the air. "Go on, Shadarii. Why don't you ask me to stop? Just open your mouth and say it!"

Shadarii stood to leave, her fists clenched and her face rigidly controlled. She began to stalk slowly down the hill.

A dirt clod smacked Shadarii's skull. She hunched, filth spattering from her shoulders, then stood very, very still....

"Go on, Shadarii! What are you going to do about it? Get your boyfriend to protect you? But you don't have a boyfriend, do you? You don't have anybody! No one's ever going to touch you, because no one's ever going to love a—!"

Shadarii whirled.

Javïra's fangs flashed in victory; she had seen the sudden pain and terror in Shadarii's eyes. "Is that what you want, Shadarii? You want it, eh? You want it! You want somebody to—"

Suddenly the air filled with slashing wings. Javïra screamed as Shadarii flew at her in rage. Fur tore and hair ripped as the women tore each other into shreds. The gardeners threw down their tools and raced to the scene.

Srïhoonii wept in fright. "Stop them! Somebody stop them!"

The chief gardener's teeth were set in a wild grin of delight. "Leave 'em! I bet three yams on the fat red one!"

The two girls brought no science to their fight, no clever moves or planning. It was simply an explosion of hate. They kicked and rolled across the dirt. Javïra yanked and tore out a fistful of Shadarii's hair, but the fatter girl wasted no time causing minor injuries. She bit and clawed, blood bursting out between her fangs as she sank them in Javïra's arse.

"Shit! Get her off her! Get her off!"

"She's killing her!"

"Poison, stop her!"

Hands tried to drag the girls apart. Shadarii clawed back to her victim, sinking in another vicious slash.

"Shadarii! Shadarii, no!"

"Stop it! You've won! Shadarii, stop it!"

Strong arms dragged the girls apart. Javïra looked like she had been mauled by angry crocodiles. Girls ran to tend her, gently lifting her battered, bloodied head. A dancer looked in horror at Shadarii.

"She's mad. The girl's insane!"

"Oh, emu shit!" The old gardener spat at Javïra's face. "It's only what the skreg deserved. I saw what she was doing! She's got just what she was asking for." The burly woman put an arm about Shadarii's shaking shoulders. "Come on, love. We'll clean you up a bit, eh? Well done! You showed 'em a thing or two for once, eh?"

Dazed and shaken, Shadarii let herself be led away. Javïra somehow managed to raise her head, spitting blood past a newly broken tooth.

"Bitch! I'll k-kill her! You just see!"

Srihoonii stared down at Javïra in distaste.

"You've done quite enough for one day! I hope you're proud of yourself!"

Javïra's lips bled. "Y-you see? I-I told you the bitch was dangerous!"

"Shut up, Javïra!" Srihoonii turned and curtly signed to the other girls. "Come on. Let's get her home."

Five

A kookaburra whirred through the air to land on a tree branch. He was a fine fat bird with plumage like a molting feather duster. The creature cocked his head and rolled his eyes, sniffing eagerly for the scent of fun. He stropped his beak and sat back to watch the entertainment far below.

"Pass Drill Seven! Even numbers, go!"

A confused mass of figures lurched into action above the meadow. The jiteng players were a gorgeous sight against the shifting forest leaves. With their bright blue armor and whirring brown wings, the Superb Blue Wrens made a brave show in the streaming forest light.

A ball flashed up through the air. Kotaru made the catch and tore off toward the goals while the other players dutifully wove up in support. They were tired and hungry. Here and there, a figure lagged unhappily behind. Nonetheless, the unit stormed forward with grim determination. Kotaru looked back across his shoulder and felt a surge of pride.

It was time to see how much the weeks of training had achieved. Kotaru punched the ball back toward the pack, grinning as two figures streaked to snare the prize. They used a perfect double-pronged assault, one to snare the ball, and one to cover the catcher's tail. The two players streaked down with the lethal grace of stooping hawks, wind streaming through their fur.

From high above, another Wren hurtled down toward the narrowing gap between the other catchers. Kotaru squawked in shock and flung his hands across his eyes.

"Mrrimïmei —no!"

All three players smacked together with a titanic crash, plowing through the daisy bushes in a tangled heap of limbs. With an awful grinding sound, the heap tumbled to a halt. The ball dropped down to thud atop one player's upturned rump.

The air split with a raucous howl of laughter as the kookaburra whooped with glee. Kotaru ignored the beast and swooped down to the aid of the injured players.

"Totoru! Tingtraka! Mrrimïmei!" Kotaru lifted a girl from the top level of the pile. "Mrrimïmei, speak to me!"

Kotaru's star catchers moaned beneath the remnants of the daisy bush. Players wearily hauled the victims to their feet and dragged them off toward the water buckets. Kotaru sighed and watched them go, failure weighing heavily on his heart.

Mrrimïmei still sat among the ruined daisies. The girl wept silently, her face twisted in shame. Thin shoulders shook as Mrrimïmei scrubbed furiously at her eyes.

"I tried! I r-really tried! I only w-wanted to... to..." The girl gave up and hurtled her helmet to the ground. "Everythin' always goes wrong! Why can't I ever do anythin' right?"

"Oh, Mrrimïmei..."

Kotaru sat down on the ground beside her while the girl shed tears of frustration. What should he do? Kotaru simply had no idea.

His new jiteng team had surprised him. Strangely enough, they all really liked him. It was a nice feeling. He trusted them, and for some reason, they were eager to please. He had intended to be their leader but instead had ended up their friend. Kotaru felt he'd found the richer path.

The memory of her still glowed like a fire within him. The vision of the girl who had rescued him hung bright before his eyes. Kotaru felt the thrill of it; the sure certainty that they would meet again.

He was captain of the Wrens. If the Wrens could win the tribal games, the king had said they would be sent against the Katakanii.

One simple win, and then they would travel to the Katakanii lands, where she would be, waiting for him, her eyes as bright and green as forest jewels. They would laugh and talk—really talk at last! He would make a song for her, and she would fill the air with the magic of her voice.

His mind whirled dizzily down from the heights of imagination. For now, reality lay here, among the daisies. Mrrimïmei sniveled unhappily beside him. Kotaru supposed he should be angry; Mrrimïmei was petulant and rash, but she always tried so hard...

"'Tis all right, Mrrimïmei. 'Tweren't your fault. We simply made a few mistakes. We're still new to it."

The girl wailed in misery.

"It was my fault. It was! I tried! I really tried..." The girl sobbed, reeling with fatigue. "I always ruin everything!"

Her nerves were worn to a ruin. Mrrimïmei was a nice girl who lacked confidence. Her accidents sometimes seemed intentional—excuses to stop trying, reasons to halt before she could be forced to put her abilities to the test....

Inspiration! Treat the cause and heal the symptom. Mrrimïmei's accidents would cease when she gained confidence. The thought was positively warming.

Kotaru gave the girl a hearty shake and smile. "Take a rest! We'll try again when we've had some food. This time, I want you to take the position of forward rover."

"F-forward rover? I-I don't know if I can."

"Surely now. I need you! I need my best people up front. You're the fastest flier in the tribe!"

"I-I am?"

"Can you think of anyone in the forest who can outrace you?" Kotaru warmed her with his smile. "Why else do you think we specially asked the king to place you on the team? Please accept the position. We need you. We really do."

Mrrimïmei looked at Kotaru, and then licked her lips, turning the information over in her mind. Suddenly she stood and wiped her hands.

"I... all right. I'll try. I'll do better this time, just you see!"

She actually laughed as they flitted out across the open meadow. Kotaru tried to outdistance her, and Mrrimïmei shot ahead at an amazing turn of speed. She looked back across her shoulders and grinned at him in triumph.

Kotaru gazed at his companions and paused in silent thought. The king had asked Kotaru to form a team for the tribal games; it was to be Kotaru's reward for his good sense during the raid against the Katakanii tribe. His team members were an odd selection. They were the strange ones—the folk that were always slightly out of place. The team contained none of the popular pinwheels of sport, and the nobility were completely unrepresented, even to the point of having a commoner as captain! A very strange team, to say the least.

"Well, boy! So fierce, so thoughtful. A mighty captain pondering his tactics, eh?"

Kotaru whirled.

King Latikai loomed from the ferns, his huge swag belly swaying as he waded through the underbrush. "So, lad! An impressive show of talents. Fast, decisive! That's what I want from my star team! You'll win the tribal championships without a doubt."

The young hunter felt a clench of awe about his heart. The king! He was actually speaking to the king! He nervously fell into a bow, trying to find his voice.

"Sir, uh, Sire. I-I thank you!"

"A fine team, my boy. Just the type of talents I'm looking for."

Kotaru tugged nervously at the collar of his armor. "Sire? About the collision, my lord, it won't happen again! It was a mistaken signal, nothing more. My folk are tired, sire..."

The king spread his hands and beamed forgiveness down at Kotaru. "Think no more about it, lad. No more about it! Recklessness is the better part of bravery."

"Yes, Sire!"

"Good! Good lad." The king threw a huge arm about Kotaru's shoulder, nearly crushing the youngster flat. "So, boy, tell me what y' need. You have the players, you have the gear. Is there anythin' I can provide you?"

Kotaru coughed. "Uh, well my lord... I was just..."

"Speak out, boy! I'm listening. Anything you want at all!"

"Sire, these players you've given me—are you sure... I mean, there's none of them as has any real practice with the game an' all. They're lovely people, but I'm wonderin' if you've not made a wee bit of a mistake...."

The king patiently shook his head. He dragged Kotaru closer and dropped his voice to a conspiratorial bellow. "Nay, lad! You've fallen fer it yourself, y' see? Always people look for the obvious talent. They think because you're big or tall or handsome, or because your family is wealthy, you've the makin's of greatness!" A huge finger waggled at Kotaru's nose. "Untrue! Greatness comes from the heart. And you, my lad, have that greatness within you!"

"I, Sire?"

"That you do, lad, that you do! You have a spark, my boy! A spark that I want cherished. So, here's the test! Do you feel the dizzy scent of victory callin' out to you?"

Kotaru saw a dazzling vision of beautiful green eyes, and his heart leapt as he thought once more of the girl. "Yes, Sire!"

"Ha! That's fine, lad. That's just fine!" He slapped Kotaru on the back "Now go back to your practice, and don't make me regret my confidence in you!"

Kotaru cracked out a clumsy salute. "Yes, Sire! I mean no, Sire! I'll do it. I'll make us win, just you wait and see! I'll make you proud of all of us!"

Kotaru sketched a bow and sped back to his men. He gathered his troops and began to fire them with a speech. Suddenly, they were spilling back onto the playing field, the air ringing to the sound of battle yells.

The king watched with wicked eyes, his teeth clenched brightly in a grin.

That's my boy! You take them and you make the bravest show since Mother Rain fought Lady Poison. You take all that optimism and dash it straight into the Katakanii's faces! They'll eat you for breakfast, boy. You and all your team of weeds and failures!

A loss to the Katakanii would salve the other tribe's pride. With a hearty laugh the king strolled back toward the village. It was all going perfectly; the game would be an utterly splendid failure.

C3 &0 &0

Mistress Traveesha planted her snout to earth in a profoundly graceful bow, remaining poised for just exactly the required amount of time before she raised her eyes to face the elders.

The leaders of clan Swallowtail met once more in solemn council.[15] Old Chitoochii stirred her teacup with a sprig of herbs and bored her gaze into the younger woman.

"So, Traveesha, what mischief have your girls brought upon us now? Fights in the village; girls tearing one another into bits, our rules of conduct flagrantly abused! We hope you have an explanation for this sorry situation."

The dance mistress folded her hands within her lap, her voice the very model of control.

"It is not the dancers who are at fault, respected elder. It is but a single rebel. A willful girl who has brought the crime of violence to our village." Traveesha kept her face held in a sad mask of regret. "Nochorku-Zha, it pains me to report that your daughter Shadarii is unbalanced. Perhaps her disability has overtaxed her fragile mind. We have tried to be kind, and she has paid us back with hate. Again, she has ruthlessly attacked, without provocation...."

"Ha!" The sudden bark of scorn made the assembly turn. They stared in outrage at a slim figure leaning insolently against the doorpost of the lodge.

Zhukora wore the simple garments of a huntress, her straight black hair streaming unbound below her slender waist. Sharp eyes gleamed as she made a wave of greeting with her hand.

"Respected elders, pray forgive my tardiness. No one informed me the council was in session."

Nochorku-Zha glanced disdainfully at his daughter.

"Zhukora, enough of your antics! We shall not forgive your ill manners again!"

---

[15]**Councils:** According to alpine legend, when First Mother became caretaker of the forest world, she took twelve advisors to be her councilors—a bird, an orchid, a fern, a tortoise, a cassowary, a platypus, a wallaby, and so forth. The tradition of the twelve-part council has remained, but formal titles such as "Brother Platypus" and "Sister Fern" are now considered inconsistent with a noble's dignity.

"Ill manners, Father?" The girl seemed quite put out. "I mean no disrespect. Quite the opposite in fact. I have come here to obey the tribal law—a law I respect too deeply to allow it to be broken."

"Broken?" Councilor Chitoochii folded her arms across her breasts. "What nonsense is this! Your father has told you most firmly..."

Leaf leather rippled as Zhukora moved, her thin body framed by her startling blue wings. "Why, surely you are aware that any person made the object of a council debate has the right to state their defense? My sister cannot speak, and so someone else must protect her reputation. Father, is it not right that I should protect my beloved sister's honor?"

Nochorku-Zha was incensed enough to actually pour himself a cup of tea.

"Don't be ridiculous, girl! That law is made only for matters of importance!"

"But surely, Father, the fate of any clansperson is a matter of importance."

"Eh? Don't be absurd! It's no one of any great position! Anyway, it's only what's-her-name."

Zhukora seemed shocked. "Father! As lord of the Swallowtail clan, are you suggesting there is a different law for young than old, for high than low?"

There was a stir of motion from outside. A considerable audience of young tribesfolk had collected by the council lodge to listen. Zhukora had conducted her campaign with care, and Nochorku-Zha played right into her hands.

"Eh? What's that you say? Different law? Of course it's a different law! Poison rot your insolence! You young idiots need putting in your place! Why in my day, I'd never have dreamed—"

Councilor Fotoki hastily leapt in, drowning out Nochorku's words. "Why come now, Nochorku-Zha! The council upholds the law for young and old, alike!" He nervously glanced out the door. "The council would be most delighted to have you represent your sister."

"My Lord, I thank you for your gracious reception. Pray, forgive the disruption of your business." Zhukora sank gracefully down upon her shanks. Her sharp face twitched as she suddenly noted the high priestess in the corner of the lodge.

The high priestess gave a nod of acknowledgment, sinking back into her talismans to watch events unfold.

Nochorku-Zha had hopelessly lost his train of thought. He stared in puzzlement at Traveesha and blinked his eyes. "You there! What are you doing here?"

"Why, my lord, surely you remember! I am Traveesha, dance mistress of the pastholders. I came here at your request, to provide evidence against the dancing girl Shadarii."

"Shadarii? Damned cheek! What's she been up to this time?"

Traveesha heaved an impatient sigh.

"She has been implicated in a fight, my Lord! She struck another without just provocation."

"Lie!" The word struck home like an ax.

The councilors blinked and stared over at Zhukora while Traveesha's jaw dropped in outrage. "I beg your pardon!"

Zhukora idly examined her gleaming claws. "Are you hard of hearing? I said you are a liar."

The high priestess folded her hands and smiled. Zhukora was a sheer pleasure to observe at work; the girl had a master's touch.

Old Fotoki scratched his mangy neck. "My dear! What exactly are you saying?"

"The dance mistress is deliberately perjuring herself. She is hiding facts in order to mislead this sacred council."

Mistress Traveesha's fur stood stiff with shock. "You dare! Why you arrogant little upstart!"

"Are you claiming that Shadarii acted without due provocation?"

Traveesha's eyes were wide with anger. "Respected elders, my niece was attacked by this—this cowardly Shadarii and beaten within an inch of her life!"

Zhukora studied the set of a silver ring on her finger. The ring was Daimïru's, borrowed just for the occasion, and Zhukora rather liked the effect against her smooth black fur. "Mistress Traveesha neglects to inform the council that Shadarii was provoked beyond all reason. Law requires three acts of provocation as justification for a violent act. The girl was jeered at, pelted with filth, and finally actually challenged to the fight! I can produce at least twenty eyewitnesses who will so testify."

A murmur of astonishment passed around the council, and Lord Nochorku glared down at the hapless dance mistress. "Mistress Traveesha, were these facts known to you before you made your statements before this council?"

The woman gulped. "Well, ah, why no, my lord. They-they were not..."

Nochorku-Zha gave a sniff. "In the future, I suggest that you avail yourself of full information before daring to approach the council! To do otherwise could compromise our judgment, a situation that is quite unthinkable!"

"Yes, Lord!"

"Hmph! So are we to understand that this girl, uh..."

"Shadarii."

"Eh?" Nochorku blinked. "Oh, Shadarii—yes—that Shadarii has actually caused no fights?"

Traveesha tried to salvage her damaged pride. "My Lord, I have told you the truth as I see it. Shadarii-kai-Nochorku-Zha has been central in two incidents of public violence! I say that she is a disruptive influence and a danger to the other girls. My poor Javïra has lost three teeth! The healers have had a dreadful time grafting her fangs back into place."

A soft, calm voice gently soothed the ïsha as the high priestess radiated matronly good sense. "Please, good people, there's no need to unbalance our harmonies over such a little thing. Perhaps this honored council might allow a poor old woman to make a small suggestion."

Nochorku-Zha dared not risk a bow—his back was in no condition to withstand the strain. Instead, he gave the high priestess a firm nod of consent.

"By all means, Revered Mother. This—this whole damned argument has lasted far too long!"

The fat priestess folded her hands across her bulging belly. "A simple solution seems to suggest itself; since the girl unwittingly causes trouble, perhaps she should be eased out of such a public profession. Future harm will thus be avoided before it ever gains the chance to form."

Nochorku-Zha seemed utterly delighted. Now here was wisdom! He looked about in satisfaction at his council, noting with some puzzlement the look upon Traveesha's face.

The dance mistress coldly laid her antennae flat. "And what, pray, would the Revered Mother suggest as an alternative future for this newly freed young dancer?"

"Oh, she might prosper better in an atmosphere of calm reflection. I'm sure the wise Nochorku-Zha and his talented eldest daughter would agree."

"Calm?" Traveesha's fur bristled instantly with fight. "You mean the priesthood!"

The priestess spread her hands in logical appeal. "If this is where Shadarii can find true happiness, I suppose it must be so. I'm sure we can find a way to welcome this poor, unwanted little waif."

The lean gray dancer whirled toward the council. "The past-holders have precedence! My lord, this is utterly forbidden! Shadarii is ours. Ours by right and custom!"

Old Nochorku-Zha was a touch confused. "But, my dear, you were just now saying that you wanted to be rid of her!"

"I? Never! I merely dutifully pointed out the troubles she had caused."

A polite interruption came unexpectedly from the sidelines. Zhukora's voice shone with pure, sweet reason. "My father has always been most pleased to see his youngest daughter prospering as a dancer."

"Have I?" The old man looked confused until Zhukora gave him a reassuring smile. "Yes, well I suppose I have."

"Why, Father, of course you have!" Zhukora's isha field stoked across her father's mind. "It's a family tradition. Shadarii is following in the wind-wake of our beloved mother. You really have no intention of releasing Shadarii to the priests."

"Don't I?" Suddenly the old man's stubbornness took hold. "Yes, of course I don't! The very thought of it. She can stay where she is and learn to like it!"

Zhukora gave the high priestess a look of triumph. The older woman narrowed her eyes, not yet content to concede victory.

"Zhukora-Ki, I wonder if you aren't overstepping yourself in this regard?"

"I think not, Reverence." Zhukora smiled. "I know exactly what I am doing."

The look that they exchanged spoke far more than mere words, and the priestess cursed herself for letting greed force her hand too soon. "Bah, the girl shouldn't remain a past-holder if she can't fulfill her function. The girl can't even speak a word!"

Zhukora combed her hand through her exquisite hair. "There's a simple way to meet your challenge. Shadarii should prove her skill. If she can truly dance, surely the past-holders is where she belongs. If she proves she lacks talent, perhaps another profession might reasonably claim her."

A capital suggestion! The elders murmured in approval, muttering eagerly to one another.

"Very well, Zhukora. Produce this sister of yours one hour after the evening meal, and we shall judge this tongueless storyteller's talents."

Fotoki smiled and nodded. "You are a most honorable girl, Zhukora. Your duty to your sister has been nobly discharged."

There was a general motion of assent, and Zhukora graciously bowed. "Respected elders, I thank you. My heart flutters when I try to imagine how our tribe would fare without your leadership."

The girl cruised serenely from the lodge while the council members congratulated themselves on another job well done. The high priestess heaved herself onto her feet and stalked off on Zhukora's trail.

Outside the lodge, the trees were filled with loitering young hunters. The high priestess saw Zhukora waiting for her on a branch, and the two women walked side by side in silence. The high priestess slyly tried to probe Zhukora's aura, but her efforts were to no avail. Like her younger sister, Zhukora had an ïsha field that burned with terrifying power.

The old woman glanced sideways at Zhukora's face. "I congratulate you on your rhetoric, Zhukora-Ki. The council are like putty in your hands. You handle them well."

"There is no art in leading fools; only in avoiding becoming one."

"You would be a fool indeed to cross the priesthood, girl! A fool indeed!"

Zhukora glanced archly down her nose.

"Why, Revered One, do I have something you desire? How very interesting! Now that gives us something to talk about, doesn't it? You see, there are a few things I might want from you...."

At last the bargaining began.

The high priestess halted and planted her fists on either side of her swaying belly. "Do not fight us, Zhukora! We have plans, my girl—plans that can advantage both of us. We can go far together, you and I!"

"Ooooh! You have an offer to make me, Your Reverence?"

"Give us what we want! Give us Shadarii, and we will talk!"

Zhukora gave an evil smile. Her fine blue-black wings opened and closed behind her as she eyed the high priestess.

"Do you wish to bargain, Your Reverence? Shadarii is still negotiable trade goods! Convince me. Who knows? Shadarii might yet be yours. I shall be most interested to hear your offers, Reverence. I shall be waiting with... anticipation."

With a swirl of her tail, the girl departed. The high priestess stood grinding her fangs in fury, muttering dire oaths beneath her breath.

CS ଅ ଋ

The council fires burned bright against the forest night, catching the gleam and flicker of two thousand watching eyes. Nochorku-Zha sat enthroned amid the clan council; hunters and gardeners made silent ranks inside the gloom. News of Shadarii's trial had spread, and so the clan had gathered to witness the judgment of Nochorku-Zha.

Within the shadows, a small, soft figure slowly rose against the ferns. Firelight lingered on shining orange curves, and the flames were shamed by the figure's glorious hair.

Shadarii wandered down into the light.

While deities such as Wind or Rain were always represented naked, lesser spirits were depicted through formal dress. Tonight Shadarii's limbs bore crisscrossed swirls of color, and a painted wooden mask hid her pretty face. Shadarii's clothes hugged close against her plump young curves, and her eyes sparkled with a secret laughter that made the night seem bright. Shadarii warmed the senses with a homey glow, like the taste of golden honey upon fresh made bread. One by one, the audience relaxed, basking in the softness of Shadarii's subtle light.

The costume was instantly recognizable; tonight Shadarii became First Mother, Zui-Kashra-Zha, daughter of the Wind and Rain.

Shadarii knelt and bowed before the council, her heart pounding in her breast. Fail, and she was finished; Zhukora had made it all too plain. The council settled back to watch and judge, their eyes hard and unforgiving.

A ritual dance required at least two dancers, yet no other dancer had offered to give Shadarii aid. None of the dancing girls would risk the displeasure of Zhukora or the priesthood. Even so, little Kïtashii had come to Shadarii's rescue. The children had flocked into Shadarii's arms, and with their help, she might just triumph yet.

Shadarii had chosen tonight's tale with loving care. It was a story of her own invention; the legend of First Mother and the coming of the flowers.

The expectant hush was broken by a distant trill of sound. Gourd flutes made a haunting, dreamy melody. First Mother looked about and wondered at the beauty of her world, and then stretched up to thank the Wind and Rain for the gift of life.

Shadarii's interpretation of the character felt strangely soft and gentle; the First Mother seemed like a little child left to run and play. She thrilled to the feel of life within her wings, marveling at the forest air and the soft caress of ïsha. First Mother drank from clean, pure streams and danced in golden sunshine.

Shadarii lost herself in a reverie of love. Each pose and motion held a world of meaning; each tilt of head and glint of fur told a tale all of its own. Where Shadarii danced, the ïsha swirled with wondrous, subtle hues.

First Mother ate of the bounty of the forest. She supped on fruits and ate eggs straight from the shells. Someone in the audience laughed as Shadarii rubbed her belly fur. For once, Shadarii's weight was an asset.

The novelty of food began to wane, and First Mother grew bored with her tasteless fare. The girl sighed and slowly let her eating cease as a supple creature slithered from the shadows.

The newcomer had the figure of a little girl, skinny as an eel and strangely alien. She had fur as gray as ash and hair the pale silver of a winter moon.

Kïtashii made Shadarii's heart swell with pride! The girl seemed as eerie as a mantis creeping on a leaf. The Fire spirit made a mocking dance and turned to address the world's first mortal.

Why are you so downcast? Why are you not eating fruits and tasty meats? Is anything wrong with the pretty mortal's world? Fire posed in thought, a sudden sly tint of craftiness stealing through its ïsha field. *Is the food losing its taste? Aaaah, but there I can help you! I know a secret—a secret to make your meals taste good again!*

First Mother looked up in hope, and her stomach growled in anticipation. *Power to make good food? Show me! Oh, show me now! Sweet Fire, I will do anything you ask.*

The audience members bit their lips as Fire sidled closer. *Anything? Why little sister, let us make a bet. We shall play a game together, you and I. If you should win, I shall grant you the use of my power. But if you lose, you must pay to me a penalty.*

A penalty! First mother crept cautiously closer. *What-what kind of penalty . .?*

Why, you must give me your pretty tail.

First Mother snatched up her tail in shock! She clasped it hard against her breast and stared in accusation.

My tail! My lovely tail! She backed away from Fire in horror. *Never! Never will I risk my precious tail. Begone!*

Fire looked with greed at First Mother's broad backside, then sidled closer, crooning in her ear.

Come, come. If I offer a thing of value, then so must you! Make the bet with me. Make the bet and play a game with Fire!

Zui-Kashra-Zha hesitantly lifted her antennae.

Wh-what sort of game?

Why, my dear girl, it is really very easy. We shall both go out for one day and try to make the most beautiful object that we can. Whoever creates the most perfect beauty shall win the bet.

It all seemed fair. Zui-Kashra-Zha licked her lips and thought about the lure of food.

Very well! We shall make our bet. We shall both see what new beauty we can make to give the world!

The audience was spellbound; Shadarii's gift for theater had snared them. Kitashii played her part with waggish style, and what she lacked in skill she made up for in enthusiasm.

Shadarii faded out into the background as the Fire spirit swirled off on its wicked quest. First Mother's beautiful, soft tail would soon be in Fire's grasp!

The spirit flew until it reached the sparkling lodges of the stars. The five starlets of the Southern Cross were played by tiny girls from Shadarii's magic class. They sat and twinkled as best they could, putting on a brave show before their grinning audience. Fire approached the stars with an elaborate air of innocence.

Oh, graceful stars, I have long admired your shining beauty from afar! I have come to pay my homage to you. I have here some combs of fine new honey. I present them to you with my profoundest compliments.

The stars eagerly snatched the honeycombs. Although each now had a comb, an extra piece still lay before them. The Stars fell to quarreling bitterly over the delicious tidbit until Fire intervened to calm their feud.

Now, now! The extra comb should clearly go to the most beautiful of all the stars. The star that has the prettiest sparkle should rightly claim the prize.

This started the argument all over again. The stars each posed and preened, claiming superiority over the others.

Fire, you decide! Which of us has the prettiest sparkle? Make your decision so that we may eat this delicious honey.

The Fire spirit hemmed and hawed, fluttering thoughtfully around and round the twinkling stars. Finally Fire shook its head.

Little stars, I fear I cannot judge. The sun is too fierce for me to properly see your shine. Give me your sparkles! I shall take them down into a cave and examine them there.

The stars grumbled and each gave up her shine. *Very well, but hurry back! We wish to eat the honey.*

Fire flew swiftly back to earth, then rolled the stolen star shine into little balls. Fire held up the world's first gemstones and laughed with glee.

First Mother's tail was as good as won!

Meanwhile, Zui-Kashra-Zha wandered disconsolately through the forest. Night drew near, and still she had no thing of beauty to show the Fire spirit. Zui-Kashra-Zha cradled her tail lovingly in her hands, listening to the sounds of little birds.

Birds!

First Mother raised her eyes in sudden wonder, then spread her wings and raced to meet her foe.

Fire lay in wait beneath a tree. The spirit sidled closer, ready to snatch away its prize.

What have you created, little mortal? What have you brought to me to rescue your pretty tail? Can it be better than these lovely sparkling gems? What can possibly match their beauty?

First Mother smiled and raised her face to the sky; a hush fell as she brought a brand new gift into the world.

Softly, quietly, the girl began to sing.

Music rose, playing out the sounds that Shadarii's throat could never form. First Mother's song swirled like a rain of orchid petals. The audience gasped as her aura spilled across them, caressing them with love.

The song rose to its finish and trailed off into silence. The Fire spirit sagged in defeat. She sprang to her feet and dashed the gemstones down into the ground. Beaten! Beaten by a mortal! The spirit tore her hair and pranced in rage.

Suddenly a shadow fell across the scene. Fire looked up in apprehension as the stars of the Southern Cross descended to the earth. Mother Rain and Father Wind loomed overhead; Fire tried to hide the fallen jewels, but it was far too late.

The stars angrily confronted Fire. *Vile, deceiving beast! Give us back what you have stolen!* They snatched back what sparkle they could still find. Far too many fragments had been lost inside the earth. The stars glared at Fire in anger.

You have taken powers from us and used them for deceit! We insist that you pay your wager to this mortal girl. You must grant the Kashra use of fire so that she may cook her food and work the metals of the earth. Furthermore, since you have cheated on your bet, we decree that you must pay a penalty. Otherwise we shall speak to our parents in the Milky Way!

Fire looked at the Milky Way in fright, then fell down before First Mother and begged for pity.

It was but a joke! A jest between two friends. Would you rob me of my powers out of cruel revenge?

First Mother wavered. Though she knew it might be wrong, she took pity on the weeping spirit.

Hush, now! I want no powers from you but my tail, and I demand a penalty. Since you tried to steal my tail, you may give my tail a gift.

Fire felt deliriously happy to have escaped so very lightly. The creature touched the mortal's tail and made it shine with light. With a last hasty glance at the assembled stars, Fire dashed deep into the earth.

With a sudden cry of joy, First Mother danced off through the forest. She threw her store of colors to the little plants, bringing brightness to the world of dripping green; and so the first flowers came into the world. Zui-Kashra-Zha had invented song, discovered cooking, and created flowers all in a single day.

Though her body eventually passed away, as all mortal things must, still her spirit lives to guide her children; and when First Mother flies up to meet her parents, the passage of her tail can still be seen behind her. For when Wind and Rain come down to visit earth, their loving daughter rises to join them, leaving a sparkling rainbow in the sky.

The dance done, Shadarii sank down in a graceful bow and covered her face with the petals of her wings.

Not a sound came from the audience; there was silence, even from the great, dark spirits of the trees. Shadarii slowly wilted, her worst fears suddenly realized.

Someone thumped his spear on the ground; another hunter joined the first, and then another and another. Others swiftly followed, until the clearing thundered with applause. Shadarii stared around herself in wonder.

They had liked it! She was saved!

Shadarii blushed beneath her mask, then swiftly called the children in to kneel beside her. A renewed outburst of cheering rose from the clan. Shadarii's inner ears flushed bright red; she ducked her head, thankful for the cover of her mask.

"Delightful, girl! Absolutely delightful!" Councilor Fotoki spread wide his hands. "Nochorku-Zha! You've kept her hidden from us far too long!"

Nochorku-Zha sat coldly in the shadows, glancing at Traveesha through slitted eyes.

"Traveesha—an opinion! Is the brat truly qualified to dance?"

The dance mistress made to speak, licking at her lips as she tried to force her words. She looked from Javïra to Shadarii, her heart hammering loudly in her throat. She wilted. Her whispered reply trembled. "She—she is the finest dancer in the tribe...." Mistress Traveesha closed her eyes and looked away. "She can stay. She has won her place among us."

The high priestess immediately leapt to her feet. "No! It cannot be! This was not a traditional story. She invented the whole tale! This is close to blasphemy!"

Councilor Chitoochii snorted irritably, glaring at the priestess. "Oh, nonsense! I agree the tale was improvised, but it has a most innocent charm. Shadarii—did you really invent the tale yourself?"

Shadarii gave a hesitant little nod, trying to avoid the high priestess's eyes, and Chitoochii beamed with delight.

Nochorku-Zha stirred himself once more and beckoned little Kïtashii closer. The girl slipped off her mask and hesitantly approached the chief. She bowed clumsily, her skinny rump tilting high in the air. The chief's voice blew cold and humorless. "Shadarii has had great fortune in her companions. Where did one so young as you learn the skills of dance?"

Kïtashii answered in a sweet, grave voice that seemed far wiser than her age. "Shadarii teaches us herself, my lord."

"Teaches you? But the creature can't even speak!"

The little girl paused as though finding the question strangely full of meaning. "We understand her well enough, my lord. Perhaps you have simply never listened."

Nochorku-Zha sank back into his cushions, then steepled his fingers and glared out into the dark. Finally the old man reached his decision. "Very well. Shadarii, a dancer you remain! It is done."

A wild whoop of approval thundered from the crowd, and Shadarii's face lit with joy. To her father's embarrassment, she flung her arms around him and hugged him till she cried.

Traveesha sucked her teeth and glared about the cheering crowds. Her eyes lighted on Kïtashii, and the little girl quailed beneath her gaze. "Kïtashii, come and see me in the morning! You are a dancer as of now."

The trial dance dissolved into a storm of merriment. Tribesfolk sang as the instruments rang out through the darkness. Couples laughed and swirled into the sky. Traveesha watched it all through pain-dulled eyes, as with a heavy heart she turned back toward her lodge.

Damn that Javïra! Now she had been forced to contradict herself before the entire blasted clan! The last few days had been an absolute disaster.

"Traveesha-Zho? A word with you if I may!" Zhukora silkily detached herself from the darkness, her lean curves shining beneath the light of distant stars. "I have been waiting for you, honored mistress. I pray there are no hard feelings between us. You surely understand that I must fight to protect the interests of my sister."

Traveesha-Zho sourly turned away. "Your sister's interests have filled enough of my time for one day. Forgive me if I retire to my bed."

"Please! A moment more! I wish to speak with you about a matter of some— ah—some delicacy. An embarrassment to the both of us. I wish to speak with you about the problem of my sister."

Traveesha-Zho reluctantly faced Zhukora. "Forgive my lack of manners." Ïsha flared around the woman like a sullen, fitful flame. "I am tired, and I cannot quite face more thoughts of Shadarii tonight. She has cost me face before the council. She has made me break faith with my own niece. My one and only wish is to go to bed! Perhaps this nightmare will all look different in the morning."

She began to walk away, but Zhukora strolled amiably along beside her. Zhukora's bodyguard, a quiet blonde girl with haunted eyes, kept silent pace with both of them.

Traveesha sighed, wearily sat down on a log and let Zhukora have her way. "Oh, very well, Zhukora, crow just as you like. I have little choice tonight except to listen."

"But Traveesha-Zho, your authority is not lost! We all saw the way you stood against the high priestess. You are a hero! People will long speak of the day that Traveesha held her ground against the mighty priesthood!"

Traveesha blinked, then stared into the face of hope. She looked in wonder at Zhukora. Why hadn't she seen all this before? Of course! She was the ultimate victor! Traveesha had triumphed after all!

Zhukora warmed the older woman with the power of her eyes. "Yes, so now you see! There's no reason to be glum." She leaned closer, drawing Traveesha beneath a veil of intimacy. "As to our mutual problem... Shadarii has pushed our pity much too far. She is stubborn, willful, and unlikely to cooperate with other girls within a dance." She gripped Traveesha's hands. "Perhaps you can do us all a great service. Give Shadarii a past-holding task of no account; perhaps the preservation of something special—something old and forgotten? Something she will never be called on to perform. Shadarii is kept occupied, your dance class is at peace... nobody loses, and everybody gains!"

Traveesha saw the simple beauty of it. Inspiration stuck home like a lance.

"Yes, of course! She may learn knife dancing! Why no one's performed a knife dance in living memory!"

"A knife dance?" Zhukora's predatory ears pricked high. "Yes, that sounds most interesting."

"Yes! A brutal, vulgar dance performed with dao. Hero spirits wield such weapons when they enter battle! Dao—ugh! I shudder just to think of it."

"I trust the dance is safe? I should not want to think of my beloved sister being in any danger... ?"

"Safe! Ha! She'll never get to demonstrate the art! Illegal—forbidden! No one may demonstrate the battle tales. Yes, knife dancing it is!" The dance mistress eagerly dusted off her hands. "I hope this has sorted out your problems?"

Zhukora bowed, her wings sweeping out to hide her face.

"Why, yes, indeed, wise mistress. I am forever thankful for your wits."

Hours later, Zhukora fluttered outside her family's lodge. It had been a most satisfying evening. She swept the curtain aside and was puzzled to find the lamps still alight. Zhukora stalked into the lodge, a frown scored across her haughty brow.

"Aaaaah, my precious beauty! Come in, my treasure! Come in and hear the joyous news we have for you!"

Her father's voice bubbled brightly through the air. Zhukora smoothed her face into its accustomed mask, flicked her streaming hair across her shoulders and advanced into the light.

Her ears suddenly went flat in rage; Prakucha beamed at her with a malicious smile. Nochorku-Zha had invited vermin into their home! Here—and on her mother's rug! Zhukora somehow managed to jerk her gaze down to the floor, then knelt and bowed in obeisance to the high chief of the Swallowtails.

"Father, Prakucha," the last word was spoken with a spit of venom, "pray forgive my tardiness. Had I realized we were expecting guests, I would have remained here to serve you."

"No matter, no matter! Your sister—the fat one—she saw well to our needs before I chased her off to bed." The old man waved his hands. "Come! Come closer! Come share the marvelous news we have for you."

Her own father poured Zhukora a brimming cup of tea. Zhukora pursed her lips in puzzlement.

What on earth was going on?

She felt revulsion slither up her hide as Prakucha watched her hungrily, his eyes drinking in her every curve and swell. He stared at the slim lines of Zhukora's rear, and his smirk made Zhukora crawl with nausea.

Nochorku-Zha reached out to take his daughter by the hands. Zhukora blinked in shock; he had never touched her with affection in all his life. What was the old spider up to now?

"Aaah, Zhukora! Fairest of my little brood. It is always such a pleasure to see my young ones come of age. Sometimes the years just slip us by..." He shook his head and eyed her fondly. "We have been unfair to you, my daughter. You have had to be a mother before you could even be a bride. Well, no more! Finally I shall give you what I know you crave so dearly. I have just arranged for your marriage to Praku-cha!"

It was like being hacked down with an ax. Zhukora sat back, her disbelief still frozen on her face. "What?"

Had she heard right? Zhukora blinked and tried to make sense out of her fathers words.

Nochorku-Zha slapped his thighs and boisterously nudged the groom-to-be. "Ha, ha! I told you she'd be overwhelmed! Do you see the joy on her face? Do you feel the thrill of romance in the air?"

Indeed, Zhukora remained utterly speechless. She swayed, almost falling in a faint. Her father wiped a tear from his eye.

"The waiting time is over, Zhukora. At last you may give yourself to eggs and children, and discover the joys of love that you have left untouched for oh so long."

The groom chuckled evilly and gave the girl a sickly smile. "Zhukora! My dearest love, come embrace me! We have so much to talk about, so many plans to lay...."

He reached out to cup her face. Zhukora snarled and struck.

Prakucha rolled with the blow, then dabbed gently at his bleeding lips, smiling in anticipation. "Yes, my dear, an exciting wedding night to plan for. We shall be joined at last...."

Nochorku-Zha gaped at his daughter, aghast at her behavior. "Daughter! Have you gone mad?"

Zhukora's fangs flashed. "Father! Get this vile creature from my sight! Out! Get out of my lodge!"

"What? Don't be mad, girl! He's the finest catch in all the clan. We gain status, security...."

"While he gains the chieftainship! You old fool, can't you see you're being used?"

"Zhukora!"

The girl bore the old man down with sudden hate. "How dare you! How dare you try to sell me off to this impotent poser!

"You'll do as you are ordered!"

Zhukora threw back her head and laughed. "I run this family, old man! I, not you! I'll marry whom I please and when I please, and this pleases me not at all!"

Her father gaped. "How dare you speak to me..."

"Silence, you old fool!" Zhukora leapt to her feet, snatched her dao from its sheath, and loomed above Prakucha. "You cringing bastard! You can't beat me at the hunt! You can't beat me at the game! Is this the last way your sick mind can think to best me? Never! I'll choke myself with maggots before I let a beast like you lay hands on me!"

She slashed out with her blade, gouging wood chips from the lodge posts. With a scream of fury, Zhukora raged from the room, spread her wings, and launched herself out into the dark.

Nochorku-Zha hurtled himself to the door. "You'll marry him! As I live and breathe, I'll make you marry him! Zhukora, do you hear... ?"

The huntress clenched her fangs and tore wildly through the air. Old bastard—he'd pay for this! Zhukora felt the hatred washing through her like a thrill of lust. Her mind whirled with rage, blood searing though her veins.

The demon of the cave would know what to do. Zhukora snarled and sped into the night.

Six

Far from Shadarii's village, a brown and kindly creek meandered through the forest's hush. Noonday sun streamed through the trees as Mistress Traveesha led Shadarii by the stream.

"Now, Shadarii, we have thought long and hard about your talents, and we've come up with a fascinating suggestion. You do like researching ancient knowledge, am I right?"

Shadarii nodded, her eyes sparkling bright with curiosity.

Traveesha inclined her antennae in satisfaction. "Good! Very good! I see we have not made a mistake. We are counting on you to help revive an almost vanished art!" The dance mistress led the way beneath a screen of weeping willow trees, sending grasshoppers fleeing from her path.

"Now Shadarii, pay attention! You must be responsible for your own research. This is a special project of your own. The caves beneath the river gorge hold paintings of the dances you must recreate. As far as I know, there is but one other dancer specializing in this field, a nice girl from the Bird-Wing clan. You should meet and compare techniques at the toteniha ceremonies."

Shadarii came closer as Traveesha threw back the wrappings on a mysterious bundle.

"Now, these are just for practice, mind! We'll have a presentation set made for you sometime in the future."

Shadarii leaned forward, only to recoil in confusion as Traveesha impatiently held out a set of knives.

"Well, go on, girl, don't be shy. Take them!"

Shadarii gingerly touched the pair of gleaming dao. She had never really had much time for weapons. The dao was a heavy cleaver, halfway between a knife and an ax. It topped a hardwood haft half a tail long, with a broad blade of pounded steel. Most gardeners and hunters carried a dao at all times. One could use it to chop wood, split cane, or carve the family roast.

Unfortunately, as far as dancing props went, dao came a poor second to dead frogs and lumps of coal. Shadarii looked unhappily at Traveesha, but the dance mistress paid no attention to the girl's distress.

"I believe the dancing style used choreographed blows exchanged between two dancers. Your admirable skills at dance design will finally have a use!" Both knives were roughly thrust into Shadarii's grasp, and Traveesha clapped her hands together in delight. "You see? You're perfect for the task! Few girls have the strength to hold a blade for long—but to you? Pah, a simple task! Experiment and see what you can do!"

It seemed an important assignment. Shadarii tried to raise her spirits as she thought of all the trust Traveesha-Zho had placed in her. A revival of an ancient dance, research and development; dance designs of her very own... This would clearly be the one great chance of Shadarii's lifetime.

She would do it somehow. A program began to form inside Shadarii's clever mind, and the girl began to slowly move in swirling loops and pirouettes. The knives ponderously swept the air around her as she tried to grow accustomed to their weight.

Traveesha watched carefully for a moment, turned her tail, and left the clearing, a cunning smile on her lips. She never saw the stealthy figure lurking in the treetops nearby.

Javïra glared down at Shadarii, her blue eyes filled with hate. The girl watched in silence for a long, long while, finally drawing back into the shadows.

ଓ ଞ ଞ

Thou hast done well, my lovely warrior. Very well. I expected nothing less of thee.

Zhukora leaned against the cave wall as she spoke to Serpent, her eyes dazzled by the visions playing through her mind

"My plans begin to form. I have moved among the people. When I speak, the people listen. They need me as the hand to wield their anger!" Zhukora trembled with the power of her Dream. "I must bring freedom to the alps! We will break the bondage of the councils. Why cower in a forest when there is a whole world to explore?"

The girl stared off into the dark.

"No more fear, no more hiding in the trees, no terror of mere things unknown! Ideas shall be treasured like precious jewels! The age of stasis shall die at last!" Zhukora stared into a future built of dazzling hopes and dreams.

The ancient spirit danced at her side. *Thy path is difficult, Zhukora, but the Dream shall always burn for thee. It is a lonely, glorious road thou seek'st to travel.*

Now tell me; thou hast troubles. Speak thy mind, and we'll see what wisdom we can brew.

The glittering presence of the spirit ebbed and flowed above the hollow corpses on the cavern floor.

Zhukora leaned her head on her hand and scowled into the darkness. "My father has just disrupted all my plans! The fool's betrothed me. Bargained me off like a piece of meat!"

Is it a valuable match?

"Ha! A sniveling coward who can't beat me in game or hunt! He needs the status of a chief's daughter for a bride."

Seduce him, marry him, and dominate him. A man is all too easy to control.

"Never! I'll die before I let that creature touch me!" The girl bared her fangs in hate. "They want to use my flesh to drag me down. Chain me to a nest of eggs like some bloated mother ant!"

Aaaaah! It has wounded thy precious pride? Does it hurt to know they see thee only as chattel? Feed on the hate, girl! Suck on its strength!

Serpent slithered like a coil of liquid night.

It is the age-old burden of inner greatness, Zhukora. Lesser creatures will seek to pull thee down. The first great test of will shall be to triumph over thy obstacles.

Thou art ruthless, Zhukora, but art thou cold? Can thou plan an act? Dare thou craft a death...?

Chilled, Zhukora's ears rose. "Death?"

The old regime must die before thy Dream can finally come true. Had'st thou thought of it, or art thou afraid?

"I'm not afraid. I'm not!" Zhukora's voice rose to a shout. "I—I fear nothing. It simply isn't time!"

The Ka flowed down to stir among the corpses on the cavern floor. They rattled softly as the creature passed.

Do'st thou see these husks, Zhukora? This broken filth? They are the remnants of doubt, of failure and self-deception. Fear it, Zhukora. These creatures died because they were too terrified to reach for greatness. They drowned in their own mediocrity.

"What—what are you saying?"

Why, nothing. Nothing and everything. Thou must make thy decisions for thyself.

A corpse rose into the air, brittle bones snapping as fragments rained onto the floor. The withered jaw hung open in a silent scream.

Serpent's voice shook with strain.

It is... hard for me to influence matter. My power is weak. To influence thy world, I need a living partner, someone to channel my powers. Senses to see and feel! The corpse turned slow circles in the air. *Thy life task lies before thee. Thou shalt take thy clan and then thy tribe, and finally thy people. Thy race shall tremble in the dust before thee! The glory that is Zhukora shall set them free!*

The Dream, Zhukora! Embrace thy Dream!

With a sudden burst of power, the floating corpse tore asunder, and the skull tumbled at Zhukora's feet.

Take it! I have eaten that which dwelt there. Part of me now lies within. Speak, and I shall hear. Call, and I shall come. I am yours, Zhukora! Use me to make thy Dream come true!

Zhukora laughed aloud. She snatched the skull and flew out into the forest, her battle cries ringing out across the tired old trees.

ᛦ ᛦ ᛦ

Shadarii wandered happily through the forest, little Kïtashii fluttering in her wake. The two companions flew in sunny silence, drifting from flower to flower like aimless butterflies.

Skinny, lanky legged, and gray as a moonlit night, Kïtashii peered sideways at her companion, her mind brimming with suspicions. Shadarii's eyes were bright, her mood gay... Kïtashii sucked her fangs and twirled her silver hair.

Shadarii landed in the grass beside a tiny purple lily. The dancer bent and breathed in its warming scent. Her beautiful orange wings flashed out to catch the sun. Shadarii smiled and softly beckoned her student closer. Cupping her hands about the flower, she wove a gentle ïsha haze. A tiny Ka rose forth to dance between her fingertips, twirling up to trill a little song of love. Shadarii lifted her eyes to smile into Kïtashii's face.

The twelve-year-old stared in utter rapture, spellbound by Shadarii's skill. "How do you do it? I've never seen the like!"

Shadarii made a rapid string of motions, cradling an imaginary something in her arms.

Kïtashii watched and gave a snort. "You have to love the plant? Oh, Shadarii, you've only just met the funny thing!"

Shadarii reached down to touch the flower and smiled. She placed a hand against her heart and then opened her fingers.

"You love it just the same, hmmm? Oh, Shadarii, I wish I had your romantic nature."

Shadarii shook her head, then beamed and spread her hands. Her message had an innocent simplicity.

Feel it. Open yourself to the love! It's really not so hard. Everything is special if we only take the time to care.

Shadarii pointed to a lovely coppery dragonfly, then closed her eyes and let her ïsha flare with light. The dragonfly dipped closer, buzzing low to hover between Shadarii's ears.

You see? So easy, if you only try.

The twelve-year-old eyed Shadarii with suspicion, her sharp nose wrinkling in thought. "You seem merry, my lady! No sighs, no tears... One would think something special has occurred."

Shadarii gave an airy wave. *Oh, nothing special. Nothing that's worth mentioning.*

"Oh! So you say there is no reason for all these sudden smiles?"

Shadarii simpered and waggled her long black fingers.

Ah ha! So there was something going on; Kïtashii pondered, wondering what it could be.

"Mistress Traveesha let me in the junior class today. I was the only commoner there. Traveesha-Zho says I have talent but I've been beneath the cloud of irregular influences. I think she means you...."

It was only to be expected. Shadarii gave her funny silent laugh.

Kïtashii's small, thin face was all too serious. "It was strange learning from someone other than you. Can we still learn together? Will you keep on teaching me? I-I'd like to, if that's all right by you."

Shadarii touched Kïtashii's nose. Of course it was all right! Shadarii was delighted she had finally found a friend.

Kïtashii smiled. "Traveesha-Zho says she wants to nurture me. I hope it's not too painful. It sounds like something done to plants...."

Shadarii made a face, stuck out her tongue, and made quacking motions with her hands. Kïtashii gave a snort.

"Fussy? Poison, yes! The woman's worse than my maiden aunt. Is she always so?"

Shadarii ruefully sighed and shrugged.

Kïtashii nodded softly. "Ah, well, at least I'm in! I'd almost despaired of ever being a dancer. Mother hates the whole idea. She almost screamed, but since the chief decreed it, she has to let me try." The little girl stared sadly out into the ferns. "I really wanted her to be happy for me. For once, I thought I might have made her proud."

Shadarii sat down beside her friend, then touched Kïtashii's heart and head, her face framing a simple question. Kïtashii understood.

"What do I really want to be? I-I want to be like you, Shadarii. Someone people will look up to!"

Shadarii reached out to squeeze Kïtashii's hand. The two of them sat together in the sunshine, listening to the breeze move through the ferns. Shadarii's mind began to wander. She remembered the warmth of another body and a smell like new-baked bread. Eyes so fine and deep a girl could almost drown....

Kïtashii's voice broke into her reverie.

"So, how long have you been in love?"

Shadarii gave a guilty jump. The twelve-year-old grinned in triumph, her tail thrashing craftily behind her. "Ah, ha! So there it is! Come along, confess your sins. You've been stringing me along all day."

Shadarii excitedly looked around them, then wriggled nearer, her eyes bright with hidden secrets. Her hands wove a rapid little pantomime while Kïtashii watched and grinned.

"So, you are in love! You found someone special, eh?"

Shadarii squeezed shut her eyes. She hugged herself and touched her breast, heaving a little sigh.

"Yes, I know he's beautiful. Now, who is he?"

Shadarii swiftly began to shape a story with her hands. Kïtashii watched, her ears rising ever higher.

"Him! The-the one who saved me? But when did you... ?"

The tale was swiftly told, Shadarii lingering dreamily upon their parting kiss.

Kïtashii pursed her lips in a smile. "Well, this explains it all, and all those questions you've been asking of me. But Shadarii, will we ever see him again?"

Shadarii barely heard; her thoughts had drifted off into some dreamy never land. Kïtashii had seen this foolishness before. Love turned perfectly sensible people into besotted twits. Not her! Kïtashii gave a superior little sniff and proudly smoothed her whiskers. She clapped her hands, trying to draw Shadarii back to earth.

"Shadarii? Come along! Shadarii?"

Her friend paid no attention as she stared into an imaginary pair of eyes.

Kïtashii harrumphed and took her companion by the hand. "Well, there's nothing on your mind now except for kissing! Come along then. I suppose I'll have to fetch you back to work."

Shadarii gave a heartfelt sigh and drifted off into her dreams. Kïtashii flattened down her ears and stamped on through the brush, thoroughly disgusted by the silliness of it all.

ꙅ ꙮ ꙅ

"Zhukora! Zhukora, where have you been?"

Daimïru hurtled down her fishing spear and raced to meet her leader. Zhukora paused at the forest's edge, laughing as Daimïru's long golden hair streamed in the sun. Wings spread, Daimïru swiftly knelt beside her leader's feet.

"You—you just left! You didn't say where. Your father says he's betrothed you!" The blonde girl suddenly looked sick. "Is—is it true?"

Zhukora alighted on a tree branch and folded back her wings. "If my father thinks he can force me to do anything, he is gravely mistaken." Zhukora took Daimïru by the hand. "There's no need to be excited. Everything is under control."

Daimïru swiftly shook her head. "No, that's not it! Councilor Chitoochi's dead. Stone dead! She just died in her sleep. Council meets to choose her successor today. Fotoki and the high priestess have put your name forward! You have two nominations, and that means it actually has to go to vote."

Zhukora sat stock-still as her mind raced with possibilities.

Daimïru swiftly bowed and finished her report. "Councilor Chitoochii was found dead in her bed this morning. The high priestess says her Ka has already flown. Council is meeting to gather mourning gifts and elect a successor to her position. Thus far, you are the only nomination. Prakucha and Traveesha are likely to be put forward as alternatives."

Zhukora's sharp eyes flashed.

"We might just do it! If I can snatch a seat on the council... Think of the hope it will give the people! Finally we'll have a voice!"

Daimïru stayed in her bow, simply waiting for Zhukora's will.

"Time is short, Zhukora. Council is about to start. If we hurry we can still reach the council lodge in time!"

Zhukora plunged down off her perch and dived through the trees. Her companion swiftly followed, taking her place behind Zhukora.

Within the council lodge, ïsha cracked with tension. Eleven elders, the clan chief, and the Katakanii's high priestess were bitterly at odds.

A gnarled old councilman slammed his fist against his bony thigh. "The girl is dangerous! My lord, I should not have to tell you yet again!"

"Oh, nonsense!" Old Fotoki firmly stood his ground. "Go back to bed, Gegachii. Dream your fantasies on your own time, not ours!"

Gegachii's sticklike figure shook with rage. "Lord Chief, three nights ago my granddaughter stumbled back into our lodge with stars in her eyes, prattling nonsense about some glorious new future. She's left her deportment class and has taken up jiteng—as a Skull Wing!" A knotted finger jabbed out in accusation. "And all because of your wretched Poison-spawn of a daughter!"

An elegant nobleman uncoiled from his cushions. "My learned comrades, this is no way for us to act! We must use calm and reason."

"Zhukora is a wild woman! Mad as a tiger-cat!"

"You go too far!" The dandified councilor made a twiddle of his fingers. "She merely has a thrilling energy of vision."

"She is a manic, violent, undisciplined child!"

Nochorku-Zha rose out of his torpor with a burst of senile energy. "What she needs is a damned good thrashing, and I'm of a good mind to give it to her!" Nochorku-Zha cracked his fist into his palm. "Spoiled brat! I'll not have her in this council! I'll not have her in my lodge! She's no daughter of mine until she obeys my word!"

A cool, calm voice broke through the chief's tirade. "But, Lord Nochorku, only this morning Zhukora spoke to me about her wedding. She was too afraid to approach you since she knew of your displeasure."

The high priestess sat calmly in the shadows, her eyes brimming with sorrow.

Lord Nochorku's thoughts tumbled in confusion. "Eh? Eh, what's that you say?"

"A maid can look upon her wedding night with terror, my lord. Surely a man of your experience can understand." The priestess wore a kindly face. "Poor blossom! With no mother to help raise her, she has no knowledge of the ways of silk and flowers. Please look kindly on her, my lord. She has had time enough to recover from her shock. She asks me to convey to you her sincere apologies, and to ask you to tell Prakucha of her love."

A female councilor leaned forward, her old eyes filled with concern. "Poor child! Has she no one to advise her on the pleasures of a married life?" The burly woman folded her arms. "Nochorku-Zha, you have been most lax as a father! Have you no idea how a young girl's fears can multiply?"

"Bah! She's old enough to go learn such things for herself! 'Tis not my fault she's still a virgin."

"Well, apparently there's still some moral virtue in the world! You should be bursting with pride for her, and instead you sit here spitting poison like a warped old viper."

Nochorku winced and flattened his ears. The elder of the hunters spoke into the silence. "She is the most generous hunter in the clan. The youngsters all look up to her. We could keep them in line far better if they felt they had a voice in council."

Gegachii's cracked old voice rose to a shriek. "Madness! Madness!"

"Oh, shut up, you old fool!"

"Don't you call me an old fool, you bloated wart!"

"Order! Order!"

Old Gegachii pranced about the lodge, looking like a clutch of walking bones. "I propose we recess for ten minutes and then vote. No more discussion! Once this farce is finished, we can discuss more suitable candidates."

The need for adjournment had grown urgent; Gegachii's bladder was no longer what it used to be. The old man raced outside to take advantage of the break, leaving the high priestess to approach Nochorku-Zha.

"My lord, a word in private? I would be grateful for your time."

"Certainly, Reverence. Your Holiness is most kind to ask."

The high priestess looked about herself and lowered her voice to a subtle murmur.

"Chief Nochorku, I did not wish to discuss your own interests before the council members, but I feel it's time we spoke. You have given many years in selfless service of your tribe. It is high time you decided to think about yourself."

"Eh? Myself? What's that?"

The priestess winced, motioning the old man to keep his voice down. "Think, my lord! What happens if you should decide to retire and take a well-earned rest? If Zhukora gains a seat on the council, she can still see that your policies are implemented. You will gain the power without the endless weary trouble."

It seemed a sensible, attractive proposition; Nochorku-Zha tugged slowly at his whiskers. "Surely we could simply let young what's-his-name—Prakucha—be elected to the council now! Then he can carry out my policies! Why should the girl be burdened with the task at all?"

"She will be a happier wife if given just a little freedom. Position will give the girl stability. A sense of independence can be a valuable thing. Surely your own flesh and blood deserves some happiness?" The priestess glanced slyly sideways at Nochorku-Zha. "Your wife, Rain caress her Ka, had such high hopes for her elder girl..."

That had been the shot that told. The old man's eyes immediately went misty. He smiled as he remembered the face of a wife long dead and gone....

"Yes, why so she did...."

One by one, the council members returned to their seats. Nochorku-Zha straightened and firmly set his jaw.

"The vote shall now be taken! In place of our deceased member, the high priestess shall cast a vote. Your Reverence, how do you cast your ballot?"

"The priesthood votes yes. The girl Zhukora should claim the vacant council seat."

Nochorku-Zha snapped his finger toward the man beside him. "Gegachii! How do you vote?"

Gegachii slammed his knotted claw upon the ground. "No! I say no! Zhukora has no place upon this council."

The curtain jerked as Zhukora thrust into the room. She stared about herself in confusion. The vote was being taken! She was too late! The girl licked her lips, trying to see if there was anything that she could do.

"I vote yes!"

"I, also."

One after another, the ballots were cast. Zhukora felt a dizzy wave of heat; six votes each way! With a sinking feeling, Zhukora saw that the last vote belonged to Nochorku-Zha. She flattened her ears and closed her eyes.

Get it over with, you old bastard. Enjoy your power while it lasts! I'll pay you back for this. This time I swear...

"I vote in favor ! The woman Zhukora-kai-Nochorku-Zha is hereby admitted to this council."

Zhukora rocked back on her heels, her eyes staring wide. The room exploded into uproar, while Zhukora wandered slowly out into the light.

Daimïru sank down on her knees and made the formal bow of obeisance. Her ïsha field quivered in triumphant adoration.

"The first victory, my leader! The first of many! Finally our journey has begun!"

A heavy tread sounded on the tree branch as the high priestess spread her wings into the light.

"Rain and Wind bless your wisdom, Councilor Zhukora. I trust the vote has pleased you."

Zhukora slowly turned, glancing at the high priestess in cold appraisal. "This was your doing, of course."

"Of course." The priestess let the breeze pick at her hair. "I said that you and I could be of use to one another..."

Zhukora's eyes never left the priest. Her face remained a frozen mask of steely, perfect black. "Chitoochi's death... such a terrible tragedy."

"Yes, and I was taking tea with her only the night before she died. Ah, me, how fleeting life can be."

"Aye, Reverence. Indeed."

Zhukora looked the priestess in the eye and then slowly gave a nod. "Shadarii's yours. Take her." The huntress smoothly turned and walked away.

The priestess drew a long, deep breath and let the chill of power fill her soul.

ᘓ ᘔ ᘔ

The Lurking Mantises made a splendid sight above the jiteng field. They were the finest team in all the western mountains; noblemen and women from the finest families of the Vakïdurii tribe. They were the pride and glory of the clans—the very best the Vakïdurii had to offer.

Ranged against them was a shifting cloud of royal blue. Agile shapes whirred casually from side to side with an easy, affable camaraderie. Kotaru's Wrens chatted back and forth as they wheeled eagerly through the skies.

The ball rose, and the Mantis captain snatched it with almost casual ease. She snapped her fingers, signaling her teammates to advance. From the Wrens' team, a single figure speared out toward the Mantis lines.

"Follow me!"

Suddenly, the air blurred full of wings as Kotaru soared high into the sky, followed by a whooping stream of players. They curled and dived, streaking down toward the Mantis captain. The Mantis stumbled, squawking to her wingmen in alarm.

Noblemen lunged forward, each eager to be the first teammate to engage. With a ringing cry, the Wrens shot past them. Wings folded, bodies dived; a rain of ïsha blows punched one after another at the Mantis captain. The girl dropped the ball, watching helplessly as a Wren snatched it in passing.

There was no discipline, were no orders! The Wrens called vulgar greetings as they tossed and caught the ball. Their captain flew everywhere at once, always covering the teammate with the ball. The Wrens whooped for joy as Mrrimïmei dashed home to take the goal. The crowd croaked in shock, stunned by the disaster on the field.

The Mantises, the prime team of the Vakïdurii, were being thrashed by an untutored group of commoners! Here and there, groups of dissidents cheered the Wrens, but the bulk of the audience was too deeply shocked even to cry.

Three nil! The Wrens were winning three goals to nil!

Perched on the royal tree, Chief Gingïkai of the Lacewing clan gnawed at his fists in rage.

"Fools! They're making themselves a laughing stock! Can't they see the Wrens' fast forward cannot turn? She's fast, but she's too fast to maneuver! If they'd just get off their arses and make a strong rear defense line..."

"Rear? I'll show their rears something!" A second chief smashed his dao into the branch. "This is the worst disaster of the decade!"

King Latikai sat grinning like a great fat caterpillar, bringing a glare of disapproval from one of the suffering chiefs.

"My lord king, have you no comment at all? Has the horror of it rendered y' speechless?"

"Comment? What's to comment?" Latikai snatched a sausage from a grill. "I've got sixty fingers of iron riding on the Wrens!"

Clan chieftains stared aghast as the Wrens stole the ball and skipped nimbly clear of the Mantises' pursuit. The king beamed in approval.

"I've a bolt of silk that says the Wrens will win four nil!"

Chief Matishah of the Lacewings jerked her jaw. "You're on! An' there's dinner tonight to say your upstart Wrens won't touch the ball again this game."

Groans sounded from the crowd as the angry Mantises rushed off in pursuit of the Wren's agile young fast forward. Mrrimïmei whirled her staff and stuck out her tongue, flitting gleefully just out of reach of her pursuer's claws. With a howl of rage, the Mantises screamed off in pursuit; not one of them had noticed she no longer had the ball.

The Wrens' captain watched the Mantises with something akin to weary sorrow before casually flipping the ball down through the goals. The crowd stared in absolute astonishment.

The Mantises had lost; it was a Wren victory four goals to none.

Suddenly, the crowd seemed to find its voice, and a shout of triumph roared through the air. They cheered because it seemed the thing to do. For years afterward, jiteng enthusiasts would talk about the day they saw a legend born.

Out on the field, the Wrens flung themselves into each other's arms. They had played in a state of dreamlike shock, watching themselves in disbelief as goal after goal went home. Kotaru ripped away his mask and shook his whiskers free of sweat.

"We won. We—we won! I don't believe it!"

"Believe it! Wind and Fire, believe it!" Mrrimïmei crushed Kotaru hard against her armored chest. "I have never, ever won anything in all my life!"

Another girl, Tingtraka, kissed Kotaru on the nose, and his teammates cheered as their captain's ears blushed red.

King Latikai waded through the crowd to pound Kotaru on the shoulder blades.

"Well, boy, you've done me proud. I knew you'd not disappoint me." He slapped Kotaru's shoulders once again, nearly blasting the smaller man clean into the ground. "Four nil! Four nil, who'd believe it? There's one to tell your grandchildren, eh? The day you beat all odds and won your fame!"

The king gave the lad a victory hug that audibly cracked his ribs, then whirled Kotaru around and bellowed for the crowd's attention.

"People! People o' the Vakïdurii, I present the winning team, the Superb Blue Wrens!" The king ruffled Kotaru's hair, nearly rattling his brains. "It is my pride, nay, 'tis my privilege, to declare the Superb Blue Wrens our champion team...." The wild cheers of the crowd nearly drowned him out. "And to further declare that they shall represent us against the Katakanii tribe!"

The air roared as the tribesfolk surged their wings in applause. Kotaru reeled around in wonder, scarcely able to believe his fortune. He stared out into open space, seeing nothing but a pair of deep-green eyes....

The victors were swept away into the arms of the crowd.

King Latikai straightened his jewelry and sidled off to find the captain of the Mantis team. He discovered her stripping away her wooden greaves, and duly slapped the woman on the back. "A fine game, lass! Well played and quite convincing. Aaaaah, if only my son had been here to give you the benefit o' his leadership. I'm sure..."

The captain ripped off her helmet and hurtled back her plaited hair. "Tekï'taa? Ha! That bugger's never held a catching staff in all his pampered life!"

The king blinked, taken aback by the woman's foul temper. He cleared his throat and mustered his dignity. "Hmmmmm-ha, in any case, an admirable demonstration, although perhaps laid on a mite too thick. Four nil? Fire and Poison, girl, who's going to believe that? Three to four would have been a better margin! Y' took your orders too literally. In the future, more initiative and less..."

"My lord! What in Poison's name are you babbling about?"

The king puffed out the royal chest. "Your instructions, woman! Have you no brains? The instructions my son gave you!"

The exasperated player shoved aside her mask. "What instructions? What's this damned nonsense?"

"The special instructions, girl! The orders for the Mantises to lose the game."

The Mantis angrily stripped off her gloves, glaring out at the jubilant Wrens. "No one gave me any skreggin' instructions! Damned fool idea in any case. Special game—intertribal matches! Whose brilliant notion was this?"

The King's antennae rose in horror. "What d' you mean no special instructions?" He grabbed the woman by the chest. "You were supposed to lose! That's how it happened! Y' don't mean to tell me that a bunch o' untrained commoners..."

The Mantis angrily tore free from King Latïkai's claws. "All I know is that we just got our tails whipped! Beaten by a flock of fledgling Wrens."

The king whirled to stare as the Wrens surged off into the village, thrilled with their outrageous victory. Latïkai could only sag down on a moldy log as an endless stream of disasters opened out before his eyes....

Shadarii frowned in concentration, her green eyes fixed on empty air. Two glittering blades swung into guard as she settled her grip and crouched in anticipation.

Suddenly, the girl streaked forward. Orange wings swept out like sheets of fire, and bundles of dried grass tumbled down in fragments as she passed. Shadarii folded and turned a somersault, splitting a target at the midpoint of her roll. Her dao cleaved the target, sending wood and straw spinning to the ground.

Damn!

Shadarii screeched to a halt, angrily hurtling down her knives. She had missed by almost half a handspan, enough to take someone's head off! Days and days of work, and still she had no progress to show Traveesha. The girl furiously sat down on the grass and thrashed her tail in spite.

Skreg it, skreg it, skreg it!

"Shadarii! Shadarii, are you there?"

A great fat figure stood by the stream, gesturing imperiously. The high priestess! Shadarii rapidly smoothed her hair and tried to make herself presentable.

"Shadarii! Come, lass. I have the most wonderful news for you. Your sister and I have made the most marvelous plans!"

Shadarii landed neatly in the grass and dropped into a formal bow. She remained with eyes downcast before the priest, her wings shading her from the woman's gaze.

The high priestess gave a loving, predatory smile.

"Oh, do get up, my dear! Come, come, formality is only for the mundanes. You are almost one of us now. There's no need for ducks and bows!"

Shadarii went quite stiff. She looked up at the high priestess in sudden fear, and the old woman laughed aloud.

"Yes! Isn't it the most delightful news? You are to become a priestess."

Shadarii simply folded and fell. She sat and stared emptily across the grass, her eyes blank and dazed.

"Aaaah, I knew you'd be excited! Think of it, my dear; an exulted position among the tribe, status beyond your wildest dreams! In the future, you could even rise to become high priestess."

Shadarii scrabbled frantically to her feet, her eyes wild with panic. She looked at the priest and tried to plead. The old priestess saw the girl's alarm and crowed.

"What? Tears and panic? Don't be silly, girl! 'Twill be the adventure of a lifetime. Don't you want to be a priest?"

Shadarii frantically shook her head. She looked about herself in fright, trying to find some means of escape—someone who could help! Father! Did Father know?

The wily priestess changed her tack, and her voice became an insidious, subtle croon.

"Shadarii, I have planned this for your own good. Haven't you heard them laughing at you? Haven't you seen them sneering at the girl who has no voice? It hurts, doesn't it, to be the laughingstock? Always the odd one out! Always the girl without a friend...." The old woman bent to whisper in Shadarii's ear. "It can all be yours, my dear. Power to stand in pride! Status to hurtle straight back in their faces! Her Reverence Shadarii-Zho[16] will be a name to love—to fear. No one will dare laugh at you again!"

Shadarii wept, trying to tear words out of her throat. She tugged at the priestess's robes and tried to form a pleading little pantomime. She touched her forehead and made the sign for "dancer."

"Your Ka? Oh, your soul longs to dance!" She beamed and spread her hands. "Hush, dear, dry your tears. We have a great need of dancers. Shadarii, you will discover stories that you never knew existed. All the tales of the past will be yours to

---

[16]**Zho:** Literally "learned"—a suffix title somewhat different from that of "Zha" ("revered").

treasure, yours to dance. Come, take my hand! Take my hand and join our special world."

Shadarii's pathetic pleas continued, but the high priestess reached out to crush Shadarii beneath her will. The girl's ïsha field lashed back with monstrous power. The priestess spun backward, blasted by Shadarii's frantic energy.

Shadarii stared in horror, barely aware of what she had just done. The old woman's eyes were lit with rage.

"Don't be foolish, girl! What else does the future hold for you? Even a girl without a voice can prosper as a priest!"

Shadarii sobbed, and then cradled something invisible against her breast, hugging it as though it would be torn from her.

"What? Babies? Don't be a fool! Who'd want a cripple for a wife?"

Shadarii jerked, and the priest cackled as she saw her barb go home.

"So, that's it! You've found yourself a man to dream of? Well keep dreaming, girl! You know as well as I just how far he's going to run when he discovers you can't speak!" Shadarii fell down to her knees and wept as the priestess spitefully twisted home the knife. "A virgin you are, and a virgin you'll remain! You'll not miss it, girl. Just thank the Ka that the priesthood wants to take you!"

Shadarii pawed the ground in silence.

The priestess snorted. "Get up! Go and learn your knife dance. After toteniha, you shall be ours. You have eight days to make all your good-byes." The old woman spread her wings and flew off into the forest.

Shadarii crept across the grass in agony and felt her spirit bleed.

ဃ ဢ ဢ

"Flowers for my bride to be! Gifts for the mother of my unborn children! A perfumed rose to grace the hair of my devoted ladylove."

Massive, polished, and perfect, Prakucha unfolded from the darkness and proffered a tiny flower. He had lain in wait outside Zhukora's lodge, knowing eventually she must pass. He made a mocking bow and grinned as he saw Zhukora's hate-filled eyes.

"What? No kiss? No trembling hug or breathless promises? You disappoint me. Surely you have at least heard how a bride should act?" The huge hunter barred Zhukora's way, leaning his enormous bulk against the door. "You know, my dear, you worry me. You lack the gentle feminine graces. Sometimes you seem barely female at all! You have the body of a spratling boy and the soul of a tiger. It will be a great pleasure to break you in at last."

Zhukora's breast heaved in rage, and she glared at Prakucha with murder in her eyes. "Withdraw your offer of marriage, Prakucha! I will give you but one warning!"

"Ooooh! Do you think to kill me through an excess of wedded bliss? I think not! We'll soon have the wild Zhukora well and truly tamed!"

Zhukora rammed the man aside. She stood in her doorway and gazed at him slowly and carefully, like a hunter gazing at unwanted, butchered prey.

"You were warned, Prakucha. The consequences will be no one's fault except your own!" The girl turned and disappeared into the shadows.

Prakucha backed away, the humor slowly dying in his eyes.

ങ ൽ ൽ

"Javïra, dear—don't play with knives, darling. Your mother wouldn't like it."

Mistress Traveesha looked up from sewing beads upon a costume, scowling as she saw her niece's latest antics. The girl pranced up and down the hearth, waving a disreputable pair of dao. She posed herself in the firelight, admiring her shadow on the lodge-tree's trunk.

The first act of Zhukora's tenure as a councilor had been to change the schedules for the totenïha ceremony. She had insisted that her sister make a farewell dance before she departed the tribe.

So, now, a knife dance was to be played in public! A knife dance! Zhukora had insisted on it, backed by a chorus of her followers. The young people were all eager to see it; a vulgar delight seemed to be overcoming all good taste and tradition. Annoyed by the clash of knives, Traveesha jammed her needle through her leaf-leather costume and gave an irritated sigh. "Javïra, put those things down! You'll cut yourself."

"I'm practicing, Aunt. Shadarii's moves looked so good I couldn't bring myself to resist!" Javïra gazed at the clean lines of her delicious body. "I think I might make a good partner for Shadarii in the dance. Wouldn't that be nice?"

Traveesha put her sewing down.

"I don't think that would be a very good idea, Javïra. We shan't go looking for any trouble."

"Anything she can do, I can do better!"

"Competition can become a fixation, dear, but I suppose it's good to see you occupied again."

Javïra's eyes glittered spitefully in the dark.

"Shadarii's going to dance the most important dance in the cycle. I thought I was going to dance the fourth performance."

"I'm sorry, my dear, but there's really nothing I can do. The priests are most insistent. We shall find lots of other dances for you. Now, do put those wretched things away!"

Javïra laughed, and her teeth flashed as she swung her knives. "Just practicing, Aunt, just practicing! I have a feeling that it still might come in useful." Javïra hurtled a dao through the air. The knife smacked into the tree trunk, spearing the shadow on the wall. Javïra stared at the weapon, her whole body thrilling to the sight of gleaming steel. "Yes Aunt! It might just come in very useful, indeed."

Seven

The dawn came cruel and bitter. Cold sliced beneath the fur to draw pain straight from the skin. Clan Swallowtail sat in suffering silence beneath the gray predawn light. Wisps of steam curled from their nostrils to hang like twisting wraiths. Here and there, a child coughed, the sound lonely in the eerie forest hush.

Deep among the ferns, a speck of brightness wavered. Faint cries and chatter carried on the breeze as, piece by piece, the forest echoed with glorious drifts of song. It was the appointed hour. The Katakanii clans were filtering through the leaves.

Voices rose as Swallowtails yelled greetings through the green, and some tribes-folk dashed to meet old friends. The forest erupted into chaos as ten thousand voices pealed out in joy. Dancers from a dozen villages whirled into the air. Hunters hammered one another on their backs, and married daughters clasped themselves in their mother's arms. It was the yearly binding of the tribe, the time of totenïha.

In the middle of the pandemonium, solemn ceremonies were taking place. The councilors of the five clans[17] all spread wings before King Saitookii, and the high priestess made blessings while her dancers consecrated a circle for the jiteng games.

The common folk paid these ceremonies not the slightest heed. Those with kin in the Swallowtail villages wandered off to dump their gear, while others streamed out into the woods to snatch the prime camping spots beside the streams. Old women gratefully followed younger folk toward the baths, keen to steam their bones and forget the rigors of the march.

All in all, the totenïha ceremonies were off to their normal start.

C3 &0 &0

Totenïha brought its usual gift of joy, and for a few brief days the tribe pretended that famine had gone. The people sang and danced beneath the trees, whooping with laughter as they spread their wings to fly. Children tumbled in the waters. Hunters scoured the riverbanks for food. Young women flocked to watch the jiteng players at their games, gazing adoringly at their latest heroes.

Out of all the Katakanii, only one small group had no time for play. The past-holders were scarcely allowed to stop and catch their breaths. They labored day and night to make the holiday a triumph for their tribe. The girls woke at dawn, snatched a hasty meal, and dashed to start their warm-ups before the other tribes-folk had even stirred from bed.

At night, hunters coaxed the girls into the bracken, showering them with gifts and soft enticements. For once, though, even Javïra could scarcely find the energy to smile. The hunters sighed and irritably waited for the times to mend. Once the

---

[17]**Clan Wing Forms:** Alpine clans were originally differentiated by the shapes of their butterflylike wings—distinctions slowly disappearing with successive generations of inter-marriage.

main ceremonies had come and gone, the girls would spark back to life. Wingshedding had always been one of the finest times of year. The nights were warm, the bracken soft, and the girls would soon prove more than willing....

Far off in the forest, two girls sat and painted masks beside a stream. They were surrounded by an arsenal of gleaming knives. A Swallowtail and a Bird-Wing, Shadarii and her companion worked in silence, their brushes moving with gentle, fluid grace.

Shadarii's companion was a compact, white-furred girl with delicious amber eyes. Hatïkaa had an overbearing character and muscles hard as iron. Shadarii primly tried not to take offense at the other woman's manner. Sometimes Hatïkaa could be funny, but otherwise wore down Shadarii's temper. Hatïkaa's only interests were her sex life and her child; she had been married for nearly half a year and already had an egg about to hatch. Shadarii had nervously edged away from inquiring about the details.[18]

Shadarii lived inside a world of pain and misery. All her hopes were dying before her eyes. Even her little dream of love had begun to wither. Hatïkaa looked over at Shadarii and wrinkled her snout.

"Fer skreg's sake, girl, cheer up! Not still moping, are you?"

Shadarii gave the other girl a hurt, resentful look.

Hatïkaa wiped her nose and sniffed in disgust. "Oh, stop looking at me with those bloody awful eyes! If you can't change it, don't worry about it. There's naught you'll get from fretting but a set of wrinkles."

Hatïkaa jammed her brush into the paint and babbled on, ignoring Shadarii's silence.

"Your sister's the talk of the tribe. Been like this long, has she? Regular tiger-cat, they reckon! Still, my younger sister's heard her talk—says the girl speaks sense. She's off to listen to her again, tonight. There's some sort of meeting every evening, now. Hundreds of folk come to see her!" Hatïkaa gave a shrug. "I don't know why anyone bothers. Keep away from 'em, that's what I told my sister. She called me a reactionary! Said a new age of justice was about to dawn. Ha! Do you get that?" The woman gave a snort. "Justice? There isn't any justice in this world 'cept what we make ourselves! Keep friends in high places and try to play the game."

Hatïkaa scratched herself in a most unseemly fashion, then pointed her dripping brush straight at Shadarii's nose. "Take your problem, now. Is that justice? No! But there's bugger-all you can do about it 'cause you've let 'em walk all over you! Now if it were me, I'd tell 'em all to stuff it! There's ways and means of disqualifying yourself for the priestly life, if you get my meaning."

Shadarii didn't understand at all; she scowled and tried to concentrate on her work.

---

[18]**Kashran Gestation:** Approximately three months in the womb. The young are birthed in the form of a hard-shelled egg. The egg must be nurtured for a further six months until it hatches. The young are then nursed at the breast until they are of an age to fly.

Her companion rudely looked Shadarii up and down. "Pretty little wretch, aren't you? You're a quiet one, but ye've got a backside that some guys I know would die for." Hatïkaa stopped and changed her thoughts midstream. "Hey, do you have any blue? I've let the brown mix in with mine."

Shadarii sighed and passed the paint. She had long ago learned to ignore Hatïkaa's prattle, and barely heard a single word the other girl had said. Feeling tired, Shadarii rolled her eyes as Hatïkaa started her monologue again.

"I like the story of the dance. You do a good job when you get moving. Mother Rain fights Poison for the love of Father Wind, eh?" The woman shook her head in admiration. "Pure magic! We'll show 'em a fight like they've never seen before! Scare the loincloths off 'em, so we will!"

The woman shifted, scowling as she compared her figure with Shadarii's. "Don't fancy playing beside you if you're shakin' it in the buff. Maybe we should both wear body armor?"

Shadarii primly straightened up; most certainly not! There was a proper way of doing things. Had the woman lost all sense of decorum?

Hatïkaa shrugged and made a face. "Aaah, who cares? I suppose you're right—it's a chance to air the fleas in any case." She gave a snort. "I'll play the bad guy. You're soft and cuddly, definitely a Mother Rain if e'er I saw one."

Shadarii beamed in sudden pleasure.

"You're as fat as a pregnant wood mouse anyway! Get 'em all thinking about mother's fresh-made bread. Good image, eh?"

Shadarii angrily went back to her painting and glared resentfully at Hatïkaa, wishing the creature would shut up and go away. Hatïkaa had no intentions of doing either.

"I thought this dao dancing would come in useful! After I was expelled from my deportment class, my father reckoned I should be a dancer. Said anything I wanted to do would be just fine as long as I did it far from home. So I take up dancing. Lots of folk to talk to. Oh, I talked myself hoarse, I did! They hadn't heard good gossip in years! We talked and talked.... No dancing done, but you can't have everything, now can you? 'Course, some of the girls got their noses out of joint. I mean, there's no one else to blame if you let other people see your private life, now is there? Anyway, we had some fun. Then all of a sudden the dance mistress comes over all bright and eager and asks me to go play with knives—waaaaay out in private where no one else could see me. My very own secret task!"

Shadarii silently applauded the Bird-Wings' dance mistress. The woman was a genius! Unfortunately, that didn't bring Shadarii any peace. She set her mask aside to dry, carefully propping it on a stick beside the stream; Mother Rain seemed to glow with life all of her own.

Masks were always worn with reverence and pride. The wearer lost identity, giving themselves utterly to their role. The dancer rose above the world of flesh and became one with a greater whole....

Shadarii's moment of artistic reverie was all too short. Hatïkaa tossed down her brush and wiped her hands off in the grass.

"Hey, red-tail! Come on, shake it honey! We've got only two more nights to get the sequence right." She snatched Shadarii's heavy dao and twirled them nimbly around her fingertips. With a careless toss, she threw them to Shadarii, who caught both weapons with a thoughtless ease.

The two dancers rehearsed their choreography of blows and parries. The weapons slashed and chopped in graceful arcs, steel ringing as the knife blades crashed and glittered in the air. Points and handles, butts and edges all had astounding, lethal possibilities.

Shadarii spun out in a graceful kick, her foot scything just above Hatïkaa's nose. Blades sang as a double cut was blocked. The women see-sawed back and forth in perfect concentration, their weapons moving gracefully inside a swirl of ïsha.

A duck, a kick, a savage slash. Blades blurred as the tempo became blinding. Hatïkaa let herself take a very convincing kick straight to the stomach. With a sudden flourish, she let her knives be knocked clean from her hand. She fell down to her knees and threw wide her hands, laughing as Shadarii leapt into her arms.

"That's it, we'll knock 'em dead! Shadarii, you and I have it made!"

A singsong voice pealed out from the trees beside them. "I say, lassies! Would y' any idea where the Katakanii tribe might be hidin'?"

The women whirled to find fantastic blue-clad creatures clinging to the trees. The strangers gazed in unashamed amazement, tilting their beaks this way and that to marvel at the Katakanii girls.

Armor. The blue clothes were jiteng armor! It seemed a flock of marvelous birds had descended from the sky. Shadarii blinked up into the boughs and smiled in delight.

A pair of elegant Kashran noblemen bowed before them. The eldest of the pair, a burly black old man, spoke in an accent that rumbled like a waterfall.

"Forgive our startlin' you, dear ladies. We had no wish to disturb such a magnificent performance. I am Chief Batookii of the Vakïdurii Bird-Wing clan. I have the honor to present Prince Tekï'taa-kai-Latikai of the Vakïdurii tribe. We are emissaries come hither to participate in the totenïha ceremonies, and we've traveled three hundred swoops to be here[19]. We'd be grateful if you'd point out the way to your encampment!"

A single jiteng player leapt onto a closer branch, peering down through the foliage at Shadarii's mask. Meanwhile, the old nobleman eyed Shadarii's knives.

"That's—aaah—that's an unusual hobby you'd be havin' there. Is it fashionable or somethin'? It looks damned dangerous!"

Hatïkaa found her tongue. She looked down at her dao and grinned. "What, the dance dangerous? Oh, no, my lord! Not until we sharpen the knives! Once that's done, it's time to watch your tail." She planted her fist on her hip. "So you're all Vakïdurii, eh? Well that's a switch! I'll show you to the village, sire. 'Tis a pleasure to be of service to you." The girl tugged Shadarii's tail. "Come on, Shadarii. Can't you see the gossip? We'll be the talk of the tribe!"

Shadarii never even heard. She sensed an aura—a delicious tang of something wild and precious. The girl began to shiver, her hands trembling in excitement.

---

[19]**Swoop:** A distance measure. A fist of fist of spans—approximately 940 meters.

The strangers moved away, leaving a single figure in their wake. The remaining jiteng player hesitantly moved toward Shadarii. Hatïkaa was already a dozen yards down the path, her arm linked firmly through Chief Batookii's own. She looked back at Shadarii and gave an impatient whistle.

"Hey, pudding, are you coming? Shake it, girl! We're not waiting for you!"

Shadarii stared at the waiting stranger, her heart pounding. Hatïkaa's voice faded off into the trees. Shadarii slowly took away her mask, letting the light stream across her face. Long red hair tumbled down her shoulders, her mass of curls flashing like liquid fire.

She stood there waiting, hardly daring to draw a breath. The jiteng player slowly raised his hands. His mask and helmet slipped away, and brown eyes shone like forest pools, reaching out to bathe Shadarii's soul.

"It's you! Mother Rain, I'd hoped so much!" The poor man stumbled over his own words. "Shadarii? Is that your name, Shadarii?"

The girl nodded, her hair spilling down in copper curls around her face.

"Shadarii..." He sighed her name as though it were a song. "I—my name's Kotaru. I'm a hunter. A—a jiteng player. We came all this way.... I mean, what I thought was—well, a chance to find you. To—to thank you. Just to see you once again!" He caught himself babbling. He'd had this planned!

Over dreamy days and restless nights Kotaru had lived this meeting through and through. They would see each other through a crowd. She would look deep into his eyes and slowly walk toward him, her hair streaming in the wind. Suddenly the girl would be there in his arms. Her mouth would reach up to take his kiss, her green eyes closed as both their senses swam in ecstasy....

An imperious voice bellowed through the woods, "Kotaru! Where've you gone, you dozy beggar? There's work to be done!"

Kotaru reluctantly began to back away. Shadarii followed, reaching out to take his hand. Their fingers intertwined. Kotaru stared at her in shock, seeing the adoration in her eyes.

"Tonight! Can you look for me at the council fire tonight? Please? There's something special I want to say!"

Shadarii nodded helplessly, her pulse hammering in her throat. Kotaru reluctantly let her go, his fingers slipping through her own. He backed into the ferns and quickly dashed away.

Shadarii whirled, her eyes dancing with a thousand stars. She threw her head back and let the sun stream into her upturned face. She danced in joy, ïsha blazing with soaring colors of delight.

He was here, he was really here! Hope was still alive! Suddenly the world seemed wild and beautiful.

ଔ ଯ ଯ

That evening, the council fires blazed high, but the meal was a pale shadow previous feasts. Food had grown scarce, and the cooks made do with whatever they could find. Still, the tribe had song and laughter.

Javïra and Srïhooni danced before the fire, light licking across their fur. Beside the royal fire the highest nobles were arrayed in luxury. They ate and spoke with rigid protocol, completely segregated from the free and easy lifestyle of their subjects.

King Saitookii crouched like a withered spider in its web, his ancient eyes glaring out across the crowds. He had ruled the Katakanii for two hundred years, rarely noticing whether his subjects lived or died. He cared for nothing except the Katakanii's unbending code of tradition. No matter what the cost, the rituals were maintained. Even now, in the face of famine, rules took precedence over need. A huge portion of food had been laid out in the center of the meadow, enough meat and fish to feed an entire clan. It was a ritual offering to the Spirit of the Fire. The whole huge meal would be burned; crisped in an instant while the people filled their bellies with tree fern pith and worms.

Zhukora had gone about her own affairs. In her place, Shadarii knelt to serve her father's needs. The old man barely even knew her name. There were more important things on his mind than useless daughters, and he never once noticed the nervous trembling of Shadarii's hands.

The high priestess watched the girl in puzzlement.

Shadarii gave a guilty duck of her head, trying to avoid the woman's eyes. Rain— if the priestess were to find out... they would lock her away. She'd never get to see Kotaru ever again! Never discover if the kiss... the kiss lingered on both their lips....

Would he want her? Had the kiss meant what she thought it did? Had it been the same for him? What if he didn't love her—or did? Shadarii's brain whirled like a cloud of butterflies.

"Shadarii, dear, don't jitter so. Do try to sit quietly. You shall have to learn how to deal with royalty once you become a priestess. We have great plans for you, my dear."

Shadarii shrank back from the priestess's view. Thankfully the old woman grew preoccupied with Prince Teki'taa.

Shadarii brought the teapot over to the prince. The long, lean youth lounged bonelessly beside Prakucha, and the men seemed to enjoy each other's company. Kotaru had been trapped by a busy circle of jiteng officials. Shadarii watched him anxiously, seeing him look in her direction with a helpless gaze of love.

Love!

Shadarii felt herself grow weak as her world swayed dizzily all around her.

"My dear, if you must pour tea, for Fire's sake let it be inside the cup!"

Shadarii gave a guilty jump as Prakucha scowled at her, his empty cup proffered in one enormous fist. The girl swiftly poured the man a drink.

Prakucha sprawled at ease and watched Javïra dance. He assessed each line and curve with the air of a connoisseur.

"And so, Prince Teki'taa, do you find our little tribe to your liking?"

Javïra danced closer, the light lingering on her. She stared at Prince Teki'taa with a hungry glitter. Teki'taa leaned forward, his eyes riveted on Javïra's charms.

"To my liking, Lord Prakucha? Oh, aye! One could say that. You seem well stocked with dainty sweets...."

Prakucha gave an oily smile.

"I shall see to it that some 'sweets' are sent for you to sample later. I'm certain Javïra can serve you delicacies to your liking."

A snort came from somewhere behind him; Prakucha turned, but saw no one except the dumb girl Shadarii. He irritably signed for her to serve the prince some tea.

Teki'taa held out his cup and idly watched Shadarii. "The Katakanii seem a most well-appointed tribe." His eyes lingered thoughtfully on Shadarii. "Very well appointed, indeed...."

"Ha! That we are, my lord, that we are! I am sure we shall all get on together famously."

Down beside the dancing circle, a disturbance had arisen. Zhukora argued bitterly with an umpire, ramming the man slowly back into a corner. The man writhed and tried to struggle free. Zhukora backed him up to the fires. Teki'taa watched with interest as the game officials reluctantly gave in.

"A veritable taipan snake! Who is she?"

"No one of consequence. Damn! I believe our plans to keep her team out of the jiteng finals have failed. How tedious. I suppose I'll have to face my dear fiancé in battle once again."

"Fiancé? How terribly interesting!" Teki'taa stared at Zhukora's lean, exquisite figure. "She has a certain savage charm."

"Of a kind, of a kind. Breaking her promises to be a challenge."

Shadarii closed her ears to their mindless prattle. Kotaru had edged free of the crowds and was searching for her. Shadarii set her tray aside and edged stealthily back into the bushes.

"Shadarii?"

Shadarii froze as the priestess' voice cracked through the air.

"And just where are you going now, girl? Well? I'm waiting!"

The girl gulped, but then held out her hands and mimicked the motions of grinding tea. The priestess curtly waved her away.

"All right, all right—don't take all night about it! Go and get to bed! Your performance is only two days hence. You must make sure it's a good one."

Shadarii hastily gave a bow and scampered off into the dark. She searched anxiously through the bushes, her tail curling high behind her. Antennae quivered as she tried to find Kotaru's rosy aura.

There!

She felt him. Shadarii spread her wings and cruised silently across the ferns. She landed softly behind a tall shape that hid uncertainly in the shadows. Kotaru was looking anxiously toward the royal fire, trying to catch sight of Shadarii.

She softly tapped him on the shoulder. Kotaru gave a yelp, leaping high into the air. He crashed down in the bushes in a thrashing pile of wings. The high priestess whirled, her nose sniffing suspiciously as she searched the dark. Shadarii swiftly dived beside him.

Kotaru's head popped out of the grass.

"It's you! You nearly scared the life out of me!"

The girl frantically motioned him to be quiet. She cringed beneath the bushes, desperately hoping that the high priestess hadn't seen.

"What's wrong? I only—awk!"

She grabbed the man and yanked him down. Shadarii blew her forelock out of her eyes and motioned him to follow her, shuffling off into the shadows with an undignified crawl. Her great soft tail waved in Kotaru's face, tickling his senses.

Once through the bushes, Shadarii rose into a crouch. With her finger to her lips, she took to the air, leading the way into the tallest trees. The girl alighted softly on a branch, her wings fanning as she tried to still her racing heart.

With a gentle flap of wings, Kotaru fluttered to land beside her. Even in the dark, she could feel the heat of his blushing ears. The two young Kashra eyed each other shyly, neither daring to meet the other's gaze.

Shadarii had no idea what to do with her hands. The pair of Kashra sat in speechless silence, the air filled with the hammering of their hearts.

Kotaru's mind spun with fright, his spirits wilting as he realized what a fool he was making of himself. "Uh... m-my lady? Shadarii-Zho?"

She thrilled to hear him speak her name; Shadarii's ears rose, her face pathetically eager in the darkness.

Apart from some beads, Kotaru wore nothing but a loincloth and a pair of hunter's leggings. Kotaru had a nice, square build, and a chest just made to snuggle up to. He smelled of sweat and warm, soft fur. Shadarii felt her skin tingle in a sigh.

Kotaru coughed and tugged nervously at his necklace. "My l—Shadarii. I... I wanted to ask you... that is, I just wanted to say... well, about how grateful I am—for rescuin' me, I mean...."

She nodded, half swooning as his words caressed her.

Kotaru looked down at his hands. "About kissin' you and all... I never meant... I mean, it was a liberty. I hope that I didn't... that I..."

He looked up at her. Shadarii crept closer, her eyes like great pools of gleaming starlight.

"It's just that I... That you..."

She edged closer, her pupils wide with yearning. He leaned toward her, and his fur tingled as he felt her warmth. Did she want him to touch her? What if he was wrong? What if he frightened her away? Kotaru froze, too terrified to even move.

Shadarii tilted her head up, her eyes closed as she craned expectantly toward him. Kotaru felt his spirits leap in sudden panic. She was warm and soft, sweet and oh-so-frightened. Kotaru leaned toward her, slowly closing in to take a kiss....

Suddenly, they were falling. They flapped frantically as they spiraled down into the ferns. Shadarii landed with a thump, her legs splayed awkwardly before her. Kotaru gave a yelp and crashed onto the grass, his face thudding down between Shadarii's thighs. Kotaru coughed and spat out grass, then recoiled from Shadarii in surprise. He looked up at Shadarii's staring face, a dead leaf still sticking to his nose. Shadarii grinned despite herself, reaching out to pluck the leaf away.

Kotaru laughed; he laughed even though the joke was on himself. Shadarii smiled to hear him, grinning at the foolish spectacle the two of them must make.

Kotaru leaned his face against his hand and looked ruefully at Shadarii.

"Awwww, skreg it! I had this all figured out! I'd look into your eyes and tell you I'd been thinkin' day and night about you! You'd blush—you'd almost turn to run, and then all of a sudden we'd be in one another's arms...." He blew irritably at his whiskers. "Ah nothin' ever goes right! It's all true though. I have been thinkin' of you. I came all this way just in the hope of seein' you once again."

Shadarii sighed in bliss, and Kotaru lay back on the grass.

"I've been dreamin' about you, my lady of the lovely eyes! Your kiss stayed with me night and day. Did you kiss me, or did I kiss you? I only remember how beautiful I felt. 'Twas as if I'd only just now opened my eyes—as though I'd been blind and now could see."

He looked adoringly at Shadarii. "I made a song for you. I made it with my flute. I'd like so very much to play it for you. Just—just to have you hear..." Kotaru reached into his pouch and drew out a round clay flute. "I'm a musician y'see. Not much of a one—not a professional, mind. I play all the time, though. When I'm out hunting or just thinkin'. I do a lot of thinkin'."

He sighed.

"I'm poor, Shadarii. I've got no right to talk to a fine lady like yourself. You're a talented woman, a dancer. And here I am, shabby as a wood mouse and twice as poor. But... a man has a right to dream, doesn't he? I mean, sometimes dreams come true...."

Kotaru sighed wistfully, then looked across at Shadarii and suddenly gave an eager smile.

"Hey, d'you sing? Oh, Rain, but I'd love to hear your voice!"

Shadarii drew away, her face frozen, and Kotaru felt a sudden blaze of embarrassment.

"Oh, Rain! Here I am, babbling again! I'm sorry, I didn't mean to drown you out." Damn! It was his one great fault. He'd let his mouth run away again. "Sorry! I just... well, I just want to know you, that's all. I'd love to hear you tell me everything there is to know, every precious little detail. But slowly. Oh, so slowly. Let me savor you piece by little piece...."

Shadarii looked sick.

The man gazed dreamily at her and sighed. "When I thought of you, I knew you'd have a voice just like a songbird. Sometimes I'd close my eyes and imagine I could hear you sing. I always knew the woman of my dreams would sound just like a... my lady?"

Kotaru jerked upright as Shadarii stumbled away from him, her hands clasped against her throat. She looked at him in anguish, tears streaming from her eyes.

"Lady! What—what's wrong? Tell me, what did I say? Please! Just speak out! Tell me what I've...."

With a sob, the girl turned around and fled. She hurtled herself into the dark, her wings flapping frantically behind her.

"Lady, stop! Tell me what I've done! Please! Just tell me!"

Shadarii slammed into a tree and staggered onward, tears streaming though her fur. She was a fool; she'd let the fantasy go on too long. She wasn't a woman, she wasn't anything! She had no voice to speak to him, no words to sing. She was nothing but a cripple. A cripple!

The girl wept and sped away into the darkness.

ᘓ ᘔ ᘔ

Piece by piece, a mighty crowd assembled in the trees. They had come in their thousands from every clan, from every walk of life; come to hear a message of the future.

Zhukora sat beneath the tree ferns with Daimïru by her side, while skull-faced guardians crouched in watchful silence. The jiteng team was slowly transforming into something more. They were the elite inner circle of Zhukora's chosen. She had touched each one of them with the fire of her dreams. They had been baptized in her light and had emerged reborn.

Daimïru stirred, her black armor rattling softly.

"More people are sure to arrive, but most of them are here. Is it time to begin, Zhukora?"

Zhukora gazed out across the shifting crowd. They lined the valley, filling the chasm with expectant faces. She had called them here, all her nation's restless and oppressed—the youth who had been denied their future. She stared at them in wonder, her eyes slowly opening wide.

"Look at them, Daimïru! Look at them! Could you ever have dreamed so many would want to hear?" Zhukora shook her head. "Why? Why have they all come? What can I tell them that they don't already know?"

"They come because you offer them a vision! Vision is all that makes life precious."

"But what if I am wrong? What if I begin a dream that turns into a nightmare?"

"Nightmares are nothing but old dreams left lying in the dust to die." Daimïru knelt at Zhukora's feet, adoration blazing in her eyes.

Zhukora absently stoke her hand across Daimïru's hair. "Oh, Daimïru, why do you care so? Without your faith, I could never find my strength. So much stands against us. It frightens me at times, my love. Can we really succeed against so much?"

Daimïru clenched her fists, her young face alight with power.

"Nothing must stand in your way. Nothing! There's no deed I would not do for you, no part of me I would not give! You are my beginning and my ending, my purpose and my soul! Without you there is no joy in life. Without you I have no reward in death! We will follow you in our thousands and in our tens of thousands!"

The black huntress stared at Daimïru in silence, then turned and slowly walked out before the crowd. A pool of radiance began to spread about her.

A breathless hush rippled through audience; they craned their ears toward her as Zhukora began to speak:

"We are the young." Zhukora calmly looked out across the vast wall of expectant faces. "We are youth. Ours is the dream of bright tomorrows, of family and friendship, of challenge and triumph. The future is our inheritance.

"My people! Youth of the Katakanii. You have come here because there are questions you believe need answers. You have come because our future is dying here before our eyes. It is dying, and the chiefs and councils will not listen!"

The girl's voice rose to a bark of sound. People jumped as her words cracked out with power.

"Can any fool not see disaster? Our way of life is dying. This year, there is folly. Next year, there will be famine. The year after—death! The children first, and then the old, the weak, the helpless. Maggots will fatten on the dead flesh of our young! The Katakanii, the alpine tribes, gone! Gone because our leaders cannot break free of their rules!"

The crowd began to rise. Sudden waves of anger swept across the people. Zhukora rode its energy, flinging her hair back from her face.

"The older generations have betrayed us! They cling to their rules and customs, rules we had no say in making. The councils claim to represent us, but do they listen? Do they care that in a year your children may be dying? And what of their 'One Great Rule'? Do the plains tribesmen starve on weeds and worms? No! They live and grow and breed and laugh while we squat upon our hills and die!

"We are told to live within the forest. We are told not to till the soil or herd the beasts! If this is the way of the alpine tribes, I say this way is wrong! I say it is the way of death, the way of starvation! It is a betrayal of our greater destiny. The ancient customs will be the death of the alpine people!"

Zhukora shook her fists in rage, her whole body wringing in an ecstasy of anger. She tore at her clothes in fury.

"I am a noble! I! I have seen the chieftains living in utter luxury. I have seen the king with his necklaces of silver. They laugh at the commoners! Laugh! You give up your food to keep them in splendor while your young go hungry! You toil, you suffer, and yet power is in the hands of the nobility, not in the hands of the people!"

The answer was a snarl of fury from the crowd. Zhukora whirled and whipped them on.

"They tell us lies! They tell us the true way is the way of peace, of submission! To grovel before them while they betray our very future!

"Lies lies lies!"

The crowd's responding roar was like a waterfall—a pounding, raging rush of energy. Zhukora rode their power, feeding it with words.

"Mother Rain fought for what she wanted! She won the love of Father Wind and created the Kashran people. The Kashra are born of struggle! The fight for what is right is holy!"

Zhukora's fists crashed against her breasts. She screamed her challenge to the very stars. "I say we fight!"

The crowd had leapt to its feet. Thousands of voices thundered in an awesome roar of rage. They took up Zhukora's cry and let her anger fill them with its strength. Her people cheered until their throats were numb—they hammered on the trees and shook their weapons in the air.

Zhukora swept out her hands, and the crowd suddenly fell silent.

"We shall bind the alpine tribes together into one great nation. This has been our time of testing! The forge burns hottest to make the strongest steel! The alpine peoples are the chosen of the Kashra. We have lived the way of purity—the way of Rain and Wind. We are sanctified and strengthened, and now our time of mission has begun!"

They roared. They shrieked out Zhukora's name. She closed her eyes and let the hysterical cries wash across her soul.

"We have the right! We have the will! We shall grasp the future with our claws and drag the Kashran race into the light. Our passion is invincible! Long live the Kashran race! Long live the Dream!"

The people screamed in adoration. A shock of fury made the very earth begin to shake. Zhukora folded her hands across her breast and bowed her head, basking in the raging heat. Skull-Wings kept the crowds at bay, their own eyes fixed upon their savage black messiah.

Zhukora slowly turned and sought Daimïru's adoring face. Her voice was thick with power.

"Go among them, my faithful one! Go tell them of my love. I am theirs now. Tonight we have seen the birthing of a nation."

Daimïru fell upon her knees and covered her face. She shivered in Zhukora's wake, her eyes wild and bright with love. Zhukora passed into the dark, leaving her Dream to burn within the hearts and minds of thousands.

Eight

A single, perfect note hung sadly on the cold dawn air. It rose above the ferns and slowly died, withering piece by piece into the fog. Birds stopped in their tracks and ceased their cries, while tree frogs and lizards emerged to sit and stare. Down by the stream a platypus rose dripping on the banks, touched by the sheer misery of the music.

Kotaru sat beside a clear, still pool and poured his anguish down into his flute. The round clay pipe lay cradled in his long, expressive hands as he gave himself to his music, shaping his grief about himself like a weeping cloud. At last, his hands dropped down, and Kotaru hung his head, a single tear slowly gathering in his eye.

"Oh, lady, what did I do wrong?"

A small sound crept into Kotaru's grief, and he reluctantly raised his head, his drooping ears twitching listlessly.

A young girl stood beside the stream, her skinny legs clad in hunter's moccasins. She had a thin, grave face and fur of fine dove-gray. Her hair shone whiter than a stream of stars. The girl looked at him through weird silver eyes, examining him carefully. When she spoke, her voice rang with a wisdom far beyond her meager years.

"Your name is Kotaru. You saved me from the raiders."

The hunter's red-rimmed eyes looked blankly at the little girl. She stalked across the stones and sat down on the rocks beside him, drawing her face into a scowl.

"Your team is looking for you. They've been worried sick. What are you doing all the way out here?"

Kotaru felt too crushed to even speak.

The little girl tucked her heels beneath her skinny rump and spoke on; she had the sensible, no-nonsense voice of an elocution teacher. "No one comes out here— only Shadarii and I. Shadarii is just down there, along the stream. I found her crying by the water. She's heartbroken. Even the pool spirits were weeping with her." The grave gray eyes looked up at Kotaru. The girl finally huffed in impatience. "Well? Are you just going to sit there all day not talking? It's really very rude you know, even if you did rescue me. Shadarii says we should always be polite. She's even polite to spiders, though I really don't know why. You were terribly brave to rescue me! I should hope we could be friends."

A tear slid slowly down Kotaru's cheek.

Kïtashii looked away as he wiped his eyes. "You can't be in love like that, you know. It really isn't done. She's spent weeks dreaming about you! Poor girl's gone quite off her head. Now the two of you are crying in the woods." Kïtashii propped her cheek upon her hand, lecturing to no one in particular. "I say, is this supposed to happen? It seems a very wretched business if it is! I don't think I shall fall in love at all."

Kotaru hung his head, and the little girl gave an impatient sigh.

"I suppose I shall have to wring it out of you! What did you do to make Shadarii cry? We can't have you both weeping. The ground is damp enough as it is. Come along, speak up!"

The hunter looked at the little girl with awful, empty eyes. "We-we met... I tried to tell her how I feel about her. All of a sudden everything went wrong! I—I don't know what I did! I—I only wanted just to talk. I'd dreamed about our kiss for so long! All I did was beg to hear her voice...."

Kïtashii slapped her hand across her eyes and groaned. "Oh, Rain and Poison!"

Kotaru sobbed in agony. "I hurt! M' heart feels like it bleeds. I canna' eat, I canna' sleep, all for the want of her! I don't know what I've done! To think that I might have-have hurt her... !"

"Yes, Shadarii told me the very same." The girl sighed resignedly. "Ah well, you'll just have to stay in love with one another I suppose. I really can't see any way of saving either of you now." Kïtashii frowned and propped her chin in her hand. "I was once told that there is a great art to catching a precious bird. If you fail to grasp it hard enough, it will fly off and escape you. If you clutch too hard you will choke the poor wee creature." She shot a sideways glance at Kotaru. "One wonders whether you both snatched this thing too hard. All these tears and sighs, all this misery... Kotaru, do you even know anything about Shadarii?"

"I..." Kotaru hung his head. "No, nothin' at all—exceptin' she saved me. And... and that there's something sad inside her. Something I'd give anything to heal."

"You really ought to become friends if you ever hope to be lovers. You must learn to listen, Kotaru. Not everybody speaks the way you and I do. Sometimes Shadarii's way seems to say much more than words."

Kotaru simply didn't understand; Kïtashii shook her head and patiently explained.

"She cannot talk, Kotaru. Shadarii has no voice. Didn't you ever notice that Shadarii never spoke?"

Kotaru's jaw dropped and his pupils shrank as he realized what he had said and done. "Oh, my... ! I-I'm not sure that I ever even gave the lass the chance." He clutched his hand across his eyes. "Oh, Wind forgive me! I'm a fool...."

"As to that, I surely wouldn't dare to judge." Kïtashii's tone indicated otherwise. "In any case, I owe you a great debt for rescuing me. I shall try to set you both on the right path since I suspect that you really do care for her."

"I care! Oh, Rain how I care!"

"I know you do, otherwise I would not let you see her. But mark my words, Kotaru! If you cannot face a voiceless woman—if you cannot respect her, then turn your back and go your way! If you hurt her, I shall tell Zhukora you were in the raid on the village! I recognize your Prince Tekï'taa as well. I should not like to be in your moccasins if she found out, so keep well away from her!" She looked up into Kotaru's yearning, shame-filled face. "Oh, get away with you! Stop looking at me with those bloody awful eyes. She's downstream at the little waterfall. Go talk to her, and for Rain's sake don't make more of a skreg of yourself than you have to!"

Kotaru shot off into the bushes as though a snake hung on his tail. Kïtashii watched him blunder through the trees and shook her head. With a snort of derision the little girl spread her fine quicksilver wings and drifted off into the fog.

Shadarii sat among the rocks and wept, letting her tears merge with the stream. Cry as she might, the pain stayed with her. Why? Oh, why had she been such a fool? She didn't even know him. She had built a whole fantasy romance on nothing! There was no way to tell him how she felt; no way to ask him the questions that burned for answers.

If I had a voice... I could make him love me if only I had a voice!

Shadarii croaked and tore at her throat, hating herself, loathing the world that had forced her to live without words to speak or songs to sing.

The girl's head shot up as she saw Kotaru facing her across the stream. Shadarii stumbled back, and tried to flee.

"Stop!"

Shadarii staggered through the trees, her ïsha fields whirling drunkenly about her. Kotaru gave a cry and soared in pursuit.

"Lady please, I beg you! Stop! Please!" He caught her as she tried to scrabble up the slippery rocks.

Suddenly her spirit seemed to leave her. Shadarii folded into a little ball and wept, her orange wings trailing brokenly beside her. Kotaru hung his head in shame. He knelt beside her in the moss, his face bowed toward the ground.

"I'm sorry. Oh, Rain I'm so sorry. I've no excuse to offer you. I've done the one thing I prayed I'd never do." Kotaru stared down at the dirt. "My Lady, I know I presume far too much, but if—if you can forgive a fool, I'd be grateful for a second chance. I never meant to hurt you." Kotaru swallowed hard. "I'm an idiot, and I'm in agony, and I'm so desperately in love! Please just let me be near. Just let me stay, I beg you!"

Shadarii made no attempt to move; her fur trembled as she wept. Kotaru fearfully sat beside her, his hands shaking in his lap.

"Kïtashii says you can speak in your own fine way, if someone will only take the time to listen. I'm listening, lady. Please, I want to understand. If you'd do me the honor of being my friend, 'twould be more than a mere fool has the right to ask."

Shadarii slowly uncurled, peering out bit by bit from beneath her mop of hair. Slowly she sat up, scrubbing at her puffy eyes, then made a few weary motions with her hands.

Kotaru watched Shadarii, his antennae rising in wonder. She molded the ïsha all around her with an awesome, unconscious power. Her every mood, her every feeling were spread out across the aura. She hung her head and tried to wave the man away.

There is no need to pretend. I am as I am. Take back your pity and go away.

"Shadarii... I—I don't pity you, but I need to understand you! Please let me listen. I'm here for you if only you'd lift your face and see."

She made a few curt signs with her free hand. Kotaru kept his mind open, waiting until she had finished before putting a meaning to the whole.

I have made a fool out of myself. I forgot just what I am. No man could love a cripple. It was stupid to forget.

Kotaru's voice was soft and gentle, and his words glowed like summer stars. "You're wrong, my lady. Any man who'd not look past your voice is not worthy of your love in any case."

Shadarii resentfully looked into Kotaru's eyes, then signed toward his breast and touched her heart. *Why? Why do you care so? Why should you bother? You are handsome, you are brave! You could have anyone you wanted! Why waste your time upon a freak?*

"I want no one else. No woman has ever caught my heart before, and no other ever shall."

She stared at him in disbelief, her breast heaving. *You know nothing about me! How can you say you love me?*

Kotaru looked into her eyes and tried to speak his heart. "Oh, my lady, I know so much already. I know that you are kind, for you helped me when my hope was gone. I know you are brave, for you risked yourself to save me. I know you are clever, for I have seen the beauty of your art. You stole my heart away with but a kiss, and now I'm lost without you."

Shadarii ran an adoring hand across his face. She wept, her whole face wracked with shame. *But my voice! I have no voice.* Shadarii sobbed in agony. *There is no future for us!*

"All I know is that I will try to make you happy. I'm brave enough to take the risk, if you'll but take it with me." He took her face into his hands and slowly brushed the tears away.

She closed her eyes, feeling dizzy at Kotaru's touch. Despite herself she felt her body move up against him, and he wound his arms about her, cradling her quietly. The girl's trembling slowly ceased. At last, she lifted her beautiful, tear-stained face to peer at him in wonder. Shadarii looked into Kotaru's eyes and gently touched her heart, her lips, his mouth. *I love you....*

Shadarii's wings began to droop; her breathing gradually slowed and deepened as her lashes closed. Comfort was an utterly seductive drug. Safe in Kotaru's arms, Shadarii simply closed her eyes and fell asleep. Her ïsha field wrapped around Kotaru like a lover's gentle arms.

He basked inside her perfect light and was content. "Sleep, my lady. Sleep and let your dreams be dreams of love." He tucked a glorious copper curl back from her tufted ear. "There's no hurry, my silent lady. We've all the time in the world, eh? All the time in the world..."

Kotaru sat back in the sunshine and held Shadarii in his arms. Slowly he began to nod, his eyes drooping as sleep rose to claim him.

 G৪ ৪০ ৪০

Zhukora drank her tea with pure delight, savoring every scalding drop. Her body felt more alive than ever before. The whole world seemed crisp and new as she looked down across the village roofs.

Daimïru sat quietly beside the teapot, stirring in a spoonful of dried leaves. Her long blonde hair glittered in the sunlight, making Zhukora's heart strangely warm. Zhukora broke a seed loaf in two and offered the larger piece to her devoted friend.

They ate their frugal meal together, enjoying the feel of sun across their fur. Finally Daimïru sat back and brushed the crumbs from her thighs.

"The village seems quiet this morning. Last night's revelries have left the people tired. I've sent hunters to gather food to feed those villagers who hunger."

"Good. You have done well, my love." Zhukora smiled and swirled her teacup. "Is there any news to report?"

"The dancing girl Javïra spent the night with Tekï'taa. The priests are attempting to gather yet more power. Other than that, all is quiet."

Zhukora nodded, losing herself inside the caress of a perfect cup of tea. She breathed a great sigh of anticipation and looked over at her friend.

"The priests are no stumbling block. I have a tool to deal with them when the time is right." Zhukora's tea had been fresh picked from high mountain streams that only she and Daimïru knew. "The games begin in three short hours, Daimïru! Great things are finally afoot. Soon the flight path to the future shall be ours!"

"The team will be ready. We match against the Sword-Tails' Rainbow Gleams at midday. And tomorrow—the Orchids."

"Yes... the Orchids. Finally we can clear the first obstacle from our path." Zhukora smoothed the white fur across her chest. "We shall win, Daimïru. We shall take the tribal title, and then we shall face the Vakïdurii team in battle. With their defeat, we shall become heroes!" The huntress's blue eyes gleamed with predatory lust. "The Wrens shall rue the day they were mad enough to come near us! Finally, Katakanii honor will be avenged!"

Daimïru blinked. "You—you suspect the Vakïdurii were the ones behind the raid?"

"Oh, yes, I know it's them. Our vile king may sit and swap pleasantries with their ambassador, but I still remember the day our goods were stolen. I remember the day my father trampled our pride in the dust!"

"Then we should strike! Drag them before the clans and have them slain!"

"Patience, my love! Patience. We'll make them pay on the field." The girl's fangs gleamed like ice. "Oh, yes... we'll make them pay in blood...."

The mood passed; there was tea to drink and another day to share. Theirs was a friendship strengthened over many precious years. The wind stirred, mingling black and blonde hair in a single fragrant stream. Zhukora stared across the village toward a distant future.

"It will be a strange life for us now, my love. There will be no more dawn hunts together, no more wild flights along the winding river. We will have to travel from clan to clan, even tribe to tribe, keeping the Dream blazing in their hearts. We'll have to become people of the race, not of the clan. The lazy days of forest life are gone...." Zhukora sighed. "I can't see that we'll have time for jiteng anymore. But still, we'll see the stars together as we camp out beneath the sky. I think we will still find beauty in our lives."

"A fine wind and my companion by my side. A vision to follow and a cause to serve. What more can I ask for? What could make me richer?" Daimïru drew a breath and let Zhukora's strength flow through her. Finally she put aside her teacup and prepared to leave the lodge.

"The team will be ready for training in half an hour. I have planned everything. Nothing will go wrong." The blonde girl bowed. "Rain and Wind bless you, my leader. I will prepare myself for my part."

Zhukora looked down at her friend and smiled. "There's no need to bow, Daimïru. We will do away with class distinctions. Our new world will have no need of them."

Daimïru smiled and shook her head. "I bow to you because it is my privilege to do so. Would I do it if it were not a pleasure?" The girl spread her wings and poised herself upon the brink. "I am proud to serve you, Zhukora. One day I will show it to the world!" The girl swept out her wings and soared into the sky.

Zhukora watched, a smile shining in her eyes. "And I am proud to be served by you, my love. The trail will be long and hard. I am grateful a companion travels with me."

The woman sipped her tea and turned her head to gaze out across the village fields, where the people sat to gather foodstuffs and make their songs. A proud people—inventive spirits fired by incalculable passion. Zhukora gazed across her village with a quiet surge of love.

"Lord Serpent. Are you there?"

Ïsha coils arose from the shrouded skull hidden on a shelf.

I am here. What do you wish of me?

"Thoughts." Zhukora sipped tea and gazed in sharp concentration at the sight of the high priestess far below; the old woman sat with councilors, pouring her poison in their ears. "The priests will eventually be my enemy. How may a warrior defeat magical power?"

The beautiful ïsha of the Serpent spirit looped and coiled about the roof poles of the room.

Power must be fought with greater power. Take a 'rider'[20]. It will trade you power for sensation from your body.

"Good!" Zhukora settled back against the door and simply drank her tea. "Then I choose you."

Serpent flashed with colors of arrogance.

I am no mere sparrow spirit, girl! I am a great one of the ïsha! My race was old before your own was even born! My power would burn your mortal body into ash!

"Courage will prevent it." Zhukora looked carefully at the skull, new intuitions flooding sharply through her mind. "You fear it, don't you. If I were to die, you might die with me."

I am beyond death! I fear nothing! Serpent looped and coiled in irritation. *I wish only for glory to come back onto the Earth!*

"You do not fear death? How interesting." Zhukora regarded the villages across the fine steam rising from her cup. "I wonder. You see, it seems to me that of all things, love is the one thing that goes beyond mere life." The girl's slim black form turned perfectly still, her eyes staring unseeing out into the trees; when she spoke, it was with her gaze focused on something strange and fragile that only she could see. "It came to me at last, do you see? I now know I have a gift to give—perfect value, but at ultimate price. And it is love that banishes my fear of the giving...."

---

[20]**Riders:** Allied spirits tied to the body of a sorcerer. The process is dangerous, and has rewards usually of interest only to a priest.

Zhukora sharply tossed the dregs from her cup out across the leaves. "I will call on you, Lord Serpent. Until then—let glory run like fire through your dreams...."

CŽ Ž Ž

To walk through the forest with Shadarii was to discover a whole new world. The background aura of the forest bloomed around her as she passed. Shadarii spread wide her arms and grinned for joy, and the touch of her silent laughter made Kotaru smile.

They ambled merrily beside the stream, their wings folded behind them. There was no need for speed—no need to fret or worry. The sun streamed through the forest canopy in a rain of warmth, and the wind grew soft and mellow as it ruffled their fur.

Shadarii led the way down a dripping maze of ferns to a place of dank, primeval peace. A wide brown pool spread out beneath a gleaming waterfall, dashing spray across the bracken in an icy sheet of rainbows.

Kotaru stretched and breathed in the cool, clear mist. Shadarii stood watching him, her fur rippling to the rhythm of the breeze. With the sun and spray behind her, she seemed some strange spirit of the rain.

Kotaru smiled and waved a hand toward the rocks.

"How beautiful! There's no Ka here? I can't feel one."

Shadarii sat herself down on a log and fanned out her precious wings.

No Ka. Not here, not now. When enough love is lavished here, a Ka will come.

"It's so perfect! The waterfall, those rainbows... however did you find such beauty?"

Shadarii looked at the streaming mists and gave a smile.

The rainbows? Ha! I made them with my tail! She grinned as Kotaru blinked in puzzlement. *A story. A silly story I will tell to you sometime.*

The girl breathed in the peace and ran her fingers through her hair. Her great green eyes were slitted in pleasure. Kotaru watched as she framed a question with supple fingers.

"Do I like stories? Yes! But there are just so few these days...."

Shadarii gasped, then sprang to her feet and excitedly danced before him. Kotaru blinked and tried to follow her motions.

No stories? There are thousands of them, Kotaru! Every rock and tree holds a tale if only we listen. There's so much to know, Kotaru! So much to do! Who can mope and moan when such a wide world opens out before us?

"Ha, and is there a story inside me?"

Shadarii grasped Kotaru's chin and peered critically into his face.

Aaaah, yes. Here I think we might find a story worth the telling. Her hand lingered on his cheek before she shyly withdrew her touch.

The girl bent down and drank, her tail lashing back and forth before Kotaru's eyes. He watched her dreamily, his face softening.

"Why do you come here?"

Shadarii flicked water from her hands, then touched the lilies and the bracken all around her, stroking their rich green leaves.

I come here to tend the plants. This stream here; people had choked it with rubbish. I cleared it all away and made the plants feel better.

"Do you come here often? This could be a lonely place."

Shadarii faltered. She half tuned away, her tail hanging down behind her.

Sometimes it is good to be alone, Kotaru. I used to think I needed no one but myself. The girl raised her head. *I have been a fool...* Shadarii quietly came to sit at Kotaru's feet, looking at him with great green eyes. *You do not mock me, Kotaru. For once I am not the butt of someone's joke. I thank you for your friendship.*

Kotaru dared to touch her hair, allowing himself to stroke her for one brief, precious instant before timidly withdrawing. Kotaru had no wish to spoil the fragile magic by letting his heart fly free.

He softly drew a clay flute from his pouch and nervously turned it over in his hands. "I really did make a song for you, Shadarii. May I play it? Only if you'd really like to hear...."

She sat expectantly at his feet, her whole being waiting for him to begin.

The man transformed as soon as he raised the flute to his lips. Kotaru played with gentle grace, his love coloring the ïsha all around him. The girl's eyes closed as she drifted on a dreamy cloud of joy. Finally, the song drew to a close; Kotaru softly laid aside his flute, his music still shining in the ïsha like a forest dawn.

The girl stood and kissed Kotaru on the cheek. Kotaru ran a hand across his tousled hair, suddenly bright and filled with life.

"Well! Shall we eat? I can find us lunch. Do you mind?"

Shadarii's eyes filled with eager light. *Hungry!*

"Can we eat here? I mean, it's your place and all. You care for all the plants."

Shadarii ruefully patted her nice round belly. *I like my meat, although I shouldn't. We all have to eat.*

"I'll see what I can find, then. Just you rest and watch a master at his work!"

Kotaru hastily began to strip away his moccasins. Shadarii pretended not to watch as he peeled off down to his loincloth. Her heart almost skipped a beat as Kotaru bent down to pile his gear.

She hastily looked away as Kotaru peered questioningly in her direction. The girl's ears blushed hot, and she wriggled in her seat.

Food is scarce around here. I don't think you'll find much in the water.

Kotaru shrugged his nice broad shoulders.

"Ha! Back home we're living on nothing but boiled bracken starch. Next year's crops are gone as well! The food's run out, and Rain only knows what we'll eat next season!" The hunter snapped his fingers. "I still eat well enough. No one else knows where to look, that's the trouble. You have to use your brains!"

Small holes dotted the mud beside the water hole. Kotaru knelt and cocked his head, bringing his antennae close to the ground.

"Yep! Crayfish livin' in the mud bank. They've all gone out into the water for a midday stroll. How d'you like shellfish, eh?" Kotaru edged slyly into the shallows and began to peer beneath logs and stones. "There they are! All squabblin' over territory beneath the rocks. What say we just make the argument a wee bit simpler, eh?"

Kotaru edged back out of the water and stood dripping on the bank. He dug beneath the mud and found a fine fat worm, which he threaded on a fishing line. A few deft turns and he had a tiny baited noose held in his hands. The great hunter wriggled out along a mossy log, his snare dangling across the drink.

"We used to get big emus up the valleys—long time ago, now. You can chase 'em down, but I tried another way. Ever notice how nosy those critters are? Well, I just laid back and waved me legs in the air. Sure enough, one of the buggers came my way to see what was up. Bam! I had him in the pot before you could blink and whistle!"

Kotaru bent over the cool brown water, and Shadarii moved to give herself a better view. The girl lounged back to enjoy the show, her isha field touched by tendrils of warmth.

A girl can always dream....

"Ha!"

Kotaru jerked the line and hauled out a fat crayfish, bigger than his hand. Shadarii clapped politely as he brought her his first catch of the day. He made a great show of laying his bounty at her feet, and Shadarii simpered properly, holding out her hand above her vassal's head in blessing.

Kotaru tottered back across the log, and Shadarii regretfully ceased spying. It was high time she made herself useful. The girl gathered kindling for a fire, clearing out a likely spot beside the waterfall. A flock of tiny finches whirred and flitted through the trees. She reached out her hands and gave a little kiss, bringing the birds to land all about her hair. She checked their eyes for sickness, smiling as she felt the eggs ripening within the little hens.

"That's another! Ha, I thought y'said there was no food?"

Shadarii smiled and kissed a tiny bird on the beak. The creatures flitted back into the trees, their gentle cries filling the air with song.

"Come back here, you bugger! Damn!" One of Kotaru's victims refused to snare itself in his noose, and fell back into the water with a splash. Kotaru thrust his hand in after it, and then yelped as the crayfish locked its pincers on his finger. With an awful splash, Kotaru fell into the pond.

Shadarii laughed, clutching at her middle. Kotaru erupted from the water, slapping at the vicious crayfish clinging to his hand.

"Ouch! Stop laughin' woman and come help me. Aaawwwk!"

The man gave a yelp and catapulted from the stream. A second crayfish had latched onto his tail. Kotaru ran across the bank, his little enemies grimly sinking in their claws.

"Aaah—fire! Arson! Murder!"

Shadarii fell to her knees and laughed so hard she gave herself a stitch. Kotaru ripped a crayfish from his hand, cursing with words Shadarii had never heard. He turned to deal with the creature dangling from his tail, only to have the first beast latch onto his toe.

"Fire and damn! You beastly little vampire!" He ripped the creature free, falling down and landing on his backside in the grass. The crayfish scuttled toward Kotaru's groin. The hunter gave a squawk and frantically backpedaled on his rear. "Shadarii! Help!"

Claws clashed shut just short of Kotaru's loincloth. Shadarii deftly flicked it away with a stab of ïsha. The hunter sullenly jerked the last crayfish off his tail and coldly stalked down all the others, his pride stung by Shadarii's laughter.

Shadarii had the hiccoughs; Kotaru glared at her, his ears flattened in annoyance.

"A fine thing! The damned beast could have circumcised me! Aaaah skreg it! Nothin' ever goes right!"

Shadarii simply closed her eyes and slowly spread her hands; Kotaru felt a warm glow spread up from his toes as she dried his fur with a tight spiral of ïsha. She grinned slyly as the whirlwind almost lifted him from his feet.

The last wisps of moisture evaporated from Kotaru's fur. He ignored the miracle and irritably dusted dried mud from his hide.

"Why hasn't anyone else noticed all this tomfoolery o' yours? I'm sure they'd love you in the healers or summat! In the Vakïdurii they'd tattoo[21] your hands blue in a trice!"

Shadarii grinned maliciously and crossed her eyes. *I have no voice! They all think I must be stupid!*

"Ha! Well someone should take you. We could make you the world's first silent priest!"

Priests! Oh, Rain, she'd forgotten! She was promised to the priests! The girl swiftly turned away and began to see to dinner. Her eloquent body was her own undoing. Kotaru saw the fear flickering through her aura.

"Lady! What is it? What's wrong?"

The girl sighed, put her hand across her eyes, and then finally looked up at Kotaru and shook her head. *It doesn't matter. Nothing is wrong.*

It would all solve itself somehow. She shook her wings and threw away the mood. The girl's ïsha flashed as she sparked the fire ablaze, and the crayfish were set to toasting while Shadarii skinned a brace of cool, crisp lily bulbs.

Lunch tasted magnificent, and fresh, sharp air had made for a pair of hungry appetites. Finally full, Kotaru rolled belly up toward the sun and stretched luxuriously in the warmth. Shadarii obligingly began to scratch Kotaru's ribs. Kotaru's face went slack with pleasure, and his left leg began to twitch. Shadarii scratched him harder as she felt him groan in bliss.

Shadarii's hands finally grew tired. The girl tapped Kotaru's snout and pantomimed a question. *Was dinner good?*

"Oh, yes, lady! Mmmmmm. Dinner was very good, indeed."

Better than stolen catfish? She looked sideways at Kotaru, pleased to see him give a guilty jump, and then curled a finger idly through his fur. *Why did you do it? Stealing is bad. Forbidden! Why did you go along?*

Kotaru's face was troubled. Shadarii patiently waited for an answer, her antennae drinking in every nuance of his ïsha posture. There was no hiding from her; there never would be. Shadarii read a man's soul with unnerving ease.

---

[21]**Palm Tattoos:** Healers tattoo their palms with symbols of the Wind and Rain. They kill no meat, nor handle unclean objects, thus preserving them from the attentions of malicious Ka.

"The raid?" Kotaru sighed, unhappy with the stupid decisions of his past. "I—I don't know why I really came. Everyone else was goin' along, I guess. Only that's not really why.... I regretted it the moment we all left home. The prince, he seemed to be takin' it all as somethin' a bit more sinister...."

Shadarii's eyes were pools of strange, deep thoughts.

Kotaru faced her with utter honesty. "I don't know, Shadarii. I used to listen to stories once. Stories about folk who rescued people—folk who made a difference. I always dreamed about bein' a hero.

"There's no food left back home, Shadarii. The game's all gone, far worse than here. Children get ill without meat. Rickets—malnutrition. I think they might begin dying soon. And—and the Katakanii are rich! Everyone knows that. I just thought.... well, you know, that maybe it would all be for the better good."

The hunter hurtled a piece of grass into the bushes. "Aaaah—it's all gone and done now. I did what I could to make amends. What do you want to know all this for anyway?"

The girl motioned gravely in response. *Shadarii is very simple. Her I already know. Kotaru is another matter. What makes Kotaru what he is?*

Kotaru gave a smile. "There's really not so much to tell." The man idly ticked points off on his fingers. "I'm the sad result of an unmarried dalliance. Someone decided to make me captain of a jiteng team. I don't like grapes, but I do like onions. I can't play the pipe half as well as I'd like. Most of all, I just like thinking." Kotaru's eyes were shy and anxious. "Is that what you want to know? Is it a start? I really can't think of much more to say...."

It was worth another scratch on the belly at least. Shadarii roughly plied her claws all up and down his fur. The hunter sighed and let ennui take hold of him. His lashes drooped as he felt the sweet warmth of the sun. Finally Kotaru stretched and gave a sigh.

"Hey, should we be getting back? I've a team who'll be wonderin' where I am. Don't you have dancin' to do?"

Shadarii's eyes grew wide; Hatïkaa would have been waiting all day for their practice session! The girl held her face in dismay. Kotaru saw expression and rose to his feet.

"Oh, you do, eh? Well, I suppose I can bear to go back now." He smiled at her. "It's been a precious day. Thank you for bein' my friend."

Shadarii licked her lips and edged closer. Suddenly she lunged in, kissed Kotaru's mouth, and swiftly fled.

"Hey!"

With a silent blaze of laughter, the girl shot into the ferns, and Kotaru whooped as he raced off in pursuit. They whirled into the endless green, the whole forest shining with their merriment.

Nine

Shadarii danced and whirled, hacking her knives into an old dead tree. Chips flew. The weapons blurred. She swept back into guard, ducking and twisting as she accelerated.

The Wrens were gathered by their campfire, finishing the last few crumbs of breakfast. Totoru, the Wren's massive goal guard, leaned against a tree, watching the buxom noble dance. "She's good."

"She's very good!" Mrrimïmei stuffed her mouth full of bread. "Mmmph, I've never sheen anything like it."

Kotaru's breakfast lay untouched. He watched Shadarii practice, his fluffy tail waving merrily behind him. The poor man heaved a heartfelt sigh and murmured something to the breeze.

Mrrimïmei glanced slyly at Kotaru, then clasped her hands to her heart and fluttered her long lashes. "Oh, Kotaaaaaruuuu...."

Kotaru dreamily cocked an ear. "Hmm?"

"Would you like to be alone, darlin'? Your rear end's on fire."

"Mmmm? That's nice...."

Mrrimïmei sighed. "Bloody hopeless! D'you reckon he'll snap out of it by practice time?"

"Aaaah, he'll be all right. We'll just move that girl's tail down to the practice field. Kotaru'll follow sure enough."

"A quiet girl, if you ignore her hobbies." Mrrimïmei scratched her chin as Shadarii cleaved a branch clean in two. "Me sister has a girlfriend like that. All knives and spears and such. Neither of 'em ever did get married...."

Shadarii had finished her routine. She scrubbed her sweaty palms with a piece of rag, grinning at Kotaru. He gazed adoringly down at her. His tail quivered as he caught the scent of her, all warm and salty on the morning air.

Slim, lanky and guileless, Mrrimïmei leaned on Kotaru's shoulder and tugged at his antenna.

"Psssst, Kotaru! Helloooo.... Hey, who's the lady?"

Kotaru blinked. He looked blankly around at Mrrimïmei as if seeing her for the very first time. "What? Shadarii? Oh, just a friend of mine. No one special."

The girl gave a snort. "Oh, come on! 'Tis the first time we've ever woken to find a noblewoman makin' breakfast. 'Tweren't us she was doing it for, either! The look on your face when she knocked on the door was priceless." Mrrimïmei idly studied her nails. "You were out awful late last night; any special reason she was makin' you breakfast?"

"What? No, no special...." Kotaru's eyes grew wide as her insinuation suddenly sank home. "Most certainly not!"

"Ah, and here's me thinkin' you always liked your meat lean. By the bye, isn't that your necklace she's wearing?"

Kotaru absently raised his hand to his own neck. "Oh, I suppose so. Yes, I guess it must be."

"Ah, well, never mind. Where there's a will there's a way, eh!"

Kotaru leapt to his feet as Shadarii walked toward the camp. "Here she comes! Just stay here, I want to introduce you! You'll like her, really you will!" Kotaru began to dash off toward Shadarii, then screeched to a halt and swiftly ran back to the team. "Oh! Look, just—ah—just one little thing. She doesn't speak, all right? So just bear it in mind."

"She can't talk?"

"Oh, she can talk, she just can't speak. Come on, she's dying to meet you all!"

Kotaru eagerly ran down to meet his friend, his tail wagging like a dizzy little pup. He chattered gaily as he led Shadarii toward the waiting Wrens.

"Ah! My Lady Shadarii-kai-Nochorku-Zha, may I present the Vakïdurii champion jiteng team. This is our forward rover, Mrrimïmei, the fastest thing with wings! This is Totoru, our movin' mountain. Tingtraka, our magic specialist—the other lady on the team. Rotïka, Kefarii..." Kotaru reached out to grip each player's arm, warming them with his special smile.

Shadarii shyly bobbed her head, then swept out her hands and clenched her fingers above her heart. A great warm rush of ïsha swept across the team.

Kotaru grinned. "She says 'hello' to you all. Most pleased to meet you."

Tingtraka looked in amazement from Shadarii to Kotaru. "You understand her?"

"Of course. I told you she talks. You only have to listen!"

Shadarii prodded Kotaru on the rump, then wagged her fingers and danced a little dance, seeming to scold him over something.

Kotaru's ears wilted guiltily. "She—uh—she says I have practice to be gettin' on with. She says she'll sit and watch, but I'm not to stop until we've all put in two solid hours."

"Ha! I like her already!" Mrrimïmei had an arm about Totoru once again. "We'll all take him off and make him work, my lady, never fear."

Shadarii gave the thumbs-up and curled herself upon a log to watch them practice. Kotaru reluctantly lead his team across the open meadow.

Kotaru gathered his folk around him, shuffling his feet through the soft green grass.

"Uh, people? I just thought I'd let Shadarii meet you all. I know we're here to win a game, but still, this is important. The lady is very special to me."

Kotaru looked from face to face, seeing their enjoyment. Kotaru gave a cough and briskly clapped his hands.

"All right, all right! Ïsha thrusts and parries will be gone through after lunch. Shadarii can show you all how to improve control. Rotïka, Totoru—your ball handling is atrocious! Mrrimïmei, what do y'call those turns you've been tryin' to pull on us?" Kotaru whirred into the sky. "Up! Up! Come on, there's a game to win tomorrow! Tomorrow we beat the best the Katakanii have to offer!"

High in the trees, a flock of Katakanii dancing girls on their way to class peered down into the clearing.

Srïhoonii twitched her antennae in puzzlement. "What on earth is fatso up to now? Who are all those people?"

"Who cares? Just some ragamuffins from another clan."

"I've seen them somewhere before. Who's the dopey looking one who keeps on staring at her?"

"Who knows. Come on. There's practice to be done! Javïra, are you coming?"

Javïra stared down at Shadarii, her eyes suddenly intense and bright. The dancer's tail waved slowly as she let out a long predatory hiss.

"Javïra?"

The girl's breath seemed somehow faster. With an agile flip of wings Javïra raced off after her companions.

Far below, Shadarii drew her knives and danced beneath the gentle morning sun.

ෆ ৪০ ৪১

"Now, watch carefully, Kotaru! The winners will be the team the Wrens shall have to play tomorrow."

Prince Tekï'taa sat on a platform high above the ground. Below him, a crowd of ten thousand had gathered around the jiteng field. It would be a match to end all matches—two teams from the same clan fighting bitterly for the tribal title. The Skull-Wings and the Orchids were to clash at last.

The Swallowtails had turned jiteng into a hard and violent game. It was going to be a foul match, and for once the people seemed thirsty for blood. Food shortages had frayed tempers to the breaking point.

The Katakanii priests sealed the sacred circle. Once the game had begun, no one could pass onto the field. Prince Tekï'taa watched the ceremonies while he ate a tiny peach.

"Kotaru, do pay attention. I'm sure you will find the local playing styles most interesting."

"Never fear, my lord!" The young captain tried to be all attentiveness and eyes. "We'll bring you a victory! I'm sure we will."

"Quite." The prince leaned forward to prod Kotaru with a peach pit. "It is important to me. See to it that you do."

Shadarii knelt quietly on the rear edge of the platform and made the prince's tea. It had taken her a whole string of beads to bribe another girl into giving her the post, but it was worth it just to be beside Kotaru.

The prince was treating Kotaru like a piece of dirt. What's more, Mrrimïmei said that the man enjoyed beating girls. Shadarii peered at the prince, her tail slowly lashing through the air behind her.

The prince idly clicked his fingers at Shadarii. "You, there—fat one! Go find us more tea, and be quick about it."

Shadarii looked at Prince Tekï'taa and gave a slow, sly smile. She retreated far too innocently for Kotaru's liking. He'd almost formulated an excuse to dash off in pursuit when the prince deigned to speak to him once more. "The Katakanii seem blessed with a fine crop of tender beauties. That last one was a touch overripe, perhaps. Still, she seems entirely pleasant." The prince sighed. "A virgin and a noble, too! Ah me. Too bad she is already spoken for."

Kotaru was suddenly all ears. "My lord?"

"Nothing. Clan business is far above your understanding."

"But, my lord! You—you mean she's engaged?"

"Oh no, of course not, boy!"

Kotaru sighed in relief. All worries faded from his mind as he saw Shadarii alight back on the platform. She beamed at him, adoring him with her lovely eyes while steam curled from the iron teapot in her hands.

"Aaah, the tea! Thank you, m'dear. I shall take a cup now, I think."

Shadarii smiled sweetly at Kotaru as she opened the pot, daintily sprinkling into it a pinch of herbs and grasses. The girl sighed in anticipation as she reached into her pouch. She held up a pair of purple seed pods and jiggled them merrily in the air, then winked at Kotaru, twirling the herbs with a malicious sense of anticipation.

Behind Teki'taa's back, Kotaru frantically tried to signal her.

No! For pity's sake, don't!

The girl seemed mildly surprised. She held the pods before her eyes, looking sideways at Kotaru before picking up the prince's teacup. Kotaru angrily flapped his hands.

Shadarii! I forbid it!

Shadarii gave a helpless little shrug and dunked the seed pods down into the prince's tea. With her green eyes all wide and innocent, she proffered Teki'taa his drink. The prince reached for it without a second glance and raised the cup to his lips; Kotaru jerked and tried to intervene.

"Uh..."

The Prince slurped his tea and scowled. "What is it now, Kotaru? Rain, man! Your nerves are getting irritating!"

Shadarii sighed as she watched the prince drain his cup. He smacked his lips and asked to have another, and Shadarii gleefully complied. Kotaru watched helplessly as she dipped the seed pods in his cup once more.

With undiminished gusto, the prince drained the second cup. Kotaru bit his nails, his tail twitching fitfully behind him.

A scream came from the audience as the jiteng players arrived. The Orchids whirled into the air, posing for the adoration of the crowds, their bright costumes shining with all the colors of the rainbow. They flexed their muscles and shook their staves, as exquisite as the flowers they emulated.

Suddenly the spectators rose to their feet. The air shook to a roar as a wave of demons surged onto the field.

"ZHU-KO-RA! ZHU-KO-RA! ZHU-KO-RA!"

Hunters leapt and screamed while the cruel black shapes of Skull-Wings clattered down from the sky. Kotaru stared at the leering skull masks and felt his face drain blank with fright.

Prince Teki'taa politely clapped his hands, delighted by the gruesome costumes. "Aren't they delicious! The Katakanii field eleven major jiteng teams. The Skull-Wings are the only team that crosses clan boundaries. Such a team! Three hundred members! They're the most vicious group to ever play the league. Seven days of jiteng trials, and not a single game lost!"

Kotaru's eyes were riveted on Zhukora's cruel, lithe form. Prince Teki'taa slurped his tea and glanced irritably at his companion.

"What is it this time? You have a comment about your opponents?"

Kotaru swallowed, his eyes riveted to the evil figures swarming through the air.

"I... nothing! I—I just saw the uniforms once before."

"Ha! Hard to mistake. They say Zhukora is a witch, and that each team member consorts with demon Ka and vampires...."

Prince Teki'taa shifted uncomfortably on his seat, frowning slightly as he rubbed a hand across his stomach. Shadarii helpfully topped his cup. The prince frowned and drank more tea, irritably settling back to watch the game unfold.

"Wings spread, ball high!"

The ball arced into the air. High above the open field, the battle had begun.

Zhukora hovered in midair, sweat dripping down the inside of her mask. Two goals down against the Orchids, and two goals scored against themselves! Prakucha had caught them by surprise, deliberately slamming two Skull-Wing players between his own men. He had taken a foul just to break the wings of Zhukora's best fast forward.

It had been a stupid move; not only had it cost the Orchids a penalty, but it had also stirred Zhukora's anger. She hung like a vast black bat above the field, her mind seething with plans for revenge.

Daimïru speared up from the tangled grass of the meadow. Her long blonde hair streamed out beneath her helmet, marking her far better than any flag or painted armor. She raced around Zhukora and nimbly halted.

"Ootïka's arm is broken. He won't leave the field."

"Good man! Put him on guard by the goals."

Daimïru's fangs gnashed in fury. "Two of my team out of action!" The girl gripped her staff. "Let me take him now! Why wait?"

Zhukora's eyes stared across the field. Her voice never changed its measured tone. "We will stay the course. You are stronger than the provocation, Daimïru; always remember that. We must move only in the final goal run."

Daimïru's tail thrashed. "Zhukora, I would never question your orders, but I simply must protest. It is my duty to protect you! To risk yourself in this fashion might cause you to be hurt."

"It is the only way to draw Prakucha out. It is the best plan for success."

"I would rather take any injury myself and leave you whole."

Zhukora nodded. "I know, my love. I know."

The crowd's roar ebbed and flowed around them like the endless wash of leaves. Zhukora slitted her eyes and rode the storm, feeling anger slowly fill her with strength.

"Signal the umpire we're ready to take the penalty play. Echelon formation on Nataku's lead."

The Orchids sullenly positioned themselves, and the umpire tossed the ball to Zhukora. With a curt snap of her fingers, she ordered her phalanx forward. The Orchids lifted a single scream of anger and lunged into the attack.

"Go-go-go!"

Zhukora flung her formation into the Orchid's claws. Figures smashed into each other at breakneck speed. Zhukora punched out with her fist, an ïsha bolt smashing back an Orchid who had been fool enough to block her path. She ripped the power from Prakucha's wings, shrieking triumphantly as he crashed to the ground.

Ïsha pulsed all around her. Every day her powers grew, and her people's faith filled her with a dizzy rush of strength.

Zhukora threw back her head, laughed, and tore clean through the Orchids' heart. Nobles yelled in fury as Daimïru clubbed them from the air. With hair streaming behind them, the women streaked to the Orchids' goals. Zhukora folded her wings and rolled, screaming past the guards to smash the ball down through the hoop. She curved up in a mighty loop, basking in the savage adoration of the crowd.

Daimïru flew beside her, aura burning bright.

Zhukora caressed Daimïru's hair, sharing the pure thrill of the moment. "Now, my love! Now! Finally you may strike!"

The blonde girl gave a sob and whirled around, her mad eyes searching hungrily though the players. Finally they alighted on Prakucha, and Daimïru gave a hiss of ecstasy.

Behind her, the Skull-Wings gathered for their final, devastating play.

"Fools—idiots! I said I wanted her destroyed!"

Prakucha slammed his fist into his palm, his purple mask shivering with rage. The hunter shoved a player backward with one huge hand. "Can't you even carry out the simplest plan? Just get Zhukora! I want her out of the game! Break her wings!"

Players hastened forward.

"Captain, her ïsha strength is unbelievable! She smashes us aside like insects! Forïta's being treated for convulsions. That black bitch did something to his aura!"

"The blonde one is always there. She'll take a blow herself rather than let her captain fall!"

Prakucha's rage was terrible to behold. The enormous man rammed a player back against a tree. "Then bring her down! Evade her! I want Zhukora taken out of action!"

"Wings spread, ball high!"

The ball spun into the sky. With a howl of fury, the Orchids stormed toward the prize.

Two Skull-Wings hurtled through the air and curled into defensive balls, cracking full-tilt into the Orchid leaders. Wings and limbs exploded in a blast of pain. The Skull-Wings uncurled in midair, wings expertly flipping out to break their falls while two injured Orchids spilled helplessly to earth.

Players slammed into one another in a furious melee, and Zhukora shot away from the combat, racing for the ball. Prakucha saw the move. With a roar, he dived toward his prey. This time he would break her ribs and give her something to remember him by! A small piece of pain to last until their marriage day. With a scream of triumph Prakucha cracked his staff between her wings, and Zhukora tumbled to the ground.

Somewhere in the distance the Skull-Wings snapped home their final goal. Prakucha turned his head in shock, looking toward the goal posts even as he speared downward in his dive.

A shape stabbed down from the sun. Something smashed between Prakucha's shoulder blades. His wings shattered as Daimïru collided with him from above. Prakucha screamed and hit the ground, tumbling end over end.

Prakucha's helmet broke against a stone. The huge hunter sprawled semiconscious on the ground, half smothered by the tall grass that towered all around. Another figure skidded to a halt beside him. Prakucha gave a croak, reaching feebly toward his rescuer.

Something knelt across his twisted spine and wrenched his helmet back. Prakucha writhed in sudden fear, huge muscles helpless against an even greater force. A wooden staff jerked back his head, cutting off his air.

He stared up into a snarling skull. Long blonde hair streamed in the wind around eyes glazed in homicidal lust.

Prakucha squealed. Daimïru heaved back on her staff. Prakucha's huge body bucked between her thighs as she clung and twisted. Finally with a crack of bone, she snapped Prakucha's neck. Daimïru stared into his eyes, thrilling to the sharp feel of his dying. Her loins jerked in release, her body shuddering in wild spasms as she let the moment take her. Beneath her, she felt the corpse's heat. Her breathing shuddered harshly in her throat.

The afterglow roared in Daimïru's ears. She tottered to her feet, absently brushing aside Prakucha's Ka.

The grass had hidden everything. Prakucha's headlong fall would explain his injuries. The deed was done; the first obstacle was finally gone....

Daimïru wandered in a daze. Her legs were weak, and her limbs trembled. In a strange state of exultation, she sought Zhukora, and found her in the milling crowd. Zhukora held her tight, sharing the precious triumph.

The first few players were circling toward Prakucha's corpse. Daimïru looked into Zhukora's eyes and smiled in adoration, reaching to stroke the face of death above her.

Two snarling skulls locked in a kiss of death. The first blood had been shed, and strangely, Zhukora no longer cared. The first step had been so easy. She took Daimïru's hand and slowly led her from the field.

In the background, the vast crowd stirred like a restless animal. The news of Prakucha's death slowly spread, souring the air with a noxious, hungry smell. The emotion felt strangely familiar, yet somehow sharply alien.

It was something like... anticipation.

Prince Teki'taa gritted his teeth and held on for dear life as he clutched the latrine. Tortured eyes rolled in agony. He lifted his tail and heaved.

Ohhh, Raiiiiin! Please let it end!

A hand appeared over the edge of the privacy screen waving a sheaf of fine soft paper bark. Teki'taa weakly grasped the paper and dropped it at his feet.

"Th-thank you child.... I f-fear I may be here for quite some ti—"

Aaaargh! Not again! The prince flailed for support as his guts knotted in agony. The poor man shut his eyes and prayed feverishly for his life to end.

Shadarii dusted her hands with satisfaction and danced off to find Kotaru. With the prince regrettably taken ill, the Vakïdurii entourage had discreetly retired from the game.

The river shone clean and bright in the hot afternoon sun as Shadarii swooped down to circle high above rapids. Jiteng players lounged in the grass while smoke swirled above a cooking fire. Kotaru leaned idly back against a tree trunk, the music of his pipe casting a cozy spell. Shadarii turned an agile somersault and landed by his side. Kotaru smiled at her across his flute, his music suddenly becoming lit with swirling moods of joy. Shadarii nestled as closely as she dared.

Clams and roots had been wrapped in parcels of paperbark and then stuffed beneath the coals. Plain, tall, and with a long, sagacious nose, the girl Tingtraka arranged the sizzling packets to their best advantage. Pulling her long black hair back from her red-furred face, she shyly bowed to Shadarii, disturbing the girl's adoring reverie of Kotaru's face.

"My lady—uh—Shadarii? We all heard shouting just now by the field. Is there some sort of trouble with the game?"

Shadarii shrugged; the jiteng game? Who knew? Who cared. She went back to gazing at Kotaru, her tail waving softly.

Kotaru looked down at her, and she melted beneath his big brown eyes. The man softly blew a short phrase on his flute. Shadarii heard her own name lingering in his music as he played the song that he had crafted just for her.

Sha-da-rii...

Sha-da-rii...

This time it was played without sadness. She luxuriated in the caress of music, feeling him worship her with his art.

Sha-da-rii...

Shadarii opened her eyes and blinked. Her mind snapped into crystal clarity. She snatched a piece of paper bark and a piece of charcoal and began to hastily sketch down symbols on the sheet.

What—what if a word was divided into segments like the notes of Kotaru's song? Word segments! Instead of using one picture to depict a word, she could use many! One for each sound. Make each picture an object who's first word segment was the same as the segment being pronounced! Of course!

Her hands trembled with excitement; Shadarii's whole world suddenly centered on a tiny sheet of bark.

Sha—da—rii. Three word segments. Three separate pictures.

Sha—say "shattra", the full moon. That was an easy thing to draw. The girl swiftly sketched a great round circle on the page.

Da—The girl frowned unhappily. The choices were endless. Dapokuko were monsteria plants. Dadakanii were tasty river clams. Daka was an adz....

Dathra! A river rush. Why not? Sha-Da....

Rii? Riitra! Waterfall; a wavy line. And there she had it! Three word segments; three pictures. Place each one beside the others, like building a tune upon a music stick. Picture words! It was actually working! In a state of wild excitement Shadarii reached for another sheet of bark.

Kotaru. Ko-ta-ru. The mind simply had to sing the word—divide it into sections as if making notes to craft a song. She would have to get a flute to play the words out one by one. It would be a work of months, perhaps even years to unravel all the word segments used within the language, but it could be done. One day she would finally be able to write down words for everyone to see.

A dozen Vakïdurii gathered all around her. Tingtraka combed her long black ponytail across her shoulders, completely fascinated by Shadarii's work.

"Shadarii, what are you doin'? Is it a picture?"

"A game? Maybe it's a game board for playin' Katakanii dak-dak[22] ?"

Little Kïtashii came wandering across from paddling her feet in the river. The girl came to stare intently at Shadarii's page, seeming suitably impressed.

"Goodness, how elegantly simple! Did you really think of all that just then?"

Shadarii nodded eagerly. She began to point out symbols in the page, gesturing to the dirt or river water all around them. Kïtashii and Kotaru watched her closely, while jiteng players scratched their heads, utterly at a loss.

"What's she doing? Is it a dance or something?"

Kotaru's worshipful eyes never left Shadarii's face. "No. It's beautiful! She—she says she's making something new. Pictures that mean words and sentences."

A huge goal guard slowly shook his head.

"I don't see the sense of it! If you couldn't talk (beggin' yer pardon, my lady), then maybe there'd be a need. But if y'can speak, why waste your time with pictures?"

Kotaru caressed Shadarii's hair. "Oh, it's useful. I know that now. She'd never create a thing that wasn't needed."

Shadarii glowed with pleasure. There was no one's praise she would rather have. She felt Kotaru twitch, his ears glowing as he saw her staring up at him in hope.

The moment was broken by a riotous whoop of laughter from the others. Shadarii irritably looked up to see Mrrimïmei staggering over to the river, her clothes disheveled and bracken in her hair. Her legs were weak and shaky—a fact noted with hoots of approval by all her friends.

Kotaru thoughtfully stroked his chin, peering over at Mrrimïmei. "Hey, love, are you feelin' any better this afternoon?"

The girl combed fingers through her hair, smiling down at all her friends. "Who, me? Aaaah there's nothin' wrong with me that my Totoru can't cure! 'Twas just an upset tummy at breakfast time, is all."

"Sick again this morning? Have you been eating ought that we've all missed?"

"Nothin' I can think of. Don't matter! The game's not until tomorrow afternoon. I'll be over it by then." She grabbed Kotaru's nose and gave it a friendly waggle. "You worry too much about us all. Just get us on that field tomorrow! We'll win, never fear!"

---

[22]**Dak-Dak:** A chesslike game played on a board that is made anew for every game. Colors on the board indicate ïsha flow, affecting the possible movement of the game pieces.

An indefinable air blazed in Mrrimïmei's aura.

Shadarii suddenly knew a secret. She sat up to clap her hands for joy, and all eyes turned to look at her. Mrrimïmei laughed as she saw Shadarii's smile.

"Oh, ho! So you've somethin' to tell us all, eh? Well out with it! Don't keep us in suspense!"

Shadarii pointed at Mrrimïmei and stroked her own soft belly. The other girl blinked in puzzlement, trying hard to understand.

"What's this? You're hungry?"

Shadarii frowned and shook her head in annoyance; she patted at her belly and then cradled an imaginary something at her breast.

"You want a cuddle? Well, I can't help you there, love. This dopey man's been missing every hint you try to give him!"

Shadarii's ears blushed. She hastily waved her hands and tried again. Mrrimïmei and company shook their heads in confusion.

"Shadarii, love, I just don't understand you!"

"She says you're pregnant, you dizzy female!" Kïtashii stamped her feet. "For Rain's sake! Can't any of you understand the simplest little thing?"

Mrrimïmei's smile froze on her face. The other players blinked and looked at her in wonder. From somewhere in the back, a voice sang sweetly through the ferns.

"Ooooh, Totoooo-ruuuu! Are you still lying down? We have a little surprise for you... !"

Mrrimïmei gave a nervous titter. Her hands drifted down to touch her abdomen. "You—uh—you can't really be serious...."

Shadarii gave an eager nod, beaming happily at the mother-to-be. Oh, to know such joy, such happiness! To feel the wonder that Mrrimïmei must be feeling now!

Mrrimïmei staggered. "Totoru!" Someone caught her. Shadarii blinked in confusion and tried to puzzle out just what was wrong. Didn't Mrrimïmei want a baby? Why ever not?

Kotaru looked at Mrrimïmei and numbly shook his head. "No, she can't be!" The team captain looked around himself in horror. "She just can't be!"

Kïtashii planted her fists upon her skinny hips and glared.

"Mrrimïmei is pregnant. If Shadarii says she feels the baby, she feels the baby! Haven't you learned anything?"

She was right. Of course she was right. Kotaru hung his head while the whole team erupted into an excited babble. Totoru burst from the bushes, bracken still clinging to his fur. Mrrimïmei went to him and whispered urgently in his ear. The two of them clung tight together as they tried to make sense out of their future. Totoru suddenly laughed aloud, then picked his lover off the ground. Mrrimïmei threw back her head and gave a wild whoop of joy.

Kotaru looked at Mrrimïmei with lost little eyes, desperately running fingers through his fur. "But—but what about the game?"

Everyone jerked to a halt. Mrrimïmei dragged a piece of bracken from her hair. "What? Is there a problem?"

"You're pregnant!"

"I'll be fine! 'Tweren't a problem yesterday. Didn't slow me down in this mornin's practice. I'll be fine!"

Kotaru staggered to his feet. "You're joking, girl! Did you see the way they played out there today? Did you see those animals rippin' into one another?"

"Oh, bosh! Kotaru, you sound like you're my mother!" The girl suddenly slapped her hands against her face. "Mother! My stars, she's going to kill me!"

Kotaru began frantically pacing back and forth. "Mrrimïmei, I just can't let you risk yourself. Think of what could happen!"

"Oh, Kotaru, you're very sweet!" She kissed him on the nose. "There's no need to worry, love. I can take good care o' myself. Everything's going to be just fine."

Kotaru kept up his pacing, his tail switching back and forth behind him. "I cannot allow you to play. I'm sorry, but there's more at stake than a silly game of jiteng. I'll not risk your life or your wee one with Zhukora."

"No!" Mrrimïmei clawed Kotaru's fur. "I can play! Don't do this to me!"

"I'm not doin' anything to you. I care for you too much to let you risk yourself. Totoru, I expect you to back me up on this!"

The huge guard took his lover in his arms. He unhappily tried to calm Mrrimïmei down. "He's right, love. One good tackle and the baby's history."

The girl wept in anguish. "No! You can't do this to me! After all this work, all this struggle!"

"We made a wee mistake, my love. 'Twill all turn out for the best. There's a baby for us now, eh? We can play jiteng another time."

Mrrimïmei wrung her hands. "But we'll lose the game! There's no reserve players. Who can you possibly find to replace me?"

The other players stared around in shock. Kotaru helplessly shook his head. Where could they find a replacement? The game was as good as lost.

Shadarii dropped a jiteng helmet on her head. It was at least four sizes too big for her, and only the tip of her snout protruded. The girl tugged at Kotaru's leggings, peering up at him from the helmet's shadows.

Kotaru looked down at her and felt his ears stand high in surprise.

"What? Oh, no! Shadarii, you can't be serious!"

Shadarii nodded eagerly, the helmet slipping down across her eyes.

"Oh, my love, you can't even play the game. You haven't practiced!"

A ball rose from over in the grass, hovered before Kotaru's nose, and then drifted down into Shadarii's lap. Kotaru rubbed the back of his neck, loving her for her loyalty.

"What if your sister sees? 'Twill mean trouble for you."

A mask joined the ball, hovering in the air.

See, my face will be hidden. Why should Zhukora know?

"You have two other assets that are a wee bit harder to disguise."

Shadarii peered down and shrugged, folding her arms in tight. *Beneath a breastplate, who would ever know?*

"I don't want you to be hurt!"

I want to be with you.

Kotaru was reluctant; he loved her for it, but all his instincts told him no. Finally he reached down to take her hands.

"All right, my love, all right. But we'll go practice now. There's much work to be done before tomorrow morn." His voice dropped down to a whisper. "You rescue me again, my lady. Bless me, but I love you...."

Shadarii gave a little gasp and clung on tight. Finally held in Kotaru's arms, she never wanted to leave his grasp again. Everything would be all right; after all, jiteng wasn't really dangerous. Who'd ever gotten hurt over a silly game?

ෆ ෨ ෩

Two lovers walked hand in hand along the riverbank, listening to the slow play of the wind. There was no rush—no need to hurry; beneath the drowsy summer sun. Love seemed slow and wonderful.

The breeze moved through Shadarii's orange fur. Kotaru drank in the sight of her as though she were a vision from beyond the sky. She looked coyly sideways at him, her long lashes fluttering in embarrassment as she saw him catch her gaze.

Kotaru coughed and spoke into the nervous silence. "I don't like the idea of your playing with us tomorrow, but I thank you for the rescue. You risk a lot for me. I don't quite know what the future holds for us, my love. I just can't seem to see..."

The future? Shadarii stood posed by the riverbank and felt the ïsha stroke her soul, while Kotaru stared down at the ground and gave a troubled sigh.

"Aaaaah, Shadarii, I just don't know anymore. My heart fights my head. Where are we going together, you and I? I wish I could tell."

Shadarii held up a finger, and then turned and led Kotaru over to the river. They sat down together on the rocks above a deep part of the stream. Kotaru watched in confusion as Shadarii settled him in place. With a long, slow sigh, Shadarii bowed her head above the waters.

Kotaru blinked; when Shadarii raised her face, she was lost in utter concentration. The ïsha began to throb as Shadarii's hands poured light across the river. Far beneath the surface, something began to swell and grow.

Movement swirled in the deeps. Light gleamed from two enormous saucers that stared at Kotaru in cold appraisal. The hunter gave a croak as a vast catfish surfaced from the murk.

Shadarii smiled and swept down into a reverent bow, her fluffy tail sticking high in the air. She raised herself again and plunged her hands into the water, reaching down to rub the monstrous catfish on the chin.

Kotaru kept well and truly clear. The catfish disdainfully ignored him, far preferring to bask in Shadarii's glow. The fish gulped water with its yellow mouth and stared unwinkingly up into the world of light.

Shadarii turned toward Kotaru and shaped clear patterns in the air. *This is Grandfather Catfish. He comes here from time to time to let me see him. He is the most handsome fish in all the world!*

The girl looked down at the hideous fish and smiled. The creature could have swallowed her with a single bite. She pointed fondly to white scars behind the creature's neck.

I healed him. One day he will tell me a tale in return. A long, slow story of the river.

Kotaru looked aghast.

"Y-you mean you went into the water with this thing?"

He is most polite. Grandfather Catfish is an ancestral catfish Ka. You should bow and say hello.

The young hunter swiftly did as he was told. The catfish swirled its huge fins back and forth, unmoved one way or another. Shadarii closed her eyes and sent her thoughts toward the giant fish.

Grandfather Catfish, here is everything that is precious to me. This is Kotaru, a good, kind man.

The great fish twitched his whiskers, and only Shadarii could have seen the subtle icons in its aura. She bowed in gratitude as the fish swam slowly back into the dark.

Shadarii turned her face toward Kotaru and shaped words upon the air. *Looking at the river shows you nothing but bubbles. The monsters are not so frightening when we look on them with love. We should never fear the river, Kotaru. It is as it is.*

Kotaru slowly shook his head.

"I'm not quite sure I understand."

She reached out to touch Kotaru's face and smile up at him with her strange, wise eyes. *Don't worry about the future, my love. Who knows what might lie ahead? Let us just float along together and see what surprises we may find....*

It was time to let the river flow; Shadarii slowly closed her eyes and tilted up her mouth. Her lips parted as she drew Kotaru down into her arms. Kotaru gently lay Shadarii in the grass and lost himself inside her embrace.

Far above them, sharp eyes glittered in the twilight. Kïtashii perched high on a rock, watching out for spying priests. The little girl peered down at the lovers cuddling in the grass, then gave a sniff and turned away, going back to her silent sentry duty.

It was all really very silly. So much pain and worry, and all for that? If they'd simply kissed each other to begin with, all this nonsense could have been avoided. Kïtashii would never understand adults. Puberty put a mildew on the brain.

Maybe...

The little girl hugged her skinny knees and stared out into the darkness, feeling strangely young and free.

Ten

It was a dreadful morning for a jiteng game; fog hung sullenly between the trees and turned the whole world ghostly white. Even the brave uniforms of the players were strangely sad and dull. The audience shivered and peered fearfully about the field. It was as though Prakucha's Ka still moaned across the grass.

The Skull-Wings hovered like evil spirits. Cold light pierced the mist and fell into the blank eyes of their masks. They hung like corpses in the trees and waited for their prey.

A crowd of ten thousand had come to see the game, but the audience lay hidden in the gloom, present only in the restless ebb and flow of sound. The Wrens shivered in the cold, swinging their staves to ease their nerves.

Kotaru gathered his team, trying to keep the tension from his voice.

"All right, people, we've seen the way the locals play. My only priority is to get my team out of here unhurt. If they attempt one of those crash attacks, you will dodge aside. You will not pursue attackers. You will not be provoked into a brawl." Kotaru's held his listeners firm and calm beneath his spell. "We've all heard about the death upon the field here yesterday. This is what can happen if we don't keep our wits. So, stay cool, stay fast, stay safe.

"Another problem is that we're missing Mrrimïmei, so we no longer have our fast strike ability. Shadarii will try to shore up our ïsha defenses. She maneuvers better than we do, so we can use her for tight flying and sudden double backs."

Kotaru removed the mask from his helmet. Today protection took second place to calming his team's fraying nerves. They needed to see his face.

"We've seen them at work. They don't use pre-set patterns like the Mantises. So, stay with your mates and work with one another. Sing out if you have any bright ideas!" Kotaru scratched his snout and sighed, unable to think of anything more to say. "Well—well, that's it, I suppose, 'cept to say... well, we've all worked real hard an' all. I know how much you've dreamed of doin' this. I just have to tell you..." Kotaru looked down at his feet and gave a sigh. "Awwww, skreg it! I love you bastards!"

He threw his arms about his teammates, and the Wrens clasped tightly together.

Kotaru hid his eyes and turned back toward the playing field. "Now come on! Let's get out there and show them how real artists play the game!"

The players cheered and thundered into the air. Kotaru lingered on the ground with Shadarii; she came into his arms and kissed him as he ran his fingers through her hair.

"What I said goes doubly for you, my love. Stay well clear of the Skull-Wings. They'll try to hurt you if they can." Kotaru bent to kiss her once again, sighing as he felt her perfect touch.

She pulled away from him and carefully mastered his attention. *I made a decision today. Very, very important. I must talk to you tonight. I will dance, and then we will talk. Do you understand?*

Kotaru felt mystified. "What do you need to say, my love? There's no need for words between us. I always know just what you mean."

Tomorrow wings will shed. Then one week later, you will go home. Back to your tribe far away.

"Aye..." Kotaru swallowed. "I just haven't thought... about you and I, I mean. I'm not leaving you! Not now, not ever!"

You must go home, my love. Where you go, so I too will go.

"You'll come with me? You'd do that? I have nothin' to offer a fine lady. Nothin' save a poor man's love...."

Her whole being yearned toward him. Shadarii carefully mimed her next few words, her hands trembling in fright. *I will go with you because I love you. As a friend, if that is what you want. As a wife, if you will bond with me....*

Kotaru's jaw dropped in shock.

Shadarii swallowed hard and tried to keep the fear from her eyes. *Will you take me as your wife, Kotaru? I most humbly ask you to twine with me in marriage....*

The young hunter's eyes filled with tears.

"Oh! Oh, Rain! Oh, sweet Mother Rain!" He flung his arms around her in delight. "Oh, of course I will, you silly girl! Oh..." Oh, was about as far as the poor lad's tongue could get. Shadarii was in paradise; she grabbed him and kissed him, pouring burning energy through his soul. Hand in hand, they sprang into the air.

"Wings spread, ball high!"

The game of the century had begun.

The crowd's cheer shook the mist like a mighty storm. One point up! One point to the Skull-Wings. The Katakanii tribe went wild. High in the treetops, observation platforms shook with laughter. Nobles slapped each other on the backs, howling praise for their champion team.

Amid all the revelry, a single figure sat in silence. Prince Tekï'taa looked pale. He had passed a grim night on the latrines, praying for a tree to fall on his head. Even so, he had managed to crawl out to see the game. It was a moment he had planned for so many weeks, and no illness would come between him and his triumph.

Play began. The Skull-Wings snatched the ball with a surgical slash through the Wrens' formation and raced for the goals. The Katakanii crowd roared.

Tekï'taa struck while elation filled the air. He leaned past his father's ambassador and raise his voice above the noise. "King Saitookii, your team plays well! I commend their skill. No one has yet stood firm against our Wrens."

The king flicked his eyes in Tekï'taa's direction, his skeletal old face showing no expression.

Tekï'taa leaned closer. "The game intrigues me. Perhaps a wager? Two yam fields along the riverbanks against your peach orchards. Accept?"

Appalled, the ambassador sputtered helplessly, "My prince!"

"Silence! King Saitookii, do you accept the bet?"

The king muttered in the ear of his attendants. Finally a young priest looked from the ambassador to the prince. "Very well, oh prince. The Katakanii accept your foolish wager!"

Down on the field, the Wrens tore free of the Skull-Wing team, swirling up to hover in the branches of a tree. Tingtraka held the ball aloft, grinning as she shook her catching staff.

They had the ball! The Skull-Wing's weren't invincible. The Wrens gave a whoop of joy and gathered about their captain. He made a few brisk signals and rallied them for the attack. Heavy men like Totoru rose into position to flank the others in the team.

Why? Shadarii barely understood. Her breath rasped painfully beneath her mask, and the catching staff felt awkward in her hands. She felt like a third leg—a useless encumbrance to the others. How stupid she had been to think she could help....

Kotaru swooped in close and clasped an arm about Shadarii's armored shoulders. "All right, everyone! Take your cues from the ball handler. Stay close to Shadarii. She's our best asset once we get in close!" He gave the girl another hug. "We need that sorcery of yours! Just tell us how you want us; we'll listen!"

She blinked through her mask holes in amazement. He trusted her. He trusted all of them.

"Tingtraka, we're all yours!"

The skinny scholar climbed high above the field. The others followed, fog streaming from their wings. With a howl of rage the Skull-Wings rose in pursuit.

Zhukora's team were deployed in depth, expecting one of Mrrimïmei's famous fast attacks. In the fog, one girl with red fur looked much like another. Tingtraka split off from Shadarii, copper tail gleaming in the gloom, and raced toward the flanks. The Wrens broke into two swirling streams behind them as Shadarii folded her wings and dived down into a screaming storm of enemies.

Black shapes flashed past. Shadarii ducked as a staff lashed past her ear. She punched out with a plane of ïsha, shearing an enemy from Tingtraka's path. More creatures raced to block her. The little dancer dived at breakneck speed between her enemies, curled into a ball, and tumbled past a skull-faced helm. The Skull-Wing gaped in amazement, slamming into a teammate in a grisly shower of wings. Shadarii flipped out of her tumble and rolled away with a dancer's easy grace.

They were through!

With terrifying precision, Zhukora's team snapped into new formations. Suddenly, Wrens were being torn out of the air. Tingtraka flung the ball just moments before being clubbed across the skull. Shadarii gave a gasp and lashed out with her mind, dragging the ball into her catching staff.

She had it! She had the ball!

So what now?

A predatory howl rose from the Skulls. They hurtled past their opponents and toward Shadarii. The girl fled in panic, coincidentally racing straight toward the enemy goals.

A snarling pack of demons raged behind Shadarii's tail. The girl grimly whirred her wings and closed the ïsha behind her like a clap. Skull-Wings tumbled down in ruins as ïsha abandoned their wings. Shadarii looked across her shoulder and stuck out her tongue, flipping her tail to show the Skulls her furry backside. *Ha!*

There came a piercing scream from above. Shadarii rolled aside, feeling a breeze rip past her wings.

Zhukora snarled and stabbed into the attack. The girl whirled her staff toward the dancer's throat. Shadarii lashed out with her mind to blast the thing away. The catching staff suddenly exploded into fragments, and Zhukora gasped in shock as Shadarii soared on her way.

Kotaru plunged between the sisters, rolling into a ball to crash into Zhukora's back. She hit the ground and tumbled through the grass as Shadarii dunked the ball clean through the goals.

A goal! The Wrens swirled through the air and cheered. Shadarii's head swam. She had finally done something right. She threw her arms about Kotaru and hugged him tight, thrilled to be sharing his victory.

Down in the grass, Zhukora angrily dusted off her greaves, Skull-Mask glaring into the air in hate. "Who is she?"

Daimïru stood staring at the plump red girl inside the Wren formation. "She's not the one we watched at practice. They've swapped her for their fast striker."

"The Vakïdurii must have kept her hidden from us. She's a surprise, and I hate surprises." Zhukora drew her gauntlets firmly on her hands. She took a spare staff and stared at her enemy. "Take her out. Break her, Daimïru. I don't care how."

The two black banshees rose and clattered off into the fog.

A new play raged across the playing field, and the audience stared at the flash and bang of ïsha deep within the fog. Here and there, the mists melted away, revealing Wrens and Skull-Wings grimly battling in the air.

Up on the royal platform, the high priestess leaned forward in alarm. "Who is that? Kanoohï, who's the player flinging all that power?"

"Red ribbons on the helmet. The girl's name is Mrrimïmei, a fast forward. No one of importance."

"Well she's blasting a hole clean through the Skull-Wing line! Have the Vakïdurii priests investigate the girl once they return. She could be valuable."

Out on the field, a battle raged around the ball; Tingtraka and Shadarii hovered high above the teams. Tingtraka grinned, her long black ponytail gleaming in the wind. She pumped her fist and thrust it out toward the milling demons far below. The two girls dived gleefully through the middle of the Skull-Wing team, Tingtraka's laughter trailing in their wake. They swooped past the Skull-Wing rovers and knocked the ïsha from their wings. Tingtraka snatched the ball and hurtled it toward Kotaru's men. Shadarii gave a victory roll and threw her arms out wide.

Suddenly Zhukora erupted through the air and slammed her staff into Shadarii's face. Shadarii crashed against a tree branch and spun to the ground. The girl somehow staggered to her feet, half blinded by the lights dancing in her eyes.

Daimïru dived out of the fog, streaking straight toward Shadarii's throat. Another figure instantly smashed into Daimïru's back; Kotaru ruthlessly pinned her wings flat and rode her to the ground.

Kotaru and Daimïru rolled apart, and the crowd roared as the Skull-Wing kicked Kotaru in the crotch. She smashed his face into the dirt, screaming as his blood spattered the ground.

Other Wrens left the game in panic. The Skull-Wings snatched the ball and raced off for the goals.

Totoru landed by Daimïru, plucked the girl up in his arms, and dashed her against a tree. The huge guard turned away and went to help his captain. Daimïru shot back into action, lunging on Totoru's back to gouge the eyeholes of his mask. A dozen Wrens hauled Daimïru from Totoru's throat.

The umpires ordered Daimïru off the field; the Wren's magician was still in play, but now Zhukora lacked her bodyguard.

The score was two to one.

Kotaru leaned back against a tree stump as Shadarii stripped away his helm. Blood ran from his mouth to stain his chin. Shadarii whirred into the branches of a eucalyptus to pick the fine new leaves.

Kotaru turned to face his team. "Wh-what did I say about fighting!"

Totoru eased his mask off, dabbing at the blood that ran out from his brow. "Are you mad, man? We just saved your tail!"

"We—we lost the point!"

"Point be damned! They attack us, I snap them clean in two."

"We lost the point! They won that goal because we all behaved like fools. We brawled like animals instead of worrying about the ball!"

"We have to do something about their play! We can't just let them kick us about and then kiss their arses in thanks!"

Tingtraka passed the water bottle among her fellow players. "They want Shadarii-Zho! It was planned! Did you see the way they peeled off after her?"

"They'll take out anyone who seems a threat!" Vast and dark, Totoru flexed the massive muscles of his shoulders. "We have to fight violence with violence. Show 'em what it costs to fight us!"

The others muttered in agreement. Shadarii broke the moment by alighting in the middle of the team. She scowled and molded ïsha with her hands.

Kotaru rolled his head. "She says you are stupid. She says Zhukora will fight, and we will fight, but what will we achieve? We must beat her by winning the game as quickly as we can."

Shadarii spat leaf pulp into her hand and cleaned Kotaru's wounded jaw. Her aura bathed his wound with light.

Kotaru blinked and absently ran his hands along the smooth, healed cut. "We're still twelve strong, and they're down to eleven. We shall not be provoked. We're stronger than they are. We can beat them without falling to their level." Sharp eyes looked from face to face. "We're going to play for fun, just the way we always have."

He knew his friends too well; they shuffled their feet and reluctantly agreed. Kotaru gripped their hands and led them back into the air to play another round.

Shadarii hung back behind the others and stared at her sister. Her tail thrashed as she watched the demons whirl. Zhukora was the Skull-Wings' weakness. Without her, they were a viper with its head struck off.

The ball whirled into the air. This time Shadarii took the whole field by surprise. She rammed aside the other players, snatched the ball, and dashed into Zhukora's team. Before anyone could stop her, she clouted her sister clean across the backside with her staff. A legal hit! Shadarii whirled and flung the ball back into her team.

Zhukora was out, and only seconds into play! Her team floundered. Wrens moved to the attack. Kotaru flung his people at the Skull-Wings' weak points, slicing through their lines to dunk a clean goal home.

Seething with fury, Zhukora climbed to her players. She glared toward the Wrens and flexed her claws. "Bitch! I'll do her for that! Kukutu, split your squad left once we engage the center. We'll turn them there. I'll take the lead! Go two to one on their main players. Clear the field as quick as you can."

The ball sliced up from the ground. Zhukora lashed out with an isha whip and took the ball. She lead her screaming team toward the goals, laughing as she felt her play strike home.

Blue figures suddenly plunged past Zhukora's face. The Wrens had swooped down through a tree to blast into her formation. Staves cracked and rang as players battled, a few tails short of the goals.

Zhukora turned and fought. The ball plunged out of the wild melee and fell down into the grass—right into the catching staff of a plump little figure in the shadows. Shadarii fixed her eyes on Zhukora and gave a malicious grin, then flung her staff with all her might, shooting both stick and ball toward Zhukora's team.

"Look out!"

Zhukora whirled as Shadarii's staff thumped into her chest. Zhukora shrieked with rage. The rule's were clear—anyone within ten spans of the ball was fair game. She had been struck out again! She seethed as the Wrens tore the initiative from her team, slamming home with yet another goal.

"Three to two! Three to two! Who'd ever have believed it?" Councilor Fotoki desperately mopped his brow. "They'll climb back! Just you wait and see!"

"This never would have happened if the Orchids had been allowed to play!" Mistress Traveesha's face screwed up in disgust. "That damned fool girl is going to cost us the game!"

Fotoki swiftly gulped his tea.

Far out on the field, something screeched rabidly.

Chief Nochorku stuck his finger in his ear and jiggled it about in irritation. "Gaaah! What's that dreadful noise?"

Traveesha cleared her throat. "I can't quite say. I suppose Zhukora is having some gentle words with her team before they once more begin to play...."

The Katakanii nobles edged forward in their seats as the ball was brought back into the center of the field.

Shadarii was rewarded by delirious hugs from all the Wrens. The girl turned a somersault before them, waggling her tail in delight.

Kotaru drew his team in close and hunched down to confer. "People! People! Three down, one to go. This time I reckon they'll be plenty mad!"

Tingtraka waved her antennae. "Let's try' somethin' silly! That Zhukora's goin' to charge straight down at that ball like a flash o' lightning!"

Kotaru licked his injured lips and let his eyes light up with inspiration. "Right.... Yes, all right then, we'll let her! Coax her down our end, picking off the supporting members of her team. We'll thin the numbers, block her shot, and then double forward. Totoru, we'll need you by our goals this time. Shadarii, you stay with him. We'll need everything we've got to make sure that ball doesn't get through."

The team shook themselves out into a rough formation.

Kotaru took Shadarii by the hand. "All right now, my fine young miss. I've seen just what you're up to, and I'm proud of you. You're a mischievous little bugger, an' no mistake! Just remember that Zhukora's dangerous. This time keep clear of her. I don't want you hurt, and we also can't risk her findin' out just who you are."

They kissed carefully, Shadarii trying not to hurt Kotaru's mouth.

The umpire saw that all was ready and swung his staff round in an arc. "Wings spread, ball high!"

Zhukora came in low and fast, just as Kotaru had predicted. She furiously snatched the ball and flung her team out like a lance. This time she protected herself with a shield of guards. Her team reacted to its orders with terrifying precision, driving relentlessly onward to the goals.

Wrens dived in to the attack; Zhukora's team ignored their casualties and screamed onward down the field. Another man fell, and then another. The Wrens struck and wove, whirling like a storm of darts. Zhukora ground her fangs as she forced herself to even greater speed.

She would have her victory!

The goal ring loomed before her, but ïsha dragged back at her wings. She felt like an insect trapped in amber. She thrashed her wings as a huge Wren sprang up before her. Zhukora parried a sharp stab of his staff, losing the ball in attempting to save herself. Blue figures dived down and snared the prize, dashing off toward the Skull-Wing goals. Zhukora looked around, gaping as she realized her team had dropped to half its former strength.

A sparkling presence made Zhukora turn. The plump girl from the Wren team hung below her, her mouth wide open in a smile. The cause of the drag on Zhukora's wings suddenly became all too clear; the girl had done something to the ïsha! She had cost the Skulls the game!

Zhukora shot off in pursuit. This time she'd rip the bitch's wings to shreds! She blind the little bastard in one eye!

Darting away, Shadarii felt a thrill of fear. Her speed failed her. She was too fat for speed, too broad of wing to outrace an opponent. Shadarii threw herself into a numbing turn. Wings bowed; muscles creaked. Grass whipped across her breasts, and suddenly she was free.

There was an explosion high above her. Zhukora overshot the turn and plunged into a tree. With a dreadful scream, she hurtled end over into the grass. Shadarii quickly sped away. Somewhere in the distance, crowds cheered. The final goal went home!

Shadarii swirled into Kotaru's arms. She had won. Hand in hand with her beloved, she soared into the trees.

ເຊ ເຊ ເຊ

Zhukora hacked with her dao. She butchered an innocent tree, ignoring the Ka that screamed out in protest. She met it with a blast of force, viciously hurtling it back into its trunk.

"Zhukora! Zhukora, stop it!"

The woman didn't hear. She raved and swore in dreadful rage, smashing the tree with all her strength. Daimïru hovered helplessly in the shadows.

"It's only a game, Zhukora! Only a game!" Daimïru scrubbed tears from her eyes. "Just—just listen to me! It doesn't matter! It's just a game. We have to move on from here. Zhukora, stop it!"

Zhukora screamed and threw away her knife, hammering the tree with her bare fists. Daimïru hurtled her arms about Zhukora and dragged her to the ground. She grimly held on as Zhukora bucked. "Let me go! Let me go, you bitch! Let me go!"

"I'm here! Hit me all you like, but I'm not letting go! We'll just sit here, my love. We'll just sit here until you're calm."

Zhukora writhed and fought with all her strength; Daimïru simply closed her eyes and rode the storm. It would last only a little while. There would be new plans made soon, new orders, new direction. Until then, she must be protected. Zhukora's genius blazed so bright she could burn herself with its heat. Daimïru held Zhukora tight and did what must be done.

ເຊ ເຊ ເຊ

Village fires lit the sky. Distant music thrummed. Down beside the bathing pools, Shadarii hopped on one foot, fighting to strip away her moccasins. The Ka helpfully heated the water as Shadarii tore away her clothes. The girl swiftly plunged into the drink, and then surfaced in a shower of spray and frantically scrubbed her hair.

Rain and Fire, she had only half an hour to prepare! The fires were lit, the circle drawn... Shadarii snatched a fist of soap-root and scrubbed furiously at her fur. Hosts of little Ka foamed the water to a froth. Together they might just have time to make ready for the dance.

A warm presence blundered through the bushes. Kotaru bounced his way over to the water's edge and dashed his hair back from his eyes. "Shadarii? Ha, found you at last! We won! I still can't believe it. The rest of us are all just going to..."

Shadarii posed beside the pool, long lashes lowered coyly as she stood in the firelight. Bright wings flipped out to frame her figure to perfection. Suddenly Kotaru turned himself around and stared out into the empty forest, his ears blushing hot.

"Uh—Oh, Rain, I didn't mean to—to intrude! I-I just wanted to tell you that I've talked it over with the others. It's all set. You and I can elope tomorrow during the totenïha dance. We can get married once we reach my clan, then there's nothing anybody can ever do to part us!"

Shadarii's head appeared above a bush in front of him. She was brushing out her hair and looking at him with those delicious eyes. *Tomorrow we will be free! Tomorrow will be a very special day. Tomorrow night I have a special gift to give you.*

Gift? Kotaru's antennae quivered. "Oh! A gift? Ah... I-I don't have anything for you."

Shadarii looked into Kotaru's eyes and slowly gave a smile. She leaned across the bushes and drew him into a kiss.

Kotaru sighed and softly ran his fingers through her fur. "My love... what gift? Can't ye tell me what it is?"

Shadarii kissed Kotaru's snout and felt a delicious tingle deep inside her. *Uh-uh-aah! No cheating! That is the delicious thing about a gift. The anticipation is half the fun. Now off you go! Some of us still have work to do!* Shadarii shoved Kotaru on his way.

The young hunter stumbled off into the gloom. "Shadarii! Shadarii, I love thee!" Tomorrow. A world of promise hung on one little dawn. Kotaru fluttered off into the dusk with stars shining in his eyes.

Halfway across the village, other women were hard at work. Javïra stirred a cup of pigment and delicately dusted it across Hatïkaa's fur. Mistress Traveesha bustled in the background, seeing to the instruments. Pipes and whistles, long-necked flutes, and drums all had to be polished to perfection.

Hatïkaa posed with her arms high, trying not to sneeze while her assistant stroked blue highlights across her. "Dong it on! Anything to get the right kind of notice, eh?" Hatïkaa gave Javïra a crude nudge in the ribs. "My husband's had a headache for a week! Too tired, he says! Too tired I ask you! If he says he has a headache after the feast I'm goin' lookin' for my own dessert! No way am I sleepin' alone tonight!"

Javïra fastidiously dusted off her fur. "I want to thank you for consenting to practice with me, Hatïkaa. It has been an honor to learn some small part of your skills."

"Aaaaah, that's all right, love. You're not half as bad as they say. There's not so much wrong if a girl likes her heels in the air once in a while!"

Javïra put her hand across her eyes. "Uh—yes, quite..."

"That prince, now! He's a nasty character. Still, I reckon I envy you! Could be interestin' to let royalty take a dip in me every now and then!"

"Now look you! I didn't..." Javïra screwed shut her eyes and tried to start again. "Let's—let's not talk about fun just now, hmmmm? We have to get you ready for what's coming, don't we!" The girl's blue eyes glinted as she smiled. "Why don't we have a nice cup of tea and just relax?"

Hatïkaa idly scratched, "Naah, love. I reckon it's time I did some warm-ups. There's no sign of that dozy partner of mine, either! Where do you reckon she's gotten to?"

"Oh, she won't be late. She's just making a few plans for tomorrow." The girl reached out for the teapot. "Why don't you just have a cup of tea to soothe your nerves? There's no need to rush ourselves, now is there?"

"I dunno, I really ought to find her."

"Well, you can't go prancing around the village naked. Anyway, you're not allowed to see each other before the dance. Not outside of the sacred circle. You're both spirit dancing tonight. We're not allowed to risk any conflicts. Particularly when you've both got those nasty knives."

Hatïkaa slopped some tea into her cup. "I suppose you're right. No point in getting stage nerves, now is there?" She noisily slurped her drink, nodding in approval. "Mmmmm—It's good! What is it?"

Javïra picked up a gleaming dao and ran her thumb across the blade, staring hungrily at the razor edge.

"Why, it's Shadarii's special blend, Hatïkaa!" She smiled absently as she held the blade before her. "Shadarii's special blend!"

The girl laughed and swung the weapon through the air. "Drink up, Hatïkaa! The night has only just begun!"

Eleven

Night had clamped across the silent world. There were no stars. There was no moon, no light to penetrate the vast depths of the forest. Only the leaping council fire and a thousand watchful eyes pierced the night.

Silence fell across the crowd. In the dancing circle, a bonfire spat and hissed. A fire sprite had made a nest inside the sacred blaze, and the little creature chittered as it dragged its talons through the ashes.

Something soft and lovely shone against the night. Firelight touched the curves of warm flanks. The mask of Mother Rain slowly rose to stare across the faces of the crowd. How long she had stood there, no one could have said. The drums might have lifted her from the very earth to battle once again for her true love.

Shadarii's fangs gleamed in the dark. This was not the gentle maid of legend. Lush curves clashed with the nightmare imagery of her thirsting knives. The dancer swung the weapons in a glittering arc as she searched for traces of her enemy.

Where was Poison?

At the front of the audience, a single figure gazed at Shadarii in rapture. Kotaru's eyes glowed in awe. For the first time he saw Shadarii's skill in all its glory. Each pose, each move, each tiny breath she took spoke into his mind. The girl who lacked a voice shouted out for all the world to hear.

Shadarii felt the fire's warmth against her back, and the crowd's eyes burned across her naked fur. Hidden behind her mask, Shadarii stretched her wings and gloried in the dance. As the drums rose in crescendo, Shadarii whirled to face the enemy who had mocked her for so long.

Lady Poison screamed in feral challenge, her blue wings spread to sweep the crowd with cold. White fur shimmered with bitter highlights, and long white hair spilled down to caress a figure that made men gasp. The girl turned to lift her leering mask toward Shadarii, snarling for the blood of her enemy.

Poison's fangs gleamed beneath her mask as she slid toward her prey.

Srïhoonii fought her way through the audience to whisper frantically in Traveesha's ear. The dance mistress whirled around to stare wildly at her niece.

Councilor Gegachii grabbed Traveesha and hissed in alarm. "Traveesha, what madness is this? Who let Javïra out there with that-that fat girl?"

"An accident, my lord! The other dancer has taken ill. She can't be budged from the latrines." Traveesha's face grew sick with panic. Srïhoonii gulped as the dance mistress took her by the neck. "Srïhoonii, why wasn't I told before? You stupid little wretch! Why didn't you inform me?"

"M-mistress, forgive me! We didn't know! Hatïkaa is in agony! Javïra had to take her place at the last instant."

Old Gegachii clawed at the dance mistress. "My Lady, your niece is out there with that mad woman! The dance must be called off at once!"

"It is a sacred dance. We cannot interfere unless either girl breaks the circle!"

Down in the audience, Kotaru's fur began to rise, and his senses prickled in alarm.

Poison lunged. The crowd gasped as blades swept a hairbreadth from naked flesh. The two warriors fought inside a glittering arc of death. The audience stared in fascination at the spectacle.

The routine went without a hitch, precisely as rehearsed. Poison's knives lashed out at an easy tempo, and Shadarii matched her, driving the woman back with the expected swipe toward her middle. Poison made the next moves in sequence. Steel rang as the patterns wove faster through the air. Knives slashed—Shadarii ducked and almost didn't make the second parry.

Poison pushed the tempo. Hissing in triumph, she drove Shadarii back toward the fire. The attack ended with a vicious double slash. Shadarii took the weapons on her lower staves, steel biting home just beneath her fingers.

Poison was pushing the dance too fast too soon. Shadarii tried to signal her to move more slowly, but Poison merely purred and came at her again.

Steel spat; knives howled. Shadarii met a blur of light with a pair of lightning parries. She licked out her weapons at the proper speed, only to have Poison backslash at her eyes. Shadarii jerked her head back as something burned across her neck. She punched out with her hands to shove the other girl away. Poison spun in a somersault and landed on her feet. Her eyes stared in mad hunger at Shadarii, and she whirled her blades en guarde.

Shadarii wonderingly raised a hand to her throat. It came away glistening wet with blood. The crowd gave a sharp intake of breath, eyes gleaming in amazement as the girl's blood flowed.

With a shriek of hate, Poison launched into the attack. Shadarii rammed forward and locked blades. The girls snarled face to face, their weapons quivering at each other's throats.

Poison filled the air with a vile reek of musk as she hissed venomously in Shadarii's ear. "This time I'll kill you! Your Kotaru can't save you now!"

Shadarii gave a jerk of shock. *Javïra!*

Javïra shoved against her and purred, "I've seen you with him! I know your little escape plans. Do you want him? Fight me, Shadarii, or I'll tell the whole tribe about your plans! You'll never see your precious Vakïdurii boy again!" She sought to ram her knife home, but Shadarii held her in a deadlock. "If you want your love, you'll have to fight me for him! Fight me, you bitch! Kill me, or I'll kill your love forever!"

All around the royal seat, the elders whirled in anguish.

Chief Ohputa tore frantically at his hair. "Stop her! Lord king, drag them out of there!"

Nochorku-Zha jerked his head around in anger. "Control yourself. We cannot interfere! There are rules. No one may cross the circle until one of the dancers elects to break it."

"But your daughter... !"

"The rules are the rules!"

Down in the sacred circle, Shadarii hurtled Javïra back across the fire. She landed on her feet and tore away her mask. Kotaru tried to lunge into the ring, only to be held back by a dozen burly hunters.

"Shadarii, no! Get out! Run! Run to me!"

The girl sobbed. She stared at Kotaru in agony, her eyes shining bright with fear. *I love you!*

Shadarii hurtled herself straight for Javïra's throat. The crowd gasped, stirred— and then suddenly a girl stood to raise a hunting scream.

"Kill Javïra! Finish her, Shadarii!"

The shout set off a sudden storm of howls. The watchers leapt their feet and screamed for blood. Months of hunger, years of frustration and futile anger, suddenly boiled forth.

Within the sacred circle, the battle raged. Javïra rolled away as Shadarii's knife hacked into the dirt.

Shadarii fought in a blind red haze of love. Javïra must die—she must die for Kotaru!

Blades blurred, sparks flew. Shadarii lashed out for Javïra's face in a furious rain of blows. Javïra kicked Shadarii in the groin. Shadarii hissed and stood her ground, cracking Javïra across the snout — Once! Twice! Blood flew from Javïra's mouth. Shadarii hacked out with her dao, and Javïra met the swing with her weapons crossed. She heaved Shadarii back and slashed for her throat. The blow rang against Shadarii's blades.

Both women crouched, chests heaving as they dashed sweat from their eyes. The crowd's roar felt like a drug.

Shadarii opened her jaws and hissed like a striking viper. Ïsha currents crawled across her fur. A massive punch of force hurtled from her toward Javïra.

Blasted off her feet, the girl screamed in pain.

Shadarii sprang and tried to hack Javïra's head clean off. Javïra rolled and cracked the flat of her blade against Shadarii's skull, and Shadarii fell, her hands clenched against her face.

The women sprawled beside the raging fire. Javïra tried to ram Shadarii's head into the flames. Shadarii's aura flared like lightning. Blazing coals lashed out to smash Javïra's face. Bright tongues of flame raced up Javïra's streaming hair. With a howl of panic, the girl rolled across the sand.

Shadarii stood, green eyes blazing in dreadful lust. She opened her hands, and her fallen dao flew up to settle in her grasp. The crowd howled, and all around, voices screamed for blood. Shadarii stalked relentlessly toward her prey.

Javïra scrabbled back to her feet, stumbling away from Shadarii's grim advance. Ïsha lashed out, whiplike. Javïra jerked. The blow crashed against her shoulder. Shadarii struck again, and her victim staggered back, blood streaming from her nose. A third blow shattered Javïra's ribs and spattered blood across her fur.

Javïra gave a dreadful scream of fear, and then whirled and launched into the air. Shadarii punched out with her fist and seized the fleeing girl's mane of hair, whirling her down beside the fire. Shadarii ground her down into the dust and wrenched back at her hair. Her dao whipped around beneath Javïra's throat. Her arm tensed as she prepared to slash Javïra's jugular.

"Shadarii! No!"

Shadarii whirled.

Kotaru screamed at her from the circle's edge. "Don't do it! Don't murder her! Don't!" Kotaru wept in agony! "Shadarii! No! Please!"

Shadarii seemed mesmerized by the victim under her. The knife bit into Javïra's flesh, blood gleaming on the blade as she slowly ground it home.

Kill? Kill for love...? No!

The mob snarled in fury, screaming for blood.

Shadarii looked at their mad eyes and felt her stomach twist with revulsion. Shadarii whirled back to her victim. The crowd gasped as Shadarii sawed her blade. With a final rip the knife won free. Shadarii pulled free Javïra's severed hair, bound the girl with it, and tossed her aside.

The crowd fell silent as Shadarii dropped her knives and walked from the circle. Their fury drained away as she swept them with her sad green eyes. Shadarii wept for her people, a people lost in their own despair.

Kotaru caught her as she abruptly swooned and fell, trying to still her trembling with his simple love.

One by one, the crowd walked away, too ashamed to meet each others' eyes.

                                    ၷ   ၸ   ၸ

A new day broke across the forest; the great moment—the Day of Shedding. Totenïha dawned blue and fine—a flawless sky gleaming down on a universe of restless trees. Entering the family lodge with breakfast in hand, Shadarii swept her antennae beneath the door post and looked in on a place of tasteful furnishings and crumpled sleeping rolls.

Father was missing, Rain be praised. Shadarii felt rumpled after a night asleep in the open grass. She dug about to find a brush and briskly worked the night dew from her fur.

"So, there you are at last! Where have you been?" Zhukora lounged cross-legged on the windowsill, happily primping her headdresses for the totenïha ceremony. "We were looking for you! We need you and that girl to teach those dance moves to the Skull-Wings!"

Shadarii didn't seem to hear. She went to her sleeping space, unrolled her little mat, took her comb, and began to tease the knots out of her tail. Soon her gorgeous brush shone like sunrise. She slipped out of her crumpled skirt and drew on her ceremonial gear.

Zhukora was remarkably content today. She lay back on a mat and idly sharpened her claws. "Have you seen it? The priesthood think they are being clever, Shadarii. They aim to control the councils—and through the councils, to utterly dominate the tribes." The girl stroked a steel file along one jet-black talon. "But you touched on it at the dance last night! Anger; a power made from a desire to be something greater—something far more wonderful! Can the priests give the people that glorious energy? No. Glory is found by reaching out for dreams...."

Zhukora's sister went on with her own affairs. Hidden behind a room partition, Shadarii silently slipped her belongings inside her belly pack and pulled the drawstring tight; she needed only food, and she would be ready for her journey.

Shadarii would leave home without regrets. The girl rose, took her pack, and headed for the door.

"Shadarii!" Zhukora briskly snapped her fingers. "Take that good skirt off and get back into your normal clothes. You can dance in old leathers. We don't want you drawing any more attention than we have to."

Shadarii's ceremonial robes were her only possessions of pride. She wanted Kotaru to see her in them. The girl obstinately turned her back and headed for the door.

"Shadarii, I said take them off! Did you hear me?"

Shadarii thrashed her tail and walked grimly on.

Zhukora leapt to her feet and dragged the girl around. "Do as I say!" She shoved Shadarii in the chest. "Do as I damned well tell you!"

Her hand cracked out to slap Shadarii on the face. Shadarii caught her fist before it could connect and held Zhukora's arm at bay, glaring coldly into her sister's eyes. Matching strength for strength, Shadarii pushed Zhukora from her way. She shoved past the astonished huntress and whirred out into the sky.

Stunned, Zhukora breathed out slowly. She watched her little sister disappear into the forest.

Sleeping mat, water gourd, spare clothes, spare moccasins... Shadarii knelt beneath the ferns and furiously stuffed her pack. Kotaru's gear already lay there beneath the hollow log; the same log where they had stuffed themselves with crayfish just a few days before.

The girl's mind reeled; to have dreamed so long, to have hoped so high, and now to have it all come true! Her hands trembled as she shut her pack and stuffed it down beside Kotaru's.

Her antennae jerked. Someone was coming! Shadarii faded into cover and camouflaged her isha field. No mere hunter could have even guessed she was there.

A skinny little girl flew down through the eucalyptus leaves. Strange silver eyes searched sadly among the trees. "Shadarii? Shadarii, it's me."

Kïtashii! Shadarii heaved a sigh and clambered out into the open. Her little friend lugged a heavy pack toward the waterside.

"I rather thought you might be here. I brought you some old hunting leathers and a digging stick. An ax... some steel needles. I know you don't have much useful gear. A—a hunter's wife is going to need some tools." Kïtashii angrily scrubbed away a tear, and then prattled onward, scowling down inside her pack. "There's food, too. We all went out and got you some—the other girls and I, I mean." Another tear slid down her nose, and Kïtashii let it fall. Her voice quavered with false cheeriness. "Well! So there we are, eh? You are leaving tonight, of course. Have we all guessed right?"

Shadarii nodded miserably and slowly reached out to take Kïtashii in her arms. The little girl began to cry, her fingers twisting through Shadarii's fur.

"Now-now you just take care of yourself. I don't know what you'll do without me to watch over you."

Shadarii gave a broken sob. She held the girl against her breast.

The little girl turned her face away. "G-go with you? Don't be ridiculous. My mother needs me." The girl snuffed. "Anyway I c-can't, you see. Someone has to help her look after my baby brother. She's not very good with him...."

The two girls held each other tight. Shadarii's soul tore itself clean in two. *My friend. My one and only friend. I love you Kïtashii!*

Finally Kïtashii drew away; her hands lingered on Shadarii's fur, trying to hold the memory of her touch. "Well! I suppose one day everything comes down to a good-bye. We-we really shouldn't cry, should we?" Kïtashii trembled, the words sticking in her throat. "I love you, Shadarii. Good-bye, my friend."

With that, Kïtashii turned and fled, leaving nothing but a lingering touch.

෪ ෨ ෫

All through the forest, the air trembled to the throb of drums. Ten thousand dancers stamped in unison. Girls trilled their tongues. Choirs sang out in glorious harmony. Great lines of dancers wavered back and forth. Painted headdresses blazed in a thousand rainbow sky. [23] King and commoners, old men, and tiny babes, all had their place in the surging totenïha dance.

Shadarii crept backward through the bushes. There was something wildly power-ful about the spectacle of tribal dance. It steeped the soul in an awesome sense of majesty. The girl closed the ferns and forced herself to steal away, sliding silently off into the forest.

Shadarii had decked herself out in all her finery—painted skirt and painted halter, with a headdress of feathers streaming through her hair. Her wedding gift to Kotaru dangled from her belt. Fluid sloshed inside the hollow gourd, making Shadarii grin with wicked glee. It was a gift to make Kotaru laugh and the high priestess rage and scream. The girl dived through streaming shafts of light and let her imagination soar.

Down beside the little waterfall, Kotaru jittered in agitation. The young man stood and chewed his nails. Fear battled common sense. Sunset had come, and still no Shadarii! Was she coming? Was she having second thoughts? Perhaps she'd been discovered! What should he do? Fly back to the village to rescue her, or seek his team for help? The poor boy clutched his addled head.

Love is a debilitating disease. Kotaru jumped and jittered, paced back and forth.... It took a full minute to see the soft figure standing expectantly before him.

"Shadarii!" He breathed her name like a prayer. Kotaru spread his arms and pulled her in against him. She buried her face against his fur and filled him with her precious light. He held her at arm's length and drank in the gorgeous sight of her.

Kotaru gave a husky sigh and shook his head in wonder. "Sweet Rain! You look so—so beautiful!"

---

[23]**Dance Costumes:** The centerpiece of the totenïha costumes are headdresses made from tall sprays of pampas grass and a great many living flowers. Fine weather allows for a more elaborate show of costume than that used in the Rain dances of wintertime.

The lovers stared into each other's eyes. They slowly sank to their knees beside the tiny waterfall. "So we're ready? There's no regret, now? I want nothin' but your happiness."

Shadarii shook her head.

Kotaru's smile reached out to light his shining eyes. "I thank you for your love, my lady. There's no greater gift a man can receive."

Gifts! Shadarii jerked the gourd from her belt, proffering it impishly toward Kotaru.

The hunter eyed it with suspicion. "What's this?"

Shadarii laughingly mimed the act of drinking. *Drink it! An engagement gift. Share it with me!* Shadarii took a swig and heaved a sigh, then thrust the gourd beneath Kotaru's nose. *Now you!*

The hunter gingerly raised the gourd and drank. The liquid had a delightful creamy taste. It warmed his stomach, spreading out to soothe his frazzled nerves. "Mmmmm—it's good! What is it?"

Shadarii gave a sly smile and made a sign.

"Milk mead!" Kotaru almost choked. Sacrilege! They could fling him from the tribe for this! To take a drink meant for nobles—[24]

Uh—was that any different from carrying off a noble girl?

Shadarii took another long pull at the flask, and then passed it back toward Kotaru, blowing her hair back from her eyes. He took a final drink and firmly put the gourd away.

Kotaru had picked a perfect route for their escape. They would curve wide away from the shortest path, circling around the mountains to throw off pursuit. Once across the river, they would shed their wings and go on foot.

The packs were swiftly donned. Kotaru took his spears and woomera, his throwing sticks and dao, and then reached out to take his bride by the hand. "So, my love, are you ready?"

Shadarii stood staring back toward the distant dancing, taking one lasting glance at the home she left behind.

Kotaru softly stroked her hair. She was giving up her whole world for him; every face she knew, every place she haunted. Kotaru swallowed, brushing his face against Shadarii's cheek. "I love you, Shadarii."

The lovers gripped each others hands, shared a final kiss, and with a whisper of wings, rose into the forest sky.

The tribe broke from its dancing for a brief but well-earned rest. Beside a stream, Zhukora sat and laughed with her devoted circle of disciples. A passing hunter handed her a cup of water, blinking in amazement as she smiled at him and thanked him by name.

---

[24]**Milk Mead:** Fermented Kashran mothers' milk is the only alcoholic beverage known to the tribes. It is drunk only at the height of the sacred *toteniha* ceremony, and only by the nobility and priesthood.

Zhukora disdained to wear a noble's robes for the ceremonies. She had dressed herself in the same leathers as the commoners. Even so, Zhukora blazed with charisma. Her lean body glowed with health—virginal, untouchable, and strong. Her eyes could grab a man and hold his very soul.

The girl spoke to a growing crowd, her voice somehow reaching out to grip her listeners' hearts like a hypnotic spell. "The moral decay of a society arises from its failure to grasp one essential truth: Power must be coupled with responsibility. To be given the people's sacred trust is an honor! No person should merely take it as his or her due!

"When anyone takes without giving in return, that is theft! When any noble takes deference and obedience without acknowledging duty, that, too, is a crime! Such a one has lost the right to rule!"

A silent ring of people had gathered all around her, and Zhukora reached out to take them with her eyes.

"We are at the toteniha, the sacred time of shedding when our tribe remembers who we are. We remember what it means to be a Katakanii!" Zhukora looked each listener in the face. "What does it mean to be Katakanii? Does it mean venerating leaders who have no right to our respect? Does it mean living in terror of the future? Think on it as you dance. Speak of it with your families while you wait for new wings to grow. There are answers! The future calls to us. We need only gain the will to act!"

She released them to spread their questions to their friends and neighbors. Zhukora sat back to talk quietly to her inner circle. Daimïru knelt at her feet, her golden hair shining in the sun. Zhukora felt faith glowing in her like a storm.

Javïra edged out into the open as the last few listeners departed. The girl looked completely wretched. Her butchered hair hung limp with sickness. Bandages bound her ribs. Hate consumed her like wasp larvae chewing through a spider's flesh. One of the hunters laughed at her. Zhukora gave the girl a contemptuous glance before turning to her friends.

"What do you want, Javïra? If you're looking for another beating, I'm sure we can find Shadarii somewhere."

The Skull-Wings chuckled. Javïra shivered, her voice somehow bubbling brightly out between clenched fangs. "Oh, really? And where will you find her, Zhukora? Can you tell me where your sister might be?"

Zhukora gave the girl an icy glance. "She is where she is supposed to be, among the dancers! She was brave enough to show herself in public, even if you could only cower in the shadows."

Javïra's face gave a twitch; she smiled sweetly past her swollen lips. "Is she out there with the dancers? Why, how very odd! Mistress Traveesha hasn't seen her all day." The girl's mad eyes gleamed with malice. "Do you know where your sister is, Zhukora? You see, I rather think you've lost her. I think you might have just lost her permanently. Now, whatever will the high priestess have to say?"

"What are you saying?"

"I'm saying your sister has made plans for a husband, for a nest filled with squealing brats. She's running away, Zhukora! She's leaving you for good!"

"What?" Zhukora shot to her feet. "Where? How long ago? Speak!"

Javïra tittered and made a little dance of glee. "She's running, Zhukora. She's already left, but I know where she's gone! I know where!"

"Where?"

Javïra hissed in triumph. "Ha ha! Our little cripple has a lover. In a few hours her maidenhood will be gone. Poor Zhukora! No shiny bauble to trade off to the priests." The girl grinned and flexed her claws. "Oh, yes, I know where you can find Shadarii, but there's a price! I'll tell you where she's gone if I get something in return."

Zhukora merely looked at her.

Javïra stroked her claws. "You'll go far in this tribe, Zhukora—very far! I want to get back all she took from me and more. You're on the council. I want you to have me promoted to the first circle of dancers, second only to Traveesha herself! I want power, Zhukora! A fair exchange; my promotion for your precious little sister's tail!"

"Where is she, Javïra. I will ask you only once."

"Do I get my reward?"

"Certainly. Where is my sister?"

"Why she's flown off to meet her lover and escape. The Vakïdurii team captain—would you believe it? They're heading west toward the Vakïdurii tribal lands. I can show you where to find their trail."

Zhukora clicked her fingers, and Daimïru snapped into a bow as she received her orders.

"Daimïru, I want your best trackers. Armor. Weapons. Food for three days. There is a parcel in my lodge, a skull wrapped in an oilskin. Bring it to me."

Daimïru cracked her wings out in salute and barked orders to her men. Zhukora held out her arms as hunters relieved her of her clothes, and then began to strap her inside her armored uniform shell.

Within seconds, her transformation was complete. The skull face turned to stare coldly down at Javïra. "Show us where to find Shadarii. Lead me to her lover, and you shall have your reward."

Javïra threw back her head and laughed. Finally revenge was hers! Javïra looked up at the face of death and felt a thrill of joy. She had won at last; Shadarii was destroyed!

Raindrops thundered through the ferns as the storm crashed against the forest roof.

Kotaru whooped with laughter as he led Shadarii in a dash beneath a cliff. They dived down into the mouth of an enormous cave to shelter from the gale. Kotaru snorted and gleefully shook the water from his fur. "Whoooo! Well, it looks like we'll be flying no further tonight, eh? Old Mother Rain and Father Wind are feelin' a wee bit frisky!"

Shadarii's eyes were bright. It was so exciting! Shadarii gripped Kotaru's hand and stared out across the churning trees. The leaves tossed and whipped like wild things, and rain brought a fresh, clean smell that made the world seem new.

Kotaru thrilled to the sight of his lover's tossing hair. He nuzzled her and laughed as she buried herself in his arms. Shadarii's silks felt impossibly warm and soft beneath his hands. She slipped reluctantly from his grasp, shed her belly pack, and then stood to peer around their refuge.

The cave formed a vast shelf slicing back into the living rock. Wind dashed leaves and grit across the walls. Shadarii raised her hand and let a bright glow spill between her fingers. Shadows writhed and faded as she filled the cave with light.

Ah ha!

A sheltered cleft of rock drove further back into the mountain, well and truly hidden from the bitter wind. Shadarii flew up onto the rock shelf and gave a grateful sigh. Kotaru clambered up behind her, peering at Shadarii's eerie ball of light.

"How do you do that? Your bag of tricks is bottomless. Is it the result of a deprived childhood or somethin'?" He stopped as he saw Shadarii's find, and then clapped his hands for joy. "Ha! Now we're lookin' good! I'll go get those packs, and we'll see about a meal!"

He dived off to fetch their gear while Shadarii stood and quietly laid her hand against the rock. The roof towered overhead, peaking like a pair of praying hands. She felt the mountain whispering in its endless slumber, filling her with its timeless gift of peace.

Kotaru stumbled up the rocks behind her and opened their packs. He gathered wood and crackling twigs, his tail twirling merrily as he turned the cave into a home.

Behind him, Shadarii trembled slightly. She opened their packs and dragged out the things that would be needed for the night. It had to be perfect! There would never be another first time. There had been no mother to tell her what to do; no older sisters to advise her. Still, she had heard other girls talking about the art of making love. Shadarii laid their sleeping mats side by side and rolled spare clothes into a pillow for the bed. Her hands shook so badly she could scarcely put it in place.

There should be flowers; why weren't there any flowers? Shadarii wilted in dismay.

Kotaru innocently went about his own pursuits, quite unaware of the preparations going on behind him. He heaved a sigh of satisfaction and dusted off his hands. "Well that's that done! Tea'll be a while, but we've some warmth now, eh? I'll just get everything ready, and then we'll..."

His words faltered as he swung around to look at her. Shadarii knelt beside a wide, soft bed. The sleeping robe lay well turned down, beckoning in silent invitation. Shadarii stared at him, her pupils wide with fright. She turned, seeming suddenly mesmerised by the fire.

Kotaru had no idea what he should do. He remembered the jiteng game. Nervous faces, fear and trembling. Kotaru slowly moved to settle on the bed beside his love, and she felt stiff as hardwood. He softly laid her head across his lap and stroked her hair. Moving with slow, careful grace, Kotaru drew his old flute from its sheath. With the firelight sparkling in his eyes, he raised his pipes to play.

The fire gave warm protection from the storm. Kotaru's music rose to fill the night with peace. Shadarii sighed. Her fear vanished as she snuggled deeper down into Kotaru's lap.

The music slowly trailed away, and the lovers nestled closer on their little bed. Behind them, the fire rose bright and clear against the restless sky.

CB ᘓ ᘓ

Black shapes ripped through the bushes as the air flashed with lightning. A skull face bent beside a pool. Antennae sniffed at faint marks in the soil. The tracker crumbled earth between his fingers, nodding slowly in the wind.

"Two Kashra. One male, one female. The male's moccasins are cut differently from ours—Vakïdurii style."

Daimïru coldly gazed across the mountain peaks, the storm stirring her hair. "Where did they go?"

"West. The trail is faint, but the girl's ïsha spoor is unusually powerful. Can't follow it, though. Lightning is dispersing the traces."

Daimïru cursed and spared a glance toward Zhukora, her tail twitching fitfully. Soon it would be impossible to fly; her wings already itched and burned like fire. Sometime tonight, their wings would break and fall away. New wings would come, but days would pass until they hardened. It might take days to walk back home.

"Daimïru. What have they found?"

"She was here. They've gone west. The storm gives us no chance to follow."

Zhukora slowly nodded. She stroked the shaft of her spear and gazed out across the waterfall. "Gather the hunters and prepare to move. We will follow on their trail immediately."

"Zhukora, the trackers say we have no hope!"

The leader gave a slow smile in reply. She reached out to touch Daimïru's shoulder. "Gather the people, my love. My sister has her role to play within a greater destiny. I will show you powers to put a storm to shame." Daimïru hesitated, but Zhukora pulled off her mask and smiled down at her friend. "Go. Go! This is something all of us must share! Something wonderful."

Javïra paced beside the pool, tugging at her bandages. She watched in suspicion as Zhukora placed a strange bundle on a rock. "What are you doing? Why aren't you going after them?"

"All in good time. We must meet someone else before we go. It shan't take long. You might even find it rather interesting." Zhukora uncovered the withered skull. Her faithful followers knelt all around her.

Daimïru drew aside her mask, her thin face staring up at her beloved leader. "We are here, Zhukora. We are ready."

Zhukora reached out to take the skull in her hands. She shivered as she felt her mission filling her with power. "The time of conflict comes upon us. Our enemies will use every weapon in their power to bring us down. Armed struggle is inevitable.

"We must be ready to face our terror. To succeed, we must hurtle mercy behind us! We must lay our lives as sacrifices to our Dream. Let no person follow me who fears to give as much as I!" Zhukora raised the skull toward the storm. Its power suddenly burst forth above the crowd. Ïsha blazed. Lightning streaked behind Zhukora's hair. "All our weapons must be gathered! Each spear, each mind, each spark of energy must be ready for our struggle! Finally, we have the means to destroy the people's enemies!"

Energy blazed forth. Zhukora screamed out in triumph. The storm reached its height.

"Lord Serpent! I, Zhukora summon you! I draw you to my body and make your power my own!"

The skull burst into a ball of light. A stream of living energy crashed against Zhukora's heart. She screamed and threw back her head. Force raged through her soul. Rocks and trees exploded into flames.

Suddenly the lightning stopped. Zhukora clutched her head and writhed in agony. Sparks arced across her body, wreathing her in pain.

Zhukora gave a scream of rage and hurtled the pain aside. She stood, arcing energy into the rocks, the rain, the trees.

Blinking, her hunters hastened to her side.

"I'm all right! Leave me. I can stand!" She stared off into the emptiness, her face blank with shock. Zhukora blinked and felt ïsha spill like syrup through her claws.

"Poison—the power! I never thought it could feel so sweet!" Zhukora stretched out her hands and slowly closed her fingers. Energy dripped like liquid fire to splash upon the ground.

Serpent, do you feel? Do you see?

Something stirred inside her, and she felt a tingle running through her limbs. Lord Serpent shivered, rippling through her body like a glorious blaze of laughter.

I see! I touch! I feel! Zhukora felt his thrill like a delicious drug. She ran hands across her curves, feeling Serpent gasp within her. *So this is life! This is beauty? Too long I had forgotten! Oh, Zhukora, this is a bargain, indeed! Thou shalt have thy power and more. I shall give thee fire in payment for the softness of thy lovely hair! I shall give thee healing as thanks for these hands to touch! I shall show thee undreamed of weapons—tools to blast thine enemies to ruins! We shall laugh at their destruction and feel this body blaze with life!*

Zhukora laughed. He was there inside her—a rider such as mere priests had never dreamed! Zhukora lashed out to shear a boulder clean in two. Then she screamed and threw her arms out to the storm, thrilling to the brilliant crack of lightning in the air.

The demons knelt in obeisance to their shining queen. Daimïru bowed at her feet and reached up to take Zhukora's hand.

"Zhukora, are you all right? What did you do?"

The leader reached down to touch Daimïru's golden hair. "I have tamed the spirit of the cave, my love. Now we finally have a weapon in our hands."

"Does the power work? Can you track Shadarii?"

"Oh, yes, my love. I feel her! There's no hiding from us now. We shall drag her from her hiding place and fling her to the priests!"

Daimïru snapped her mask back into place. The hunters rose into the air and sped out through the darkness. Zhukora raised a demonic howl of hunger. With a savage shout, the hunters plunged into the heart of the storm.

CR EO EO

In the light of dawn, Shadarii dozed, snug and warm beneath Kotaru's arm. She glowed with satisfaction, nestling happily in her lover's strong embrace.

Lovers! They were really lovers! Weary but happy, Shadarii sighed, her head pillowed on her own beloved man.

Kotaru heaved a yawn and nuzzled at Shadarii's ear. He reached up and scratched his lover between her long antennae. "Mmmmmm—how are your wings? Are they itchy yet?"

Shadarii gave a shrug, and then reached out to touch her wings, groping in confusion as her hands reached only empty air. Shadarii sat up, blinking at two great swathes of orange that lay beside her in the bed. Her wings had dropped off in the night, and she had never even awakened. She laughed her silent laugh and snatched one old, discarded wing. Black and orange, red and white... such a pretty thing, such a shame to toss it all away.

Kotaru's wings were intact. Shadarii lay beside him, letting him kiss her as she combed her fingers through his hair. The smells of a warm shared bed were new and strange. Shadarii smiled and felt morning breezes stream across her fur.

In time, the girl felt the urgent tug of an impatient bladder. She eased out of bed, and then danced merrily outside to find a convenient bush. The sun was bright. The sky shone blue. The day grew warm and fine. All she needed was a cup of tea to make it a perfect dawn.

Her business done, Shadarii pranced along the rocks beneath the cliff face. Below her, the river wound its way toward the edges of the forest. Shadarii leapt along the boulders like a child, dancing out her happiness for all the world to see.

Shadarii clambered back into the cave and went to stir her lazy man from bed. Kotaru lay tangled in the sleeping robe, his delicious body gleaming in the filtered light. Kotaru gave a growl and pulled her down into the bed. He nibbled at her neck, making Shadarii kick and wriggle in delight. She grabbed him by the ears and tried to slap his groping hands away.

Not now. There's years for all this nonsense! It's time for us to be up and gone!

Kotaru sighed and wistfully nuzzled at her. "Ah, me! Now there's the rub! Once she gets what she wants, it's all just thank you and good-bye!"

Shadarii gave a snort and pushed him back across the bed. Kotaru crept reluctantly from the covers, rubbing sleep from his eyes. His lover held up the teapot and jiggled it around before his nose, and Kotaru's face filled with naked lust. "Oh, please! Rain, woman, tea in bed! You're a queen of mercy!"

Shadarii twirled her tail and scampered from the cave.

Kotaru yawned and followed, watching as she bent to fill the kettle from a rain pool. His voice hooted gleefully down to her from high above. "Hey, brush-tail! I'll break that seed loaf for breakfast!"

She turned and waved merrily back at him, her eyes sparkling bright with love. She swung back to fill the kettle.

Something dark slashed through the air. A throwing stick cracked against Shadarii's skull. Her world went black as she spun, unconscious, to the ground.

Kotaru leapt forward, blinking down at her in shock, and then threw himself aside as something flashed toward him. A spear shattered on the rock face, inches from his head.

Kotaru spread his wings and dived. He lanced between the rocks, desperately racing for Shadarii, and then swerved as a shrieking figure burst up from the ground. A spear whipped past him, parting the fur across his neck. The naked hunter roared and crashed full tilt into his enemy; the creature tumbled back, bones breaking as it slammed against a rock. Kotaru roared and smashed his fist across the creature's grinning skull.

A second figure burst out from the bushes. The Skull-Wing warrior lunged a spear. Kotaru spun and ripped the weapon away. He jammed the butt hard into the Skull-Wing's crotch and cracked the staff against his assailant's neck.

Kotaru ducked and grabbed Shadarii by the arms. He had her half lifted from the ground when a flock of Zhukora's demons tore down from the trees. Kotaru snatched a fallen spear and hurtled it with all his strength. It shot toward the enemy, only to explode into a shower of ashes at one wave from Zhukora's hand.

Kotaru blinked in astonishment. He leapt high into the sky. His spears lay bundled in the cave; from there he could hit anyone trying to touch Shadarii. The hunter shot through the air with blinding speed, a dozen shrieking enemies behind him.

Something erupted from the weeds below. Daimïru lunged. Kotaru screamed as her spear rammed through his stomach. He spun into the cliff face, falling a hundred spans to smash against the river bank and sink beneath the foam.

Daimïru stared down at the trail of bloody bubbles in the water, twitching at the thrill of killing. Zhukora came to touch her, and Daimïru trembled beneath her soft caress. She relished how the spear had sunk home, how horror had flashed in his eyes as he had stared death in the face....

"Is he dead?"

Daimïru numbly nodded, still incapable of speech. Zhukora drew in a breath and gripped Daimïru in excitement.

Javïra scuttled forward, cackling as she circled her fallen foe. "Ha ha! He joined her last night! Blood was shed! Now your prize is useless to the priests!"

The skull masks gathered in forbidding silence. Zhukora slowly paced the rocks, her long hair streaming in the breeze. "What the priests don't know will not concern them. My sister lacks a voice to even tell them what she has done."

Javïra purred in triumph, and her white fur shone like winter ice. "Aaaaaah! So we shall keep an ax above her head? Finally I have her in my power! I'll make her beg my forgiveness before the entire tribe!"

Zhukora glanced down to spear Javïra with her eyes. "Fool! Three times she has beaten you. Have events entirely escaped your notice? Do you remember the witch-girl on the Vakïdurii jiteng team? Has it never occurred to you just who that player might have been? I thought as much! Shadarii is dangerous. I have underestimated her once. I shall not do so again." Zhukora coldly looked down at Javïra. "You have pursued my sister beyond all reason. You are stupid, and stupidity is dangerous."

"Stupid?" Javïra peered smugly sideways at Zhukora. "Perhaps I am, but I know advantage when I see it. If the priests find out Shadarii is no longer a virgin, her value to you is lost! You need me, Zhukora. You need me to keep our little secret safe and sound. And so I shall, but it will cost. I want to be paid what I deserve!"

The girl spat down on Shadarii's face and gaily danced across the stones.

Zhukora watched her with sardonic eyes, then lifted her hand. "Javïra."

The dancer turned.

Light exploded from Zhukora's claws. Javïra gave a scream as her fur exploded in a sheet of fire. Lightning blasted through her flesh. With a bubbling hiss, her skeleton slammed to the ground. Javïra's Ka screamed as it whirled away into the winds.

Zhukora gave a pretty smile and reached out to take Daimïru's hand. "Payment in full, just as you deserve. Yes, I should say our little secret is quite safe. Thank you Javïra! You have been most entertaining."

The demons triumphantly closed about their queen, then bore Shadarii down into the forest depths for sacrifice.

Twelve

Light flickered on the floorboards of an empty room, while high above, leaves whispered in a restless breeze.

Lost in a daze, a girl stared down at their shadows on the polished floor, her green eyes wide and empty. The tree house swayed back and forth like a mother's arms. The girl sat and listened to the trees, drifting away upon the ebb and flow of sound.

It was all so nice and restful.

Sun.

It felt rich and warm against her fur, warm, like being held so nice and tight. There had been a time once when she had felt a touch like that. Soft breath against her fur and arms about her waist while she had slept in a delicious dream of peace.

Or had she?

It was hard to know for sure. Why bother when the sun was so comforting? She felt the warmth stream down across her face and gave a gentle smile.

Someone was coming. It would be the blonde one again, the one who felt so tight and hard inside her. She yelled more easily than the others. The girl blinked unhappily and lifted her face toward the door.

Still, at least it was food time. Food was always the best time of the day!

A bar was dragged free of the door, and the blonde one tramped into the room, hurtling down a bucket and a box of food. She was in a shouting mood again. The sunbeam girl's antennae wilted. No matter how small she made herself, trouble always found her....

"Food's up! Roots and greens. I'm not dragging anymore water up here again, so you can just stick with what you've got!" The blonde girl snatched the prisoner's previous meal box and crammed the empty leaf plates inside. She went to nudge a bucket in the corner, turning around in anger.

"What? This thing's empty again! Have you been yet?"

The prisoner shrank down, wishing to disappear.

"Come on! You're not fouling yourself again, filthy bitch! Get on with it!"

The girl sighed and dutifully squatted on the pot. The blonde winced in disgust, staying far away until the business was done. The prisoner rose and approached the food box, drooling happily.

Her guardian backed off in disgust. "That's our girl! Eat all your nice food. Eat up and be nice and quiet for Auntie Daimïru!"

The prisoner stuffed boiled roots into her mouth. Food was good! Food was when she did something with her day. It was always the same food, though. She remembered other times, tasty things to eat and crunch. There had been wood grubs toasted in ashes or boiled clams or simmering codfish! One time, there had been crayfish....

Crayfish... Shadarii drew her brows together in thought. It was hard to think these days. So very hard....

The drugged food did its work; the girl's eyelids drooped, her eyes went dull, and her head began to nod. The old tree dreamed ever onward, while Shadarii slept the dull sleep of a rotting log.

"A representation! We should make a representation." Nochorku-Zha's hands shook as he furiously addressed the council. "I won't have it! I won't! Foreigners stealing our dancing girls? It's just not done! There are proper channels for this sort of thing."

"I agree, my lord. The procedure was most irregular!" Councilor Fotoki gave an imperious scowl. "If the Vakïdurii intend cross-national marriages, they should place a proposition before the council."

"Hear, hear!"

"Quite so."

"Damned impertinent...."

The elders thrashed their new-grown[25] wings in anger.

A smooth, cool voice reached out to soothe their nerves. "Colleagues, colleagues! We must remember our dignity." Zhukora leaned forward, her figure stark and hungry beneath her hunting clothes. "There is no need for alarm. Why turn the world upside down over a lovesick girl!"

Gegachii was in fine form today. The old man shivered in a purple fit. "Lovesick? Kidnapped! Poor Javïra's been dragged off into the wilds by some thieving commoner!"

"Oh, to the contrary! Their departure was planned. Mistress Traveesha had noticed poor Javïra acting oddly just before her disappearance. The hunter must have taken pity on her after her humiliation. Javïra did have a certain talent for wrapping men about her little finger...."

Gegachii flapped his mouth open like a gulping catfish. "Fraternizing? W-with a commoner?"

"Alas, she always was a headstrong girl...."

At a loss, Councilor Lakïka raised a hand to his brow. "So, now where are we supposed to stand? Javïra is missing, but she wants to be missing! The Vakïdurii will think poorly of us if we take her back, but if we fail to act, they might think us weak. What shall we do?"

Zhukora gave a wise nod as she listened to his words, and then slowly lifted a finger, as though inspired. "I have it! I recommend the creation of a subcommittee at once. We shall carefully examine every option."

A capital idea! The elders were delighted. Finally their young firebrand was speaking sense! Nochorku-Zha gave a nod of approval.

---

[25]**Wing Cycles:** Despite the presence of healing magic, Kashran wings still tend to accumulate damage in the course of an active life. The yearly shedding provides a necessary replenishment. The wings drop away, to be regrown in approximately one week's time.

The discarded wings are burned as a pledge of thanks to the Fire spirit—although brightly colored wing scales are collected for use in paints, contributing much to the splendor of alpine jiteng costumes and ceremonial garb.

"Order! Order! The motion is before the council. All in favor? All opposed?" He swiftly counted hands. "Done. The subcommittee will be organized by Zhukora-kai-Nochorku. With the tribe dispersed, we have six months until our next tribal gathering. I require a committee report at that time."

Zhukora gave a gracious bow. The council moved on to other business, never once disturbed by Zhukora's silent smile.

Nochorku-Zha was well pleased. The totenïha had ended, and after a week's relaxation, the tribe's wings had regrown. With the other clans dispersed to their territories, the strain on local food supplies had eased. All was well, and peace reigned—even that little fight during the ceremonies was forgotten.

Oh, yes, The fight... Nochorku-Zha managed to focus on that memory. "Zhukora! How is what's-her-name? The fat one?"

"Shadarii?" Zhukora sadly folded her hands. "Still despondent, I'm afraid. We really can't give her to the priesthood until she's thrown off her stomach flu. I'm sure she'll be quite recovered in a week or so."

"Bah, useless wretch. Her mother will have a thing or two to say to her!"

Zhukora's eyes grew cold. "Aye, Father. I suppose she shall." She slowly rose from her place and graciously inclined her head toward the council. "I shall take my leave and tend to her now, Father. With Shadarii ill, the household duties are mine."

"Eh? Who's ill? Oh, yes, quite. Well, off you go, then. And, remember, no roots for supper!"

Zhukora turned on her heel and slowly left the council lodge. She flicked her wings out with an imperious snap and waved them in the sun.

Daimïru's slender figure speared down from the canopy above. The girl landed in a stream of long blonde hair, bowed, and raised her face to report.

"Shadarii has been attended to, Zhukora. I checked her myself. The poison roots are working perfectly."

"Good." Zhukora took her companion by the arm. Far below them, the village prepared for evening. "I take it she's quiet?"

"Oh, aye. Quiet as a baby. She'll be fast asleep by now."

"Excellent!" Zhukora's ïsha flared. "Let's go see her, shall we? It's time to let our friend Serpent have another little chat."

The two women grinned together. With a flash of wings, they sped off into the trees.

Little Kïtashii sat in the grass, warming up for her dance rehearsal. She bowed her head onto one straightened leg, gritting fangs against the painful stretch. The other girls made their moves with effortless grace. Why was she the only one incapable of bending? The skinny little creature blinked back tears and tried again, pushing herself far past her limitations.

Without Shadarii, Kïtashii felt alone. She was surrounded by noble girls—caustic, superficial bitches whose only joy in life came from slashing one another down. Their greatest wish was to see Kïtashii hurtled from the dance class.

Kïtashii's days bloomed into a nightmare. She worked on chores around the lodge, caring for the baby when her mother went away. She did the family's cooking, tended the garden plots, and wove mats to trade for food. Each day she grew more tired—a little less able to keep up with the strain. Her mother sat back and waited for Kïtashii to admit defeat.

She wouldn't! Never! It was her only chance to be a dancer. If she gave up now, her dreams were finished. The girl switched legs and tried to hold another stretch. The physical strain proved almost more than she could bear.

All around Kïtashii, the other students whispered back and forth. The girl felt a sly glow of delight. By now, Shadarii's disappearance was known. A noble girl had taken a commoner as a husband! The scandal was too delicious to ignore.

"Girls, girls, girls—gather round!" Mistress Traveesha swept through the clearing as if a storm brewed beneath her. "Girls! Come here, please. I have a most upsetting announcement."

Traveesha pressed her fingers against her face. The girls rose from their exercises and silently gathered.

"My dears, I have the most dreadful news. Absolutely dreadful! The council have officially announced that one of our sisters of the tribe is missing. Gone! She's run off with the Vakïdurii team. Gallivanting with a commoner lover!" Traveesha suddenly looked down at Kïtashii and clapped her hand across her mouth. "Oh, I do beg your pardon, child. Still, it's just not done. It simply isn't! There are rules of conduct we all must follow. Girls, let this be a warning to us all! We must never, ever allow passion to overrule common sense. Now one poor girl has lost everything that matters in her life!"

Kïtashii gave a little smirk as she thought about Shadarii's joy. That's what you think!

"Oh, girls, I just can't think of what our poor Javïra could have been thinking of..."

Kïtashii's face fell in shock. "Javïra? You mean Shadarii!"

"What? Don't be foolish, child! 'Tis our beloved Javïra who's been spirited off by those Vakïdurii beasts." The tall, old dancer wrung her hands. "She was unbalanced! The fights had cracked her mind! Now some villain's taken advantage of her—made all sorts of unspeakable promises, and then dragged her off into his filthy hovel."

"Shadarii! What about Shadarii?"

"Shadarii?" Mistress Traveesha couldn't have cared less. "Wretched little freak! She's the one responsible for this! Driving my poor Javïra clean from her senses. Well, I'll have no mercy on her this time. She's finished in this clan as far as I'm..."

"Mistress! Shadarii—where is she?"

"Oh, she's shut away ill somewhere. Ashamed to show her face now that she knows just what she's done. Her sister's looking after her until she recovers."

Kïtashii whirled and made to race into the bushes, only to be grabbed by the wing roots and hauled back into line.

"Not so fast, young miss! There's a dance to rehearse."

"But..."

"I never want to hear of you consorting with that—that creature Shadarii ever again! She is an evil, twisted girl. You will not seek her out. You will not speak with her. You will not speak of her. That is my direct order." Kïtashii rolled her eyes in panic. Mistress Traveesha held the little creature off the ground. "I will be watching you, young lady. Every minute of the day, every moment of the night. You do want to be a dancer, don't you? Make your choice. Follow orders or go right back to what you were."

Traveesha dropped her victim in the grass. The little girl gave a sob, and her hand trembled as she pressed it to her mouth.

When the other girls moved back to class, Kïtashii turned and followed close behind.

It was cold—so very cold. Shadarii shivered, curling into a fearful little ball as icy winds jabbed at her fur. Shadarii looked around. A vast emptiness stretched all about her, soaring off into the dark. She shivered with fear.

Winds moaned. Ïsha creaked and splintered in the dark. An evil presence slithered nearby.

Daughter...

Shadarii gave a convulsive jerk and curled tighter.

The voice swirled around her like a polluted stream. *Thou art alone, daughter. So alone. It is how it was always meant to be. Alone in the darkness...*

Shadarii sobbed for breath, hands jammed tight against her ears. *No! There was someone! Someone who cared! Someone who loved me....*

No. There never was! See? Look into your mind to find the memories. The presence coiled closer.

Shadarii desperately sought for memories of her love. There were there, faint and ephemeral—pictures scored on ice. Even as she tried to grasp them, they melted clean away.

See? No unsightly memories. Nothing but emptiness.

Shadarii reeled, clawing at her skull. *They will come back! They will!*

They were never there, Daughter. Only fantasy. And fantasy is best left in the dust to die.

I hate you! I am light. Light withers darkness!

Light can never reach all of the darkness, little fool. All light eventually must fail.

The presence rattled once more through the husks of her empty dreams, and then was gone.

Zhukora opened her eyes and smiled, drawing a smooth, deep sigh. Lord Serpent purred, coiled above Shadarii's sleeping form.

The creature's memories of love are all but gone.

"Good. You have done well, my friend. We have all done extremely well." The huntress opened her arms and gathered Serpent against her heart. "And how may I reward you for your skill?"

Let us fly! Go with the girl of gold and soar high into the sky.

Zhukora laughed, then turned to Daimïru and reached out to take her hand.

Daimïru brushed a trailing lock of hair from Zhukora's eyes. "Is he speaking to you? What does he say?"

"Nothing of consequence. Senses still delight him. He is a child with a new plaything."

"What's it like? How does it feel to have that—that thing inside you? Does he read your mind?"

"No, not really. I don't even know he's there until he speaks. He can hear me only when I decide to call on him."

"I fear for you, Zhukora. Be very, very sure you can control him."

"He'll not harm me. We share the same needs—the same desires. Serpent is my thrall."

Zhukora knelt beside Shadarii. The plump little dancer lay huddled in a ball, her fur dulled by drugs and long neglect. Zhukora stroked her fingers through Shadarii's tangled hair.

"Love... physical love is so ephemeral. Already she has forgotten his face, his smell, the sound of his voice. One by one, we shall slice the memories from her mind."

"Will she still be useful? The high priestess will fast for three more days. When she returns, she'll expect her prize. What happens if we hand her a dreaming idiot?"

"Oh, my sister will be whole in mind. We'll just wall away a few memories that might be embarrassing to us."

Daimïru looked down at the forlorn little figure on the floor. The last rays of the evening sun lingered on Shadarii's softness. "A shame really. She's quite beautiful in her way."

Zhukora gave a derisive snort and shoved the sleeper with her foot. "Beautiful? No. Too soft! No strength, no will, no vision! Beauty? No. You are beautiful. Your passion rings out like a glorious song! But this—this pudding?" Zhukora gave Shadarii another brutal kick. "Dust beneath our boots! A tool to use—no more." Zhukora swept back her hair. "Come. 'Tis time we were gone. We don't want anyone to find our little prize."

The two women retreated from the lodge and firmly barred the door.

Behind them, the sleeper whimpered, and a single tear slid down into her fur.

ওও ৪৩ ৪৩

A heavy drumbeat pounded though the darkness, and the air thundered. An entire tribe shook the trees with mourning. Feeling drained from a long, hard march, Mrrimïmei hung on Totoru's arm as the horizon glowed with fires.

"A funeral dirge—and so big? Now, who warrants that kind of send off?"

Prince Teki'taa's ears lifted as he pondered the distant music. He smiled and waved one hand toward the Vakïdurii village. "Come along, my little Wrens. It seems we are almost late. Do try to show some of that agility you're famous for."

The group of travelers emerged from the forest night at the edges of a jiteng field. A vast funeral pyre blazed at the center of the clearing. Smoke boiled furiously into the air while hundreds of dancers leapt and swirled across the flames. Dust hung heavy in the air, and the world trembled to the crash and boom of mighty drums.

Prince Tekï'taa wandered through the crowd, pushing toward the ring of priests who knelt solemnly before the blaze. The man hung a suitably grieving expression on his face and stared at his father's funeral pyre.

The high priest of the Vakïdurii came to stand beside him, leaning to whisper in the prince's ear. "Thy father died two nights ago, quietly in his sleep. We are now a tribe without a king."

"How tragic!" Tekï'taa placed a hand across his heart. "He died without warning, I suppose."

"Quite suddenly. Ah, well, he was always overweight. The healers had warned him of the dangers to his heart."

"Just so. What an appalling tragedy." Tekï'taa looked sideways at the priest. "So, tomorrow the tribe must select its new king?"

"Quite so. And who should arrive upon the scene than Tekï'taa? Tekï'taa the provider, the man who brings us a glorious jiteng victory!"

The flames licked ever higher; when Tekï'taa concentrated, he could almost hear his father's fat sizzling in the fire.

The priest laid a hand on the prince's arm.

"Celebrate well, my prince, for tomorrow you shall be king." The man leaned closer, his long fangs gleaming in the firelight. "But remember, oh king. Remember who it was that placed the power in your hands."

Out at the edges of the crowd, Mrrimïmei fought her way toward Totoru. The girl shouted to be heard above the deafening sound of drums.

"He's not here! No one's seen Kotaru!"

"His lodge is empty. The other bachelors say they've not seen hide nor hair!" Looming huge above the crowds, Totoru creased his muzzle in thought. "He must have never made it home with the girl."

The lovers clung together, wincing as the crowds surged back and forth, and Totoru bellowed into his fiancé's ear. "He's the smartest man alive! How could anything have gone wrong?"

"He's a lovesick fool! Anything could've happened to him." Mrrimïmei looked around in panic. "Why? Why did we ever let him do it? The whole idea's too dangerous! I should have known something bad would happen!"

"They must have changed their plan and gone another way."

The girl shook her head, her eyes bright with panic. "No, I can feel it! Somethin' is wrong!" Mrrimïmei clenched her fist. "Call the team! We'll search. Comb the likely routes, and then all the unlikely ones. If he's out there, we'll find him!"

Totoru reluctantly began to move. "There's a whole forest out there, love. How can we ever hope to find him?"

"He's ours, and I'll never give him up! That man's done everything for me!" Mrrimïmei glared bitterly toward the fire. "I knew this would happen! We search! I'm damned if I'll ever give him up."

The two Kashra pushed off into the churning crowds to find their team. Behind them the drums crashed with the sound of ancient storms.

ᜃ ᜋ ᜌ

Kïtashii lay beneath her sleeping robe, listening to the approach of dawn. A magpie warbled somewhere in the distance. Leaves rustled. The little girl blinked, wondering if she could see the ceiling of the lodge. Was it dawn yet? Would anyone be stirring in the village? Hunters might be; dawn was the time to catch possums returning to their lairs. Zhukora's men might already be combing the trees....

The room lay still. Kïtashii strained to hear if her mother was awake. With painful slowness, the girl rolled over. Each rustle of the sleeping mat sounded as loud as a snapping branch.

Night still hung above the forest. Vast tree trunks shimmered in the dark. Kïtashii balanced awkwardly on one leg, pulling on her little skirt and halter. Finally done, she spread her wings and sank into the treetops.

No one would tell her where the ailing Shadarii was hidden. She wasn't in her father's lodge or with the healers or priests. That left Councilor Chitoochi's lodge. Since the councilor had died, her house had been left sealed and deserted, and Zhukora was warden of Chitoochi's keys....

Why? Why didn't they want Shadarii to be seen in public? Had they hurt her somehow? She wouldn't have come back without a fight. The poor girl might be lying there in pain, needing her!

With reckless speed, Kïtashii flung herself through the dark. She slowed only as she neared Chitoochi's lodge.

She swept in to cling beneath the boughs of a nearby tree and searched the darkness for signs of danger. Half hidden in cobwebs and mistletoe, a haze of ïsha shimmered in the gloom. Someone sat above the lodge, quietly keeping watch.

Kïtashii hung upside down and thoughtfully waved her tail. Any aerial approach would be seen. On the other hand, the guard's view was blocked by the huge bulk of the tree house below him.

Kïtashii withdrew her claws and fell silently toward the ground, plunging through the dark for long seconds before finally flicking out her wings. Wind roared around her. She curved into a loop and began to rise. Tree bark brushed her belly. Above, the tree house floor neared. As Kïtashii's momentum slowed, the girl reached out her claws to catch the rugged bark of the trunk.

Ha! Easy! The little creature swarmed busily up the trunk, scuttled beneath the tree house, and twirled her tail in glee.

The windows of the lodge were covered by sturdy wooden bars, and the front door was locked. Kïtashii crouched uncomfortably in the dark space beneath the floor and tried to think. She couldn't break the bars and couldn't force the door. Kïtashii took her tongue between her teeth and tried knocking softly on the floorboards overhead. Five minutes of effort yielded no result.

Kïtashii petulantly rammed herself back against a branch. Wood creaked alarmingly behind her. Kïtashii froze, and then pushed back against the branch once more. Overhead, the floorboards gave slightly.

Ah ha!

Clever little hands began to run across the planks. The wooden pegs that held the boards together had started to work free. Kïtashii plucked the pegs out one by one and stuffed them down her tiny halter. The girl softly drew a plank free and placed it between the branches.

She whispered hoarsely into the dark gap. "Shadarii! Psssst, Shadarii? Shadarii, are you there?" Kïtashii's ears pricked as she heard a sluggish movement overhead, and her sensitive black nose caught hold of Shadarii's smell. "Pssst! Shadarii, it's me!"

Still she heard no answer. She must be hurt! Kïtashii began tearing at the floorboards, her ears flat in anger. "Hold on Shadarii. I'm coming. Just stay still while I come to get you." A second board came free, and then a third. Kïtashii flattened her wings and pushed up through the hole, wood scraping her ribs.

Shadarii's orange wings fluttered limply in the gloom.

Kïtashii gave a little cry and raced over to her. "Shadarii! What have they done to you? Oh, sweet Rain what have they done? Oh, my poor friend!"

Warm arms fumbled out to hold her. Kïtashii buried her face in Shadarii's breast and whimpered in relief. "Oh, Rain! Thank the spirits you're all right. I found you. They tried to stop me, but I found you!" The little girl ran fingers through Shadarii's tangled hair; she smelled strangely dull and sick. "I've made a hole in the floor. We can drop out and be gone before they know it!"

There was still no answer; Shadarii stirred and let her head fall back to smack against the floor.

"Shadarii?" Kïtashii blinked. "Shadarii, can you hear me? Shadarii, wake up!"

The woman's eyes were open, but she didn't seem to see. She reached out to touch Kïtashii's face and gave a dreamy little smile. Kïtashii croaked in shock as Shadarii sighed and cuddled happily against her.

A bowl of boiled roots lay on the floor. Kïtashii reached across and suspiciously sniffed the remnants. A sharply acidic scent rose to burn her nostrils. "Poison root!" she gasped, her eyes widening.

Kïtashii looked in fright at her friend. Poison root was a forbidden thing! Lazy hunters used it to poison water holes; dropped into a pool, it could stun every fish in a hundred spans. To use it on an animal was forbidden; to use it on a fellow Kashra was unthinkable.

"Come on, Shadarii! Up! Come on, wake up. We have to get you out of here!" It was hopeless. Shadarii had been drugged to her eyeballs. Kïtashii held up Shadarii's head and tried to meet her gaze. "Shadarii! Can you hear me? Come on now, blink twice if you can hear me. Come on! Just try for me...."

Yes! Shadarii smiled happily and blinked her eyes—once! twice!

Kïtashii lifted Shadarii's face and shook her by the hair. "All right Shadarii. Now you listen very, very carefully. We have to get you out of here. You mustn't eat the food, all right? Don't eat the food they give you! Empty the bowl down the hole in the floor."

Shadarii's head lolled. Kïtashii wrenched her face upright once again.

"Shadarii! Listen! Don't eat the food. Not one bite. They're poisoning you! You mustn't eat anything today. I'll bring you food tonight.

"Drink this water now. Drink up! We have to flush the poison from your blood. Drink all you can today, you hear? Drink all the water they can give you."

Footsteps scraped on the roof overhead. The guard had begun to stir, and soon he would come check on the prisoner.

"Shadarii, I have to go now. They'll find me if I stay. You just hold on tight, and I'll come back again tonight. I'll help you get away and find Kotaru."

Shadarii suddenly blinked at the mention of Kotaru's name.

"That's it! Kotaru. You remember Kotaru! He's waiting for you. We have to go to him." Kïtashii began to squeeze back through the floor. "I'll be back tonight! I love you!"

The little girl blinked in shock as she saw how light it had become. She crouched in hiding and replaced the floorboards. Her task done, Kïtashii turned nose down to the ground and simply let go of the branch. She fell silently into the gloom and made her way back home.

Her mother's tree house lay hushed and silent. Kïtashii slipped through the curtain and tried to creep back into bed.

"Kïtashii?"

Mother! Kïtashii froze. "Uh... Mama?"

A sleepy voice yawned somewhere in the dark. "Draw water for tea and get breakfast going. Must I do everything?"

Kïtashii felt her spirits wilt. "There's last night's bread, Mama. There—there isn't anything more!"

"Then go dig in the gardens. And weave more mats for sale!" The woman snorted and rolled over in her bed.

Kïtashii looked toward the pile of half finished rugs. "I have to dance today, Mama! It's important. There's five rugs made already. You can sell them today. I'll do the rest tonight, really I will!"

"You do the work I give you. We'll cure you of this dancing."

Kïtashii bowed her head and wandered out into the morning light. Behind her, the baby cried as her mother went back to sleep.

Flying possum.

It was a flying possum—a little creature no bigger than a mouse. Shadarii lay back on the floor and looked at the tiny creature through befuddled eyes. The world turned beneath her as the sun began to shine. The bad time of the night had passed, and everything was good again.

Sun. Nice sun to warm her. Sun and a little possum high in the sky.

She beamed dreamily as she held out her loving hands. The tiny possum sprang from the skylight and wafted down into Shadarii's grasp. The dancer gave a sigh and held the creature to her breast, where the little possum promptly snuggled into a ball and went to sleep.

A cup rose and dipped into the water bucket, then drifted down into Shadarii's hand. She drank carefully, trying not to wake the sleeping possum. It dozed like a little baby, quite oblivious to the world.

A baby...

Shadarii liked babies. She was going to have one soon—gray, like the possum. She was going to make the baby for someone very special. A very special present all her own...

A present for whom?

Shadarii floated the possum high in the air and softly placed it in the rafters. It would be safe there. The blonde girl wouldn't see it.

Her head whirled. Thinking made her feel sick. It was nice once the sun came up. Soon it would be food time again, and everything would feel good and lazy.

No, she wasn't going to eat the food today. Why ever not? She felt so very hungry, and her head had begun to hurt. It always hurt when they took too long with the meal....

Something scraped at the door. Shadarii rolled, saliva running from her mouth. A figure came and stood inside the door; buckets clanged—water splashed, and the delicious scent of breakfast filled the room. The door slammed tight, and Shadarii made the food box slide across the floor toward her.

It was porridge! Shadarii dizzily sat up, her face alight as she dipped her paw into the nice warm goo. She closed her eyes and touched the food to her lips.

No.

Shadarii frowned and put down her hand, the food slopping back into the bowl. Moving with elaborate care, she tipped it out through a hole in the floor.

Now, why had she done that? Shadarii slumped against the wall and stared into space, her eyes troubled. The sun streamed down across her fur, but this time it brought no glow of comfort.

Her head hurt. Her senses swam.

Something was terribly wrong.

Power recoiled in Zhukora's mind; she clutched her skull and bared her fangs. "What? What is it?"

Serpent hissed, *She fights me! This creature has true power! I hurt...*

"Fighting you?" Zhukora unsheathed her claws. "Don't be ridiculous!"

She sits and watches me! When I approach her, she attacks. Her overmind is not properly subdued.

Daimïru lifted the lantern and came swiftly to Zhukora's side. "Zhukora! What is it?"

"The bitch is fighting us! Somehow her mind's still active. Serpent just took a beating! What went wrong? Did she take her food?"

"Every scrap. It was the usual dosage."

"Damn! Why did I pin any hopes on this stupid cripple? Was there something unusual today?"

"She was pacing around the cage all day. She's never even moved a muscle any other time."

Zhukora clenched her hand about the handle of her dao. "Our schedule is tight! We have only one more night to work on her. After that, the high priestess will come."

"We can do without the priests! They have no place in our new order."

"They are a tumor we shall slice from the heart of our society!" Zhukora whirled and slammed her fist against a wall. "I'll see their blood run in rivers! We shall tear them apart, just as they have torn our people into classes!" The girl's wild eyes froze. She unclenched her fists, her breathing calming. "For now, we need them. They legitimize us in the eyes of king and council. We can't move against them until we're more secure."

They turned back to the wretched creature shivering on the floor. Shadarii's fur lay dull and matted, and she twitched in her sleep, lips drawn back from her fangs. Zhukora sneered down at the little dancer. "We'll come back to finish her tomorrow. I'll conquer her if I have to burn her mind out like a husk! Double the dosage—and double the guards! I want nothing to go wrong tomorrow night." The two women whirled and left Shadarii to her sleep.

Shadarii jerked fitfully on the floor, her body battling the pull of drugs. The girl dragged memories from their hiding places and swelled them out with power. In time, Shadarii had found a name—a face—a feeling.

Kotaru...

The girl's hands clenched into fists as her dreams drove on.

Zhukora and Daimïru whirred through the night skies. Kïtashii emerged from cover, watched them go, looked about herself, and felt the stillness of the night. There would never be a better time than now.

Kïtashii bent to pick up her belly pack. With her tongue slyly touched against her lips, the little girl edged through the shadows of her mother's lodge.

"So! A little nighttime stroll, Kïtashii?"

The girl gave a convulsive jerk of fright and whirled.

Mistress Traveesha!

The dance mistress loomed above her like a storm. Kïtashii blinked as she saw her mother standing in the background.

"Well Kïtashii? Have you nothing to say?"

Kïtashii helplessly tried to open her mouth.

Mistress Traveesha's eyes narrowed as she glared down at her victim. "Well, since you're so active tonight, perhaps we should have a little talk. It seems your dance career is not as important to you as we all thought! Let's chat about your future as a gardener or a weaver, shall we?"

Kïtashii sobbed, tears streaming down her eyes. She tried to back away. Traveesha caught a fistful of silver hair and twisted it until Kïtashii squealed.

"Yes, a little talk will benefit us all. First I think your mother wants a word or two about stealing from the family larder."

Her mother scythed a jagged cane through the air and started toward her weeping daughter. Kïtashii sobbed and jerked in terror. Traveesha dragged her down across a log and ripped away her skirt. The cane struck; Kïtashii flung back her head and wept in silence, too proud to scream.

Traveesha watched in sickly fascination. If she couldn't have Shadarii, she'd have this skinny little wretch instead! The mistress laughed in the darkness as the punishment went on.

Thirteen

The world swooped and spun as Shadarii tried to bring her senses under control. She reeled and shook her head, fighting the fog from her brain.

Where was she?

Shadarii blinked and screwed her eyes shut tight, and then tried to focus once again. Something had hit her head—she remembered it. Shadarii put her hand to her skull. No lump, no pain, no sign of a wound... The girl dragged in a breath and tried to still her whirling mind. Something felt wrong—something was missing.

Kotaru!

The dancer drew a breath. Kotaru! Where was he? What had happened? Zhukora must have found them at the cave. What then? Shadarii had memories of Kïtashii whispering to her in the gloom. She stared around the empty lodge in sudden understanding; Kïtashii must have come to speak to her. Something—something about escape.

Where was Kotaru? Kïtashii would know! Shadarii whirled to face the door, her green eyes flashing fire. She had been attacked, drugged, betrayed! Pity help anyone fool enough to come between her and her love.

Shadarii lowered her head and spread her hands, looking clean through the walls of her prison and out into the currents of the world. It was dawn; there were two guards outside the house and a lock upon the door. The guards were coming closer, a box of food and a bucket of water swinging from their hands.

Breakfast time.

Shadarii took stock of her prison, seeing a lavatory bucket, an empty food box, and a heavy wooden water pail.... She curled up beside the water bucket and softly closed her eyes, feigning sleep.

Locks grated as the door swung open. Her guards plodded across the floor. "Hey, cripple! Breakfast!"

A girl's voice sneered cruelly. "Aaaah she'll never hear you. They doubled her dosage. She's out like a lamp."

"She's filthy! Her ladyship Shadarii-Zho. So much for the mighty!"

The female spoke again—a thin, high voice that held a strange ring of fanaticism. "My mother whored herself to nobles to find the food to feed us! I listened to her squealing in the bed like a pig in rut!" She kicked Shadarii in the ribs. "They've preyed on us like larvae burrowing through flesh. Priests, chiefs, kings.... We'll pour their blood across the ground in rivers. Zhukora will lead us on into an age of justice!"

The first voice gave a snort. "We should be out there training. Instead we're stuck here wiping some damned cripple's arse."

"We serve the Dream. And if this trash will help make it live, I'll wipe its arse and blow its nose—even kill it if I have to. I just wish she'd give me a reason! Attempting escape... or even calling for help!"

Shadarii's felt a chill ripple down her spine, and her fingers fastened about the handle of the empty water bucket.

"...well here's a rag! You can give her a bath since you feel so keen. I say we should let her fester in her own muck until she..."

Shadarii erupted from the floor, the bucket lashing out to crash across the guardsman's skull. She grabbed his throat and smashed his head against a post, feeling him turn slack beneath her claws. She ripped the dao out of his belt and spun to face her other foe.

The room seemed stuck in time. Shadarii's eyes blazed. Rage took hold of her again.

The girl snarled in hate and hurtled a spear straight at Shadarii's eyes. It cleaved slowly through the air—a smooth, dreamy arc. Shadarii let it fly past, feeling the flow of energy around her. She rode the streams and her whole soul came ablaze with brilliant color.

Shadarii moved between the huntress and the door, blocking her escape. Her enemy reached for a second spear. Shadarii whipped around in a circle and cracked the flat of her blade against the other woman's skull, bowling her down across the floor.

Kotaru.

Both enemies lay unconscious; Shadarii spread her wings and launched herself into the sky, a dozen spirits glittering at her tail.

Kïtashii wept, tears soaking into her bed. Her backside leaked blood from a maze of cuts, and she sobbed in agony with every move. She was sickened—numbed by a horror she had never thought possible. Any parent who dared do such a crime would once have been hurled from the tribe! Yet, here she lay, torn to ribbons while Traveesha watched and laughed from the shadows.

Kïtashii clawed her bed in shame. She had failed Shadarii. Her friend had needed her, and she had failed. Kïtashii trembled, her shocked mind struggling to make a plan.

A sudden scratching sound came from the door behind her. The little girl screwed shut her eyes and felt her spirits tremble. Rain—please don't let her hit me again! Kïtashii didn't know if she could bite back the agony a second time. She cringed upon her bed and tried to hide beneath the covers, her whole world turning gray with fear.

A hand touched her. It was a caress like sighing music, stroking lovingly across her face, pouring care and comfort into her soul. Kïtashii blinked in wonder; her mother had never touched her so in all her days. Her antennae rose as she felt something pure dawning within her heart.

Shadarii!

Blessed ïsha flooded across her flesh, washing away the memory of pain. Kïtashii buried her face against a soft expanse of fur. She gave a sob and wound her fingers down into the warmth.

"I—I failed you. I tried to come and help you, but I failed." The caress of healing never faltered, and the last of her pain began to fade. Still Kïtashii wept. Her heart filled with shame and anger as she clutched her skinny arms about Shadarii's waist.

"You're going to go away again. You have to. Kotaru's not here, so you have to go and find him."

The little girl rested her face against Shadarii's heart. "I believe in you, Shadarii. You're all I have. Take me with you. Let me help you find Kotaru. I want to be with you."

Kïtashii felt herself being clothed, and soft hands combed the tangles from her hair. The little girl looked up into Shadarii's haunted eyes. "I won't ever fail you again. Not as long as I live, I swear!"

Shadarii reached out to take Kïtashii's hand. Together they walked through the door and rose into the sky, flying off toward the distant Vakïdurii lands.

က ဠ ၈

"Gone! Two guards are down." Wings spread in a formal bow, Daimïru glittered in the firelight. "She has a day's lead on us."

Sitting cross-legged on a tree fern log, Zhukora seemed darker than the night all about her. Black fur gleamed like liquid silk. She regarded her beloved with cool blue eyes. "Both guards down?"

"Knocked unconscious, and the Ka inside the lodge tree refuses to speak! Shadarii may have had an accomplice who helped her escape."

"Or perhaps not. I begin to see why the priests were so avid to make her theirs." Zhukora finished polishing her spear and stroked the chittering spirit in the weapon with her mind. The white tip of her tail switched slowly in the gloom. "The priests we can deal with—I will neutralize them tomorrow. But Shadarii remains a problem. Her escape is inconvenient. She cannot be allowed to return."

"I can find her, Zhukora. It's not hard to guess where she has gone. She cannot know her lover is dead. She will eventually seek Kotaru at the cave where they made love."

The leader's cool blue eyes looked out on the stars. Zhukora sighed and let the forest breeze blow through her hair. "You are my one, my only. You are the better half of me, Daimïru. I must ask you to kill for me again. Do you mind, my love? There is no one else I can trust."

"Ask and I shall give. I do it out of love for you."

Zhukora's gaze grew troubled; she turned away and slowly bowed her head. "Kill her quickly, Daimïru. This is not her fault. She... is still my sister. It would be a... kindness to ensure she does not suffer...."

"Zhukora? Are you all right?" Daimïru hesitantly approached.

The black huntress squeezed shut her eyes and rubbed a hand across her brow. "The first one was easy, Daimïru. But it just goes on and on! Each death leads to another. Prakucha, Javïra, Kotaru. Now my own sister must die. She... must! It's the only way we can be safe."

"I'll do it, Zhukora. I promise you it will be quick."

"Sacrifices must be made if great dreams are to live. I must take the guilt upon myself so that our people can be free." Zhukora reeled and wiped her lashes. "Guilt must... It must be mine. In the end, it must be only I..." Zhukora raised her eyes.

"Stay with me tonight, just for a little while? Stay and watch the stars. I sleep better when I know you are near."

"I'll fetch my pipes, and we'll sing, like we always used to."

"Thank you, Daimïru. Thank you for your kindness."

The two hunters sighed and looked back up at the moon. Somewhere in the forest, their prey was waiting.

03 80 80

Kïtashii pushed her way between the bushes and brushed her skirt to remove travel stains. The skinny girl then walked boldly through the Vakïdurii village, approached a washer woman, and gave a solemn little bow. "Pray, excuse me, Madam. I am looking for a hunter called Kotaru. Do you know where I might find him?"

The woman scrubbed her wet hand across her cheek, blinking in surprise. "Kotaru? Kotaru? Rain, no, child! No relative of mine!"

"Please, Madam, it's very important I find him. He's a jiteng player for the Wrens."

"Wrens, eh?" The woman peered suspiciously at the child. "You don't sound like you're from around these parts."

"I'm from another village. Please, I have a message for Kotaru."

"Ha! Well if it's jiteng players you're after, the royal village is the place. Our fine new king's been holding games and feasts for the better part of a week!"

"I bid you good day, Madam. Thank you for your help." Kïtashii turned to go.

The washer woman calmly put aside her chores. "Katakanii by the look of you. And not a scrap of food's been past your lips for the better part of a week. By yer 'ma'am's and manners' I'd say you were a dancer. You have the look about you." She wrung out her dripping laundry, her eyes fixed on Kïtashii's face. "Now what brings a wee girlie so many days from home?"

Kïtashii began to walk away.

The woman propped her hand on her chin. "Going already, lass? And what if I were to tell our hunters there are Katakanii poaching on our land?"

"It would be a lie, and it would do you no good. You'd need more than mere hunters to find us."

"Us? Aaah, so there's more than one of you. I thought I saw a pair of green eyes watching from them trees." The washer woman poked a finger at Kïtashii's nose. "You're skinny as a snake! When did you last eat. Come on, out with it!"

Kïtashii gulped. "We...we ate... maybe the day before yesterday. Shadarii found us eggs. I think Shadarii hadn't eaten for a day before we left."

"Sweet Rain, girl! Get your friend and come along. The wind's passing between your ribs." The woman thrust at Kïtashii's skinny rump. "Well, go on, go on! I'll not have a pair of corpses on my conscience. I'll swap thee a meal for a smile—I never seen such a grim, wee face. Go on!"

Some time later, the travelers slumped beside a fire. The sensations of warmth and food wove a drowsy spell. Shadarii blinked her eyes and let Kïtashii drag the knots out of her filthy fur. Kïtashii worked on in silence.

The washer woman spared nothing. Tea bubbled on the hearth, yams steamed in the ashes, warm sleeping robes were piled beneath Shadarii's rump. The dancer hung her head and felt her world spin dizzily around her. Hope blazed in her heart. She had escaped her sister. She had broken through the dreams and darkness. Kotaru might be only a hundred spans away! Shadarii smiled even while her head nodded to her chest.

Kïtashii dragged a ball of fluff out of her comb and went on with her grooming.

The Vakïdurii woman looked at Shadarii's face and pulled her chin. "She looks tired. She doesn't say much, does she?"

Kïtashii's voice rang strangely soft and cool. "No. No, she doesn't say much."

"She looks a strange one. Eyes like a poet, soul of a healer."

"She's not like you and I, Pekaka. She's not the same as anybody."

The comb moved in hypnotic patterns down Shadarii's fur, and Kïtashii stared at the even furrows left gleaming in its wake. She sighed as Pekaka reached out to touch her hair. Strong hands lowered her down onto a sleeping mat and tucked her beneath a robe. The little girl fell asleep before her head even touched the ground.

Shadarii dozed where she sat. Pekaka went back to tending her hearth fire, hardly sparing either of her guests a glance.

An old woman sat across the coals, her arms firmly locked across her scrawny breast. "I don't like it! We ought to tell the chief. Ragtag foreigners sittin' on our doorstep? It just ain't done!"

Pekaka shot a sour glance at her mother. "We keep 'em here. There's more to all this than meets the eye. They've come running, and they're welcome beneath my roof until I say otherwise."

The old woman scuttled closer and pawed at Shadarii's wings until Pekaka slapped her hands away. "Get your damned hands off!"

"I weren't doin' nothin'!"

"Well, see that you don't! That girl's quality, she is, so keep your mitts to yerself!"

"I was just seein' if the color rubs off! How do you know she's quality? She might be havin' us on."

"She's quality and she's staying, so don't get no ideas!"

"Well I don't like it!"

"You don't have to, you mad old crone. Just tend the fire while I go out. I'm off to find someone who knows these jiteng players the wee girl was on about."

Pekaka gathered her shoulder bag and made to leave. "I'm not of a suspicious mind, Ma. Still, if I even hear a hint that you've spread word that these two are here, I'll send you to my sister. We'll see how well you fare with that bitch as your host!"

The old woman shrank back. She grumbled and bent down to turn the tubers in the fire.

"Aaah, be off with you! I'll guard yer two precious little vagabonds, never fear."

"Just see that you do, old hag. I'm sure m' sister's just itchin' for your company."

"Shadarii?"

Shadarii twitched, snuggling deeper into her sleeping robe.

The voice came back to croon sweetly in her ear. "Shadarii, wakey wakey!"

Mmmmmm... wake up time. Kotaru's scent still lingering in her nostrils, the stiffness of newly discovered muscles in her thighs. Shadarii snuggled down in bed and gave a sigh. Kotaru...

"Come along, then! Rise and shine!"

Shadarii's eyes flickered open. Sunlight danced across her fur, dazzling her. She ran a hand through her pelt and tried to make sense out where she was. Just to make matters worse, someone ruffled her fur and boisterously kissed her on the cheek.

"Good morning, your ladyship! And what a great pleasure it is to have you join us at last. I never knew the dead could walk until I saw your face!"

Shadarii was kissed soundly on the mouth. The girl pushed away and stared up at a grinning face, trying to force the world into some sort of sense.

Mrrimïmei!

The Vakïdurii girl grinned down at her, laughing as she saw recognition finally dawn. Shadarii flung her arms about the other girl and crushed her in a hug. She looked about and saw all her friends beside her again—Mrrimïmei, Totoru, Tingtraka the scholar girl...

"Ha ha! Shadarii! So, finally you're here! Better late than never, eh? You've had us worried sick. We almost went out on the rescue operation of the century!" The girl ran fingers through Shadarii's fur. "So, where is he? Where have you hidden him, you silly girl? Is Kotaru safe and well?"

Something cold slithered through Shadarii's heart. She let Mrrimïmei's hands drop, and the Vakïdurii girl slowly lost her smile.

"He—he's not with you, is he?"

Shadarii simply stared. It was impossible! Kotaru must be here—he had to be! She had escaped, she had come to him! It was all right now. It was all going to be all right.

"Shadarii, listen to me! Where is Kotaru?" Mrrimïmei angrily shook Shadarii by the shoulders. "Shadarii! Tell me! Damn you, what's happened to him!"

Totoru gently forced his fiancé back. "Ssssh. Can't you see? She thought he was here. Something's happened. Something bad."

"She did it!" Mrrimïmei slammed her fist against a tree. "I told him to leave her alone... !"

"Quiet!"

Shadarii desperately tried to think. Kotaru wasn't here, and he wasn't back at the Katakanii village. She would go back to the cave and trace his trail. Shadarii leapt up and began to dress in her filthy leathers. Kïtashii silently joined her, hastily snatching their paltry belongings.

"Kïtashii, wait! Where are you going?"

The little girl hastened to tie back Shadarii's hair. "She knows. Where she goes, I follow. I'll not leave her ever again!"

"But—but you're only twelve years old!"

"Shadarii needs me." Kïtashii bowed deeply to their hosts, and Pekaka bowed back in bewilderment.

Shadarii took her friend by the hand and scrabbled for the door, jiteng players stumbling in her wake.

"Stop! Shadarii…"

Shadarii swiftly took her bearings and spread out her shining wings.

Mrrimïmei leapt in her way. "No. I'm comin' with you!" Shadarii tried to wave the girl aside, but Mrrimïmei hissed and stood her ground. "I'm coming! He's more ours than yours! You'll not find a way of stopping me!"

Kïtashii narrowed her eyes and glared at the Wrens. She snapped her fingers. "We'll wait an hour, no more. Get your equipment."

Shadarii whirled, but Kïtashii folded her arms and stared the dancer in the eye. "I said I will never fail you. That includes letting you rush off like a fool. I will serve you despite yourself."

The Wrens flew off to fetch their gear.

Shadarii gave a snort. She bit back a thudding headache and signed curtly to the little girl. *Why don't you leave me alone?*

"Because you need me."

Shadarii turned away and irritably shook her wings.

Kïtashii sat down to bide her time. "Is there a route Zhukora's men won't expect?"

Shadarii irritably screwed shut her eyes. *Two ïsha streams slash past each other in the river gorge. The gap between them is only one span wide.*

"Can we take the battering?"

I can. The rest of you can go get stuffed.

"Very nice. We love you, too." Kïtashii cast an eye toward the hearth hut and scratched beneath her scrawny ribs. "Ah well, at least this way we get some breakfast. Let's see if there's any of those roots left over from last night." The little girl scratched again, wondering if she might have fleas. "Might not be such a bad idea after all. Pekaka's mother might be an old witch, but she can certainly brew a cup of tea."

Fourteen

The little band of hunters flew through a screaming maelstrom. Shadarii plunged ahead of them, swooping down cataracts and riding shock waves along the gorge. Kïtashii grimly drove the Vakïdurii on, darting back and forth behind the hunters like an angry little gnat.

Spray flashed. Shadarii banked beneath a spur of rock, diving with the river as it plunged down a waterfall. She disappeared into the roaring mists.

The Wrens pulled up in alarm, eyes fixed in panic on the sheer drop of two hundred spans. Kïtashii shot past them and tumbled in Shadarii's wake. The Wrens followed, staring straight down into destruction. Someone gave a yell as they struck the wall of mist. One by one, the Wrens shot out of the spray—eleven frightened faces taking stock and counting limbs.

Shadarii skimmed above the surface far downstream, her ïsha wake splitting the water behind her like a knife.

They had flown like maniacs for two whole days. Shadarii never tired. She pushed herself to impossible speeds, uncaring whether anyone followed. The girl now circled high onto a cliff and went to ground, and the other Kashra pursued her in an exhausted blur of wings.

Hunters collapsed on the grass while Mrrimïmei folded over, almost vomiting with fatigue. Shadarii ignored it all. She saw a familiar cliff face across the river and reeled for joy. The cave was only a hundred spans away! The girl spread her wings and soared toward her goal.

Kïtashii lunged into Shadarii's path and instantly brought her teacher to a halt. "Stop! We don't know what's down there. Zhukora might have come looking for us!"

Shadarii whirled, antennae twitching as she searched for ïsha traces. She stiffened. Subtle currents were hidden in the shade.

Kashra lay in concealment near the cave mouth. They were extremely skilled; the Wrens had noticed nothing. Shadarii picked out her enemies one by one and sank down into cover.

"Kïtashii, what is it? What can she see?"

"Hunters." The little girl crept back across the ridge. "Twenty of them hiding below."

Tingtraka hunched in the dust, her chest heaving as she tried to catch her breath. "Hunters? You mean Skull-Wings? So, what the skreg do we do now?"

Kïtashii ran fingers through her tangled hair. Her arms trembled with fatigue, and the river sounded cool and soothing at her back. "I don't know. Let's rest for an hour—wait for dark. Maybe we'll think of something by then."

The Wrens collapsed. Here and there, a hunter groped for a drinking gourd. Shadarii lay on a rock and stared down toward her enemies.

Kïtashii closed her eyes and sighed. They had until sunset. She had to devise a plan, something to draw the guards away. Now, what would make a Skull-Wing want to leave his post... ?

CR &D &D

"It's never going to work! Mrrimïmei, don't be ridiculous!" Tingtraka wrung her face in distaste next morning as she watched her teammate stepping into Shadarii's clothing.

Mrrimïmei rammed grass into the halter top in an attempt to mold herself into Shadarii's shape.

"Mrrimïmei, don't go!"

"Ha! You're just jealous!"

"It was my idea! I have red fur, too!"

"You're not fast enough. No one flies faster than me! Kotaru's in trouble, so I'm damned-well going!" The girl shoved more grass beneath the belt of her borrowed skirt. "Anyway, you have black hair. They'd spot you a mile away!" Mrrimïmei tightened the belts and straps. "There we are, all ready to go! Now, let's get this over and done with."

Mrrimïmei jittered with excitement, having difficulty even sitting still. Shadarii delicately dabbed the girl's wings with bright ochre dust. They would soon shed their color, but for a brief while, they could fool the waiting enemy.

Mrrimïmei rose and gazed through the trees.

"Right! We all ready?" Nods came all around. "All right, then! I'll be off. Give me a fist of seconds, and then move out."

The girl spared a warm kiss for her fiancé, and then rose high into the air. She glared down at Shadarii before disappearing into the shadows.

Shadarii checked her knives, paced in silence, and scowled as she counted off the seconds.

Eight, nine, ten...

Tingtraka dug her spear tip in the ground.

"I still say I should have gone! I'm fast, too! What if the Skull-Wings catch her?"

Totoru whirled and looked at her; the girl saw his eyes and wisely shut her trap.

Thirteen, fourteen...

"What if they don't all follow her? What if some of them stay by the cave?" Rotïka tugged nervously at his mask straps. The tiny little man had spoken for them all, and the ten remaining Wrens swapped nervous glances, slowly fingering their weapons.

Eighteen, nineteen...

Kïtashii hefted a borrowed spear. "Does anybody have another spear? I think I can throw one just a little way."

Totoru coldly folded his arms. "Oh, no, not you! You're stayin' right where you are."

Shadarii glared at the huge hunter and gave a sharp snap of her hands.

She comes. She has the right.

It was time to go. Shadarii tugged at her borrowed hunting leathers and took to the air. The other Kashra swiftly leapt to join her. They clattered off into the shadows, following the gleam of Mrrimïmei's ïsha trail.

A hunter gripped Daimïru's arm. The girl went stiff, her breath hissing as she glimpsed motion in the clearing. A figure wandered out into the open, walking cautiously across the broken stones. Sunlight shone from a pair of startling orange wings.

Shadarii!

Damn! She stood in the only place where Daimïru's men were out of reach. The open rock face had offered them no place to hide. Shadarii stood well out of spear cast. She was among clumps of mountain ash, small trees surrounded by great mats of resin, leaves, and crackling bark. It would be impossible to creep up on her by foot. Daimïru chafed, casting a quick glance all along the waiting line of hunters.

A twig snapped beneath a hunter's heel.

Down on the rocks, the prey's antennae swiveled and then stopped. Suddenly, Shadarii shot into the sky and raced downstream.

Daimïru burst from the trees. "Don't let her get away! Kill her! Kill Shadarii!" She hurtled herself into the pursuit.

Twenty hunters thundered on Shadarii's trail.

Mrrimïmei swept out to hover high above the riverbanks, staying just long enough to be seen before dashing through the ferns. The Skull-Wings took the bait and shrieked for her blood. Mrrimïmei gave a snort and whirled off through the trees, leaving her pursuers far behind.

"All right, they've gone! Fan out and look for trails!" Kïtashii and her friends spread out across the clearing to comb for ïsha spoor.

Shadarii dashed up the slopes and plunged into the deserted cave. Her fur shivered as a thousand memories whirled into her mind: Kotaru's smile, Kotaru's laugh, the pain, the joy, the ecstasy! The girl squandered ïsha in her wild search for clues.

"Shadarii! Be careful, someone will see the light!"

Shadarii never even heard; she thrust past Kïtashii and scrabbled up the rocks. They had only minutes before Zhukora's hunters returned; Shadarii chewed her fist and tried to think just what to do.

Tingtraka carefully sifted through the ïsha auras of the cave, and then followed the trail back to the little alcove where Shadarii and Kotaru had made love. After long minutes, the girl drew back in defeat. "It's too faint for me. I just don't know where to find his trail. If he'd only left a mark—a clue!"

Kïtashii paced swiftly back and forth, her face drawn into its customary frown. "We must find where he left the clearing. Shadarii, where did you last see him? Retrace those steps. Relive the moment."

Shadarii closed her eyes and tried to remember. The sun had shone; there had been cool, fresh water. She had smiled and waved. Something had smashed against her skull, the teapot shattering in her hand as she fell...

The water hole!

Shadarii whirled and dashed down among the boulders. The girl thrilled as she retraced her actions, move by move. She had stood right here in this spot. She had turned and looked straight back toward... Kotaru...

Icy scorpions scuttled up her spine. Shadarii's whole world narrowed as her gaze settled on a single darker patch of shadow. She found herself moving toward it, staring without comprehension. She gazed down, unable to make sense of the horror at her feet. A strange, light-hearted trance settled across her mind. She fell slowly to her knees, her head cocked as she peered at the weird thing in the grass.

It lay like a burnt, dead log—foul, rotten, and violated... shriveled... desiccated, like meat left too long on a fire. Shadarii reached out to run her fingers across the ashes. She slowly sank across the corpse, clutching the stinking thing to her. It fractured as she clawed at it in incoherent agony.

Kotaru! No! Not my Kotaru!

Tingtraka sank into the dust, her eyes drained of hope. Kïtashii hung back, terrified of intruding on either woman's grief. The little girl tried not to weep, stifling her tears. She mustn't cry! They needed her. Someone had to be strong! Someone had to be strong! Someone had to…

Shadarii slammed herself against the corpse, willing it to break and stab her through the heart. She tried to rip her dao from its sheath, but small, strong arms wrapped about her. Kïtashii dragged Shadarii back from the corpse and held her tight.

"Hold me! Hold onto me! Don't let go." Kïtashii rocked the older woman back and forth just like a baby.

Tingtraka hesitantly approached, tears leaving wet tracks through her dusty fur. The Vakïdurii hunters stared in disbelief at Kotaru's corpse. "We have to go now. We have to run."

Kïtashii hung her head. "Not yet. She can't go yet."

Shadarii threw back her head and tried to shriek Kotaru's name. *Why! Why can't I scream? Oh, my love, I can't even scream for thee!*

"Shadarii, look out!"

Shadarii's head snapped around in time to see a figure framed against the rocks. The creature stared down at her and staggered back in shock.

"Daimïru! Leader, she's here! Shadarii is here!"

The Skull-Wing shot into the air to find reinforcements. Kïtashii hurtled a spear with all her might. It arced up and struck the hunter, jabbing beneath his wing. The Skull-Wing fell into an ash tree. He whirled around to fix his blazing eyes upon Kïtashii. His woomera flashed forward, and Kïtashii could only gape as a spear streaked straight toward her breast.

Shadarii flung herself in the way. The spear tore to splinters as ïsha blasted it from the air. With a silent scream of rage, Shadarii lunged for the Skull-Wing's throat.

"Shadarii, stop! What are you doing?"

The Skull-Wing screamed and punched out with his aura. Flame showered the dried leaves at Shadarii's feet. The girl smashed her enemy's head against a tree and hurtled the unconscious body aside into the dirt.

Sparks caught in the tinder. The ash trees erupted in flame. Shadarii and the Wrens dragged their unconscious enemy aside, too stunned to fight the blaze. The trees, one by one, were swallowed up in the spreading fire. Their seed pods burst, showering kernels across the blazing soil.[26] Kotaru's corpse was suddenly engulfed by a spreading storm of flame.

The Wrens backed away. Brush fires spread into the surrounding forest. Soon, the entire mountaintop would be engulfed in flame. Shadarii stared as the funeral pyre closed over her beloved's corpse, the hilltop disappearing beneath the blaze.

She let the others take her away. They drew her into the forest and left the cliff top to its fate.

ᙳ ᙭ ᙭

"Snake! Conniving whore! Down on your face and pray we look on your soul with mercy!" The high priestess foamed with rage as she whirled and pointed a commanding finger at Zhukora's heart. "Did you think we would forgive? Did you think we would do nothing?" The priestess gave a laugh. "We'll have our due, Zhukora! We'll have Shadarii, or we'll smash you into the dust. I can snap you like a twig! Prakucha's death condemns you. One word from me, and you are finished!"

Zhukora leaned against a lodge post, holding back a fit of laughter. She looked like a schoolgirl trying to hide her giggles from the teacher.

The high priestess looked around her ring of acolytes in shock.

Lamplight made weird shapes in the darkness, and Zhukora's shadow flickered with an evil energy. No one saw the warning. The high priestess knew nothing but her own blinding fury. "Prakucha's death hangs over thee, girl! From this day forth, your life is at my whim! We were to be partners. Hand in hand, we could have ruled this tribe! Well, now those days are fled. We will use you, girl! You will be our puppet. The moment you fail to please me, your life is gone!" The high priestess swept out her wings. "Did you really think we—aaaahk!"

Something smashed the priestess into the air and crucified her on a blaze of lightning. She tried to scream. Her mouth half opened, but she choked on her swollen tongue.

With a vague air of amusement; Zhukora strolled around her victim, as though examining an extraordinary exhibit. Serpent swirled around her shoulders, filling the ïsha with writhing shapes of dark.

The priestess's fur began to smoke.

Zhukora clasped her hands behind her back and coolly turned to face the priests. "Now, I shall tell you the way of the future. I shall tell you because you are stupid creatures driven only by your greed. You have betrayed our tribe; you have betrayed the Kashran race. You will now serve the destiny of the people, or I shall slaughter you like insects, one by one."

A priest beside Kanoohï bared his fangs in rage and sent his spirit "rider" leaping through the air. "Die, witch!" A bolt of lightning lanced for Zhukora's heart.

---

[26]**Fire Trees:** The most spectacular of the flowering trees are children of the Fire spirit. The seeds are actually germinated only after passing through the intense heat of a fire. The cycle of fire and regrowth is thus central to the ecology.

She contemptuously flicked the blow aside, and the priest squawked in shock as his power flashed and died. Serpent drew a long, slow breath and rose like a cobra from Zhukora's shoulders. Beneath the enormous Ka, the priest shuddered. There came an agonized little whimper from the darkness, and Serpent sighed in delight. The Ka drew away and rippled in delicious satisfaction.

It left the priest sitting there, staring into space just like a corpse. A long string of drool gradually trailed down from his lips.

With luxurious sensuality, Zhukora caressed Lord Serpent as she addressed the priests. "I will warn you only once. Defy me, and I shall reduce you to a living death."

Behind her, the high priestess hung limp and empty. Her Ka was gone, sucked and eaten like a plump, delicious fruit. Zhukora looked up at her and softly smiled.

A dozen Skull-Wings slowly filed into the room. They stood behind the priests and awaited their leader's words of command.

Zhukora stared at the body of the high priestess and then walked slowly over to Kanoohï. The priest screwed shut his eyes, trembling in abject terror. Zhukora stood above him, disgusted by his cowardice.

"The high priestess has gone into seclusion to spend the last few days of her life. Kanoohï, she has passed her mantle on to you. Be glad, Kanoohï. Be glad! You are now high priest of the Katakanii."

Zhukora turned and began to walk away. She paused in the doorway, gazing back toward the priests. "Had you been people of vision, this would not have been necessary. Your pathetic power games disgust me. Where I saw famine and hardship, you saw only political advantage. You are unworthy to share the earth with the lowest gardener in the tribe.

"There is a power coming to this forest. I will not allow you to oppose the Kashran Dream."

She jerked her head toward her guards. "Take them. Guard them well. Kanoohï will now accompany me. He will explain to our king that the tribe must have an emissary—an ambassador to all the other tribes, and that the only ambassador the priesthood will accept shall be Zhukora." She looked coolly down toward the new high priest. "Kanoohï, do you understand?"

The man shook with fear.

"I-I obey!"

"Good. See that you do."

Zhukora turned and walked out into the dark. With a last glance toward the high priestess, Kanoohï scuttled hastily on her tail.

C3 &⊃ &⊃

A bitter wind swept across the empty hillside. Dust rattled in the blackened skeletons of trees. The gray light of dawn killed the last flickers of the coals.

Shadarii let the ashes bite her skin. Wind picked at her hair, snapping it out like tongues of flame. She ignored it all. Her mind turned blank; her eyes grew glazed; her breaths slowed to near stillness. Her whole world transformed into a wilderness of loss. Ashes swirled, hissing in her ears like the voices of the dead.

Slowly, she reached up behind herself and drew away her halter. Her skirt and moccasins followed—belt and beads, knives and pouches.

In utter silence, Kïtashii took her teacher's garments.

At last, Shadarii knelt naked in a field of ash. Two knives lay crossed on her lap. Shadarii slowly rose and faced the sun, then dug the knives beneath her ribs and drew them across her breasts. Blood traced bright trails across her fur. The girl closed her eyes and dragged a long slash through either cheek, blood mingling with her tears.

The girl began to dance. The dead trees wept. The wind moaned. Shadarii wove her slow ballet through the midst of the destruction. She ripped the knives across her flesh and stared into the clouds.

Kïtashii sat cross-legged in the dust, watching her beloved teacher dance. The little girl kept her wings folded down around her body like a velvet cloak, and sat with all the serenity of an acolyte at worship.

The Vakïdurii hunters were appalled. The Wrens watched in shock as Shadarii slowly tore great bleeding strips across her fur. Tingtraka sobbed in helpless agony, swaying to Shadarii's rhythm, her hands pressed against her skull.

"Oh, Rain and Poison, look at her! Why is she doing this? Why?"

Kïtashii's voice blew as soft and empty as a winter mist. "It is the Rekï'ka: The ghost dance. She dances for her dead."

"It's only supposed to be a tiny cut! A speck of blood! She's killing herself!"

"Pain can be a transcendental state. Shadarii will try to cross the barrier." The little girl never let her eyes wander from the dance. "Her world is dead. She needs to find new answers."

"Don't you understand? Look at the blood she's losing! She'll die!"

"If that is the answer that she finds, the choice is hers to make."

Tingtraka reeled in anguish. "We have to stop her! We can't let her do this to herself!"

"I swore never to fail my teacher again." Kïtashii drew her wings more tightly about her body. "I will not let you interfere."

Out among the ashes, Shadarii's dance went on. Long trails of red dripped down across her swirling ankles. She began to whirl faster. Ïsha pulsed like a churning storm; sparks spat and crackled at her feet; each fleck of blood began to smoke and steam with power.

Shadarii danced inside a haze of suffering. Slowly, the pain began to fade. The rhythm drove her on, the knives sliced across her flesh; she never even felt the cuts. It was beautiful! Shadarii lost herself in a mist of light, soaring high upon glorious wings of fire.

The world shifted—flowed like tree sap—and suddenly there was only silence. Exultation raged through Shadarii's heart as ïsha flowed around her in a living stream, each current filled with endless meaning.

She looked out upon utter serenity; a world of peace and drifting dreams. A loving presence shone down toward her from above, and Shadarii smiled and turned her face toward the light. She knelt in obeisance, raising her face toward the warmth.

I have sinned! I have turned to violence in the cause of love. Now my life is empty. Take me! Fill me or break me. I give myself utterly to thee....

The light shone down upon her with its love, lifting her, absolving her, filling her with peace. Rain streamed down into her fur, feeling cool and soft and soothing. The girl lifted her arms in adoration, sighing as she felt its ïsha pour into her soul. The Great Mother looked down on Shadarii's face and slowly raised a smile.

Shadarii's thoughts ran clear as water. She felt her mind free itself from pain. Shadarii marveled at the simple love that blazed inside her soul.

It was the peace that came with meaning. It was the beginning of a mission.

Mother Rain had blessed her with new questions, riddles that might take a lifetime to answer. Shadarii turned them over in her mind, her soul blazing bright with wonder.

I must discover why. What makes us want to kill? Why does my sister have the power to make us destroy each other? Why has a thousand years of peace now come to this?

As my sister has become the instrument of death, so I shall become the instrument of life. I must become a leader and a teacher. I must find a path to set my people walking hand in hand with Mother Rain.

I must do all these things, and then I shall finally be allowed to join my Kotaru in his grave.

Shadarii bowed before the light. She felt the mists swirl about her as she returned to the forest world.

Rain began to hiss into the ash, and Shadarii lifted her face to smile at the benediction. The little dancer slowly stood, her green eyes looking out with joy upon the world. It was as though she had never truly seen before. Shadarii walked toward her friends and wrapped them all within her love.

Mrrimïmei backed away in fear. Shadarii's skin was utterly unbroken; not a single wound or drop of blood showed on her fur. The Vakïdurii gasped, only to be held in place by Shadarii's loving smile.

Only one person showed no fear; Kïtashii knelt and covered her face with her little wings. Shadarii drew her student up and kissed the tears from her eyes. Kïtashii held Shadarii's hand and swayed in utter adoration.

"I will follow you, my teacher. Teach me the dance you dance."

Shadarii turned and wandered slowly north, heading toward the highest mountain peaks. Kïtashii gathered their goods and followed in silence. The two strange figures rose high into the air and softly fluttered out across the forest green.

In absolute bewilderment, Totoru stared after them. The ten other Vakïdurii looked to him for leadership. The hunter shook his head and tried to make sense of it all. "Where is she going? Across the mountains? There's nothing there but desert!"

Tingtraka jittered, eager to be off and flying. The girl's eyes were bright and full of joy. "Follow! She knows where she's going. Follow her!"

Mrrimïmei hissed in fright. "Don't be stupid! The girl's gone insane!"

"Insane? Didn't you see it? Didn't you feel it?"

Mrrimïmei glared at Tingtraka's eager face. "See what?"

"The Rain! The Rain fell on her. It fell on her, only!" Tingtraka stared after Shadarii, and then gave a gasp as a rainbow sprang out across the clouds. A wondrous arch of color sparkled in Shadarii's wake. "Look! A rainbow! A rainbow flowing from her!" The girl whirled and stared down at the others. "I'm going! Stay here if you want. Where she goes, I want to follow!"

With that, Tingtraka dashed off in Shadarii's path. One by one, the others followed, until finally only Totoru and Mrrimïmei still stood on the ground. The lovers clung together, staring anxiously at their departing friends.

Totoru twitched his tail. "I can't take you out there. We have a baby to think about! A future to plan!"

Mrrimïmei wept in agony. "We can't just leave them! They're all we have! What have we got to go back to?"

The lovers stared at one another. Finally they rose into the air, leaving the hillside to its memories and bones.

CS   හ   හ

Beneath bright, open skies, far from the forbidding edges of the forest, a young woman stood digging in the river for clams. She was a pretty little thing; a girl of gold with amber eyes and honey colored fur. Her blonde hair swept about her face, trimmed shorter on the left than on the right. A woolen skirt hung kilted above her muddy thighs, and her bare chest shone in the sun. The teenager sang gaily as she sank her wooden shovel in the silt, and a basket brimming with clams spoke of a morning's work well done. The girl whistled tunelessly through her teeth and bent to sift more tasty morsels from the muck.

Something heavy drifted slowly in the current. The girl stopped her whistling, gave a little frown, set aside her shovel, and waded through the river reeds. Her jaw dropped as she saw what slowly swam toward her. A gigantic catfish thrust downstream—a creature fully four spans long. Vast yellow eyes stared balefully up into her face, glaring straight into her soul.

A naked man lay draped across the creature's back, his green wings trailing in the water. Ïsha discharge arced up from the fish, wrapping the man in a wild blue net of sparks. He lolled deliriously, whimpering as he pawed the fish's scales.

The girl stared in shock, hardly flinching as the enormous fish cruised up beside her. The wounded man's breath rattled in his throat, and the Kashran girl reached out to touch his back. Raw ïsha alone must have kept the man alive; blood leaked from a blackened scar, trailing down to stain the water red.

She couldn't help herself; the girl reached out to drag him into her arms. She clutched him hard against herself and stared around in panic.

He was so beautiful—and a nobleman! Gray fur and a fine face... red blood smeared upon his mouth. The girl dragged him onto the banks as the fish slowly backed away. Roaring with the strain of it, she hauled him to the mud, then tore off her skirt and crammed it against the bleeding wound.

"Xartha! Xartha, come quickly!"

She blinked back tears, smearing one bloody hand across her face. "Xartha, you little bastard! Now! I need you. Hurry!"

A tiny girl stared out from the grass with owlish eyes. She saw her naked sister straddling a nobleman; Xartha's mouth flopped open, only to snap shut in shock as her eldest sister grabbed her by the tail.

"Don't just stand there! He's dying! Go fetch Papa." The clam-digger tore off Xartha's skirt and slapped her sister's naked rump. "Go find Papa. Tell him to bring the healers! Get your brothers to bring a stretcher. Quickly!"

The girl used her little sister's skirt to seal the man's wounds. Xartha ran for home as the clam digger clamped the makeshift bandages hard against her patient's side.

"Hold on, my lord, Harïsh is here! I'll not let you die! I'll not fail your fishy friend!" Blood soaked across her hands, and the girl wept and held on for all she was worth. Far off in the distance, the village came alive with shouts and panic. Harïsh ground her teeth together and poured her power down into the stranger's dreadful wounds.

Please, Rain... don't let him die....

Behind her, Grandfather Catfish swam down into the darkness. His duty done, he drifted back into his peaceful world.

Fifteen

The wet season came and went, bringing summer in its wake, and the world sizzled as cicadas filled the air with noise.

Daimïru and Zhukora hurtled themselves into their work. They gaily dashed from clan to clan on a dizzy tour of recruitment. Zhukora gathered the young folk, the impoverished and oppressed, giving them new hope through the simple power of her voice. Where she went, cheering followed; where she came to rest, followers appeared. Day by day, the people loved her more. She reached out to touch them with her dream, filling their empty hearts with purpose.

Zhukora could scarcely believe the new joys each day brought. Daimïru flew ever at her side, and a people's love surrounded her like a fiery blaze. New dawns saw her soaring high above the forest world, new territories drifting past her.

They were magic, precious days. The Dream had been planted in the minds of the people, and Zhukora tended it with love.

Unrest spread like a disease. With the passing seasons, hunger grew. Daimïru's elite Skull-Wing guards relentlessly trained themselves for combat. Each clan gained its nucleus of Skull-Wing warriors, selected from the finest hunters in the tribe. Zhukora smiled. Her time of destiny drew near.

బ   ఴ   ಎ

"A jiteng game? Why how terribly amusing. The Katakanii have a positive obsession!"

Idly sipping tea, King Teki'taa lounged on his cushions. He held out his cup, scarcely noticing the girl who hastened to serve his needs. The new king of the Vakïdurii favored his royal herald with a languorous smile. "So, Zhukora is outside? Do show her in! It's always such a pleasure to meet with old, old friends."

The herald bowed and hastened off to do as he was bid. Teki'taa patted the backside of his serving girl, becoming more than a little interested in his graceless explorations. The girl bore his touch in silence, her eyes screwed tightly shut as she swallowed back her shame.

Zhukora strode in, gleaming as cruel and magnificent as a hawk. Daimïru hovered at Zhukora's side, her slim face savage against her stark black uniform. King Teki'taa pursed his lips in appreciation, grinning as the woman met his eyes.

Delicious!

Teki'taa clapped his hands together, his voice rolling musically out across the air. "Zhukora! Or rather, Zhukora-Zho. What a delight to see you once again! Traders have already told us of your marvelous good fortune; ambassador, and at only twenty-five years of age! It seems that youth is finally gaining a hand in government!" The king showed no inclination to invite his guests to sit. "I presume there is a reason for this most delightful call. If you will dismiss your servant, we shall begin our discussion. Commoners are barred from the presence of the king."

Zhukora's face remained unmoved. "Daimïru is my chosen councilor. Surely as companion to an ambassador, she has the right to stay?"

"A commoner for a councilor? Really, Zhukora!" The king paddled his hands in a finger bowl and dried them on a towel. "Oh, I suppose the girl can stay. I'm sure her opinions will be amusing, at the very least...."

Zhukora sank to the floor, her long hair spilling down around her like a cloak of silk. She turned her pure blue eyes upon the King. "I have a certain amount of business with your tribe. It is tiresome, but I'm sure we'll soon be done."

Daimïru passed her a quirt,[27] and Zhukora made a great show of studying the first few cuts.

"Ah, yes. Firstly, my lord, there are allegations that Vakïdurii tribesmen have carried off two young dancers from our tribe. I am afraid there is evidence to sustain such accusations."

Tekï'taa steepled his fingers. "I should hate to contradict such a charming guest. One hesitates to point out that even if this were true, there is little that two female ambassadors could do about it." The king gave an evil smile.

Daimïru stirred, only to be stilled by a subtle motion of Zhukora's hand. Zhukora bathed Tekï'taa in the magic of her smile.

"Why, lord king! We rely only on your famous sense of fair play. Good relations between our tribes are to our mutual advantage."

"Maybe so, maybe so... but you find yourselves in Vakïdurii territory now. Here, my word is law!" King Tekï'taa swirled his teapot, pouring a drink for his guest. Zhukora cunningly passed the cup to Daimïru, forcing Tekï'taa to pour a second measure for herself.

"King Tekï'taa, my people feel they have grievances against your own. Whether we can substantiate these claims or not is quite irrelevant. The people believe they have been wronged, and so we must present their case. Justice must be done."

"Justice? For the people?" Tekï'taa sputtered in his tea. "A fine state of affairs when we are dictated to by a horde of flea-bitten commoners!"

Zhukora's tone grew hard. "They are the people, Lord. Surely they are the reason we hold power? Once we gain power, we also gain obligations."

"Obligations? Ha! Commoners have their duty, and I have my power! The situation suits us perfectly."

"Even so, Lord, my tribe demands a trial."

"Bah! Impossible!" The king insolently swirled his teacup in his hand. "A trial between two tribes? No judge could be trusted to vote against his or her own tribe. The case would never be resolved! No, no girl. You're speaking nonsense!"

"Lord King, we have no need for councils! Let Wind and Rain decide!" Zhukora's gaze glittered from beneath exquisite lashes. "We suggest a game of jiteng— your finest team against the Skull-Wings, here on your own home ground. The teams can meet in one month's time when our two tribes join together for the bo-

---

[27]**Quirt:** A mnemonic aid based upon the alpine "music sticks." A quirk is a stick whittled with marks, each mark representing a different message that the courier has leaned by rote.

gong feasts. Each tribe will wager an indemnity—say one field of yams. To the win-ner goes the spoils!"

"A game? Here, on our home ground?" Teki'taa licked his lips. "It could be a good idea at that!" The man leapt up and began to pace the floor. His popularity had suffered since he had taken on the kingship. Another field of yams would more than restore his position.

"Done! We'll hold the game at the end of the feasts. Unfortunately, the Wrens have been dissolved. No matter! The Mantises will more than match your Skull-Wings. You'll see what pure nobility can achieve against these worthless common-ers!"

A terrified young girl softly stole into the room—a delicate little creature scarcely thirteen. She bowed swiftly, pressing her face against the floor in abject terror.

Teki'taa gazed at her with hungry eyes, suddenly losing interest in his other guests. "I will ask you to leave me now, Zhukora. It seems Rooshïkii has once more come to discuss her father's debts." He smiled wickedly at the trembling girl. "We shall have a nice cozy little talk, won't we my dear? I'm so glad you've finally come to your senses...."

Daimïru hissed a breath and reached for her blades.

Zhukora snapped her fingers and held her in her place. "Lord King, is it not true that a visiting dignitary may beg one boon from her host?"

The king blinked and looked up from his prey. "What? Of course! You'll want for nothing while you dwell within my tribe!"

"Then grant me my boon now. Give me the girl Rooshïkii as my companion."

Teki'taa glared at Zhukora and gave a long, slow hiss. He dismissed Rooshïkii with one sharp wave of his hand, and Daimïru swept the girl beneath her arm. Zhu-kora graced Teki'taa with a short, clipped bow and retired from the royal presence.

The outside air smelled cleaner. Zhukora drew in a grateful breath and let the wind blow through her hair. "No need to fear, Rooshïkii. You're safe now—Zhukora protects you. Does your father know you're here?"

The young girl shook her head. She had stilled her tears, fighting back the sobs as she stared at the tall, commanding foreigners.

"You are a brave girl, Rooshïkii. A brave girl but a foolish one. Your king is evil, and we shall bring justice down upon him soon." Zhukora lifted the girl's face. "Rooshïkii, look at me! No more crying now. How much does your father owe the king?"

The young girl ashamedly smeared tears from her eye. "F-five fingers of silver, Honored One! Five whole fingers!"

Zhukora removed her jewelry of office and placed it in Rooshïkii's hands. The little girl stared in astonishment as she caught hold of a fortune.

"No debt is worth the price of your pride, Rooshïkii. Even so, I bow to you. You had the courage to try." Ïsha currents stirred through Zhukora's hair. "You can go home in safety now, or if you want, you can remain with us. The day is coming soon when tribes will no longer matter. We will need brave souls like you, Rooshïkii. Courage like yours is utterly without price."

The little girl stared in adoration into Zhukora's eyes. "I will come. I swear I will follow you forever."

Rooshïkii fell down in a bow. She gazed once more into Zhukora's face and then dived into the tree tops. The last they saw of her was the flickering of her soft beige wings.

Daimïru rested her hand upon her knife.

"Our first Vakïdurii Skull-Wing."

"Only the first. There will soon be others."

Zhukora turned and gazed across the Vakïdurii lands. A cold wind rose to ruffle through her fur.

ᘓ ᘔ ᘔ

Harïsh danced dizzily through the grass, her sweet voice filling the world with magic. The girl's skirt swirled around her soft young hips, and golden hair shimmered in the breeze. She buried her face in a bunch of flowers and gave a dreamy sigh.

To be fifteen is a wondrous thing; but to be fifteen and in love? Aaaah, now there is a magic spell, indeed....

With dizzy little steps Harïsh stole down to her favorite water hole. She hitched up her skirt and softly crept into the lovely, soothing shadows. Harïsh peered down into the pool, her golden eyes blinking at her wavering reflection. The girl pushed back her hair and stared critically at the thin face that gazed back at her.

Ugh! So dimpled. So innocent!

Harïsh sat on the gravel and plucked miserably at her clothes. Homespun wool and a sling for a headband. How tomboyish! How unladylike. Still, once per day, she had to watch her father's flock. The sling had to be carried somewhere. At least it kept her hair back from her eyes.[28]

Would he mind? Would he really mind? He was a nobleman, used to a fine house and linen bed sheets. How could he even look at a girl who dug clams from the stinking mud? If only she could be a real lady....

But then, he had smiled at her yesterday—really smiled! She had seen him looking at her with those beautiful brown eyes. Could it be that he saw something she did not? The girl peered cautiously back into the water, biting her lip as she took a second glance. Could someone really love this face? She hoped it with all her heart.

The girl dredged up all the power at her command and managed to kill the water's chill. She glanced furtively about, bared her boyish shanks, and slipped slowly into the pool.

Harïsh heaved a sigh and sank back to lounge in luxury. There was a delicious wickedness in pampering herself from time to time. One long leg stuck from the water as she contentedly soaped her thigh. The girl lay back her head and smiled, imagining her hands as his. She gave a sigh and let the image linger.

---

[28]**Slings:** The slings used by plainsfolk are employed most often by shepherds to drive dingoes and wedge-tailed eagles away from flocks. A true marksman such as Harïsh will often wear three such weapons of different lengths, intended for use at different ranges.

Something rustled in the grass. Harïsh shot bolt upright in the water, her face wrinkling in distaste. "Xartha, I know you're there! Go away." Nothing moved. Harïsh set her jaw and angrily stood up in her bath. "I'm warning you, you little horror! If you don't stop following me everywhere, I'm going to tell Papa!"

Nothing.

"I've finished anyway! You can fall in and drown yourself for all I care. Just stay out here and rot!" The girl tossed back her hair and stalked regally from the bath. She dried herself swiftly on a towel and angrily wound up her skirt. Little sisters were such a pain! With a flash of wings Harïsh headed for home.

Something black and twisted rose to crouch beside bathing pool. Its snout sniffed at the unfamiliar scent of soap. The creature leaned over to peer into the pool. It snarled down at the reflection of a fleshless skull.

The black beast sank back into the shadows. It stared across the wide green plains and gave a low hiss of desire.

The stranger lay in his rumpled bed and stared out the cottage window. He blinked and sighed, feeling pain ebb slowly through his wounds.

His thoughts were crystal clear; no memories remained to disturb his reverie. The stranger's mind had been wiped blank of all his past. Even the memory of his memories was gone. He never even realized the lack. People came. People went. They jabbered nonsense sounds that tickled his ears.

Still, he felt a dreadful sense of loss. Why? What was lost? He touched his woolen kilt and the bandages about his waist. He had his clothes; he had his wound. Everything was just as it should have been.

The stranger's world was nothing but an empty void. There was no one but himself, the villagers, and the girl of gold.

Outside the house, Harïsh fluttered gaily to the ground, dodged her father's wary eye, and ducked in through the door. She came bouncing into the sickroom and joyfully set down a bunch of flowers. Golden eyes sparkled at her guest.

"You're up! Did you do that by yourself? How marvelous!" Perhaps he was finally getting better. "How do you feel? Is the pain as bad today?"

He rolled his head to look at her. Troubled clouds drew across his eyes. Harïsh patiently touched her stomach and mimed her words.

"The hurting down here. Is it all right today?"

He gave a sorry grimace and touched his bandages; the pain must still be bad. The man gave a little smile, and Harïsh felt her young heart skip a beat.

The village speaker had been quite firm—the river spirit had given the stranger to the house of Kana; Harïsh's family would be responsible for his care.

Aaaah, the speaker! Such a wise, pious man....

A nobleman in the house! The girl's parents were ecstatic. Their status had soared like a falcon. Travelers had come from far and wide to stop and talk to Totli-kana the master potter. Her father had spun his stories far into the nights, selling more pots in one afternoon than he had previously sold in weeks.

Harïsh gazed fondly at her patient, brushing the long locks at the right side of her face. "Ah, my funny friend. Strange wounds and giant fish. What a mystery you are!

If only you really understood me. Where are you from? Will you want to go back there when you're well?"

He looked at her, not understanding a word but pleased to hear a friendly voice. She heaved a sigh and looked up at him through puzzled eyes.

"So, where might you be from, my friend? Not from the forest, even if you are a giant! You're no alpine savage, since there's no notches in your ears, no scars carved across your back...." The girl glanced across her shoulder to make sure they were alone. "You're—uh—you're not circumcised, so you can't be from the plains." She felt her ears blush hot. Harïsh pressed the back of her hand against her cheeks. Dear Rain—there had been no shame in bathing an unconscious man. She had brothers! She'd seen it all before.

The girl pulled her earring and tried to puzzle out the problem.

"Perhaps you come from the coast! The fish might have brought you from the sea. Is that it? Did you come from the great wide ocean?"

The girl suddenly puffed out her chest with pride. "I went to see the healers again. They're pleased with the way I'm taking care of you. The healer major says I show great promise."

The girl looked left and right, then leaned closer to whisper conspiratorially, "You mustn't tell my Mama, not yet—but I've taken my first examination for the healers. I've learned the herb lists by heart, and they let me study the paintings that show the surgeon's art. Isn't it fantastic! They said I have strong hands and a healing touch, with sheep, I mean. You know, setting bones and pulling teeth. But what if I could do it for people? Wouldn't that be fantastic!"

The stranger listened, reading every inflection of her tone. He looked up at her, gripping her hand as she poured out her woes.

"My ïsha power isn't very strong, but that isn't everything, is it? They say I have clever hands! I can make medicines. I fixed your fever, I really did! And I helped Usha's egg when she gave birth. If they take me, I can go on to be something! Something that really matters!"

The girl paced back and forth across the room, her brown wings thrashing the air.

"I want to do something with my life! If I could heal the sick—be someone people could look at with respect and love!" She came over to the stranger and looked into his eyes. "I mean, wouldn't that be worth fighting for? Wouldn't that be worth—well—keeping secrets from Mama?"

The girl slumped unhappily on the bed.

"Mama would go wild if she found out. Papa says I'm to be a potter, just like him! I've had enough of pots! 'Tread the clay, Harïsh! Harïsh, go mix the glazes!' " The girl gave an unhappy snort. "What sort of life is that? Clay in your fur and charcoal in your hair. Fire sprites hissing jokes behind your tail! I have a talent, a skill that makes me happy. Isn't that better than kilns and pots and clay?"

The stranger seemed to understand. He was the only man who had ever listened to her. He gazed steadily at her, filling her with a feeling that had been nibbling her nerves for days. It felt like little butterflies fluttering in her heart.

The girl dived her nervous fingers down into her pouch, looking for something to occupy her hands. She felt a round clay flute. Harïsh took it out and stared at the thing unhappily—giddy and miserable all at once.

The stranger's tail went stiff. He stared at the flute. Something sparked deep in his eyes. She handed the instrument to him, fascinated by the changes in his face.

"Oh! Have you seen one before? It's a clay flute. My father makes them. It's not like a proper reed flute. They're actually rather difficult to play...."

The stranger raised the flute to his lips and blew a single, perfect note. It sang out like the haunted crooning of a ghost. The girl gave a shiver. Hackles rose all up and down her fur.

High in the rafters, the household spirit uncurled from its sleep, and Harïsh blinked in astonishment as the Ka danced to the stranger's song. The nobleman's green wings lifted to the touch of unseen winds. Finally he let the music end. He looked at Harïsh with bright, shy eyes.

She took the flute, afraid to meet his gaze. "Thank you. I... Thank you for letting me see."

The girl hastily scrubbed her eyes and handed him back the instrument.

The stranger's eyes shone with light, and for the first time he seemed utterly alert.

The girl clapped her hands for attention, firmly pointing to herself. "Harïsh. I am Harïsh. And you, do you have a name?" He blinked and shook his head as if trying to clear his thoughts. The girl pulled his chin so he looked at her again. "Harïsh. Har-ïsh."

The stranger frowned, turned his hand toward his chest, and pursed his lips in thought. Suddenly he reached out to touch the girl's shoulder. "Har-eesh." He nodded slowly, smiled, and touched her nose. "Har-eesh!"

She was thrilled. He could speak! His deep, beautiful voice sent shivers chasing down her spine. "Yes! Harïsh! I'm Harïsh!" She touched herself again. "Harïsh." The hand went to tap him on his chest. "Your name? What is your name, do you remember?"

His fur felt warm; too warm. Perhaps he had been sitting too long in the sun? The stranger touched his breast and screwed up his eyes in thought. Finally, he gave a shrug. If he had a name, it was long gone. The loss clearly troubled him. He seemed exhausted. Too much too soon.

Harïsh gently laid him back on his bed. "My poor, sick friend. We'll get you well. The fish would never forgive me if I let him down, now would he? I'll change your dressings, and we'll let you sleep in peace."

She stroked his handsome muzzle and stared at his precious, troubled face. "We can't just call you 'stranger'. Would you like a name? Shall I give you one?" The girl looked out the window and watched the waving grass. "What if we call you Keketál, 'the river's gift'? I think that's rather strong and handsome, don't you?"

Keketál. Yes, it had a gallant ring to it.

When he grew stronger, she would teach him how to speak once more. It would take time, but he would learn. The girl stroked her patient's hair and gave a smile.

The scuff of sandals made Harïsh's ears twitch. Xartha stood staring with her big wide eyes. The tiny girl was only four years old, the absolute picture of her doting mother. Harïsh glared down down at her baby sister and gave a scowl.

"I thought I told you not to follow me anymore!"

The little girl just stood and stared. Harïsh sniffed and tried to ignore the brat as she smoothed back her patient's fur and tucked him in his bed. She let her hand linger softly on his brow.

Maybe he was too warm? His forehead felt hot. Harïsh leaned closer and ran her hands across his fur.

Xartha still stood there, watching.

Harïsh's concentration shattered. She gave an ill-tempered snarl and stomped off to find her mother.

Mama stood in the yard turning sheep's-milk into cheese. Everything about Harïsh's mother was neat and crisp and clean. Her figure was strong and youthful; her fur smelled of new-spun wool. Harïsh marched toward her, wailing all her woes.

"Mama, that little brat's following me again! I've told her and told her and she just won't go away!"

Her mother wrung out a bag of curds, hung up the cheese, and gave a sigh. "Oh, dearest, can't you children play in peace? Mama is busy right now."

"I am not a child! I'm fifteen, and I don't want to be followed by some spooky little brat!"

"Spooky? What nonsense is this now?"

"She never talks! Why does she just sit there and stare at me all the time?"

Harïsh's mother went on with her work. "All I ask is that you look after the others from time to time. You are the eldest, my love. You're of an age to be helping me around the house. You'll have a household of your own some day. There's no time like the present to learn a woman's duties."

"But, Mama...."

"Oh, Harïsh! Is it really such a bother? Why can't you just ignore her?"

Harïsh irritably kicked her feet.

"She's not just bothering me. She's bothering our guest. She just stands there staring at him! He doesn't like it."

Her mother washed off her hands and dried them on her skirt. She sat down on a tree stump and drew Harïsh to her side. "Harïsh—perhaps you and I should have a little talk. A mother notices things. I think you might be taking this business with our guest a little too seriously. I should like you to spend less time with him."

Harïsh went stiff with panic, then saw her mother's suspicious eyes and hastily ducked her head.

"Harïsh, look at me. Come on, look into my eyes."

Harïsh jerked her face and defiantly set her jaw. Her mother slowly nodded.

"I had guessed as much. I would have spared you this if I had caught it earlier. Ah, well, I suppose we all learn through our mistakes. Pain is just another part of growing up."

"M-Mama?"

"First love is always the hardest. Let it go, Harïsh. This man was never meant for little potter's girls like you."

Harïsh felt her ears burn. "Mama! I-I never... I feel no such thing!"

"Indeed? Well then, I'm glad to hear it. A man like that has a family searching for him. He has a whole life waiting, just beyond our reach. I'll not see my little girl weeping once he finds his memory." The woman's words were gentle. "Draw back a little, my dove. Infatuation with a mystery leads only to pain."

Harïsh felt tears spring to her eyes. "He's hurt! He needs my help. Mama, I have to care!" The young girl wept, her head cradled in her hands. "I'm not infatuated. I'm not! He's just so helpless. He needs me! I can help him! I really can! I won't do anything wrong—just let me care for him. It's all I ask! Please."

Her mother closed her eyes and turned her face. "Go, take the ewes for milking, and then help your brothers stock the kiln."

Harïsh's breath sobbed in her throat. She stared up at her mother through awful, pain-filled eyes. "Mama, please! Can he stay? Can I keep on caring for him?"

Her mother looked sadly into Harïsh's eyes. "Yes, my love. I cannot stop you. I'm afraid you'll care for him for a long, long time to come."

 C3 ᛒ ᛓ

Desert winds stirred the dust into a semblance of life. Tiny figures shimmered in the haze, plodding onward through a land of suffering. They walked by day, they walked by night, and still the horizon never came in reach. It was as though they walked the pathways of the damned, condemned forever to a world of thirst and emptiness.

Without plants, without life, the desert held no ïsha to lift Kashran wings. Shadarii had led her followers out into a lifeless void. They had staggered in her footsteps over weeks of utter nightmare. The pilgrims had almost reached the end of their endurance. A last few drops of salty water rattled in their drinking gourds, and no one had eaten for days.

Still, Shadarii wandered on. Perhaps she sought the world's edge. Perhaps she had finally lost her mind.

Shadarii, Kïtashii, and Tingtraka took the lead. The other hunters shambled forward over broken, crumbling earth. Mrrimïmei hung upon Totoru's arm, her waist noticeably thickened by the egg inside her. She carried it in grim silence, firmly keeping to the front of the march.

Wind picked at the branches of a dead acacia tree, and two of the hunters tottered over to inspect the wood for beetles. They found none, not even a termite. Kefiru kicked the tree and brushed his hand across his bloody lips.

Suddenly, he turned, his antennae twitching to a hint of ïsha scent.

A bearded lizard darted from the rocks. Kefiru's throwing stick spun through the air to smash the lizard's skull. The hunter flung himself upon the corpse and swiftly cracked its neck.

Food!

He laughed and snatched up his kill. The lizard was longer than his leg—a veritable feast! Kefiru ducked away from the others and made ready to devour his meal.

"No! Kefiru no!" Kïtashii glared down from the rocks above him. "Share it! What do you think you're doing? Have you gone mad?"

The hunter desperately concealed his kill. "It's mine! I've not eaten in days! Who're you to tell me what to do?"

Shadarii made a curt gesture of her hand, and Kïtashii whirled back to face Kefiru.

"It belongs to the group! As a group we live. We share it!"

"Who are you to tell a hunter what to do? Since when do I take orders from a piddling little brat?"

"No one's giving any orders. What's wrong with you?" Kïtashii jerked her head toward her teacher. "Share it! Mrrimïmei needs the blood. When she's drunk, we can all divide the flesh."

Kefiru stared around at the ring of hostile faces, his eyes glaring mad with anger. "Why? Why listen? I caught the lizard! I want to eat it! What's wrong with that—what's wrong?"

The little girl stared at him with wise, commanding eyes. "Have you learned nothing about what Shadarii's tried to teach us? Sharing, respect, community! Three simple little rules! Is it too much to ask? We share it, but Mrrimïmei gets the blood. She needs it for the baby."

Kefiru ashamedly handed over the kill. Mrrimïmei weakly tried to wave the beast away, but Totoru hacked its head clean off and drained the blood into a cup, forcing her to drink every reeking drop. She coughed and spluttered, but somehow kept the foul mass in her gullet.

Tingtraka parted the lizard flesh into thirteen equal sections. One by one, the hunters slumped into the dust to eat. Kïtashii brought a tiny morsel to Shadarii, who tried to pass her food to Mrrimïmei. Kïtashii snatched it back and forced Shadarii to eat her share.

Kefiru crammed raw lizard in his mouth, eating bones, scales, and all. He wiped his bloody hands against his tongue and glared over at Shadarii.

"She sits up there like lady muck! Look at her. She's just as thirsty as anybody else! Why won't she just give up and turn around? She's no immortal; she can die just like the rest of us!"

Rotïka cracked a lizard bone and glared at him in hate. "Well why don't you turn back, then? I'm sick to death of your incessant whining."

Kefiru turned away and gnawed his lizard bones in silence, his thoughts hanging over him in a dark cloud.

A change somehow seemed to creep across the ïsha. The pilgrims raised their antennae and lifted their eyes in wonder.

Something soft and beautiful was dancing in the dust. Shadarii spread her smile of love. The pilgrims laughed as she pantomimed an enormous hopping toad, puffing out her chest in pompous pride.

Long ago and far away, a huge toad lived beside the waters of a lake. He lived with dozens of warty little cousins, all singing merrily in the cool light of the evening sky. They dwelt in peace and harmony, growing sleek on bugs and flies and nestling in the lovely mud.

One day, the toads' peaceful world began to change. The sun grew hot, burning the toads' warty skin. The lake began to shrink, leaving a ring of mud cracking all around the banks. Every day, the water receded. The toad community grew afraid, and held a meeting to decide what to do.

The toad spokesman sat upon a majestic lily pad and waved his claws in fright. "Fellow toads! Our lake is shrinking. Soon there will be no cool mud for us to sit in—no lovely water in which to bathe our feet. How shall we deal with this threat to our way of life?"

The toads croaked among themselves in consternation. They puffed out their chests and argued bitterly, each filled with questions, but none able to find answers.

Finally one old creaky toad waddled up before the others. The assembly fell silent as he made his muttering way toward the lily pad. He settled back and spoke in an ancient voice. "Cousin toads, hear my words. The lake has dried before. The lake shall dry again. There is no need for panic and alarm. We merely need techniques for survival."

"What! What techniques could these be?" The other toads hopped eagerly up and down.

The old toad puffed out his chest and made the youngsters quiet down. "We shall create a simple set of rules. There is enough for all if we will be satisfied with a little less. Water will be scarce, but if we all share, we shall live happily through the summer. There is not enough space around the lake's edge for everyone to sit snuggled in the mud. We shall take turns, with each toad getting a fair share of what we have. When the winter rains come, the lake will swell with water. Life will return to normal. Hardship is always temporary. All bad times pass, if only we have fortitude and patience."

The other toads croaked out their applause! Only the fat toad at the back seemed unhappy with the arrangement. He waved his pudgy claws and tried to shout the others down.

"Stop! Don't listen to this old fool! What use is knowledge of the past? These are modern times! The world is changed and new. I say this is a disaster! Something must be done!"

No one listened to him. The other toads laid out plans for their survival. They would dig tunnels in which to hide their skins from the burning sun. Each would have a set time of day to bask beside the lake. They would emerge at night to let the dew soak into their hides....

The fat toad watched everything in disgust. All around him, toads burrowed into the soil. Dirt flew and mud clods tumbled. It all looked like too much hard labor! Finally, everyone had a nice deep hole to hide in. The fat toad gave an irritable sigh and dug his own hole in the bank. Although the idea was silly, he was unwilling to be left looking like a fool.

At dawn, the toads began their roster. Group by group, they settled by the water, each giving up his time when the appointed moment came. Everyone gained enough pleasure to last the day. There was just enough for each toad to get by.

Long days passed. Each morning, the sun rose high and burned the trees and grass until they cracked. Each evening, the lake grew lower. The toads clung to their plan, sure that in the end everything would turn out right. In truth, life was very tolerable.

Not everyone was happy. The fat toad scratched his belly and paused carefully in thought. He looked at the falling lake and sourly sucked his lips.

"How can I trust a doddering old fool? Of what value is the knowledge of the past? The lake is shrinking! There isn't enough water for us all. Soon it will be gone, and when that happens, I'll not die of thirst like all these other stupid fools."

So, when it was time for the fat toad to take his place beside the water, he shuffled down obediently to his spot. The creature peered shyly back and forth and then scuttled over to the shadows. He dipped his nose into the water and sucked in a great huge gulp. He stored the drink beneath his skin and hoped the others wouldn't see.

"No one will miss a little bit of water! I'll take this and keep it until it's needed."

Greed always spreads. When one person takes more than his due, another person covets it. What someone else has, we always want. The other toads saw their fat brother sucking in the water *and felt a surge of panic. Someone was hoarding water! Perhaps there wasn't going to be enough water after all. Each toad scuttled off into the shadows and slyly took a suck of cool, refreshing drink. They licked their lips and quietly crept back into their holes. At the end of the day, every toad living by the lake was smugly sitting in his tunnel, feeling very fat and full. Each was convinced he was the cleverest toad in all the world.*

In the morning, a nasty shock awaited them. The lake had shrunk overnight. The water had dropped to an alarming level. A disaster was at hand!

The toads duly shuffled out to take their turns beside the banks. Each glanced suspiciously at his neighbor, noticing how sleek and fat he seemed. When each toad was sure no one else could see, he swiftly took a gulp of water, desperate to snatch his share before the supply was gone.

It was a sour, hostile day. Toads rarely spoke to one another. Each creature glared at his companions and shot dark, suspicious looks. In the evening, each toad waddled into his hole, so grossly swollen he could scarcely squeeze through the door.

Day by day, the lake shrank with terrifying speed. The toads forgot their rosters. Each creature simply shouldered his way down to the lake and sucked up all the water he could find. The lake dwindled, wasted by the toads' dreadful, selfish greed.

Finally, the lake was dry. The toads were bloated with stolen water. Each creature burrowed down into his hole and sealed shut the door, afraid the other toads might come to steal his horde. The toads sat in their burrows in smug, suspicious silence, thrilled they alone were smart enough to survive the awful drought.

The lake bed dried and cracked. The water lilies withered and blew away. There was only dust and silence—hot sun and stifling air. Soon there was no sign that the lovely lake had ever been....

The summer fled. Autumn flourished. The wet season came again. The rain fell at the appointed time, just as it always had since time began. Only this time there was a difference. The lovely lake had gone. Water poured down into the lake bed and simply drained away. It leaked out through the cracked, dry mud, and turned the soil to dust. Other ponds began to grow, but the toads never came from their holes to see.

Deep beneath the earth, the toads hid, oblivious to the world. They sat, swollen with jealousy, guarding their little treasures even when there was no longer any need. Though each toad had more than he could use, their selfishness had made them poor. No mud, no lake—no nice evenings paddling their feet in fellowship. Nothing but an empty life of greed.

Kefiru winced unhappily, stung by the moral to Shadarii's tale. She came and kissed him warmly on the nose, then led him over to a strip of hard-baked mud. The other hunters gathered in amazement as Shadarii took a digging stick and opened the earth. She plunged her hand into the dirt and hauled up a struggling prize. Before their startled eyes, the girl lofted an enormous, bloated toad. Shadarii grinned and squeezed it to release a delicious drink of water. She drank half of the toad's stores, smacking her lips as she stuffed the furious amphibian back into his lair.

Water! She had found water in the desert!

Shadarii read the ïsha waves and found more toads far beneath the ground. She led her followers to them one by one, showing them the places they should dig. Soon the little group was covered in a cloud of flying earth. The pilgrims laughed as their prizes were hauled from the ground.

A smile growing across her face, Shadarii sat and watched her children work, and then curled beneath the dead acacia tree and quietly fell asleep.

ભ   ಬಾ   ಬಾ

Harïsh shot bolt upright in bed and blinked into the dark. Her chest heaved, and her fur was drenched in sweat. The household spirit writhed frantically in the air about her , desperately trying to drag her from her bed.

Keketál!

The girl flung herself into the sickroom. Keketál lay thrashing in delirium, dripping with sweat. He was burning hot to the touch. The girl sobbed and desperately dragged the huge man out of bed.

"Mama! Papa! Quickly, wake up!" With all her might, Harïsh hauled Keketál across the cottage floor. "Papa! Help me! Papa, we need you!"

Her parents burst into the room.

Harïsh wept as she tried to drag Keketál across the ground. "It's the wound! It's infected inside him. You have to help me!" No one moved. The girl ground her teeth and heaved with all her might. "The river! Help me get him in the river, quickly!"

Harïsh's father pushed his daughter clear, and then lifted the tall stranger into his arms. Harïsh led the way down to the river, tears spilling down her face.

She burst out onto the riverbanks. Totli-kana stared with wise gray eyes at his daughter. "What now? Where must I take him?"

Harïsh flung her arms about Keketál and dragged him into the icy water, gasping as the cold stabbed her. Harïsh tried to still the chattering of her teeth. She wiped her eyes and snapped an order to her brothers.

"Hochtli, Mixtli, fly! Go to the village of Circle-Tree and bring the master healer. Now! Go!"

The two boys saw the tears flashing in their sister's eyes and sped off to do her bidding. Harïsh barely even saw them go.

"Mama, the healers will need hot water, blankets, and boiled root bark from a wattle tree. Crush a green ant's nest and save the juice."

"I'll fetch it, love."

Harïsh wept and rocked her patient to and fro. His breathing eased as he slowly cooled down. "Papa, I'm frightened! What if he dies?"

"Well it won't be from your not trying to save him." The old potter sat on the bank. "Is it really worth such a fuss girl? If he's dying anyway, it might be kind to let him slip away in peace...."

The girl clutched Keketál against her. "He'll live! Just you see! I'll make him live."

Her father gave a shrug. He would deal with the inquiries of his neighbors, explaining why their summer night was being disturbed. His daughter would meanwhile stay at her post, blonde hair shining like a beacon in the dark.

The night dragged on with agonizing slowness. Keketál's breathing quieted against Harïsh's breast, and soon he began to shiver with cold. It seemed that hours had passed, and still the healers hadn't come. Keketál muttered something in a weird, lilting tongue; Shashashii? Shagarii? Harïsh simply couldn't understand. He spoke to her, reaching out to touch her face with trembling hands.

He could cool no more without doing further harm. The wound must be opened and drained immediately. There was no one else to do it.

Harïsh calmly called out to those gathered on the banks. "We're taking him back inside. Get me a knife, a bowl, and a hollow reed. Cloths and blankets—and someone powerful! I need someone to hold him." She hitched Keketál's face up beneath her arm. "Someone help me lift him out."

Neighbors helped lift him up the banks, and then manhandled him back into Harïsh's home. They dragged him close by the fire and scampered clear to watch Harïsh work.

The little potter's girl allowed her mother to strip away her dripping dress and wrap her in a blanket, never once pausing as she saw to her patient's needs.

"I need someone with power. There's going to be blood. I don't have the ïsha to control it."

Lord Ingatïl, the village speaker, knelt at Keketál's head. She spared him a glance of gratitude before she turned back to her task.

She held a flint knife above his wound. A sour red scar gleamed against the poor man's fur. Harïsh felt his pulse beneath her hands and knew what she must do. "I love you!"

She pushed down hard and made the cut. Keketál arched as she drew a bright line of blood across his heaving flesh.

It hadn't cut through!

Harïsh felt a wave of panic. Blood welled from the cut to spill through her steady fingers. The girl bit back a surge of bile and carefully scored the flesh again. She felt the muscle separate, and something hot and filthy spurted across her hands. A vile stench of pus sent her audience staggering in revulsion.

Sweet Rain! Keketál's wound had festered deep beneath the skin. The girl scraped the abscess clean and flung the muck into a bowl. She squeezed and scrubbed, washing out the wound with extract of wattle bark.

A sudden commotion sounded at the door as a group of healers shoved the crowd aside. Two journeymen made to snatch Harïsh back from her patient, but the master healer held up his hand and stopped them in their tracks. The girl was doing just fine by herself. The abscess had been swabbed fresh and clean.

Harïsh tossed her knife into a bowl, her hands still calm and steady. "I don't know what else to do. There's no power in me. I cannot heal him further."

The master healer gently helped her to her feet. "We'll take it now, my girl. All that's left is to tidy up and do a trick or two. The real work is done."

The tall old man led her out into the open air where dawn brushed crimson feathers against the dark horizon. Harïsh sat down upon a log as a blanket was gently laid about her shoulders. She looked out across the village roofs as though waking from a dream.

"Did I do right, Lord Healer? I didn't know. Someone had to do something."

"You saved his life. You committed yourself to the action that you felt was right. Tonight, you discovered the gift of courage."

"If—if I'd had the power... if I'd held enough magic, I could have made a spell to heal him."

"No, little one. Not with all that filth inside him. The knife and spell must work in partnership. Though your ïsha power is very small, your instincts mark you as a healer."

The old man led the girl back inside and softly sat her down by Keketál. Two healing mages bent above the patient, weaving shimmering fields of force. The master healer felt Keketál's brow and took his pulse. With a nod of satisfaction, he wandered over to see Harïsh's parents. The potter and his wife bowed before the nobleman.

"Totli-kana, Nurïman-kana, with your permission, we would like to train your daughter as a surgeon. She has the talent. She has the need. Any other future would leave her broken and unhappy."

The potter looked up in alarm. "But, mighty lord, she is to be a potter like her father! We mean to wed her to the potters of another village!"

"You have two sons who can be potters. The world will never lack for young girls to be wives. I say this maiden is very special. Cherish the treasure that Rain and Wind have brought you."

The two parents looked toward their daughter. She sat with the stranger's head cradled in her lap, staring into his face in adoration. Totli-kana started toward her, but his wife put out her hand. The woman led the villagers from the room and left Harïsh at peace.

Harïsh never even noticed that they were gone.

Keketál opened his eyes and ran his tongue across his lips. Harïsh gave him a sip of tea and carefully wiped his mouth.

He reached out to touch her face. "Harïsh... "

The nobleman smiled, falling into a gentle, healing sleep.

Sixteen

As the wet seasons[29] waned and the days grew long, the Vakïdurii and Katakanii tribes drew together on their yearly route of march. The time had come for the great moth feasts high in the mountains, where every year the bogong moths flocked to the caves. Untold millions of them sheathed whole cliff faces with their furry bodies. The two tribes joined to feast on the meaty morsels, growing fat and sleek on the fluttering snacks. Trade took place, and rituals were shared. For once, mere tribes seemed slightly meaningless as brotherhood glowed deep among the trees.

Sixty thousand Kashra gathered by the caves. After months of starvation, the people drooled at the thought of stuffing themselves sick with meat.

Zhukora looked on the teeming peoples and knew her time drew near. Power was about to tip into her hands, and all because of one tiny little thing. She looked toward the bogong caves and knew she had won.

For this year, there would be no moths.

Moths needed rain, and the trees were stiff and dry. Oh, they would come—in weeks or days; Serpent could feel them slowly drawing near. Meanwhile, though, bellies went empty and people grew angry. Once again, the tree ferns were butchered into starch. Frogs and water bugs were devoured by the enormous mobs—even earthworms and wood lice were better than starvation. The commoners hungered side by side, Vakïdurii and Katakanii suffering together. The nobility and priesthood still lived in luxury, skimming off their tithes. The people watched as their children starved and felt anger growing in their hearts.

Time had finally played into Zhukora's hands.

A vast, gangly spider blundered across a strip of bark. The hairy "huntsman" was larger than an outstretched hand. It was flat and brown and ugly, with a face even its mother couldn't love. The beast had inordinate trouble coordinating all eight legs. From time to time, it would stop to take stock of its surroundings, as if counting to see if all its limbs remained.

Down among the leaf litter, all seemed perfect with the huntsman's world. The creature sat back to lay plans for another busy day, and a long pink tongue shot out between its fangs to clean its dainty feet. The spider wriggled with satisfaction as it basked in the morning sun.

"Mine!"

---

[29]**Seasons:** The alpine Kashra recognize six seasons: Many-Wings (high summer, with plentiful insects and wood grubs), Sky-Gray (full honeycombs and overcast skies), Frog-Sing (a warm, wet season), Rain-Weeping (heavy rains, flooded rivers), Chill (deep, cold winter), and New-Flower (when the world warms and the wattle trees bloom). To this the high altitude clans will sometimes add "Wind-Battle", a time of wild rain and wind storms, which are taken as evidence that even the marriages of gods can sometimes be stormy.

"No, mine!"

A hand lashed out to snatch the spider. The creature thrashed its spindly legs and tried to fight, unable even to bite its way to freedom.

"Mine! I saw it first!"

"You Katakanii offspring of a clam! 'Tis mine!"

Two scruffy little boys faced each other. Both were wild and skinny. The Katakanii and Vakïdurii children bared their fangs.

"Bugger off! I found it. I'm gonna eat it!"

" 'Twas mine! You stole me spider, you filthy pussball!"

"Maggot!"

"Shit eatin' Katakanii!"

The Katakanii boy stooped and hurled a rock, and the other boy ducked the shot. With a squeal of fury he flung himself on the other boy. They grabbed each other's ears and fought a mighty battle in the dust.

The hapless spider landed on its back beneath a bush. It waved its clumsy legs, trying to make sense out of a topsy-turvy world. It was just recovering its sense of up and down when a pair of squealing giants crashed into the brush beside it. The spider flipped right side up and scuttled off as fast as it could.

"Needle dick!"

"Thief! I'll kill you!"

The boys were abruptly hauled high into the air. Both children blanched as they found themselves surrounded by lean, fantastic figures dressed in black.

A voice spoke—a low-pitched female voice that seemed to carry all the majestic power of the Wind and Rain. "Very well, who started this?"

The two boys stared in fear at a slender figure in the shadows. Light glittered from a pair of cobalt wings.

"Well, boys? Has neither of you anything to say? Were you fighting over nothing?" The woman shone like a figure from a dream. It was her—the lady of the skulls! The Vakïdurii boy jerked as her blue eyes pierced clean through his soul, reading his every secret, his every sin....

" 'Twasn't me, my lady. 'Twas him! I saw the spider first!"

"Hmmmm. Really?"

The boy wilted slowly. "Uh—well, we was together at the time. Takii's my friend. But—but I saw it first!" The little waif miserably hung his little head. "I—I was hungry...."

Zhukora closed her eyes and ran a hand across her face. Her voice grew sharp with pain. "Hungry for a spider? Hungry enough to kill for it? That's what you both said, isn't it? That you wanted to kill each other?" Zhukora signed to Daimïru, and the other hunters let their captives go. "If that's what you really want, here you are. Here's my knife. Daimïru will give you another. You can hack each other to your heart's content, and all over a spider."

The Katakanii boy whimpered as Daimïru pressed her knife into his hands. He dropped the weapon and scrubbed his palms against his fur.

"I didn't mean it, honest! He's my friend...." The boy scuffed his moccasins in shame. "I didn't mean it. I was hungry is all. It's all there is."

"What does your father do, lad?"

"He's a metal smith, my lady. A good one!"

"Hmmmm—and what of you, my little Vakïdurii spitfire?"

"Me pa's a hunter, ma'am! Only there's nothing to hunt. All the animals is dead and gone, see?"

"Yes. Yes, I know." Zhukora sighed. She turned her clear blue eyes on the boys. "Bring your fathers to me, and I'll show them where to find food. We'll hunt on the plains and find enough for your families and friends."

The Vakïdurii boy seemed ill at ease. "Papa says we shouldn't get too close to Katakanii. He tol' me not to be Takii's friend."

"We are not Katakanii or Vakïdurii. We are Kashra. One race—one unity. The time for tribes is past." The woman turned her perfect face toward them, and the two boys stared at her in awe. When she took their hands, they almost fainted. If she had asked them to battle monsters for her, they would have fought and died for her on the spot. The children bowed, and then clattered into the air.

Zhukora sighed and retrieved her knife, staring after the two retreating boys. "I don't like to find that. Did you see how they fought over a little spider? It's enough to make me want to weep."

Daimïru sighed and clasped the skull-shaped handles of her paired dao. "There is no choice except to wait. We can only pray the suffering will soon be over."

"They say purity of purpose may be achieved only through suffering." Zhukora bitterly gazed into the trees. "It is a hard path we fly, my love."

"It is worthwhile. Your victory will be their salvation."

The group of Kashra rose through the air on silent wings and drifted off into the light. Down in the leaf litter, the huntsman spider struggled across a mossy log. It cleaned it feet, worked little paps beneath its jaws, and then blundered on its way without a worry in the world.

03 80 80

Shadarii sat in meditation beside a broken rock. Her eyes were closed, her fur dulled, her lips parched. Even so, the girl was utterly oblivious to the world.

She let her mind wander with the desert breeze. She felt the sands and scorching heat—the careful patterns that the flies wove above her ears. A gecko's eggs lay buried in the dust beneath her tail. Sun and sand, earth and air... Shadarii reached out and merged with her world.

Even here, there was beauty. Amid the dust, Shadarii had found wonder. A desert sunset, the arid moon, dead twigs etched against an endless sky. Shadarii had learned to understand this place and, in so doing, had discovered love.

Shadarii shivered as the power flowed. She was the Chosen One. All her sufferings went to a purpose.... Kotaru, the hunger, the loss, the guilt, the pain... in suffering she would be purged. When the answers finally came, she would be pure enough to see.

Why? Why do people need to fight and kill?

She felt tired. The answers stayed as far away as ever. Perhaps she simply searched too hard. Shadarii heaved a sigh and wearily brought her mind back to the here and now.

The others were waiting for her. Shadarii opened her eyes as Kïtashii bowed and looked worshipfully up into her face.

"Shadarii-Zha, there are ruins on the horizon. Tingtraka can see them from an outcrop of rocks. They lie a little distance from our chosen path. Shall we go and see them?"

Shadarii eagerly leapt to her feet, and the other pilgrims scrabbled in her wake. Shadarii opened her wings to fly; of all the company, only she had ïsha enough to rise off the sand. Skimming along, she laughed as her squawking followers fell behind.

A noise intruded into Shadarii's mirth. She snatched her head around in shock to find Kïtashii flapping madly at her tail. Shadarii beamed and led her little follower out across the desert sands.

A line of ruins appeared on the horizon. Shadarii and her student landed on a ridge of rock, soft wings flipping in amazement as they stared in awe at their discovery.

A shallow dust bowl had been scooped from the desert soil. There were ruins at the far rim of the valley—great, mysterious towers made of stone. The corners were blurred by groaning centuries of sand and wind. The buildings stood there like the skeleton of some enormous beast—jagged bones thrusting up against the desert sky.

The girls had never seen so many buildings in their entire lives. There must have been thousands of them, clustering like trees inside a forest. Who could have built them, and why? There was hardly enough ïsha to lift a mouse. How could anyone live where it was impossible to fly?

The valley looked as though it had been carved out of the ground by a giant spoon. Kïtashii stared in astonishment at the center of the valley, where a stand of spinifex wavered in the breeze.

"Water! Look, Shadarii, there's water! And trees, and shade!" She turned to wave the other pilgrims to greater speed! "A pool! I can see a pool!"

The youngster stormed over to the water and plunged her whole head into the pool. She erupted out of it seconds later, choking out a curse. "Salt! Damn!" The little girl kicked out at the rocks in disappointment.

Shadarii wandered over and gave an idle shrug. A salty pool was no disaster— they had encountered such before. Shadarii could heat the water and turn it to steam. They could collect the vapor against a cone of leather clothes and drip it down into their water gourds. The teacher grinned as the other pilgrims wandered to her side.

See? A bath at last! No more fleas! No more dirt against our skin.

There would be grubs among the spinifex and juicy scorpions in the rocks. It was a veritable garden! They could scour the area for supplies before moving on. Shadarii thanked sweet Rain for the opportunity to rest.

But first, there were the buildings; Shadarii felt a delicious shiver of anticipation. While half the group collected food, she took the others up the slopes toward the ruins.

The pilgrims moved between the gate towers of the ruins and passed into a land of silence.

The wind dropped away, and the air became cool. Pilgrims shivered and drew themselves closer together. Their footsteps fell quietly in the sand. All about them, ancient towers leaned inward like the edges of an empty grave.

Shadarii cautiously approached a piece of broken wall. She picked at it with her claw, staring in fascination as she watched the material crumble.

Mud. They were made of mud!

She threw back her head and stared into the sky where tower tops etched dark lines against the blue. There was a sense of dizzy motion, almost as if she were falling. The girl gazed up in wonder, trying to imagine just how heavy such a tower would be. Kitashii pointed to doors high above the ground and whispered quietly in awe.

"It's almost like a forest. Like the towers are trees! They had no forest, so they made their own."

Shadarii stopped short. She lifted a hand to halt the others while her long antennae searched the shadows.

They were being watched.

Her ears flicked. She was sure there was someone here. Perhaps a few last spirits lurked in the dust. She shivered and tried to turn her back, her senses prickling. It was not so much a sense of danger. Merely one of... anticipation.

The group slowly roamed among the towers, running hands across the age-old stone and mud. The lanes led in a maze toward the center of the ruin, and Shadarii's pilgrims followed. At last, they climbed across an embankment of fallen brickwork and stared out into a wide patch of open ground.

A circular clearing had been blasted from the sand, and the nearby towers lay shattered into pieces. Broken walls gleamed like ice, fused into position by heat.

A gigantic carved image lay at the center of the clearing—a vast, weirdly shaped hunk of carved soapstone. Shadarii turned her head sideways to make out the figure, and found herself peering at a titanic face. A Kashra! They had found the fallen statue of a Kashra!

Kitashii clambered up between the figure's ears and grinned down at her friends. Her nostrils suddenly flared, and she almost drooled in greed.

"There's meat grilling! The others must have found food. Should we go back?"

Meat—real meat! The pilgrims turned and streamed back toward the water hole. Shadarii glanced one last time at the statue, feeling she was leaving something undone. The dancer paused, her antennae questing quietly. She finally turned away and led her companions back toward the valley.

Hours later, Shadarii lay back in her sleeping robes and stared at the stars. There were no leaves to hide the stars, no forest mists to sheath the world in clouds. For Shadarii, the desert sky had become a source of endless fascination.

Kotaru would have played the flute. If only she could hear that haunting sound once again, the music reaching out to touch her soul.

Kotaru...

Shadarii's eyes glittered in the darkness. The girl listened to the fireside chatter of the others.

The travelers had bathed and rested, and now fat goanna lizards roasted in the coals. In the middle of the desert peace, Tingtraka began to speak. She stared into the flames and let her thoughts drift with the smoke. Her voice whispered in the wind.

"The stars here are beautiful. When I was a little girl, I'd climb high atop a tree and see them. Not as many as this, but still, a few. The priests say that at night you can hear stars whispering in their dreams." Tingtraka stared into the night. "I was going to be a priest. Did you know that? From the time that I was small I always knew that I would be a priest. I wanted to help, you see. I wanted to do something good for everyone. That was always my problem. I only wanted to help."

The girl sadly trailed a finger down her throat. She swallowed hard, trying to change memories into words. "Mama went away. She went off with another man and left Papa all alone. He cried so hard I thought his heart would break. It was all right, though. I understood. I hurt, too. It—it was as if Mama had said she never really loved me. Papa and I just held each other and cried and cried for hours.

"It was only just the two of us together. We were everything each other had. Oh, Rain, but I loved him! He was good to me. Father traded spare food and got me nice clothes and little presents. I think he was sorry he couldn't be with me more. It was all right, though; I understood. You do, you know, even if you're only eight years old. I tried to keep the house for him just like Mama should have. I was very happy then." Her voice trailed to a halt as she remembered a little girl long gone.

Mrrimïmei laid another branch upon the fire. "Do you still want to be a priest?"

"Hmmmm? Oh, yes. I'd like to." Tingtraka's wide eyes glittered. "That would be fine, wouldn't it? To be a real priest."

"So does that mean... You know, are you still..."

"A virgin? No. You see, one night he… made me do it. My own father raped me when I was only eight years old." Tingtraka kept her face toward the fire. If she wept, the others would never know; only Shadarii could see her eyes, and Shadarii would not tell. "He was everything I loved in the whole wide world! My papa. My papa..." Tingtraka's voice caught. "I adored him! My whole world. He was all the love I'd ever known!

"I—I suppose you'd call it rape. Sometimes I don't know. One night he came home crying, I went to him, and he held me. He told me how much he loved me. For a long time he just held me close and said how much he loved me....

"Papa told me what he needed. He said only if I wanted to—only if I didn't mind. He said he loved me and that it was something very special. Something very special to make him feel good again. I—I loved him! I couldn't bear to see him cry. I told him yes. I just closed my eyes and let him, and never even tried to get away."

The girl's fists clenched in the air.

"It hurt! Oh, Rain, but it hurt! He tried to be gentle, but it almost tore me clean in two! I tried not to let him hear me scream. He needed me! How could I fail my papa? All the while it happened, he kept saying how much he loved me. I think that was what hurt me most of all...."

Kitashii stared at the girl in horror. Tingtraka spoke on into the silence, her voice sounding strangely tired.

"It happened again after that. A week later he was touching me again. I knew what he wanted without his even telling me. I cried, but he held me in his arms and said what a good girl I was for him. Somehow it made it seem worthwhile; he still loved me.

"I was frightened, you see. Mama had gone. I thought Papa wouldn't leave me if I was good.

"He started to do it to me more and more. Soon I knew more about sex than any little girl should. Sometimes I sat in class and cried. Everyone said that I was strange in my head. No one ever thought to find out what was really happening....

"One day I woke and knew I had to tell somebody. I went and asked the priests if it had been wrong to do what my father wanted. The priests were very kind. They sent my father off to the healers. He was sick, you see. Papa never wanted to hurt me. He simply couldn't help himself.

"The priests raised me. I've never seen my father since. Years later, I grew old enough to see the horror of just what he had done. I didn't ever want to see him again." Tingtraka ran dead strands of grass through her fingers. "It wasn't my fault. I never even had a name for what I was doing; but still, they never let me be a priest."

Mrrimïmei gazed down at the sand. "You've never had boyfriends, have you? I never wondered why."

"No. The thought of sex still makes me sick; it revolts me." Tingtraka turned dry eyes toward Mrrimïmei and her lover. "And then—then I see you two. I see what love can be, and I'm ashamed.

"Shadarii took my hand and let me cry the pain away. We sat there for hours and hours one night, she listening and me talking. And when I was done, the agony had gone. I had never felt so free in all my life....

"There's no sense in letting the past destroy the present. Someday, I'll find a man to love. There's no hurry; if it's right, it will happen. Shadarii helped me see. I'm going to visit Papa when we return. I want to let him know I forgive him. If I ever loved him, I can give him that small gift. I can never be with him again, but I can take away his pain.

"Taking away pain is all I ever wanted to do. Perhaps I might end up as a sort of priest after all...."

Tingtraka rose, turned the meat upon the fire, and then ran her hands across Kitashii's hair and gave the girl a smile.

Shadarii rolled over and went to sleep in the knowledge of a job well done.

 C8 80 80

Late that night, the pilgrim's camp lay still and silent. The towers loomed over-head like gigantic fingers. No wind blew; no ïsha stirred; not a single insect chirped in the dark. The ruins seemed to lie in wait for their prey.

Shadarii padded stealthily through the dust, following the footprints left earlier in the day. The sand felt cool and soft beneath her feet. The scent of heat still clung to the stones. Shadarii flowed through the ruins like a shadow—lithe, soft lines and thirsting curiosity.

The mighty statue lay as it had fallen—a handsome figure slowly drowning in dust.

Shadarii's antennae quivered. She sensed something... hidden, something interest-ing...

There! Where the base of the statue had once stood, the ïsha whirled with greater intensity. Shadarii excitedly moved over to sift the aura through her mind.

Deep beneath the earth, power flowed. The scent of it seeped out from beneath the giant rock. Shadarii stepped back and reached into her ïsha well. The girl slowly drew it up, feeding it until ïsha glowed around her like a storm. Sand erupted from the ground before her, and a slab of pavement split off and slowly moved aside. Shadarii gasped and let go, astonished by the mighty thing she had done.

A hole yawned before her, and a set of steps led down into the ground. From the darkness rose a smell—ancient air long shut off from Wind and Rain. Shadarii stared down in fascination, drawn helplessly toward the mystery.

A slight noise came from behind. Kïtashii crouched there in hiding.

It was only to be expected, and Shadarii felt pleased and touched. The dancer closed her eyes and smiled, holding out her hand. Kïtashii moved from her hiding place and took her teacher's grasp.

The two Kashra walked slowly down the old stone steps, thrilling to the icy chill of shadows on their fur.

CB ED ED

In the dreaming forest, a fire crackled in Zhukora's lodge. Quiet and drifting in a fragile, precious peace, two slender figures sat in the firelight, enjoying one another's company before the coming of the storm.

Zhukora dragged her hair out of its ponytail, and sheer black silk spilled down into the night. She smiled as Daimïru reached out to take it softly in her hands. The sensation of a gliding comb filled the air with peace.

Daimïru cleared her throat and spoke. "The jiteng match is set for tomorrow. King Saitookii and all the chiefs have gathered for the game. All of them—every elder of the Katakanii and the Vakïdurii—together in one place."

"Our players are ready?"

"Oh, yes. I've handled all the details. Each and every follower knows exactly what to do."

Zhukora gave a thoughtful nod, careful not to disturb Daimïru's gentle hands. Of course, there was nothing left to do but wait. One way or another, the world of to-morrow would be changed.

The huntress closed her troubled eyes and sighed. "And so the game begins, Daimïru. Finally it begins. I must lose myself totally in my purpose. The time for Zhukora is gone. I must transform a final time—rise from the shadows into the light."

"I will be there with you. I will change with you. You will never be alone."

Zhukora hid her face beneath a gleaming stream of hair. "I cannot ask it of you. We both know where this must end."

"I know." Daimïru's strength never faltered. "I will never abandon you."

Zhukora swallowed, then stared into her lap, unable to meet Daimïru's golden eyes. There was something that had to be said—now, before the time was gone. Zhukora trembled as she bared her soul. "Daimïru... In all my life I-I have never had a lover..." Zhukora felt her eyes burn bright with tears. "If—if things had been different... Sometimes I wish the Dream had never come. That I could—could simply be with you."

Shadows played beneath the roof; Daimïru stared into the coals and slowly shook her head. "You were never made for me—not like that. I know that now. I—I'm content. Every order that I follow, I follow out of love."

Zhukora slowly closed her eyes. "Daimïru... I'm sorry."

"Not all love is consummated in the bed." The golden woman's eyes shone bright with tears. "Wherever you go, whatever you do, know this: My love for you will never fail, my faith never fade. Whatever path you fly, I shall be there with you."

The fire crackled as logs shifted in the heat. The women sat side by side in silence, staring at the stars.

Finally, Daimïru shook herself awake. "I should go. There is much to do tomorrow." She slowly rose, wandered to the door, and turned. There, she sank into a bow, spreading her wings in silent worship. Then she was gone.

Zhukora stared into the dark and felt the fire glowing at her back; she gazed into the emptiness long after her friend had gone.

03 80 80

Far beneath the desert sands, Shadarii stared in astonishment.

The stair shaft had opened out into a chamber that echoed like a mighty cave. The ceiling stretched high overhead, vaulted like the limbs of a forest tree. Walls and ceilings were covered in fabulous painted scenes.

The people of the desert had once held marvelous powers!

The ïsha here was more than thick enough for flight. Both girls rose into the air and stared at the murals, peering in amazement at the scenes of life gone by. The art style seemed simpler than that used by Shadarii's people, lacking all sense of depth and perspective. Their ancestors had been primitives in the fields of the fine arts; still, the ancients had raised a civilization of staggering size and power.

It had been a fertile place—flat grassland with little soul, but rich in food. The hills were terraced like stair steps, with orderly rows of plants. Another picture showed women harvesting grain with little metal knives.

"Shadarii, come quickly! Come see!"

Kïtashii hovered beside another set of pictures, her face blank with horror. Tiny Kashra tore each other into bloody ribbons. Heroic figures strode through fields of corpses, their metal clubs striking down enemies. There were women pierced through with darts and hunters slicing at each others' wings.

Shadarii backed away, staring at the walls with new aversion. She straightened her back, cocked her head impatiently, and glowered. *Well? You may show yourself whenever you are ready. I'm quite prepared to wait.*

"Shadarii?" Kïtashii's antennae swiveled. "I can feel... something in here with us!"

Oh, yes, it was clever. Its patterns had merged with those of the cavern, and the Ka lay in hiding, content to spy on its visitors. Shadarii tapped her foot, looking for all the world like a school ma'am waiting to chastise her young.

Something stirred deep in the ïsha. A vast, powerful presence took shape in the darkness. *There's no need to be testy! I was going to show myself when the right time came. Moving too quickly only leads to disaster.*

Speech from a Ka! Shadarii regained her composure and swept down in a bow. The little dancer knelt and offered a glorious ïsha sculpture to her host.

The mighty Ka exclaimed in delight, wrapping tendrils about Shadarii's gift. *How beautiful! How clever! It seems art has flourished across the dusty centuries. Thou art most polite, child. It is a pleasure to see that good manners have survived.*

Shadarii's mind felt all a-whirl. Never once had Shadarii encountered a Ka who talked. The little dancer carefully covered her face with her wings.

Pray, forgive our intrusion. If we have offended, we offer our apologies. We were motivated only by reverent curiosity.

Offended? Why, no, child. Hast thou not guessed? I have been waiting for thee. I have been waiting for a thousand empty years. Shadarii jerked her head up as the spirit came to swirl graciously above her. *Thou art the little teacher—the Silent Lady. I have felt thee blazing through the desert like a star. Finally we meet.*

Felt me! From all that way?

Why, yes. For a thousand years I have slept to heal my wounds. I awoke only when I felt thy touch of beauty stir against my soul.

Hurt? It had been hurt? Poor thing! Shadarii sat on her haunches and stared into the swirling ïsha.

Spirit, my name is Shadarii, daughter of Chief Nochorku-Zha. I am of the tribe of Katakanii, the clan of Swallowtails. I was a dancer of the second circle before my journey into exile. The girl held her bow with a dancer's fluid grace. *Whom do I have the honor of addressing?*

I have never been one for labels. If thou likest, thou may call me Starshine.

Kïtashii stared with great wide eyes at the spirit. Clearly she could not hear it speak. Shadarii turned back to the Ka, losing herself in the wonder of communication.

The spirit danced and filled the air with song. *Thy curiosity blazes in thee like a fire! A kindred spirit! After all these years a scholar wanders to my lonely lair. What can we teach each other, my little one? Shall we make a trade? Let us swap knowledge for knowledge, truth for truth! I shall answer any questions thou asks. In return, tell me of the world of life! Ask; ask and I shall speak.*

How old was such a Ka? Thousands of years? Millions? Think of all the secrets it could tell!

Shadarii leapt to her feet and spread her arms. *Tell me, Lady Starshine! Tell me of this city. Who lived here, and where have they all gone?*

The city has had many names. As a mere watering hole, it was known as "place of reeds." The village became a city over many long, slow years. The Kashra of the Northern kingdom called this place Jho-Kori-Jho. This means "many trees within the wilderness."

Shadarii's eyes blazed brightly. *More! Tell me more! How did they live here in this empty desert? Why did they live in such awful desolation?*

The spirit swirled like a summer rainbow in the sky. *Desolation? Oh, no. It was once green and beautiful. The northern folk dug trenches to bring water to the desert. Alas, the canals were cut by Serpent and his minions. The plants withered, and the city was abandoned to the dust. The city fell because the people would not fight. They thought they could ignore their danger and have it merely pass them by. They paid the price for foolishness. Serpent came for them, and now there is only sand and empty bones.*

Shadarii's ears lifted high in wonder. *Serpent? Who is Serpent?*

A spirit of evil. A creature that thrived on holding power over others. He was finally slain in a war long, long ago.

The war! You saw the war? Shadarii felt a chill ripple down her spine; her mission blazed within her. *What was it like? Why did the people turn to such wickedness?*

Wickedness? Perhaps. Thy race were once powerful warriors, child. When the kingdoms of the north and south finally went to war, the very earth trembled with their might! Serpent worked destruction on an entire world! I could not stop him! Finally we met in single combat. We clashed, and he fell away in mortal agony. Though I was nearly slain, I had some small powers yet. I crept into this place and gave myself to sleep, hoping time might cure my wounds.

The spirit shrugged away her mournful mood and let new light steal through her aura. *Tell me, little sister. Speak to me of thy world. Do the flowers still shine deep in the grass? How do they feel against thy skin? How does the water sound as it goes spilling down the rocks? And Rain, and Wind, and autumn leaves beneath thy feet! Tell me! Tell me what it is to be alive.*

The little dancer cleared her mind and tried to show the spirit visions of her forest world. She thought of deep, cool glades and silent ferns; the lazy drift of dragonflies across a mossy pond....

Suddenly, quite gently, she began thinking of Kotaru. Not the rotting, blackened thing high on the cliff side, but Kotaru the man; sharp and clever, bright and gentle, with his funny, lopsided smile. She remembered long walks hand in hand, grilled crayfish eaten by a fire, dancing for him while he played his wonderful little flute... Shadarii polished her memories, reaching out to feel the forest deep within her soul.

Lady Starshine seemed to give a little sigh. *The man Kotaru—he inside thy dreams. Wilt thou wed? Wilt thou bear young to him? I should like to meet him one day. He seems a fine, strong boy.*

Shadarii's heart grew chill. *No. You will never meet him. He was murdered by my sister. He is gone, and I am condemned to remain behind. Now I wander through the world, wondering if my grief has made me strong.*

The Ka rippled with a quiet flow of rainbows. *Has it made thee strong, girl? Hast thou ever found the answers thou sought?*

I don't know. I set out on a quest to find why violence happens. All I have found is dust and fleas, and hollow towers of mud.... Shadarii miserably hung her head.

The spirit seemed to pause in thought. *Shadarii, what would thou do if thou had power? Real power! Power to heal any sickness with a simple touch. To make life bloom all around thee like a song of joy!*

Shadarii sniffed and sighed. *An idle dream. Peace has no power in the world.*

No! Not so! A miracle can move men's hearts. Make miracles, and thou shalt have thy power!

Shadarii's ears slowly rose. *Miracles? What do you mean?*

Miracles are made, not found. Join with me! Let me escape this dreary land of dust! Let me see and hear and feel through thee. In return, I can give thee sorcery beyond thy wildest dreams! Think of all the good that we can do together! Let me help thee in thy quest for peace. Starshine looped and whirled in desperate eagerness, and Shadarii felt a sudden blaze of greed. Here lay the key! Perhaps this was why Mother Rain had led her to the desert. The girl reeled in excitement, barely able to stand straight.

I-I want... I need to talk to Kïtashii. Please! Just let me speak to her.

Of course, child! Speak with thy acolyte. Take thy time.

Shadarii staggered over to Kïtashii and swiftly told what she had found; the power of it, the majesty—all it could mean to them! The spirit offered miracles, sorcery such as the world had never seen! Their mission could finally go on.

Kïtashii put her hands behind her back and slowly paced the floor. Shadarii nervously watched her, waiting for advice. Kïtashii finally whirled, her little face alive with joy.

"Yes. I say yes, take it! Oh, Shadarii, think what it means! It's a sign. Mother Rain must have led us here herself!"

Shadarii went stock still. The decision quivered there before her. This would change everything. No more little dancer moping in the moss. This would be an end, just as it was a beginning. The old Shadarii would be laid aside forever...

Kïtashii saw the thoughts inside her teacher's mind. "Don't fear it, Shadarii! The world cries out for something new. What's left to us? Kotaru's gone, our tribes reject us. Since you have another destiny, I say embrace it! Take the mask and wear it. Dance the dance, Shadarii! Dance and see where the music leads!"

Shadarii whirled and faced the Ka, then threw out her hands and opened her soul. The spirit seemed to shriek in ecstasy. Shadarii threw back her head and offered her body to the flames. Ïsha plunged down like a knife, and power poured into the dancer in blazing stream of light. Shadarii swelled in triumph and rose against the storm.

Mrrimïmei rose from her blankets, shrieking as grass bloomed beneath her bed. The sand erupted into life. Flowers shot like comets from the sand. The pilgrims shouted in alarm, snatching their blankets and dashing for the rocks.

Ancient seeds exploded with new life. Springs spewed sweet water high into the air, showering across the sands. The pilgrims stared in amazement as a naked figure danced above the miracle, ïsha swirling about her in a daze.

Shadarii!

Shadarii flung out her hands, pouring life into the wilderness. Plant Ka squealed in ecstasy as she drew them from the ground to swirl all about her in a dance of selfless love.

Kïtashii laughed dizzily as the desert bloomed.

Mrrimïmei's jaw dropped in astonishment as a tree beside her suddenly swelled with ripening fruit. "Kïtashii! What's going on? Where are Shadarii's clothes?"

Kïtashii laughed and danced her dance, too far gone in merriment to hear. Tingtraka pressed her hand against her throat and slowly walked into the grass.

"Clothes? She doesn't need them any more! Don't you see? A primal spirit is never clothed. She's taken on the power—taken on the role!"

"B-but she's not a spirit! She's just Shadarii!"

Tingtraka didn't heed. The girl joined Kïtashii in cavorting by the pool, and Shadarii laughed as her followers came spilling down onto the soft green grass. She had the power! She was the chosen one, the Avatar of Mother Rain. The girl danced for joy, thrilling to the feel of moonlight across her naked fur.

She would make a legend. She was given to the ages. Now the story of Shadarii would begin!

Seventeen

The creek shone cool and sparklingly clean. Overhead, a band of cockatoos clowned in the trees. Keketál gazed at their antics and gave a funny smile.

A line of old clay potsherds leaned against a fallen branch. With a flash, a broken milk jug passed on to the next world, and Harïsh laughed as she flicked her sling back into her hands. "See? Easy! Now you try. Go on."

Keketál stood watching the young shepherdess. She was slim, long, and lanky— great bright eyes and laughing boyish curves. Her breasts were new enough to be an embarrassment she was trying to learn to accept.

All of the village women wore nothing but skirts wrapped about their hips, and the occasional water jug balanced on their skulls. Though the sight of them should have been commonplace, Keketál still found his eyes drawn in blushing fascination.

He awkwardly hefted his sling and tried to keep his mind on the job. He picked a rose-quartz pebble from the stream and shook it free of water. A sling seemed easy enough in principle; he need only whip the stone around his head and let it fly. Keketál poised the sling, took careful aim, and fired. He stared eagerly at the target, waiting for it to shatter into a thousand little bits.

"Keketál! Look out!"

The man gave a squawk, then frantically dashed aside as his sling stone crashed down into the grass behind him. Keketál tripped and fell straight into the stream.

"Keketál!" Harïsh dashed to her patient's side as he cursed and smashed his fist against the water. Harïsh sighed and shook her head; accidents and Keketál just seemed to go together. She calmly made the offer to help him rise.

Keketál sniffed, cradling his fragile dignity. "I can be helping self, thanking very much!"

"Oh, no, you can't! Now, I'm not having you strain yourself, so accept my hand or you can just sit in there and suffer!"

With poor grace, the nobleman took Harïsh's offer and allowed himself to be dragged from the stream. Harïsh seemed rather strong for a girl her age. She had also picked up a vulgar habit of laughing at her elders. Keketál haughtily wrung out his tail.

Harïsh usually wore two or three slings about her forehead, each optimized for a particular range. She ran one weapon's thongs between her fingers as she spoke. "Look, you just whip it, see? It's just like throwing, only your arm is longer."

She demonstrated once again, hurtling a heavy stone into a shard of pottery.

Keketál glumly looked down at his sling and heaved a mighty sigh. "Maybe sling is not meant for I. Keketál make accident again."

Poor Keketál. He tried so hard to be a help. Clearly he was not used to freeloading on his hosts. Once he got up early to tread the clay, but father wouldn't hear of it. A noble, laboring? Never! What did he think daughters were made for?

That admonition had not stopped Keketál from sneaking out to chop the wood. Harïsh had been furious when she'd found out. A man with a stomach wound swinging a stone ax ? Absurd! She had told him off quite thoroughly until he had wilted like a dying flower. Her heart had softened in an instant; the poor girl was hopelessly in love.

Beside the stream, all seemed clean and quiet. The trill of bellbirds filled the air, and ïsha murmured sleepily to the caress of water. It was good just to be together. They walked along the rocks, teetering as they tried not to wet their sandals.

Keketál was not quite used to the feeling of his clothes. Sandals, kilt, and cross belts... so simple, but so very strange. And he just kept staring at Harïsh's smooth breasts... !

She noticed his interest and cocked her pretty head. Keketál felt his ears burn bright red, coughed and tried to find some way to cover himself. "Uh—Harïsh. You are to watching sheep today?"

"Sheep. Watching sheep. Yes, I'm minding them this afternoon. I have the shift after Mixtli."

"Aaah, shall I come as well? Sheep-sheep make for nice sleepy thoughts. Harïsh can talk and talk until she drops. I listen and learn some more goodly talkings, yes?"

"Listen and learn some more speech." The girl wagged her finger at him. "And, no, there'll be no lazy afternoon for you! Great leader Keketál offered to help in the house raising, didn't he? And so, now he gets to spend a hot afternoon laboring in the sun."

"Oh..."

"Yes, 'oh!' Silly man. Don't you dare strain that wound!"

Keketál's ears wilted; he had forgotten about the house building. Now he was going to lose the entire afternoon.

The girl paused on a rock and archly glanced across her shoulder. "I have a surprise for you this evening. There are rewards for mighty house builders! The day might not be wasted after all."

Suddenly the rock moved beneath her feet. The girl gave a squeak and pitched toward the water, but Keketál caught her, dragging her safely into his arms. She clung gratefully against him, laughing as he swept her off her feet.

Finally held in Keketál's arms, Harïsh simpered prettily. Embarrassed, Keketál set the disappointed girl down on the grass and dusted off his hands. Harïsh gave him a frustrated glare and sullenly launched aloft. Keketál blinked and felt his antennae drooping.

What did I do this time?

Completely mystified, Keketál followed her. He sighed and wondered how he always managed to get into so much trouble.

 CS 80 80

A blazing meteor cleaved above the desert waste. In its wake, life exploded from the desolation, grass burst out across the sand, springs miraculously appeared—the world awakened from death into life.

The naked dancer cleaved the air like a streaking spear of light. The pilgrims whooped with laughter as she led them on a merry ride. Behind them, a swathe of green sprang up beside a whole new river. Shadarii squandered power wantonly, throwing her arms out in delight as she reached out to shape a world!

Lady Starshine felt the wind whipping through Shadarii's hair and shrieked for joy. *Oh, gods, I had forgotten what the touch of life was like! To feel the power in these forms! To see the world through bright new senses! Oh, Shadarii, dost thou see, my love? Dost thou see what we can be together?*

The spirit laughed as Shadarii caressed her with her mind. Starshine thrilled to the little dancer's touch.

We shall become a power in this world, my love! Where your sister was death, you shall be life. Ashes swirl in her footsteps while you leave only petals! I shall show you powers undreamed of. We shall fight evil and scour away all pain and want. It shall be the golden age of Shadarii!

Shadarii chided the boisterous spirit. *We shall first find out what is wrong with the world, and then we shall heal it. I shall be a builder and a maker! No more killing, no more anger. I shall give the world a gift of peace!*

Thou must be ready to fight, my child. Thy enemies are legion. War lies upon thy path.

Fight? When I can do all this? Fa! The world is far too beautiful for fighting! Shadarii made a triumphant barrel roll, swooping dizzily through the air. Behind her, the pilgrims laughed in merriment as she led them far out into the desert sky.

ଔ ଷ ଷ

Girls giggled around the village stream, chattering happily as they balanced tall pitchers on their heads. It was house-raising time; a season for excitement. There were boons to be collected by the men. Who would choose whom? Girls slyly swapped opinions and filled the air with laughter.

Harïsh swooped across the stream and spread her wings for landing. The advantages of being a potter's daughter were few and far between, but tonight they made a difference. She had the most spectacular water jug any girl could hope for. Harïsh leaned down to peer into the stream, briskly checked her hair, her earrings, and her makeup. She dipped her jug down into the stream and carefully filled it to the top. Balanced serenely beneath her load, Harïsh climbed her way toward the village square.

A languid female voice flickered in her ear. "So, Harïsh, going somewhere? How very odd!"

Harïsh shot a hostile glance toward the speaker, and her tail flicked archly through the air. "Odd? I'm carrying water, Namïlii! Even though you don't work, you must at least have seen other people being useful."

Her opponent rose from the grass beside the stream. Namïlii was a thin streak of a girl with delicious bedroom eyes. She looked Harïsh up and down and gave a haughty sniff. From the lofty age of sixteen, a fifteen-year-old seemed a mere child.

"And what are you doing here? This is no place for little girls. We women are having a private conversation."

"Well I'm sure you're constantly talking about your privates. As for me, there's work to be done, so good day!" Harïsh cruised up the hill, not spilling a single drop of water.

Namílii opened her mouth to toss out a parting shot, but Harísh had already gone.

Another girl sniffed wriggled her elegant whiskers. "So, Namílii, do you have your eyes on anyone in particular? Someone with colored wings, perhaps?"

That did it! Namílii shot the girl a narrow glance and proudly took her leave. Soon they'd see just who chose boons from whom! They all might be laughing on the other side of their faces.

The village square had become the center of a bustling industry. Young men of the village thatched and wove, stripping saplings and trimming strips of wood. All through the thirsty afternoon, they drove themselves in their tasks, and the house grew with amazing speed.

A circular perimeter of saplings had been thrust into the ground, their tops bent down and lashed firmly into place. Soon the grass thatching would be spread across the dome. A house was rising out of nothing more than sticks and grass.

Everyone briskly went about his task, never once interrupting the smooth efficiency of team work—everyone except one man. The locals shook their heads and left him to his own devices.

Right now, Keketál was engaged in "improving" on the traditional house design. He diligently added diagonal braces all across the structure. Hupshu, the husband-to-be and prospective owner of the house, watched in bewilderment.

"Keketál, why are you doing that? It's time to put the thatching on. You're holding everything up!"

Keketál hovered erratically in the air, trying to talk through a mouthful of spare string. He gurgled something unintelligible in reply.

"Keketál, the others are waiting! We're keen to finish the house."

"Keketál make cross braces. Make house stronger."

"But...why?"

"Better is better! Strong house better than weak house! No fall down."

Hupshu scratched his head. Certainly the point was valid, only why bother? If the house fell down, they could simply make another.

Toonwa, the seance singer, stamped over to Hupshu's side. The man had little time for foolishness. "Hupshu, the day grows hotter! What is this idiot noble doing? The house braces look like an abomination!"

The workers muttered in agreement. Hupshu shook his tawny head and peered up at Keketál. "He's done something to the internal structure. Just try pushing it. See? It doesn't shift and flatten."

"It is a waste of time! There is a set method for building a house. Experimentation is not productive. Time is wasting and the maids are waiting!"

Keketál's tail waggled merrily above them as he tested all his lashings. "Ho, Too'vaa! If problem is, why not to helping be?"

"Because it's not my job, you dozy man! I am a thatcher, so I thatch! Yekïchi is a rope maker, so he makes the lashings. Each and every one of us has our own set task. There was no mention anywhere about extra braces!"

"Nobleman gets any job he wants. Keketál wants this job! Braces hurt nobody but make house much better. Is good, no?"

"No it's not good! You're holding everybody up."

"If want speed, why not help?"

"Because it's none of my affair!"

Toonwa stomped off to join the other thatchers. Hupshu gave the man a cold hard stare before fluttering up to aid Keketál. To both of their surprise, a group of youngsters left their other tasks to join them. They grinned through their sweat at Keketál, nodding as he smiled in thanks.

Keketál fixed a final knot and tugged furiously at the house frame. The wooden skeleton barely even moved. Satisfied at last, Keketál heaved a weary sigh and fell back to the ground. He landed clumsily, and pain stabbed through him. Keketál folded over in agony.

Hupshu raced over in alarm.

"My lord! Is it bad? Harïsh will kill me!"

"No! Hurt n-not bad! Must... must help with thatching...."

"Enough, my lord. Enough! Harïsh would have our tails if she found out!" Hupshu led his friend across to a handy piece of shade.

An old man sat there, watching the house take shape while chipping out flint knife blades on a stone. His craftsmanship was beautiful to behold. The old man dusted off his lap and pointed at Keketál's nose. "All this extra work. Y'ought to pace yourselves better, else you'll have no energy for tonight! Where's the point in house raisin' if y' can't enjoy what comes after?"

Hupshu gave a weary grin. "Ha! Perhaps Your Reverence would care to come help?"

The old man gave a snort and reached for a fresh chunk of flint. "I have a wife's ire to fret about. 'Tis not worth the lumps I'd get tonight. You youngster's enjoy it while you can!"

Enjoy it? Keketál felt his muscles tremble. It had damned near killed him! The villagers must have some strange fascination for heavy lifting. For the sake of fellowship, a whole village had dropped their work and come to build a house for Hupshu's bride.

It looked like there were some rewards in any case. The parents of the happy couple had laid on quite a feast. The delicious scent of roasted lamb sizzled through the evening air. Keketál gave an exhausted smile and thought about the coming pleasures of his dinner.

Young girls brought jugs of water for the thirsty workers, and men made haste to seem at ease and nonchalant. Tired looks disappeared; all grumbling miraculously ceased.

Keketál stroked his nose in puzzlement. The girls seemed strangely different. He couldn't quite put his finger on it, but something had changed. The girls' eyes sparkled; their lashes fluttered prettily as they spoke coyly to the men. Tails waved little hints of perfume on the drowsy summer air.

Keketál felt his ears blush hot. The skirts seemed a trifle brief today! What on earth was going on?

A tall, slender village girl walked toward Keketál. Her eyes were filled with dark, delicious promise. Each curve and valley gleamed in glorious harmony. She fixed her smoldering gaze on Keketál, melting her chosen victim to the spot.

The girl hefted a tall jug of water, and saliva broke out all across Keketál's parched tongue. A drink! The girl must have been sent down by the spirits.

Hupshu firmly shut Keketál's jaw and whispered in his ear. "Psst! Don't look! Just play 'em on a bit. The fun starts when they get really desperate for your attention."

"What?"

"Ssssh! Trust me; don't look too thirsty. Anyway, here comes another one, see? With any luck, there'll be a fight!"

Keketál blinked in wonder as Harísh cruised over in his direction, trying to move her hips just like the older girls. She looked at him with anxious eyes and suddenly faltered in her tracks.

Keketál stared at her in wonder. For the first time he really saw her. Keketál blinked. Dear Rain, had she always been so... pert?

The girl bent down to pour him a drink, her backside deliberately turned toward him. She met his eyes, jumped with fright, and then fled into the trees.

A warm voice broke in upon Keketál's whirling thoughts. The sultry female that he had seen before stood offering a water jug, her voice husky with hinted promises. "Gentle lord, would you care to sip from my sweet waters?"

Keketál's heart stammered in his breast. "Uh—No thank you! Keketál has water already."

"Are you satisfied so easily, handsome lord? Perhaps I can slake your thirst far better. Once you dip into Namílii's well, you may lose interest in more common drink...."

She cocked her head, regarding him through lowered lashes. Keketál looked around himself in panic. Harísh stared tearfully at him from afar, and Keketál hastily waved Namílii away.

"My—uh—my drink is fine, thanking you! Is enough for me."

"I understand, my lord. Still, the evening is long and hot. I am always there should you ever need to slake your thirst..."

Namílii flung a triumphant smile toward Harísh, and the potter's girl fixed a bitter glare on Keketál.

Hupshu boisterously slapped Keketál between the wings. "Ha! See, I told you it can get interesting!" He gestured with his cup toward the waiting women. "That's two aiming for you. Rain help you if Harísh sees you eyeing off Namílii again. And Rain help Harísh if her father finds out she's serving water!"

Keketál missed the point. He blinked in confusion and scratched his addled head. "Why can't Harísh serve water?"

"Cause she's only fifteen, that's why! There'll be blood to pay if old man Totli catches her!" The man heaved an admiring sigh. "Aaaah, what it must be to have a noble's wings!"

A wild storm of applause broke out as the last strips of thatching were hauled into place. Hupshu dragged Keketál to his feet.

"Come on! It's starting. Don't keep 'em waiting long or the girls might start to fight. They did that when we built Pochtli's place last summer. Clothes ripping, hair torn out..." The young man pulled his chin in thought. "One of them was the bride, too. Funny thing life, eh?"

"B-but why? Why girls fight?"

"Because... j-just go get into line."

Keketál scuttled off toward the feasting tables where Lord and Lady Ingatïl and their son were already blessing the new house. As chief noble of the village, Ingatïl had welcomed Keketál into the community. Fascinated by his flute music and fishing, the old man seemed delighted to have another noble close at hand.

"Aaaah, Keketál! So here you are, boy! A splendid job on the house. Absolutely splendid! Not normally the done thing for a noble to get his hands dirty, but we must all move with the times. I suppose labor is terribly modern, what?"

Keketál blushed and nodded, embarrassed by the old man's love. Ingatïl and his wife had made Keketál welcome in their midst without a murmur of complaint. They left him largely in the hands of Harïsh and her family, content to invite him to dinner once in a while and talk to him of "noble's business" such as alliances and marrow growing.

The feast had drawn the entire village. Hupshu laughed and served his guests meat, dealing out the food with a lavish hand. The village girls demurely clustered in the shadows, coyly sheltering behind their wings. The house builders were on the far side of the clearing, whispering excitedly as they eyed the women. Hupshu wiped his greasy hands and drew Keketál near.

"Here we go! All right, just make your choice and make it well. Remember how seriously a woman tends to take these little things...."

Women were staring at him, devouring him with their eyes.

Keketál felt a rising surge of panic. "Hsst! Keketál not understand. What is Keketál to choose?"

Hupshu ran his fingers through his hair. "Look, it's the payment for helping build a house. Tradition, you see! Everyone who helps can claim a kiss from one maiden of the village. That's what gets the girls in such a state! You can chose only one, so if you could choose any woman to kiss, and you knew she couldn't refuse you, who would you take?"

Aaaaah! Finally the light dawned! Keketál mentally applauded the audacity of the man who'd invented this one; making men eager to do hard work had been a feat of pure genius. One had to admit, the custom had a certain charm...

A hush fell across the bystanders as the fun began. A young house builder stepped forward and curled a finger toward a blushing shepherdess. "Kürimal! I claim my boon!"

The girl dashed out and stood on tiptoe to take her kiss. The young herdsman shyly brushed her lips, and the crowd made sound of appreciation. The girl pressed deeper into her partner's arms.

A stifled snarl of rage came from among the other girls. Keketál saw a young woman brushing tears back from her eyes as she fled for home. Hupshu's warning rang suddenly all too clear; this game was dangerous.

"Namïlii, I claim a boon of you!"

A tall fisherman called triumphantly out across the field, and Namïlii came forth to give the man his due. She took him and devoured him with a sizzling kiss. Namïlii left her victim dazed, eyeing Keketál as she sauntered back toward the other girls.

One by one the workers claimed their prizes, and the women met the choices with delight or disgust. Slowly the little ceremony drew to a close, until Keketál found himself finally thrust out into the open.

The little group of maidens seemed to draw a breath. Keketál stared from one face to another, his ears flushing as he saw the women gaze at him with desire. The man tried to beat a hasty retreat, but Hupshu steered him firmly back in place.

"Now look! It's an insult not to choose anybody. Just make it quick, and it'll all be over."

"B-but who?"

"Well I don't know! It's your kiss! Who would you most like to get a kiss from?"

Suddenly Keketál met a pair of frightened, hopeful eyes. Harïsh had hidden back behind the other girls. The girl jerked away, trying not to show him the yearning in her gaze.

"Keketál will claim his boon. He asks a kiss of sweet Harïsh."

Harïsh! The girl nearly swooned as joy poured into her like a stream of light. She came into his arms, craning to offer him the gift she craved to give. She closed her eyes, trembling as he slowly bent to kiss her parting lips.

A voice cracked out across the yard. "Stop!"

The partners whirled to see Namïlii charging the village square.

"Stop! He cannot claim a boon from Harïsh! Choose another. Choose a boon from the maidens! It is the law."

Keketál looked down at Harïsh in confusion. "Why? You say choose, Keketál makes choice! Why not Harïsh?"

"Harïsh is not a woman! You cannot claim a boon from a mere child!"

Harïsh flew straight for her enemy's throat. Keketál frantically dragged her back by the heels. The air was full of thrashing wings and tearing claws.

"You bitch! I'll rip your eyes out!"

"Piddling little child! I'd like to see you try!"

"Slut!"

"Tart!"

"Whore!"

"Child!"

Harïsh gave an incoherent shriek and ripped off her headband. Keketál caught her before she could find a handy stone. Hupshu meanwhile tried his best to hold the other girl at bay.

Harïsh flung dirt into Namïlii's eyes. "Who are you to say if I'm a woman or a girl?"

"Little girls should be back pissing diapers in the nursery, not planning an evening on their backs!"

"You skinny whore! Just 'cause half the village has plowed your Fire-damned furrow!"

The women lunged toward each other, murder in their eyes.

Keketál flung out his hands and ïsha flashed, sending both women tumbling in the dust. The huge nobleman dangled one female in either hand. "Enough! Be still."

Lord Ingatíl came bustling over and tapped his foot in anger. "Disgraceful! Namílii, what would your mother say if she saw you making such a spectacle? Harïsh, have you no shame? Trying to take the prerogatives of a full maiden!"

"Lord! I am a woman! A woman!" Harïsh clutched her chest in anger. "I have as much right to reward a builder as the next girl! Lord Keketál has asked me, and I want to give!"

"My dear, you are nothing but a little girl. You have not yet had your sixteenth birthday."

"Birthday?" Harïsh threw off Keketál's hands. "I'm more a woman than that Namílii can ever be! Just because I don't screw every living creature in the village..."

Namílii gave an incoherent shriek of rage. She tried to gouge Harïsh's eyes, only to be caught and shaken like a rattle by Keketál.

Harïsh stood her ground before the village speaker. "Lord Ingatíl, I am a woman, and I claim a maiden's rights! My body speaks for itself! Let Namílii prove I'm not a woman."

It was an interesting problem; Lord Ingatíl paced slowly back and forth, his long wings slowly beating the air. Finally the old man turned and tapped his nose. "Here is my judgment. The law of 'four virtues' must hold. This is the accepted measure of adulthood. Harïsh, are you adept in four separate arts? Prove to us your skill, and we shall accept you as a woman grown."

Harïsh threw herself clear of Keketál, then opened her hands to show the tattoos of a healer. "I am a surgeon! The high healer himself wishes to take me as his student. Lord Keketál is my proof of skill!"

Ingatíl scratched his nose and grudgingly conceded. "Harïsh, you are indeed a healer. You do credit to our village."

The girl furiously pointed to her magnificent water jug. "I am a potter! My father has taught me how to glaze and fire. My own wares are for sale at the markets!"

"Harïsh, you are a talented potter. Your work exhibits a considerable charm."

"I am a shepherdess. I tend the flocks. I shear and spin, weave and milk. No girl in the village makes finer cheese! No one in the tribe can match me with a sling!"

"Harïsh, your prowess with the sling has caused us trouble more than once. We still remember the incident with the high seer and the wasp's nest. As for your cheeses, their taste is... memorable, to say the least. We shall conceded that you have this skill."

Namílii whirled toward Lord Ingatíl and flung her hands out wide. "My lord, these are crafts, not arts! Is this virtue? There's no creativity in making mere pots!"

Harïsh's father spoke out from the crowd. "I heard that, Namílii-toka! You just see how long you wait for your next water jug!"

The girl hissed in spite and ignored the interruption. "I say again, where is her art? Would you compare this prancing little imp with me? I am a musician of the first degree, skilled in both the flute and the long grass pipe! I am a poetess, trained in the creation of running stanzas! And for my fourth virtue..."

A crude voice hooted from somewhere in the audience. "No one does it better!"

"My fourth virtue!" Namílii spoke on regardless "is the skill of dancing."

"What?" Harïsh snapped her fingers underneath Namïlii's nose. "Why you puffed up river toad! You dance like a pregnant ewe. I'll outdance you any day of the week!"

"Why you little she-goat! You've never danced a step in all your life!"

By way of answer Harïsh snatched her empty water jug. She glared in challenge at Namïlii. "Well?"

Namïlii grabbed her own pitcher and proudly marched to the center of the clearing. She stood there waiting, flipping her tail in challenge. Both women balanced their jugs between their ears and stood delicately poised and waiting.

Men ran for their instruments, and soon clay flutes warbled like a flock of bumble bees. The two women stood with the tall jugs balanced on their heads and held their arms out level with the dusty ground. With a nod from Lord Ingatïl, the little orchestra suddenly found its footing and began to play. A sigh rippled through the crowd as the slender dancers gracefully began to turn.

They moved with the timeless suppleness of sweet young river grass. Harïsh and Namïlii both bobbed slowly down upon their haunches, rose and turned a stately pirouette, the water jugs never once shifting on their heads. They slowly turned and closed their eyes, concentrating carefully as the music cycled through its chords.

Full circle; both women's faces were serene with concentration. They snapped their fingers once, bobbing down to start their stately dance once again. Harïsh kept her lashes closed as she matched her opponent, move for move.

The rhythm slowly gained momentum. Men began to clap in time to the rising music while women chorused admiration as the dancers dipped and spun. Keketál found himself joining in their heady beat, grinning as Harïsh calmly flitted him a glance. He blew a kiss as he watched his girl of gold; she felt his aura touching her and gave a glowing smile.

The musicians exchanged a set of evil glances, and suddenly the music increased its tempo. The dancers slid into the higher speed without a hitch. They dipped, they whirled, they bobbed in place. Each girl kept the measure without error, turn after turn, each one slightly faster than the last.

Again the music sped its tempo. Clapping hands drummed the girls on ever faster. A bead of sweat trickled slowly down Namïlii's brow. The girl gritted her fangs and tried to stop her hands from shaking. She fell behind the beat, blinking as she saw her enemy cruising through the turn. Namïlii gulped and tried to make more speed.

Her jug began to tilt. Namïlii felt the balance shift and tried to compensate. Suddenly the jug was tumbling through the air. Namïlii gave a shriek as her water jug smashed against the ground. The girl screamed words Keketál had never even heard as the crowd surged forward to Harïsh and whirled her in the air. Her father grinned at her and clasped his hands in victory.

Keketál took her in his arms. She grabbed his face and locked him in a wild, delirious kiss. Keketál dizzily clung against her, half fighting her and half lost inside her touch. It was wrong—she was only fifteen! And there was something else—something he couldn't quite remember. It burned him, shrieking in anguish somewhere in his mind.

Harïsh loved him; only a fool could fail to see it now. Keketál let the moment take him, content to drift within the wonder of her embrace.

Eighteen

The sound of the crowd surged like a forest washed beneath a restless wind. It was the sound of life, of rage and thunderous power, and its ïsha currents shook the forest to the roots.

Zhukora listened to the ebb and flow. Finally the gamble had begun; racial destiny hung teetering in the balance. On one side lay absolute extinction—on the other, Zhukora's blazing light of change.

And on both sides lay her death. Zhukora saw her ending and was not afraid. She had made her bargain with the gods; the time of Zhukora finally had come.

Daimïru knelt behind her. The stark white skull-face craned toward Zhukora in expectation. Childlike eyes gleamed in the shadows of the mask. "The jiteng teams are assembled. The chiefs and kings begin their feast. It is time."

"Yes, my love. Time to ride the winds." Zhukora reached down to touch her beloved's streaming golden hair. "I love you."

Daimïru waited for her leader to whir into the air, and then followed her across the jiteng field. The sun shone down on them both, transfixing them with light as they rode the tossing power of a people's rage.

The moth-feast had become an absolute disaster, but even in the face of starvation, traditions had been ruthlessly enforced. The nobles had been allowed to glut themselves on moth meat, leaving nothing but pathetic pickings for the poor. The Kashra were a ravening horde. Where they moved, not a single living thing remained. Paradise had become broken wasteland. Desperate hunting parties snarled and fought, and for the first time in a thousand years, violence blossomed in the people's hearts.

Zhukora's followers had hurtled themselves into a frenzy of salvation. She had taken the hunters and formed them into enormous killing teams. Forsaking the ancient laws, she had set fire to whole regions of forest, driving panic-stricken game onto the people's spears. The commoners no longer cared for custom.

The people leapt to their feet as Zhukora flew across the field, sixty thousand voices thundering her name. She swirled up to the waiting kings and sketched a graceful bow before her waiting enemy.

Teki'taa lay back, caressing a shamefaced serving girl. Old King Saitookii glared across the crowd. Beside the kings, the elders of both tribes had gathered about a wasteful feast. There were councilors and popinjays—Dance Mistress Traveesha and lordly, fat old men.

Black clad in her wooden armor, Zhukora turned toward the kings, shaping every word and moment into tools of her desire. "My lords, the game teams are ready. The our tribes are assembled. We await only your signal to begin."

Nochorku-Zha flattened his ears and glared into his daughter's face. "You have overstepped your authority! There are sixty thousand people out there! You were asked to arrange a simple jiteng game. Can't you even do that properly?"

"The presence of your own people disturbs you, Father?"

"Disturbs me? Pah! It's disastrous! What are you going to do with them afterward, eh? You didn't think of that, now did you? There's no food for all these vermin! They'll pay for their foolishness with hungry bellies and screaming children!"

Zhukora gave a smooth gesture of her hands. "Daimïru has seen to food. For the first time in weeks, there will be enough."

"We are not fools, Zhukora. We know about your bush fires! We shall take this matter up with you at a later time. Status can be a fragile thing!"

Zhukora bowed before Nochorku-Zha, her face strangely lit with calm. "All power is fragile, Father."

"Power? Power is eternal!" Nochorku-Zha spoke for all of them—the assembled chiefs and kings. "It is enshrined in our way of life!"

"That is a foolish, dangerous belief." The black-furred woman shone with an almost magical inner light. "Power is lent from one person to another. It is a gift, and a gift may be withdrawn unless it is a gift of love."

King Tekï'taa had ignored the entire exchange. Zhukora's entourage of Skull-Wings seemed to amuse his tastes. "So, Zhukora! Still you insist on consorting with commoners. I suppose a noble must be forgiven these little whims. We would never stand for it in the Vakïdurii, but there you are! Each to his own."

Zhukora turned to view her group of attendants. "They are my soul mates, my lord. I do not believe that colored wings signify ability."

"Soul mates? One of 'em looks like a child!"

"She is thirteen, great lord. An artist and sculptor. It is the girl Rooshïkii, whom you placed in my care as a boon."

Tekï'taa's pushed his attendants' hands away. "Th-that little girl is still with you?"

"Aye, my lord. Rooshïkii is my trusted friend. Although she is young, she has more intelligence than many thrice her age. She was the first Skull-Wing from the Vakïdurii tribe."

"The first?" King Tekï'taa jerked in alarm. "There are others?"

"Sire, there are now perhaps two hundred Vakïdurii members of the Skull-Wings."

Vakïdurii chiefs shot up in alarm. One old woman pointed a quaking finger in accusation. "Witch, you've deceived us! You'd have our own folk playing on the field against us!"

Zhukora's power cracked like a swelling storm. "Deceived you? You accepted a challenge—the Skull-Wings against the Mantises. I made no mention of tribes."

"But our own tribesmen might be playing against us!"

From the Katakanii lines, Mistress Traveesha rose to glare at the Vakïdurii leadership. "What? Oh, never! Zhukora would not be so perverse!"

Zhukora turned her gaze upon her fellow Swallowtail. "You are quite wrong, Traveesha. At least half the Skull-Wing team upon the field will be Vakïdurii. They no longer think in terms of tribes, but in terms of nation. They are mine, and I am theirs. That is all that matters now."

King Tekï'taa peeled a fruit, glaring at Zhukora with distaste. "This is a most bizarre jest, my lady! I hope there is good reason for your behavior."

The girl cocked her head and peered from beneath her streaming hair at the assembled company. Suddenly she seemed every inch a scheming little girl. "It is not so much a trick as a riddle. The answer to the riddle is very simple. There shall be a reward for anyone who can answer it before the game is done. The riddle is this: What does it mean if your own people wish to play against you?"

She turned to Daimïru and filled her with her power. Daimïru worshipfully pressed her face down to the ground, and then soared forth to lead the team. The crowd raised a roar as they saw her come. Zhukora watched her beloved go, her eyes flashing bright as stars.

"Wings spread, ball high!"

"First attack group, dive!"

Skull-Wings surged toward their prey; Daimïru pumped her fist and sent a shock-team smashing down into the enemy. The air shivered with the thunderous crash of impact. Armor splintered. Bones cracked. Skull-Wings snarled and slashed at Mantis' wings. All around the field, the audience shrieked in an orgy of approval. The crowd fed on the violence and drove itself into a foaming rage.

Daimïru felt the breath burn in her lungs. The Wrens had been a challenge, but mere noblemen were barely worth the trouble. She whirled around to find her own elite reserves and brought them her gift of rage. "Their captain's mine! Follow me!"

Daimïru gave a scream and split the enemy formation. Mantis masks yelled at her as she shattered them in two. She spun and rolled between a snarling pair of Mantis guards, shrieked, and broke a victim's wings.

The Mantis captain whirled in shock. Daimïru plunged down from above. He barely had time to scream. Daimïru's boots smashed into the Mantis mask, snapping teeth and crushing bone. Daimïru arched in climax as her victim's body spiraled to the ground.

The audience howled in ecstasy.

Daimïru's boots dripped with blood, sweet and fresh and smoking hot! She looked down at the corpse and let out a scream of victory. She shook her staff toward Zhukora and howled out her leader's holy name.

The cry was taken up by thousands, and then tens of thousands, until the whole world trembled to the sound of adoration.

Daimïru wheeled across her fallen enemy and flung Zhukora's name to the sky.

"Dear Rain! It-it's turning into a riot!"

"Is that player unconscious? Sweet Wind, what did that girl do?"

"They're animals!"

Crowds surged around the royal stand. The air thundered with their demented rage. Vast waves of people screamed out Zhukora's name, shaking branches and trees.

Zhukora breathed the delicious breeze, her slim young body gleaming as she turned toward the storm. "Terrifying, isn't it? Power! Pure, raw power! It needs only a hand to shape it, to guide it along a chosen path!" The girl's terrifying eyes gazed across the elders. "How does your power compare against this, my lords? Surely there is a rule against it? Will no one quote a law to the crowd?" She looked at their fear and gave a laugh. "What? Has your control faded so soon? When did it go, I wonder? Did you feel it slip so swiftly through your hands?"

Nochorku-Zha had his hands clapped across his ears. His eyes rolled in terror. "Stop it! For Rain's sake, stop it! You started it, now end it before it goes too far!"

"Oh, Father, I don't want to stop it! I have worked so long for this moment. Old fools! You have sat so long atop your tree you have forgotten to look down." She looked out across the shrieking mob and slowly closed her eyes. "My power! My people! United in a single will. We shall set a fire inside this forest that will change the world forever! The rot will be burned away, the cluttered wood seared clean! The new growth will be strong and wild and free!"

"You're mad!" Teki'taa reached for his dao. "I'll have you exiled! I'll have you killed! Guards! Guards, take this creature away!"

"I don't think so. Rooshïkii, please ensure our guests remain in their places."

A silent guard of Skull-Wings instantly rose from the leaves, and the tribal elders shrank into a panting knot of terror.

Teki'taa reeled in panic. He saw Rooshïkii's calm eyes beneath her snarling mask. The spear in the girl's small hands never left his throat, and she slowly let it pierce his sobbing hide.

"You won't get away with this! We have laws and customs! The tribes will stone you into pulp! It will take more than a mere sports team to bring us down!"

Zhukora looked sadly down into Teki'taa's face. "Do you still not understand? It is not a team, my lord; it is an army—a new way of being. The Skull-Wings are a moral elite." She smiled out at her followers, filling them with her love. "Each of us has made a single pure decision. The deliberate choice to die for our beliefs. We are already dead. Don't you see? No fear, no other cause to live for. Once we made the choice to die, we finally became free. The ultimate liberation!"

Teki'taa wept in fright. Everywhere he looked, the faces of the dead stared coldly back at him.

Zhukora gazed at him and slowly shook her head. "You will die, King Teki'taa. There is no escape for you. The people are mine now. Their power has passed to me. I shall scour your filth away and make the world anew."

The Vakïdurii king gave a dreadful, broken sob. He had wet himself in fright.

Zhukora almost felt pity for him. "Oh, you will not die yet. Not quite yet. There is a game to win, you see? I do have a sense of theater. We shall all be part of one last dance together; the final performance of your lives...."

Her father snarled and spat down at her feet. "Traitorous bitch! I curse the day your mother bore you! I wish she'd died rather than laid your egg into this world! May her soul... aaaaaaugh!" The old man stared in disbelief at the spear jutting from his chest. He croaked and spilled down to his knees, his eyes gazing in horror at his daughter.

Mad with hate, Zhukora clenched the hand that had thrown the spear and gleefully watched him die. "You were never worthy of her! She was all that is perfect! You have defiled me with your blood inside my veins. Die! Die old man! Let your soul go screaming in the dark!"

Zhukora flung Lord Serpent at her father's soul. His Ka screamed as the demon began to feed. Zhukora wept and laughed, staring down in triumph at her father's twitching corpse.

The crowd gave another roar; another goal down. Zhukora whirled and stared out across the playing field, shining like a god. The jiteng game ended in a frenzy as the teams sought each other's blood. The two formations hurtled together in a blast of force. In a single dreadful instant, the Mantis team simply ceased to be. Daimïru spun past a rain of screaming, crumpled figures and shot home the final goal.

Daimïru swooped high across the field, breaking the sacred circle. The crowd danced with her, wildly shrieking out Zhukora's name. A living ocean thundered across the grass, sweeping up the few small particles that fought against the flow. The wave exploded forward, gathering momentum and foaming about the trees. The air turned black beneath the roar of thrashing wings.

The living tide crashed against the royal platform, blasting all about Zhukora's feet. The girl held up her hands to force the torrent back. Zhukora let her hair fly free into the wind. She stood before them, virginal and magnificent, then opened her arms in blessing, thrilling to the power in their adoring eyes.

Silence spread like ripples in a pond, radiating out from the slender goddess at the center of the mob. The people held their breaths and craned to hear her words.

"My people! Vakïdurii and Katakanii! We have our Skull-Wing victory!"

The air cringed to the victory scream of sixty thousand voices.

Zhukora calmly rode the waves of love. "We have seen the Mantises defeated! It is your victory, not ours. We have fought so that you might win. We have fought to save you from the leaders who have betrayed your sacred trust!"

The crowd seemed to jerk in shock. Like a great, formless living thing it turned toward the chiefs and kings and howled in rage.

"Had you not heard? To solve our differences, your chiefs and priests made an arrangement! A victory was to cost one tribe or the other fields of yams. Food snatched from the mouths of your children to pay for your leaders' greed!"

Zhukora's voice rose. The crowd's power poured into her hands.

"The Skull-Wings have fought not to tear food from the mouths of our comrades, but to save the people from their kings.

"One race! One will! One destiny! Nobles, cast aside your privileges and join with me in my struggle! People, reach out in brotherhood to your neighbors. No Vakïdurii! No Katakanii! I say waste no time fighting one another! Fight the leaders who have betrayed you into starvation!"

Zhukora clenched her fists and howled in an ecstasy of rage. "Death to the betrayers! Long live the Kashran race!"

Zhukora rammed her fist toward the terrified chiefs, and her answer came a maddened storm of hate. The earth shook. The forest trembled. Trees disintegrated as a formless monster surged toward its prey. Chiefs and elders were drowned beneath the flood. Zhukora shrieked with laughter as the people howled her name.

Little Rooshïkii dragged a prisoner before Zhukora's feet and threw him to the ground. Tekï'taa stared at the screaming mass of people all around him and wept with gratitude.

"Oh, Rain—oh thank Rain! You saved me! Oh, Rain..."

Zhukora looked at him, her mad eyes strangely calm and wise. "Saved you? No. I made Rooshïkii a promise. I told her your life was hers to take. She is not a really vengeful girl. She merely has a sense of justice. You took something from her, you see. You spilled her blood and took away her maidenhood. Now Rooshïkii wants to take something from you in return. Do you see how simple justice is?"

Tekï'taa whirled around in fear. Rooshïkii held a glittering knife. The little girl slowly drew away her mask to reveal a face as dead and mad as any skull. She advanced toward the sobbing king, hunger glittering in her eyes.

Rooshïkii laughed as she took him in her claws. Tekï'taa screamed as the crowd ripped him from his clothes.

"No! No, Zhukora, I beg thee! Rooshïkii, please! No!"

Zhukora smiled as blood spurted on her fur. The screaming went on and on, drowned by the crowd. Rooshïkii laughed in her madness. The little girl laid her offerings at her leader's feet. Zhukora clasped her acolyte against her heart as the people gripped her with their gift of screaming love.

A young man scrabbled forward from the storm and flung himself into a bow.

"Zhukora-Zha! Zhukora, be our queen!"

The mob took up the cry; the power of it thundered through the air. Zhukora shook her head and tried to wave the screaming people down. "No! The age of kings and queens is done! We, the people, now control our own destinies!"

Women lunged toward her, holding out their bloody hands. Zhukora's name rose to the heavens like a raging magic spell. Zhukora's name shook the very stars. The people howled until leaves were stripped from the trees. They begged her, they implored her. How could she refuse the ones she loved? The girl let tears stream from her eyes as she wandered through their dream. The people lifted her into their arms and carried her in triumph.

The gift was made; the power was hers. The age of Zhukora finally had come.

CB   BO   SO

The pilgrims stood stiff with shock and gazed with wide, bewildered eyes toward the horizon. The sight before them numbed their very souls.

Tingtraka shivered as the ïsha breeze rippled through her fur. "Sweet Mother Rain! Look at it, it's beautiful!"

Waves stretched from horizon to horizon. Water glittered farther than mortal eyes could see. Bright white birds dipped and wheeled through the sky above, shrieking welcome to the children of the trees.

For the first time in her life, Shadarii saw the ocean. She reached out with her mind to feel the endless flow and wonder of it. Waves surged and pounded on the shore. Sand hissed and bubbled in froth. Ïsha trembled to the pulse of the world.

Kïtashii splashed and danced along the shore, her skinny little feet leaving puddles in the sand. It was the first time anyone could remember seeing her so happy. She took wing and turned a delighted barrel-roll above the waves. "Shadarii-Zha, you should feel the ïsha lift! So strong and free. It's like being in a storm!"

Tingtraka took a little step toward the sea. "Kïtashii, do be careful! Don't go fallin' in!"

"What?"

"I said don't fall in! You don't know how the ïsha currents flow!"

Kïtashii swept low above the waves, glancing haughtily across her shoulder. "I can handle myself quite well, thank you very much! Just because I'm twelve doesn't mean... awk!"

Tingtraka never heard the rest. Kïtashii plunged herself clean into an enormous wave. The breaker exploded into foam, tossing its victim high onto the beach. Totoru led the pilgrims in a gleeful hoot of laughter.

Shadarii moved off down the beach, the wind ruffling through her fur. Her eyes were spellbound.

Lady Starshine leapt and wheeled in the ïsha all around, drinking in the dancer's sweet delight. *Little sister, did I lie? Is this not a wonder?*

It's beautiful! I thank you, Lady Starshine. This is a gift, indeed! Shadarii stopped beside Kïtashii and dried her dripping fur. Hand in hand, they wandered down the shore while pilgrims plunged into the waves. The men played a boisterous game of catch with Mrrimïmei's clothes. Tingtraka contented herself with walking naked along the beach, turning over pieces of cuttlebone and wondering what they were.

Shadarii felt a delicious wave of peace. Her children were laughing and content. Weeks of empty wandering were quite suddenly forgotten. She smiled a gentle smile and slitted her eyes.

Kïtashii industriously scratched her skinny ribs while staring out across the far horizon. "I wonder if it rains here? What would it sound like, do you think? All that water hissing across the waves."

Tingtraka bent and retrieved a tiny seashell from the sand. Smooth and beautiful, the cowrie shell gleamed with swirling depths of color. "Look at this! How lovely! Like a little bead." She placed it against her breast and gave a smile. "There's more! We could make a necklace."

Shadarii squeezed Tingtraka's hand, and the huntress looked calmly out across the ocean.

"Where do we go now, Revered One? Left or right? Or will you take us out across the water?" She was serious; Tingtraka would fly out into all that emptiness if Shadarii only asked.

Shadarii gave the girl a loving smile and pointed westward down the shore. Far, far off in the distance, a tiny plume of smoke rose into the sky. Shadarii had found a village. The little teacher wandered off to gather sticks of driftwood from the sand.

Kïtashii watched her go, her bright eyes full of love. "She knew it would be there. I think she saw it in a dream. She wants us to find a village by tonight."

Tingtraka's slender ears rose. "Why?"

"Mrrimïmei. She will lay her egg soon. It will be a male child with soft gray hair."

"Oh, come now! How could you know all that?"

"She told me. Shadarii-Zha always knows. It will be born at midnight tonight. Mrrimïmei will have a difficult time in labor. Shadarii-Zha wants her to have a roof over her head."

Tingtraka glanced at the other pilgrims cavorting in the surf, and then sighed and began to search for shells. "Come along. There's no hurry. Rain knows, we all need a little rest." The tall huntress flipped over a piece of wood and blinked as she found a tiny purple crab. "Yes, a nice day in the water will do us all a world of good!

"You know, life is looking better all the time!"

ㄸ ㄲ ㄲ

"Zareemah-Kha, we must take the boy now. He cannot die inside the house. His spirit would be trapped by these cold, hard walls."

"Come, my lady, we must take him to the ocean. Let his soul fly into the arms of Father Wind."

The noblewoman only cried all the harder as she clutched her little son against her breast. The boy hung still and limp inside her arms. The fever had almost finished its work, and his soul had nearly fled.

Three dream walkers stood respectfully by the bedside, each dressed in a ritual mask. Brother Fish, Brother Gull, and Sister Mouse. Each had entered into the dreaming. Each had touched the heart of a primal spirit guide. They were the holy ones of the Heshtanii, the People of the Sea.

Sister Mouse wept as though her heart would break. Little Zareemii-Chi had been her student; almost her own child. Eight years old was too young to die. He had hardly even begun to live.

The mask hid her tears from the world. Brother Fish turned toward her, and then faced the weeping mother.

"Zareemah-Kha? My lady, there is nothing we can do now for his body. Please, let us tend his soul. Sister Mouse will be Zareemii's spirit guide."

Time grew short. They must do their duty for the child. Brother Fish sighed and signed for his companions. Somehow they broke the mother's frantic grasp. Gull and Fish lifted the little bed, carefully cradling Zareemii in his blankets. Sister Mouse trembled as she took Zareemah by the arm.

She tried to control herself; she really tried! But it was Zareemii—her own little Zareemii... !

"It—it will be all right. H-he can't feel the pain anymore, Zareemah. Just remember that. No more pain...."

Sister Mouse broke. She couldn't bear it! The girl sobbed against Zareemah, and other villagers hesitantly came to help them walk. Fishermen looked up from their nets and lines. They slowly turned away as the death procession moved toward the endless sound of waves.

The sun trailed gentle fingers across the far horizon. Tiny purple crabs dug tunnels in the sand. The dream walkers settled Zareemii's bed beside the shore.

It could not last much longer. Brother Gull croaked in warning as the boy's breathing faded. Brother Fish felt for Zareemii's pulse and heaved a sigh. "Zareemah, he is going. Hold your son one last time. Hold him and give thanks for the life you shared together."

Zareemah gave a dreadful choking cry and flung herself against her son.

Brother Fish laid his cape across the ground. "Sister Mouse, please do what you can."

"No, Brother, not this time! Not Zareemii!"

"I do not have the gift of sending. He has no one but you."

Sister Mouse backed away, clutching at her mask in agony. "He was my friend! My student! Please, I can't bear it...."

"Please, Sister—your student still has need of you."

She couldn't! To hear Zareemii's voice again; to touch him and tell him he was dead. To point the way for him, but not to follow...

There was no one else....

Sister Mouse laid herself back into Brother Fish's arms. To lead Zareemii's Ka, she was going to have to die. The other priests must pump her heart and breathe air into her lungs. The girl gave a hideous jerk, and then toppled back onto the ground. Her heart fought against her mind. She clamped down hard to still its beat.

Mouse! Mother Mouse, lead me! Set me free and guide me to Zareemii!

The woman's body arched in a dreadful spasm. She screamed once with the pain of death...

And suddenly she soared free!

She felt a darkness filled with light, an emptiness that flowed with laughter. Bright black eyes smiled as the Mouse Spirit swept her up with joy, and the priest-girl gave a shriek of glee. Tricks to play and things to find! They would laugh and dance and play through all eternity. Mother Mouse drew her over to Zareemii and wrapped them in her love.

The priest knew she was in danger but no longer cared. Life was pain and struggle. Why go back? Why send Zareemii on a journey when there were so many games to play? Mother Mouse led them onward in a dizzy dance of joy.

Something bright and shining filled the world with light. It hung softer than a whisper and more lovely than a flower. So beautiful, so powerful! The dancing spirits stopped and stared in awe.

The presence stroked Sister Mouse with gentle hands of love. *This is wrong, little priest. You must go back. It is not yet your time to die.*

"No! No, please, I like it here! I don't want to go back!"

This place will always be waiting for you. But now, you must go back. There is work to do.

"Oh, please! Please, don't make me go!"

Your friends are waiting for you. Think of all the grief you'll cause. Do you see? See them crying all around your lifeless body?

Oh, Sweet Rain! The voice was right! The priestess saw her friends. Brother Fish tore off his mask and wept. He thrust Brother Gull aside and crammed his lips down on her mouth. She felt air rush in to fill her lungs, and her heart began to beat. The world of spirits faded as life rushed back to fill her mind. The girl hungrily twined her tongue in a kiss, and Brother Fish sobbed as he was drawn into her softness. He loved her; why had she never seen it before?

In the kingdom of the Ka, the light reached out to take Zareemii by the hand. *Come, Zareemii, it's time to go back home now. Your mother is crying for you.*

Mother! The little boy gave a wail of anguish. He allowed the shining presence to take him back toward the land of life.

Something leapt and begged about them, weeping in hurt and loss. The mouse spirit skittered through the ïsha sea in panic.

Don't go! Stay with me! Be lonely never more. Please-please-please-please-please! Be fun; be happy! Many runnings, many matings. Tricks to play and secrets to be dug! The glowing presence touched mouse with regret. *Oh, Mouse, they must go back. Don't be sad. I shall teach them how to speak with you. You will never lose them. But it is wrong for them to stay here with you now. I must bring them back to life.*

The mouse spirit sighed and saw the sense in it. She reluctantly let them go, and the creature of light dipped and swirled in gratitude. *Thank you for looking after them, Sister. May your life be ever bright with fun and laughter!*

Zareemii suddenly felt air rushing through his lungs. Ïsha power poured through him like a river; it soothed him, healed him, and filled him with its energy. He opened his eyes and gazed into a smiling face, a face whose eyes shone greener than the eternal sea.

"The boy! The boy's alive!"

A ring of villagers stared at the naked stranger. A sense of unearthly peace and beauty swirled about her. She drew a long, slow breath and lifted her face toward the sun. In her arms, Zareemii stirred and rubbed his eyes. Zareemah-Kha gave a cry and flung herself upon her child.

Shadarii placed the little boy into his mother's grasp, then smiled and began to walk away.

"Wait!"

Sister Mouse tore herself from Brother Fish's arms. "My Lady, who are you? How did you save me?"

There were other strangers standing on the beach—lean Kashra with the girl's light shining in their eyes. Zareemah-Kha looked up from her reborn child. She called out to the stranger, her voice broken with her tears.

"Thank you! Oh, thank you! Oh, Rain, how can I repay you? Everything I have is yours!"

The woman turned and sadly shook her head. The stranger needed nothing. Her eyes somehow seemed to speak. *How much price can be placed on life? Is there a value set on joy? Where there was death, I give you life. Enjoy the gift I gave you and remember me with kindness.* She turned to leave once more.

Sister Mouse lunged forward in alarm. "Revered One, please! Stay with us. Teach us." She faltered as the strange green eyes once more touched her with their love. "I want... I-I need... Please, stay with us. Let us return kindness for your gift of life."

Grass seemed to grow inside the stranger's footsteps. She gazed into the priestess' eyes and looked into her heart. *Follow me.*

The villagers stumbled in Shadarii's wake, watching in amazement as flowers blossomed in her footprints. Fishermen fell down onto their knees as the procession passed. Women knelt and hid awe-struck eyes behind their wings.

Suddenly, a little girl ran by; a skinny little creature bearing a great string bag of toasted crabs. The Silent Lady threw back her head and smiled as the girl tossed a steaming crab toward a villager. They danced along the rooftops and swirled before a delighted crowd.

Someone gave a laugh. People caught the Silent Lady's hands and let the dancing take them. All tears were forgotten, all sorrows left aside. Villagers and priests, fishermen and pilgrims, the reborn and the laughing mother... one by one they gathered in the lady's light. They danced inside her rainbow and filled the world with joy.

> ᑌ ᕉ ᕉ

Zhukora sat quietly in her house and made a meal of simple hunter's fare. The night was hushed and quiet, glowing with the energy Zhukora had unleashed. Young men whooped overhead as they practiced fighting skills; men and women avidly debated politics while dredging streams for food. Zhukora smiled and listened to their energy and trust.

She listened, and she was content.

Revolution had spread to the other tribes, from the deepest valleys to the tallest mountain peaks. Throughout the villages, peace and order reigned. All Kashra were equal. All now had a common goal. The self-hate had finally been purged, burned out of their heart in a single night of fires. For the first time in living history, the alpine peoples were united by a single will; a single blazing love.

Zhukora.

The dark empress sighed and sipped her tea, lost within the clear perfection of her Dream.

"Zhukora! Zhukora, it's happened!" A blonde bolt of lightning streaked into Zhukora's lodge. Daimïru skidded to a halt in a spreading cloud of soot. "Zhukora, it's happened! Two casualties. One dead, one injured. Killed by plainsmen." The girl knelt and cracked her wings out in obeisance. "Everything went as planned. We made a deep raid into the plains territory. I set two grass fires to drive out game. We caught kangaroos in their thousands! Hundreds of them plunged down the cliffs! Enough food for half the nation."

The girl excitedly wiped sweat back from her eyes.

"I sent parties back on foot to carry all the meat. The rest of us followed down the river. The territory is rich beyond our wildest dreams! Fields of grass all filled with seeds. Wattle trees that have never been harvested in their lives! Ducks, emu, possums, yams... We found whole herds of meat animals. Some of the game was—well—woolly. Four legs and white thick fur. They didn't even run. We speared them in their hundreds."

Zhukora passed her friend a cup of tea.

"Daimïru, my love, I know it was exciting, but you really must tell me..."

"Yes, yes! But that's when it happened, you see! There were plainsmen guarding the herds. We chased the woolly creatures over a hill, and then it happened! Plainsmen tried to drive us off. They threw rocks with terrific force! It was just as we have hoped. The plainsmen have slain one of us!"

Zhukora paced excitedly up and down. "What happened to the plainsmen?"

"Oh, we slew them. I took one. I killed her with a spear!" The girl's eyes were filled with a sick light. "A spear is so sensual! It glides, it soars, then it plunges home. You should have seen her eyes as she died!"

"Yes, my love, I'm sure you were artistic." Zhukora softly stroked Daimïru's hair. "So you slew them? And hid the bodies? Good! The fires will have covered your trail."

"Word has spread. The people are gathering out there in their hundreds! They want revenge!"

Zhukora hastily stripped away clothes, reached for her gleaming armor, and began to buckle straps. "Our moral course is clear. We must avenge our fallen comrade. We have a debt of blood to pay." The girl hastily changed her loincloth. "Quickly! Go summon the people to a clearing. I must tell them of the crime the plainsmen have committed. We shall have our war at last, my love! They will scream for plainsmen's blood!"

Daimïru laughed and scampered for the door. She soared through the darkness, shrieking out in glorious victory. The time had come.

Finally it would be war!

ᐃ ᐃ ᐃ

Brother Fish sat in the sand beside Shadarii's feet. Overhead, the nighttime sky shone darkest blue. Women dragged prawn nets through the shallows. Fishermen speared their suppers from canoes. Food toasted over open fires while sea folk sang their strange, soft songs.

In that cobalt sky, Mrrimïmei laughed and tossed a ball toward the other jiteng players. Totoru snatched the ball only to plunge straight into the surf. Fishermen laughed as Totoru erupted from the drink, staggering out onto the beach to dry.

The people of the sea were contentedly at peace. A simple people and a complex one; there were so many new stories to hear and tell. Shadarii passed the night listening to the priests, smiling as fisher folk crept near to witness the Silent Lady's words.

The Silent Lady neither ate nor drank, nor did she ever tire. Kïtashii interpreted the dancer's hand motions into words for the crowd.

Brother Fish wound his arm about Sister Mouse and kissed her flowing hair. He looked up at Shadarii and spoke quietly into the hush.

"Revered One, we have had a crime occur inside our village. A very serious crime. Lady Zareemah says a new age comes and the old rules no longer hold. We therefore ask if you will sit in judgment."

Shadarii's fur gleamed as she framed words with her hands.

Kïtashii watched and then spoke into the night. "Shadarii-Zha says she has no desire to intrude on your affairs, but will offer her opinion."

Brother Fish formally bowed toward the Silent Lady. "Two days ago, a man called Pöshïkaa stole the boat of another fisherman, Lalalii. He took it at night while Lalalii slept. We have a rule against stealing boats—Pöshïkaa must fish for Lalalii for the next full moon. This is the old law, but Zareemah-Zha has told us the old rules are no more. Revered One, what judgment do you pass?"

Mrrimïmei whirred overhead. In the distance fisher women sang. Shadarii dusted off her hands and carefully framed shapes in the dark.

Little Kitashii translated. "Rules are used to make judgment easy, and so can create injustice. Why did your neighbor need the boat? Why did he feel he had to take it without asking?"

"Pöshïkaa's family is poor, and his boat no longer floats. He has a new child, and there was no time to build a new canoe."

Shadarii slowly nodded and began signing.

"Shadarii-Zha says Pöshïkaa was wrong to take the boat. He should have asked. The village must also take some blame. Why was Pöshïkaa not invited to share a canoe? Shadarii judges both sides guilty.

"Pöshïkaa must apologize for his fault. When times are better, he should hold a feast to thank Lalalii for lending him the boat.

"The community should meanwhile come together to build a spare boat for your village. If anyone comes into hardship, the boat can see him or her through. We pilgrims would be honored to help you, as thanks for your hospitality."

The idea had merit. The fisher folk sat back in amazement to discuss this radical new idea.

Tingtraka came wandering up from the water, straining beneath the weight of an titanic fish. Shadarii stared in amazement at the vast catch. Tingtraka coughed and idly filed her nails.

Mrrimïmei whirred low overhead, looking as fat as a pregnant bed bug, but still keen to play the catching game. She snatched the ball from her husband's arms and blundered off above the waves.

Tingtraka cleaned her dinner and glared into the sky. "Mrrimïmei, do be careful! Sit down awhile and take it easy!"

Mrrimïmei banked and fluttered past the dunes. "Why? I feel wonderful!"

"I know you feel wonderful! I just think..."

From overhead came a sudden scream of pain. Mrrimïmei hung in the air, folded in shrieking agony. Totoru had swooped up from beneath and accidentally crashed into her pelvis. The girl spun and plunged toward the ground.

Mrrimïmei clutched her belly and gave a demented scream. Something had broken; a tiny Ka squealed in agony! As Totoru caught her short of the ground, the girl lashed out with her fist and grabbed Shadarii's fur.

"Sh-Shadarii, save it! Don't let it die! Shadarii! Shadarii, do something!"

Mrrimïmei arched her back and writhed. Totoru tried to hold her. She rolled mad eyes and saw his face. "Get away from me! You killed my baby! You bastard, you killed my baby!"

Totoru croaked and tried to hold her.

Mrrimïmei shrieked and clawed him in the face. The girl jerked and felt something slicing her inside. "It's broken! Help me! Help me...."

Shadarii clapped her hands; Mrrimïmei instantly fell unconscious. The little Teacher staggered to her feet, Mrrimïmei dangling from her arms.

Totoru shook with shock, and Tingtraka rocked the huge hunter back and forth. "Shhhh, it's all right now. It was an accident. An accident, that's all. Just sit with me awhile...."

Tingtraka met Shadarii's eyes, but the Teacher helplessly shook her head. No power on earth could help; Mrrimïmei's child had already gone.

Tingtraka slowly nodded and pulled Totoru close. "It's no one's fault, Totoru. We all love you. Just hold me tight. She didn't mean it. She didn't mean a word."

Hours later, Mrrimïmei lay shivering in bed. Kïtashii and Tingtraka were still tending her, sponging with gentle, caring hands.

Mrrimïmei slowly clenched her claws and rolled to face the door. "Bitch."

Tingtraka looked up from her work, dragging sweaty hair back from her eyes. "What?"

Mrrimïmei spat onto the floor. Shadarii's scent still lingered in the ïsha. "Bitch! She just sat there while I writhed and screamed! Did she bring my baby back? Did she?"

"She cared for you. She healed you. You're alive only because of her."

"She saved that village boy! Brought him back from the dead! Why not my baby?"

Tingtraka sat up and angrily wiped her eyes. Blood left a smear across her fur. "There was no body for her to bring its soul back to. Don't you understand? The egg was crushed! I helped her drag the fragments out of you."

"Bitch!"

Tingtraka slowly washed her hands. "You're distraught. You'll feel better once you've rested. We'll fetch Totoru. He'll hold you till you sleep."

"Keep him away from me! All of you damned pilgrims keep away!" Mrrimïmei spat once more. "She has the power to raise the dead! She can make the desert bloom, bring water from the rocks, but still she won't raise a hand to help her own. We aren't important enough to bother with."

Tingtraka stiffly stood; her eyes were filled with hurt. "That's not true. She helps everybody. She almost slew herself to save that little boy!"

"Ha! It won her adoration from these simpleton villagers. Adoration and obedience. That's all she wanted! She feeds on love like a vampire on life!"

Kïtashii glared in pure hate at Mrrimïmei. "You make me sick. Shadarii saved you because she loves you, and now you betray her with your words." Kïtashii drew back from her patient. "I've had enough of you! You've never understood. Never learned! Always Mrrimïmei first! Well, we've done our duty. Your egg's dead now, so to hell with you!"

Mrrimïmei rose onto her elbow. Her eyes were sick with pain. "You stupid little brat! What do you know about it? You or your—your fellow 'priest of Shadarii'! "

Tingtraka's face froze as she carefully folded her towels. "You're right, of course; I will never know. My father saw to that when I was eight. But you can still have another child. Be thankful for the Teacher's gift."

Mrrimïmei shrieked and tried to fight out of bed. "Teacher? Teacher! She's betrayed Kotaru! She let her lover die and then turned her back on his corpse! She has the power to avenge us, and yet she does nothing! She's as dangerous as Zhukora!"

"No! No, you're wrong!"

"Go outside and look at her. Tell me she's the same Shadarii you used to know."

Tingtraka turned to go. She hesitated in the door and gazed down at the dust. "I will pray for you, Mrrimïmei."

"Don't waste your breath. Mother Rain didn't save my son."

Nineteen

"Ko"

"Ki"

"Ka"

"Ku..."

"What about a 'Ksa' as in 'Ksatra'?"

Ksatra. A heron. Yes, that could be drawn. Shadarii made four elegant swipes with her brush and added them to the master list. Kïtashii and Tingtraka smoothly copied the shapes, Tingtraka adding a flourish that reduced the moves to three. They inspected each other's handiwork with grins of excitement.

The great task was almost done; Shadarii's picture words were spilling into place like pieces of a puzzle. The three women had worked in absolute isolation for days, and soon they would return to the village, bearing the gift of these symbols. The world would finally have the means to keep its knowledge safe and sound.

The three pilgrims worked together in companionable silence. Kïtashii blew on her page and held it against the light. Shadarii had almost forgotten what a pretty girl she was. Wearing the wispy native skirt of shells, she seemed skinny, pure, silver—and utterly at ease. Now, if only they could make her smile more often than she frowned....

A petulant voice hissed unhappily in Shadarii's skull. *Shadarii! Thou art wasting thy time. Scribbles and drawing, words and stories! There are real things we should be achieving.*

Shadarii ground fresh pigment and serenely dipped her brush. *These are real things. This is very important. Now bide your time and be patient.*

Bah! Ideas are dangerous. Thou shalt cause trouble if thou insist on stirring lower social orders into thought.

Oooooh, lower orders! Shadarii smiled in amusement. She gave Kïtashii a wink and prodded merrily at Starshine. *You must tell me all about your insights into social structure.*

Don't be impertinent! The whole social order is my idea. Who dost thou think relegated milk mead as a prerogative of the nobility?

You? Shadarii blinked in sudden interest. *You invented milk mead?*

Don't be ridiculous! Milk mead is as old as the Kashran race. Silly child! Milk mead governs the color of a Kashra's wings. Once upon a time all Kashra bore bright wings. I installed a system of discipline among the patriarchs of the third dynasty, and colored wings were thence onward reserved only for autocrats. The system has remained universal ever since.

There it was again; a hint of a glorious rich past. Shadarii's brushes fell into her lap. *Tell me about it! What third dynasty? Why did they need a social structure? When was all this? How long ago?*

There is no point in telling thee. The spirit sniffed in hauteur. *It is all quite irrelevant!*

Tell me! Lady Starshine, please! I need to know!

No! I shall not tell thee. Thou art destined for greater things than childish curiosity!

Shadarii picked up her brushes with a snort of irritation. *Fine! Don't tell me. And don't expect me to fly to that hill you like, either. You can damned well sit in there and suffer. The rest of us have work to do.*

Shadarii went back to her labors. She had a symbol set to finish and a manifesto to prepare. She had just made progress into the glottal stops when Starshine's voice returned. *Not go to the hill? Not even for a while?*

Not even for a minute!

The spirit went into a huff. *Bah! Thou art becoming more difficult every day! I wonder why I ever agreed to this bargain in the first place.*

You are free to leave whenever you like. At least my head would be much quieter.

Ha! And how would the 'Silent Lady' fare without her miracles?

Mother Rain would not abandon me without power. My faith shall sustain me. Go; I have no need of you any more.

Starshine quivered. Her bluff had been well and truly called. *I shall stay. Someone must look after thee, though Rain knows, I get no thanks for all my work!*

Shadarii primly dipped her brush. *Your efforts are noted, if not always appreciated.* The girl reached for a fresh pile of pages. *Now will you kindly leave me to my work? We are trying to sow the seeds of eternal peace!*

ෆ ෮ ෨

"Here we are, my boy. Here we are. Spearhead rock! 'Tis a few years since I was here last, but the view always stays the same." Lord Ingatil wheezed heavily, utterly exhausted by the flight. He sat beneath a gigantic cypress tree and let his old wings droop.

Spearhead rock jutted high above the restless trees. Keketál and Ingatil could see the bright pasture about their little village. Other villages lay far beyond, scattered all up and down the river. From high on the rock, it seemed like some distant fairyland. Keketál drew a breath and leaned back against the gnarled old cypress tree.

"Iss beautiful. Muchly greenings, muchly peace. Food to eat and long days in the sun. Keketál thinks Lord Ingatil iss a lucky man."

"Lucky? Why do you think so?"

"Iss happy here. No problems that cannot being solved with just a little jug dance."

"It isn't all so smooth, my lad." The old man scratched his hide and peered at Keketál. "There are things I want you to understand. You've come to us by surprise, and I'll confess I like you, but you don't quite fit in. You ask questions no one else asks. You see things with a different eye. So, before you make any, well, any lasting decisions, shall we say, I feel we should share a word or two."

"Uh—decisions?"

"Let's just say I feel something in the wind, eh? If you were to settle down, you should first know us better than you do."

Ingatil guided Keketál's gaze out across the river, tracing unseen lines all up and down the land. "The river here belongs to us, the Ochitzli tribe. Downstream there is a lake, and that belongs to the painted Zebedii. They live in villages made out of rafts, and raise frogs for food—so be wary if one of them invites you to dinner! Inland from us to the south are our real neighbors, the Takoonii and Harapii. True shepherds. Good people. My wife is Takoonii."

The old man paused and assumed a pained expression. "Dreadful cooks, though. Utterly appalling! Ah, well, each to his own.

"Anyway, there we have it. That's the world I know, from the sea right up to the black lands of the demons."

Keketál glanced past the plains toward the dark line of the forest, far away. His antennae shifted to a hint of ïsha wind. "Demons? What is demons?"

"The ancient enemy. A people so savage, so terrifying that all contact is forbidden! They disappeared into that evil place a thousand years ago. Who knows whether any of them survive? Still, the old laws remain; we are forbidden to approach the mountains."

The old man repressed a shudder. He shook the thought away and turned back to his companion. "We're a people of habit, Keketál. For a thousand years, there has been peace, but we owe our tranquillity to our customs. Everything we do is ruled by precedent, you see?"

Keketál simply didn't understand.

Ingatïl tried again. "Keketál, we don't change the way we build our houses. We don't change the way we think. We have food in plenty because our population stays the same. No women fight over fashions since our clothing is prescribed according to our station. Custom, always custom. There's sense behind it." Ingatïl heaved a sigh. He could see that wild look in Keketál's eyes; there was trouble in the offing. "Ah bugger it. Enough's enough. There's eighty eight people in my village, and each one of them has a soft spot for you. I can foresee an interesting life."

The old man scratched vigorously at his hide.

"Now don't you tell my lady where we've been today! She thinks we're out fishing. There'd be hell to pay if she found out where I've been."

Lord Ingatïl passed Keketál an old stone jug, popping off the cork with an air of relish. "Beer! Hupshu's finest brew. Don't tell me you've never drunk a beer? Go on, boy, drink! 'Twill get that wan expression from your face."

Keketál hesitantly sniffed the jug. The smell of the liquid was rich and powerful.

Ingatïl borrowed the pot and took a pull, leaning back to heave a grateful sigh. "My boy, the spirits gave men beer because they knew we would have wives. Each is a comfort in its own way. Beer has the advantage of being a trifle quieter."

Keketál took the jug and hesitantly tried a little sip. It was sweet! Keketál pricked up his ears and eagerly began to drink.

Lord Ingatïl rubbed his nose and made a sour face. "Women women women! Bah! Harïsh said we were to keep you from the beer. Says your stomach can't handle it." He took a short pull from the jug and passed it back to Keketál. "No beer, indeed! Little wowser! She's hooked you, but she's not landed you yet. There's still a few freedoms left to us in the world. Beer is one, and Spearhead rock's another. Can't live without my wife, mind you. Still, sometimes a man just needs the rock, eh?"

Keketál waited for Ingatïl to finish with the jug. He stared out at the clouds and let his mind wander into dreams.

His Lordship leaned on his elbow and solemnly regarded Keketál. "I wonder, boy. I wonder where you might be from. Those eyes of yours have seen much hardship. You once knew another place than this; a place where someone tried to kill

you with a spear." The old man looked up into Keketál's eyes. "What do you remember lad? Is there nothing at all?"

Keketál stared unhappily at his toes. He wriggled his feet inside his sandals and
felt strangely ill at ease. "Always iss everyone asking about Keketál's memories.
Keketál has no memories; only sun and trees and River-Bend. Iss all Keketál needs.
He wants nothing more."

"The lack must be terrible for you."

"Terrible? No, my lord. My memories are filled with happiness. Why should
Keketál feel pain?"

"Because you've lost a lifetime, lad. Someone stole your life away, and you cannot
even feel the loss."

They lay back and shared the beer beneath the vast old cypress tree. The sun
shone down upon a distant world and filled the air with peace.

Keketál suddenly touched his lordship's arm and pointed off toward the mountains. A thin veil of smoke swirled from the woods far to the north.

"What do you see, lad? What is it?"

"Burnings! Black black smoke with the wind behind it."

"A bushfire? Heading in our direction?"

"Yes, iss toward the village come!" The boy squinted in puzzlement. "Keketál
sees specks. Is people moving near the flames."

"Firefighters from the northern villages. Probably Marsh-Side, the village Hupshu's bride comes from. They'll be coming here for help." The old man heaved
creakily to his feet. "And help we shall! There's a stream between us and the fire.
We'll do a controlled burn on the other side and dam the fire before it spreads too
far. 'Tis much the same every summer." The chieftain bent to take his bag. "You go
ahead, lad. Your young wings are faster. Find my son and tell him what we've seen.
He'll gather the men to fight the fire."

Keketál hesitated, but old Ingatïl irritably waved him on his way. "Tut tut! Come
on, I'm not so old I can't fly home. Speed is of the essence! Off you go!"

Keketál gripped the old man's hand and did something no plainsman would ever
try. He took a running leap and simply threw himself clean off a cliff three hundred
spans high. Ingatïl gave a croak of shock and raced over to the precipice, just in
time to see a tiny figure spearing straight toward the ground. Keketál flicked out his
wings mere moments before spattering. Somehow he caught the ïsha and shot off
across the trees.

Lord Ingatïl stared down at the sickening plunge the boy had taken and slowly
scratched his hide. "Well! It seems the world still has a surprise or two after all!"

Harïsh sat on her bed, busily embroidering a clean white skirt. It was a dreadful
process, full of stuck fingers, curses, and snarled thread. Nevertheless, she still was
bright and gay, humming a merry wedding song. The kilt was of the finest Zebedii
linen, the type of dress a girl might choose for a bridal gown...

Something quivered by the window. Harïsh opened one eye and glared out. "Xartha! I swear, if I stick my head out there and find you..."

A sharp scent stabbed into her nose. Smoke! Harïsh stared out the window and saw the shadows in the sky, then dived her hand beneath the windowsill and came up with a struggling handful of little sister. Harïsh tucked Xartha hard beneath one arm and raced toward the door.

"Xartha! Go to the assembly point, quickly! The teachers will take you down the river with the other children."

The men would fight the fires while the elder women would wet the thatch and guard the village. Harïsh grabbed a staff and made ready to drive her father's flocks downstream.

Something was following her again! Harïsh didn't even have to look. The little four year old had patiently trotted in her sister's tracks. Harïsh gave a gasp of exasperation and dragged the little miscreant off toward the village square.

Harïsh's mother swooped overhead, braking to an untidy halt. "Harïsh!"

"I have her, Mama! I'm taking her to the teachers. The raft will take them all downstream."

"Then hurry! The flocks can smell the fire. And take your mantle! Cover all your fur!"

Harïsh dumped her sister with the other children and raced off to save the sheep. Behind her, the village boiled like an ant nest stirred by a stick.

The world thundered to the death-screams of a hundred thousand plants. Tiny Ka swirled everywhere as village men dived into the storm. Teams dragged blazing torches through the grass, deliberately back-burning as the brushfire swept toward River-Bend.

The whole village operated in drilled, efficient teams; every man knew his place, and only poor Keketál was left aside. He watched Lord Ingatïl's son, Ingatekh, direct the building of the firebreak and wondered if there was something he should do. Minute by minute the gap between the brushfires grew smaller. Rain help anybody sandwiched between....

Refugees! The refugees! Keketál suddenly remembered the tiny figures he had seen from Spearhead rock. They might be trapped between the firebreak and the brushfire.

Keketál swooped quickly to Ingatekh, son of Lord Ingatïl. The other nobleman stood snapping orders to his subordinates. An Ochitzli nobleman wasted no time on explanations; he merely expected obedience.

Keketál alighted on a tree stump and sketched a shallow bow. "Ingatekh! Ingatekh, permission for the speakings please!"

Ingatekh whirled and looked at the intruder up and down. The older man blew impatiently through his whiskers.

"What's that? Speak properly! Rain, your accent is revolting! Haven't they taught you anything yet?"

"Accents not important now! What about the peoples we saw in front of fire? There is a way for them to leave, yes? How will they escape being caught between two dreadful burnings?"

"It's too late, the fire's already set!" Ingatekh huffed and turned to go. "It's not my affair. They're not my people."

Keketál stared in horror at the other nobleman. "But Ingatekh can't just be leave people to burn! We have to do something!"

"Why you insolent young hatchling! Who are you to criticize me?"

"I am Keketál! I am noble-wing. What makes you better than I? You have done wrong. You should try to make it right."

Ingatekh brushed ashes from his fur. "All my men have their allotted stations! I'll not disturb the drill!"

"Drill? You will kill people because of stupid customs?" Keketál gave a roar, grabbed Ingatekh by his cross belts and hauled him from the ground. The huge noble held his victim dangling in midair. "You! You are not worthy to carry your father's excrement!" Keketál hurtled the other man aside. His voice snapped villagers to attention. "Keketál needs three men! Three men to come with him through the fire!"

The men gazed in horror at the horizon. The sky blazed red with the heat of the onrushing inferno.

"Quickly! I need three. Three to help Keketál save the villagers from Marsh-Side. Please!"

No one moved; Ingatekh pulled himself up from the ground and gave a triumphant laugh. "Ha! Thus speaks the hero Keketál! Go away, Keketál. Crawl back to the womenfolk."

Someone stepped forward from the crowd. Hupshu tossed away an ax and nervously wiped his palms. "I'll go."

Ingatekh whipped around to glare in rage.

"What?"

"I said I'll go. Someone has to." Hupshu stared helplessly toward the towering walls of flame. "I suppose it will be all right."

"Don't be a fool. What about your bride, lad?"

Hupshu stared in anger at other men. "She's in there! Don't you understand? She's somewhere in the fire!" Hupshu swore and snatched a water bucket. "I follow Lord Keketál!"

Keketál soaked his fur in water, and then drenched his companion. Both men sprang into a tree and stared out across the fires. The ïsha boiled as the flame walls thundered to the clouds.

Keketál stared and watched an eddy rise. A window of empty sky suddenly blossomed out before him. "Hupshu, are you with me?"

"Aye lord!"

"Then, now!" Keketál leapt, and Hupshu sprang a whisker's breadth behind him. Wings cracked with force as they hurtled themselves into the fire. Keketál tumbled like a mad thing as he tore clean through the heat; Hupshu burst through the flames beside him and gave a shout of fright; the blaze had blackened the edges of his wings. He ran a hand across his face and turned to Keketál.

"Where to, my lord?"

"Where the others fear to go. Toward the flames!" Keketál and Hupshu sped through the burning trees. Inch by inch the gap between the fires was narrowing, closing the rescuers between towering cliffs of heat.

Coals gleamed inside the ruined skeletons of trees. The fire had ripped out the forest's life and sucked its juices. Ashes hissed and coals spat. Trees raised their arms in shock toward the sky.

There, among the ruins, a deathly creature knelt in silent worship. She shone as stark and beautiful as blackened bone. Zhukora gazed into the dead black branches of a tree and reached out to touch the beauty of its lifeless desolation.

Serpent savored the stench of smoke inside Zhukora's lungs. The spirit gazed out through her eyes and heaved a sigh.

Thou art beautiful, Zhukora! Did I not tell thee that warfare was the key? Did thou ever see thy people so powerful, so at one? Here is the spice of life! Here is the honor and the glory.

Yes, Serpent. You are a friend, indeed. Never once have you lead me astray. Zhukora gazed at the withered wilderness and gave a sigh. *I have seen my people transform into warriors! Where once there was sniveling supplication, now there is pride! The people have become a weapon. Now let the whole world tremble before our power!*

Zhukora rose to her feet. Her bright eyes peered out through the dark recesses of her mask. *My warriors sang out my name as they went into battle! Can there be any praise higher than the adoration of the people? Every day I think I cannot love them more. Every day I find myself loving them more deeply.*

The woman slowly turned around. The fields of ash behind her thronged with fantastic shapes. A thousand alpine warriors knelt there, arrayed in jiteng armor. They were sheathed in the startling colors of the parrots and the forest birds; of flowers, flames, and rainbows—leering demons and stark white bones. All the wild panoply of forest myth had embraced the joy of war.

A mere thousand warriors; a tiny demonstration of the power of the Dream. Zhukora had tested her new creation, and had found it good....

The jiteng teams were the heart and soul of Zhukora's war machine. The teams had come to her, begging the honor of fighting at her side. Now they surrounded her; the fighting elite of a people hardened by struggle. Each team of twelve had endlessly drilled in working together, thinking together, fighting together. Zhukora's army had sprung ready-made into her hands.

For a thousand years they had been crushed beneath a weight of rules. Zhukora had torn aside the barriers; now nothing was unthinkable.

They knelt in silence, disciplined in ruthless patience as only hunters could be. Their spear points shone like stars against the ash.

Zhukora's elite bodyguard of Skull-Wings lay far across the river, under Daimïru's command. Zhukora's plans were exacting and precise, and already five villages had fallen to their spears. Zhukora's warriors were utterly without mercy. They felt no remorse, no guilt; not even hate. The Dream had reduced their enemy to the status of mere prey.

A massive warrior in falcon armor handed his leader her woomera and spears. Zhukora turned her skull mask toward her waiting officers.

"Daimïru's wing is about to cross the river. Fist captains,[30] ready your attack waves."

The falcon stared at the distant wall of fire, as though the horror of it had hypnotized him.

Zhukora coolly drew gauntlets onto her hands. "What is wrong, Frukuda? Do you fear the fire?"

"My leader, how are we to pass the flames?"

"I shall part them." Zhukora looked down at her followers, and her face opened in a simple, loving smile. "I shall be beside you. The fires shall not burn us; the heat shall pass us by. Follow in my flight path, and I will bring you victory."

The leader's eyes shone like a child's laughter. The nobleman stared at her for one adoring moment before cramming his face down to the ground.

Zhukora gazed in absolute serenity across the faces of her warriors, filling them with her thrilling light. The chosen thousand knelt in shivering worship.

"I love you. I love you all." With those simple words, the black goddess of the forest turned to watch the forest fire.

At the far side of the village, a black horde stirred into action. Skeletal, demonic shapes crouched forward on the trees. Beneath a branch, Daimïru hung like a predatory bat, cruel eyes glittering as she stared down at her prey.

Zhukora's plan had been brilliant. At the very crack of dawn, she had led the Skull-Wings in an attack upon the plainsman villages. They had slaughtered men out in the fields and women in their beds, beasts in pens and eggs in nests. Zhukora used terror with all the skill of a surgeon, slicing through a patient's flesh. A few deaths now would purchase power untold. The plainsmen would surrender, and in the long run, lives would be saved. Daimïru savored the radical morality of the Dream even as she prepared herself to kill.

The beautiful girl stared with the clear, bright eyes of a psychopath. Her soft voice reached to caress their screaming lust for blood. "Let nothing live. Let no prey escape you. We shall slay the women in their huts and their babies at the breast. We shall hack down their men and open out the throats of playing children. Our sacred mission is to sweep this land clean." Daimïru turned to gaze joyously out across the swirling river. Faith swelled to fill her with its power. "They have sat there in their obscene wealth as we slowly starved to death! Now the time of retribution is at hand. We shall terrify them as no souls have ever witnessed terror. We shall show them the horror of defying Zhukora. A thousand years ago, they shut us inside the woods to die. Finally, vengeance has returned!"

She let her hair stream in the wind and shrieked out her battle cry. "Forward for the Dream!"

Three hundred voices took up the roar. Daimïru's demons raged down to sweep the world with death.

---

[30]**Fist Captain:** Commander of twenty teams of twelve warriors. He is assisted by four hand captains, each controlling five teams.

"Keketál! There's no one here! There's no sign of anybody!" Flames roared in cyclones. Hupshu flinched as a blazing branch crashed down from a tree, and he tried to shield his face from a stinging stream of cinders. "Keketál, don't go any closer! Don't let the heat get to your wings."

Keketál barely even heard. The nobleman flitted back and forth across the fire, trying to fight his way upwind into the blaze. Hupshu slowly battled up beside him.

"My lord, enough! There's no one here. If we stay, we will be burned!"

"Keketál feels movements! Maybe iss someone back behind big fire."

"If they are behind the fires, they're safe! Come, my lord, we must retreat."

Keketál's wings beat furiously at the ïsha. He'd been so sure there were figures near the fire wall. Had they been behind the fires, or in front?

Hupshu dragged at Keketál's cross belts, hauling him back toward the village lines. "My lord, please! I will not allow you to hurt yourself. Harïsh would have my balls served on a plate! Quickly, back toward the creek before we set our fur ablaze."

A strange wind began to move through the blaze. The nobleman felt his antennae rise in astonishment. "Hupshu, look! The fires are dying!"

"Don't be..."

"No, look!"

The heat boiled like a whirlpool. Suddenly debris exploded through the air. Blazing leaves and coals ripped past Keketál, and both men were hurtled backward by the blast. Keketál curled into a ball and rolled, his body remembering jiteng training long past. He slapped the ground and somehow sprang back into guard.

The flames had drawn back into a whirling tunnel. At its center hung a shrieking figure made of blackened bone. She threw out her hair and sent a horde of nightmares howling down the corridor.

Hupshu and Keketál drew slowly to their feet as all the colors of a madman's dreams came screaming for their blood. Keketál snatched up Hupshu and dragged him into the air. "Fly!"

"Keketál! What are they?"

"Follow Keketál! Follow quickly. Do as I do!"

Keketál suddenly knew what to do; every twist and turn fell into place. With a yell of fury, he folded his wings and speared between the blazing branches of a tree. Behind him, Hupshu shot through the gap, and sparks roared up to blind the pursuing creatures.

Something ripped through the brush beneath them. It smashed into a burning bramble and gave a howl of pain.

Hupshu sobbed in desperation. His eyes rolled in terror as he saw the snarling horde behind him. "Savages! Sweet Rain, it's savages!"

Steel flashed as a spear hissed for Hupshu's back. Keketál punched out with ïsha and shoved the spear aside. He shot a glance across his shoulder and let Hupshu draw close behind.

"Go! Head for the village lines. Ram the flames. We must give warnings to Lord Ingatïl!" The two young men dived off toward their home.

Behind them the nightmare surged onward in a wave of blood and steel.

Harïsh's mother cursed as she hauled water from the river and staggered back uphill. Her feet were filthy, and her fur was drenched with sweat. With two sons and a grown daughter, why was she always left to do the blasted work? There was the roof to douse, the deadwood to be cleared, and a whole pile of grain to store. There was dust and ash, livestock scattered, and the family's clothes getting filthy...

Damn! Who'd be a mother?

Nurïman-kana irritably balanced the weight of a water jug above her brow. What idiot had put the river so far from the house?

She gave a little cough and staggered slightly. Her face lit with dawning wonder as she touched a bloody shaft that jutted out beneath her ribs. She felt it without understanding what it really was.

The woman's eyes grew wide. Her mind went blank. She felt herself being pulled down to her knees.

A storm of demons blasted through the quiet streets of River-Bend. Women splashed against the ground in writhing, stinking fragments. Lord Ingatïl's wife was hacked across the middle by a gleaming metal knife. Villagers screamed and tried to flee. A pregnant girl streaked through the huts, blood streaming from her butchered wings. She ran onto an outstretched spear, sobbing as the steel ripped through her.

Nurïman watched it all. She saw her village die before her very eyes. The mothers and the matrons, the hussies and brides; all gone beneath a screaming cloud of wings. Nurïman curled into a ball and wept for the children she would never see again. She wept for a husband lost somewhere in the flames, and died with tears in her eyes.

Fire ripped at Keketál's wings as he exploded through the nightmare wall of flame. Behind him, Hupshu burst out from the firewall, and both men came sliding down into the crowd of village men.

"Fly! Get to the village! Get your families and flee! The savages attack!" Keketál somersaulted to the ground. He dragged men to their feet and shoved them frantically toward the village. "Iss an attack! Savages. Hundreds of savages hiding in the fire! They're heading for the village."

Keketál spat to clear his mouth and desperately fought for breath. "Keketál needs single men beside him. Get axes, branches, rocks; anything to using for weapon. The rest must go! We try to slow them down for you!"

Bewildered, the villagers saw the fire wall begin to swirl. It shivered, as if molded by some almighty hand. Lightning cracked, and flames hurtled themselves apart.

A storm of alpine warriors thundered through the sky. The mob of villagers broke and fled. Men shrieked as spears caught them in the back. Dao rose and fell, and the hindmost men were butchered into fragments.

Keketál took a group of villagers and led them off beneath a wave of flames. The others careered off trees and ripped through bushes, fighting one another in their mindless panic to escape.

A lightning bolt ripped among the trees, and two villagers screeched as white light blasted them to ashes.

Keketál clutched a tree and stared in horror. "They're driving them! They're driving the men toward the meadow! Sheep to the slaughter!"

Lightning blazed again. Keketál rolled his eyes and tried to form a plan. "Keketál will take you East toward the herds. We must find the sheep and shepherds. After that, we have to keep the savages away from the river! The children are still hidden on the banks."

Keketál ripped away his cross belts, tore the bands into strips, and hurtled them toward the other men.

"Quick! Make slings. Get stones, branches—anything! When we fight, get height, get speed! Try to cripple their wings. Don't go for a kill unless it won't slow you down."

He knew. Keketál somehow knew how to fight, something he must have lived through time and again. He shook the thought away and sat down to help his men. Keketál had saved six villagers from disaster. He had given them a purpose, he had given them courage.

Now, Rain help them, they were going to attack.

Twenty

Harïsh cursed and muttered as she fought through a tangled clump of blackberries. She had a headache, her feet were ripped and torn, and she'd suffered it all for a stupid lamb!

The creature thrashed and bleated as it struggled in the thorns, brown eyes guttering stupidly. With her shepherd's staff, Harïsh hacked at brambles. She spat venom as the lamb lunged even farther from her reach.

"Come here! Come here, you stupid bastard!"

A thorn jabbed Harïsh's foot. The lamb bleated as it wriggled deeper into the thicket. Harïsh bared her fangs and lunged for the creature's throat. Neck—nice thin neck! She imagined the bones splintering beneath her hands; eyes bulging, arteries bursting...

"You little woolly shit! Come here! I'm going to twist your bloody head off!" Harïsh made a snatch.

The lamb gave a little squeal of fright and leapt clean out of the thorns, then sped across the grass and ran whimpering to its mother. Harïsh fought back to open ground and glared murder at the elusive beast.

It wasn't even her damned lamb! It belonged to Haripettii. The ear-tag was red on blue.

"Bugger it!"

Haripettii lounged back against a tree and laughed. He was a handsome lad of fourteen. Harïsh glared at him and picked jagged leaves out of her fur.

The fire seemed suddenly much, much closer. Harïsh scowled as she stared off toward her home. Surely the fire would be under control by now. If not, standing inside a thicket of dry thorn would be suicide. The safest course would be to move downriver. Harïsh slowly backed away, wiping her hands against her filthy skirt. "People, get your things! We're moving the flocks out of here. Come on, lets get them down the watercourse."

Haripettii turned his back and ignored her. Less than a third of the shepherds were male, and they were the difficult ones. The girls had taken one look at the fire and packed their bags. Harïsh stalked over to Haripettii and nudged him. "Get up. We're leaving."

"Says who?"

"Says me, skreg head."

"Who put you in charge? I'll move when I say, and not when some dolly tells me to!"

Girls grow faster than boys, and Harïsh had more muscles than any of the males. She landed an almighty kick on Haripettii's rear. The boy tumbled to his feet and swung at her with his fist. Harïsh tripped him over an efficient foot and landed him hard on a bum-piercing thistle. Harïsh whirled on another boy, her eyes glaring like those of an angry golden hawk.

"Up! All of you, up! The fire's crossed the creek. We're leaving." She pointed at a gawky, leggy girl who sat binding her sandals. "Pachetta, you're our fastest. Go back to the village and tell them where we've gone. I'll take your sheep with mine."

Pachetta gave a stylish salute and launched into the air, brown wings whirring as she shot off toward the village. Meanwhile, with fliers swooping back and forth to rattle the strays, the village flocks moved slowly south, toward the river.

Harïsh sighed. The day was too hot for all this nonsense. There were sheep to move and lambs to find. So much for the peaceful life of herding. Harïsh plodded wearily along behind her sheep, tapping the laggards with her staff.

Three weeks. Three weeks, and she would be moving to the healers' school at Emu Point. She would leave behind everything she loved to start her big adventure. Day by day, the date drew closer, and now all of a sudden, she had found reasons to stay right here at home.

Keketál.

Without him, her life would have been over. He loved her. She could see it shining in his eyes. But then he would treat her like a child. Would he ever come right out and kiss her? How obvious did she have to get? How could any man be so clever, so lovable, and so dim?

A piercing whistle rang through the air as a shepherd girl flew overhead.

Harïsh cupped her hands and gave a yell. "Oi Pachetta! Back so soon? What's up?"

Pachetta ripped though the branches overhead, sobbing as she looked back across her tail. "Help me! Somebody help me!" Pachetta hurtled herself down into the gully.

Something black and hideous came screaming in her wake. An ïsha bolt ripped out to gouge her wings. The monster exploded from the bushes and shrieked for blood.

Hurt and reeling, Pachetta spun out of control and crashed into the creek. The girl clawed at the ground. Her left wing had broken, and one arm hung crooked from her shoulder. She dragged herself across the dirt and whimpered for her friends.

An evil, predatory hiss came from behind her. Pachetta turned, life draining from her face. A demon came for her. Pachetta watched, shaking her head in disbelief.

"N-no go away! Please, please let me go. I haven't done anything...."

Black claws reached out to grab her by the hair. The creature's knife swept up above Pachetta's head.

"No! No, please! Don't. No!"

Blood gouted through the air. Pachetta shrieked as something sticky vomited across her face. She went on screaming even after hands and bodies crowded in panic all around her.

"Pachetta! Pachetta, did he cut you?"

Pachetta felt her face being swiftly wiped by someone's skirt. The girl blinked, slowly realizing she was still alive.

"She's all right. It didn't cut her."

"Her arm looks funny!"

"It's a dislocated shoulder. Hold her! Hold her still!" Harïsh grabbed Pachetta's hand, shoved a foot inside her armpit, and clicked the bones back into place. Pachetta squealed, her whole body shivering with pain.

Harïsh held her tight and whispered calm words inside her ears. "Shhhh, it's all right. It's all right now. It's over. You're safe."

The demon lay sprawled across the ground, a stream of blood seeping from its skull.

Harïsh ignored the creature as she slowly smoothed back Pachetta's hair. "It's all right. I killed it with a stone, see? You're safe now."

Pachetta's gaze drifted far away, and then fixed her eyes on a eucalyptus flower and gave a vacant smile. "The village... Everyone's dead, Harïsh. Mama's body is lying on our roof. I hope she doesn't fall down. She might hurt herself...." Pachetta giggled and closed her eyes.

Harïsh ripped the leaf tips from an overhanging paperbark tree and vigorously rubbed the buds beneath Pachetta's nose.

"Oh, no! You stay awake with me! You'll be all right now. Just breathe this nice and slow."

Harïsh spread a pool of calm among the other shepherds. She tended Pachetta's wounds and spoke quietly to her friends.

"Lyrilla, go up a tree and see if there're any more black demons. Keep everyone else down low. We don't want to be seen."

The fat blonde girl paused and looked down at Harïsh. "Harïsh, shouldn't we use healing magic on her? I can do it."

"No. Not until we know if there are more demons. They'd smell the magic. Just stay calm and quiet. You're all right with me." Harïsh spoke with a healer's soothing voice.

The others felt their terror bleed away as the fifteen year old reached out to take them with a mother's guiding hand.

"H-Harïsh. What about home? What Pachetta said, about the village...."

"Shhhhh, we don't know about the village. We'll find out where we stand before we go rushing off anywhere, all right? We stay together"

Lyrilla hissed down from her perch high in a tree. "Harïsh! Harïsh, there's three more of them. I think they saw you kill the other one!"

Harïsh never once looked from her patient. "How far away?"

"Huh?"

"How far away are they?"

The girl took another look, her knees hammering in fright.

"F-fifty spans, maybe. They're squatting in the grass, keeping low."

Harïsh eased Pachetta's head back onto the ground. The potter's girl dusted off her hands, slipping her sling into her fingers.

"Everybody, find smooth stones, as many as you can. Quickly. Put them in your pouches."

A dozen anxious faces gulped at her in shock.

"What are we going to do?"

"We're going to open fire and drive them off. We must chase them all away."

Lyrilla looked almost ready to cry as she turned a rock over in her hand. "D-do you believe what she said about her mama? About the village?"

"Yes. I believe her."

The children turned and scoured the gully for rocks. Harïsh gently chivvied them along, striding behind them and keeping watch.

She could see them now; three black shapes crouching in the grass. They held their grotesque heads together in council as they decided what to do.

Harïsh signaled the other teenagers to rise. "All right everybody, they're nicely grouped. Remember the wasp nest we shot down over Lord Ingatekh's table last feasting day? We're the best shots on the river. We'll all fire together so they can't dodge." Harïsh rose slowly to her knees and tensed herself to fire. "All right everybody. Ready? Aim! Fire!"

Slings cracked as the young shepherds sped their missiles home.

In the meadow, the demons whirled in shock. A black shape spun and tumbled back in pain.

"Keep firing! As fast as you can!"

Father Wind sped the sling bullets through the air. The demons fled in panic. A last rain of stones hacked through the branches all around them. The shepherds gave a cheer, and the boys leapt the gully walls to fire a final shot.

Harïsh dragged the others back into cover. She tossed one girl her shepherd's staff and gathered her equipment. "All right everyone, we're going to abandon the sheep. We can find them again later. We're moving down to Wattle Creek, where the banks overhang the water."

Haripettïi toyed unhappily with his sling. "Harïsh, what about the village? My mama's there!"

Harïsh's golden eyes were strangely soft and sad. "I know, friend. My mama's there, as well."

She led them down the watercourse and out into the trees. The shepherds softly flitted through the bushes and left their homes behind.

A black shape knelt briskly in the dust before Daimïru and cracked his wings in salute. "War-Chief, Team Seven has encountered enemy resistance. One man dead, one injured. The injury is serious."

"Who was injured?"

"Myself. My elbow has been broken."

He said it without the slightest hint of emotion. The man's arm dripped blood onto the ground as he held his formal pose of submission. "An enemy female was discovered spying on the village, and Team Seven flew in pursuit. The prey lost us in the brambles behind the village meadow. The team split in three to comb the brush. Our detachment discovered the target fleeing down a dry watercourse. Team Leader Frakaki gave chase and was attacked by plainsmen armed with missile weapons. He was slain instantly."

"How many enemy?"

"Approximately twelve, War-Chief. Mostly immature females."

Daimïru slowly paced across the ground. She trod through a patch of glistening blood, stirring a cloud of bloated flies. "Why did you flee? Are children so terrifying to you?"

"Our officer was dead. We were outnumbered three to one. My orders were to scout and report. I held the team in place until we had assessed the lethality of their weapons. I considered my report to be of value."

"Would you do it again? Would you make that decision again if you faced such a situation?"

The man blinked. "It... it would depend on the situation, Leader. I would carry out my duty as I saw fit."

"Good. You are promoted to team leader." Daimïru glared with savage, hungry eyes at the corpse-strewn ruin of the village. "You've found aggressive females? Ha! So, they are not entirely without honor. What weapons did they have?"

"The creatures use strips of cloth to hurtle stones with tremendous force. Our man was killed by a single blow to the skull at twenty spans. At fifty spans they are still too accurate for comfort."

Daimïru caressed the skull-shaped pommels of her dao and paused in thought.

"We must develop combat tactics against their weapons. Take your full squad. The odds would be even. Let's see how well you fare against these stone flinging warriors. Bring us back a victory."

"Yes, leader!"

Daimïru snapped her fingers and brought a tiny demon gliding to her side. "Rooshïkii, you will follow Team Seven and observe. Under no circumstances are you to engage. I require your full report on the engagement."

The little girl snapped her wings across her face in salute, then followed Team Seven on its mission. Daimïru watched them go and gave a smile.

"They were here. Harïsh's ïsha trail is fresh."

Keketál knelt above a tiny patch of scuffled ground, reaching down to touch a handful of crushed paperbark leaves.

Nearby, a corpse lay bonelessly sprawled beneath a red gum tree, and Keketál rolled it over with his foot. The demon had been dead for less than half an hour. The noble retrieved a blood-stained pebble from the muck and gave a frown.

Hupshu licked his lips and leaned in closer to his friend. "My lord? What is it?"

"A rose quartz sling stone. Harïsh's stone. She shot the demon while he held a captive by the hair. She was standings over there, beside the bank."

"That's twenty spans away! To shoot one man and let another stay untouched? My lord, it isn't possible!"

"Harïsh can do it. The rock has her ïsha scent. She's killed our first enemy." Lord Keketál scowled as he sifted through the grass for signs. The six villagers watched uncomfortably, mystified by their leader's preoccupation.

The nobleman finally finished his examination. He drew a long, bent stick out of the corpse's belt and tucked it through his own, and then retrieved the demon's spears and tools.

"The sheep and shepherds were here. Twelve children carrying one injured." Keketál kept one spear and passed another back among his men. "They must have gone on foot to hide their ïsha spoor. Clever. They must know of somewhere close by where they could hide."

One boy looked from the empty ground and into Lord Keketál's hard eyes. "My lord, how do you know? Y-you can't possibly know all that!"

"Keketál knows."

Hupshu retrieved a metal knife from the dust and thrust it through his belt. "Where to now, my lord? Where have the shepherds gone?"

"Wattle Creek. Harïsh teach Keketál to shoot slings there. Beneath banks is cover place. Good place to hide." Armed with spear and woomera, the nobleman led the other villagers into the air. They disappeared with a blur of wings.

In the gully, silence reigned until the first demons drifted through the trees.

Deep in the shadows of Wattle Creek, the shepherds lay fearfully in hiding. Harïsh and Haripettii stayed on watch beneath the overhang while the other teenagers tended to Pachetta's wounds. The eerie silence of the woods made their fur crawl with alarm. Harïsh anxiously scanned the wilderness of tangled leaves above her, hardly daring to let herself breathe.

There was a crawling sense of something wrong: Twigs creaked in the breeze, and dead blackberry bushes rattled their old dry thorns. Harïsh gripped her sling and blinked out into the unknown.

Haripettii stiffened as he saw a stealthy something edging through the ferns. The boy leaned close to breathe into Harïsh's ear. "Look there, over by the tea tree. A tail."

He was right. Harïsh rose slowly onto her haunches, her slingshot held out as the tip of a wet, black nose slid cautiously around a tree. She opened fire. The shot went wide, and her target gave a pathetic yelp and immediately fell into a blackberry bush.

Only one man in the world was that consistently unlucky.

"Help! No shoot! Is me! Is Keketál!"

"Keketál!"

Harïsh joyously threw herself from cover and soared to Keketál, pulling his long tail. With a squawk he came free from the prickle bush and was smothered in her arms.

Six more village men rose into view; men with axes, sticks, and knives. They were the most beautiful sight Harïsh had ever seen.

"Oh, Keketál, I knew you'd come! I knew!" There were tears on her cheeks.

Keketál brushed them away and kissed her once again. Harïsh! His girl of gold. The nobleman grinned down at her and waggled his ears. "Keketál makes lookings. He is clever! We find you quick. There is a hurt person with you, yes?"

"Pachetta has a broken wing. How did you guess?"

"Ha! Keketál does not guess; Keketál know! Keketál is clever!"

The other shepherds spilled out into the light as Keketál's men raced across the creek. Brothers and sisters hurtled themselves into each other's arms. Keketál grinned and clutched Harïsh against his heart. He had escaped the hunt and found his girl. The demons were vulnerable after all.

The nobleman held out his hand to still the babbling villagers. The men and women shot puzzled glances toward Keketál. His caution seemed absurd. The bushes were still, and the enemy had gone. Even the cicadas had suddenly ceased their song....

As one, the villagers sank into the ferns. Keketál glared at a distant tree, slowly drawing his captured throwing stick. Without even seeming to aim, the noble suddenly hurtled the stick into the sky.

The weapon whirred, curved around in a savage arc, and sliced behind the tree. A black shape screeched and tumbled from hiding. Keketál whirled. The alien woomera flipped forward as his spear flashed and struck. The black figure shrieked in agony, and dozens of savage demons immediately burst from the trees.

"Fall back! Fall back and shoot!" Keketál's orders galvanized the villagers into action. The savages had sprung their ambush too soon, and the open gully gave the slingers a perfect field of fire. Shepherds scythed the bushes and drove the creatures back. Two demons fell, jerking like puppets as they clutched their broken skulls.

The savages reacted with blinding speed. Orders snapped out in their warbling tongue, and black demons melted instantly into cover. They tore through the dead ground behind the banks and furiously closed the range.

Spears flew; a young girl dragged herself across the stream, a shaft impaling her thigh. Harïsh fired and blew apart a demon's jaw. The remaining savages ripped into the village ranks.

The men surged forward with their clubs and staves, buying Harïsh's friends time to escape. Keketál roared. He rammed a demon back across the stream. The savages' armor shrugged off every blow. Still Harïsh and her shepherds hovered near the fight.

Keketál sought his beloved's eyes and bellowed out across the bloody stream. "Harïsh, split the slingers left! Get onto the high ground!"

Villagers died beneath the dripping metal knives. The savages fought like madmen! One demon barely even grunted as a spear rammed through its chest. He then stalked forward into battle like an impaled forest bug.

"Keketál, get down!"

The men hurtled themselves flat, and the air hissed with sling stones. Demons staggered back and died.

"Up! Kill the bastards!"

The villagers rallied behind their chief. Captured spears plunged and bit. Hupshu screamed in rage and shoved his dao into a demon's heart. He whirled and stabbed a second creature in the spine. The savage arched in agony before pitching into the stream.

Suddenly there was no one left to fight. The last two demons fled down the stream, one with a broken elbow and one with a spear impaled through its chest.

Keketál staggered sideways to collapse against a corpse. Hupshu fell to his knees and retched.

Bodies lay strewn across the creek, blood clinging thick as syrup to the stones. Somewhere in the background a wounded woman cried. The sound hung strangely soft against the sudden, deathly still.

Harïsh came to him, just as she always had when he needed her. Keketál's eyes went blank as he gazed at the horror. "It is Keketál's fault. Keketál led them here."

"No, my love. They would have come after us anyway. You saved us."

Harïsh lifted Keketál's fine hands and washed them clean of blood. In the distance, a village girl moaned as they dragged a spear from her leg. He should go help.

Keketál opened his eyes and tried to think what to do. "Harïsh, how many of us are left?"

"Three men, seven shepherds. Five of us are badly hurt. Three might... might die." Harïsh slowly wove to her feet. "I will see to them. I-I have to care for them...." She turned to her duty.

Keketál still stared at the corpses in the stream. "They should have slaughtered us. If they had attacked on the wing..."

"They did not hit us on the wing. You beat them, my love. You showed us how."

"Next time, they will come by the air."

"You'll know what to do. You always know what to do." The girl staggered as she walked across the stones.

Somewhere, an injured shepherd tried to clear his bleeding lungs. Keketál slumped back against a tree and closed his eyes, trying to still his trembling hands.

He had known—the throwing stick, the silver knives, the screaming skulls. Somehow, he had already known....

Keketál hid his face inside his hands and felt his spirit weep.

A hush sighed among the warriors. Something filled the air with a numbing spell of awe, and a thousand fighters sank reverently to their knees.

Footsteps echoed. Zhukora slowly paced among her worshipers. Ïsha swirled around her as she walked. Her armor dripped with light, and highlights gleamed across her slender curves.

Daimïru knelt before her in the dust and bared her dripping blade. "Revered One, the village has been liquidated. Their women lie dead, their men fell before our ambush. The children were slain as we overran the river. All the target villages have been totally destroyed. Your orders have been fulfilled."

In the houses, little Ka wailed in dismay. Zhukora looked about the ghastly corpses draped across the village square and gave a smile.

"You have done well, all of you. No one could have asked more. Perform the rightful ceremonies. Free the spirits trapped inside the bodies. Give them the gift and ask forgiveness. We are not butchers. Though we have come as instruments of punishment, we shall act with mercy and respect."

Zhukora gazed at the corpse of a beautiful teenage girl. Once she had been blonde, vibrant and alive. How like Daimïru...

"A dreadful lesson. They have paid for their crimes. We have shown them the price of defiance. Now, our will shall be done. We have secured the future of our people."

The leader's voice rose out to ring across her warriors. "We claim these lands in the name of the united Kashran race! Bring your families. Let your children feast on the fresh meat of the plains! We shall dig the yams and fish the rivers. We shall worship Rain and Wind and thank them for their bounty. The unholy waste of natural resources is at an end!"

Zhukora held them spellbound with her words. She stood before them, virginal and perfect; the custodian of the Kashran racial dream.

"No property! No priests! No elders, kings, or queens. We will have our Dream! Our Dream of iron! Our Dream of living space and justice. If the plains creatures oppose us, they will pay the price in blood! We are the peoples of the alps—the chosen ones of Mother Rain! We shall take the Dream across the world and push back the old limits of Kashran glory!"

The rainbow warriors screamed in adulation. Zhukora drew their faith around her like a cloak of streaming colors, bowing her head. She swayed, utterly lost in a storm of love.

Two figures rose to peer through the grass. A golden, fluffy tail waved high above the bushes, and a gray hand reached out to quickly snatch it back. "Hsst, get down! I told you to get down!"

"I want to see!"

"Get tush down! Don't stick it in Keketál's face."

Harïsh gave a 'humph' and waved her tail in his nose. "Ha! So finally you notice."

"Notice? You drive Keketál mad for weeks! How Keketál keep faith with your mother when all he thinks about iss jumping you?"

"Why, you lecherous old flea-bag!"

"Jiggle-rumped hussy!"

"Boor!"

"Brat!" The bushes quivered as Keketál's head popped up from cover. "Prickly-fire and poison! Keketál knew he shouldn't have let you come! Go back and look after hurted ones. Go back and be helping friends!"

"Now, look, I've bound and stitched until I'm fed up to the gills! I want my Mama and Papa, I want my lazy brothers, and I want my brat of a little sister! So you can go right on wasting time, or you can let us get on with the job!"

Keketál wore a suit of demon armor that still dripped wet from the creek. He angrily folded his arms and turned away.

"Pah! Always is a busy-body! Silly girl go home and tend sheep! Now shut up and let me finish put on this stupid gear."

Harïsh took her fears out on Keketál. If she had stopped to think, she would have gone stark raving mad. The girl jerked her armor into place. The helmet spilled down across her head and nearly smothered her. "Well, how do I look?"

"Hmmph. Demons not waggle backside when they walk! Why did you come? Why? It is too dangerous for you."

"Because I love you, stupid man! I love you."

The nobleman blinked as it dawned on him just what Harïsh was saying. The poor man's jaw dropped as everything sank home.

Harïsh saw his face and angrily flicked out her antennae. Her family had gone missing, her village stood in flames, and her only companion was a numbskull! She whirred into the air and sped toward her home. Keketál growled once before following.

They flew toward the village meadow. Keketál waved the girl behind him, landed, and wormed his way into the grass. She saw his wings turn stiff. For long moments the man simply lay on his stomach and stared across the fields. Harïsh crawled curiously up beside him, her ears lifting as she gently placed a hand across his rear.

"Keketál? What is it? What do you..."

The girl turned her gaze across the meadow, and words froze inside her throat. She felt her face form a vacuous smile as she stared at the murder of her entire universe.

They were all there, every man that she had ever known. Totasha the dye maker. Lasri the weaver's boy, so proud to fight fires beside his father. They were still together, lying side by side. Dead Lord Ingatekh stared in outrage as a crow held aloft one of his gleaming eyes. The bird swallowed the morsel and stropped its beak upon his lordship's bloodstained fur.

Harïsh spread her wings and gently drifted through the sky, coming to rest beside a gray old figure in the grass. Harïsh reached out and absently stroked her father's ruffled fur.

The field was black with still shapes. There would be thirty one of them; Harïsh had no need to count. Everyone was here—all the missing men of the village, all together in death just as they had been in life. Harïsh had never guessed there was so much blood in all the world.

Keketál alighted beside her, his arm about her shoulders. Harïsh paid him no attention, staring at her father and her brothers in the grass. Her voice seemed strangely gay, as though she were lost inside a dream. "Mama's dead, of course. They killed everything, didn't they? We never even knew they existed, and they came and killed us all."

The girl wove to her feet.

"She'll need me. I really ought to be with her. They're my family, you see? You really have to understand us. What happens to my family, happens to me.

"I didn't want to die. I wanted to marry you. I could have been a good wife, you know. I wanted to bear your eggs and share your house. I was going to be the finest surgeon in the tribe! I'd have given you everything, every happiness my heart could find, and you'd have loved me in return."

The girl slowly wandered out across the grass, letting Keketál's hand slip from her grasp. "I have to go. Do you understand? I simply have to go."

Suddenly the girl gave a jerk and fell. Keketál caught her softly in his arms, the heavy throwing stick tumbling from his grasp. He heaved the girl across his shoulder and bore her over to the trees.

"Keketál understands, my love, but Keketál iss family too. He iss family who loves you."

"Rooshïkii, your report."

The tiny warrior looked up to face her leader's eyes. Rooshïkii's voice rang with a supernatural calm.

"The unit was eliminated in combat. There are two survivors—the new officer and his second. Both are superior fighters. Their position was hopeless."

"How? How did mere villagers beat back our elite?"

"Our attack was engaged by missile fire before it could close. Team Seven attacked hand to hand, but the enemy combined firepower with melee action to beat them back. The key is to attack from the air at high speed. Slings cannot be fired on the wing. Our spears are the superior weapons for mobile fighting."

Zhukora stroked her chin. "Are all the enemy so dangerous?"

"No, Revered One. Only when motivated by powerful leaders. They lack our discipline and devotion. "

"This small group—it had a powerful leader?"

"There is one dangerous officer among them. Without him, the villagers would have been helpless. I would have taken him were I not bound by my orders."

"Only at the cost of your own life."

"If it serves you, it is well spent."

The little girl bent forward in a bow. Zhukora refreshed herself with tea from a common soldier's kettle. She looked across the teacup at her smallest warrior.

"I am pleased you obeyed your orders. You are far more use to our cause alive, Rooshïkii. I want you to organize our scouts and spies. You are to be our eyes and ears in the world."

The young girl glanced up, her skull mask quivering in astonishment.

"Revered One! You do me too much honor!"

"Never. Ability must be recognized and nurtured. You are the clearest thinker of all my officers." Zhukora swigged the last few drams of tea and set her cup aside. "Go. Pick your own teams. Report to me when you see fit. Let no person doubt that Rooshïkii-Zha speaks with my authority."

The officers bowed. Rooshïkii rose stiffly to her feet and disappeared among the busy crowds of warriors.

Zhukora gave a sigh and let her cup be filled again. "Daimïru, what's next? Let's get the business done."

"Food. We have found buried hordes of grain, more than we can carry. The village herds have also been discovered."

"We shall leave the supplies. They will be useful during the resettlement. Detail a hand of teams to garrison here."

Daimïru signed to a Hand Captain, and the man instantly flew off to do the deed. Daimïru turned to the next cut on her quirt and gave a predatory smile. "Aaaaaah, yes, prisoners. We have found a single living female who had hidden in a wicker basket. She 'bargained' most prettily for her life; I think Team Sixteen is already half in love with her. I must admit, the girl does have a certain charm."

"By all means, bring her in! I shall be pleased to meet a living plainsman. We will send her off to her rulers with our demands."

It had been a most wearying day. Zhukora stood and stretched her slender body in the sun, thinking suddenly of curling up in a bed of new-cut grass.

Lord Serpent suddenly hissed a warning in Zhukora's mind. *Someone watches! I feel hostility and power!*

Zhukora whirled and glared about the village square, seeing only flies and corpses. No danger lurked. No one hid beneath the trees. The only movement came from a single Skull-Wing warrior. He knelt across a female corpse, gently closed the woman's eyes, and bowed his head to pray.

Zhukora scowled and flipped her tail, annoyed beyond all reason. What did the boy think he was? A priest? "You! You there! What are you doing?"

His skull mask jerked up. The painted wood gleamed with tears.

"Are you crying, man? What in Poison's name is wrong with you? Come over here at once!"

Zhukora imperiously pointed one finger at the ground before her. The warrior detached a necklace from the body at his feet and flipped out his wings. Suddenly, Ka flew from the house posts to surround him in a ball of swirling light.

Daimïru stood, her face twisting in puzzlement. "Zhukora? Zhukora! What's he doing?"

The warrior was whirring high into the air, spirits rising from the houses to follow in his wake. The warrior dived off between the huts at an astonishing speed.

Zhukora ran a few steps forward and gulped like a landed fish. "No!"

I have smelled his soul before! He was near us in the battle of the fires! It must be the enemy officer!

Zhukora gave a shout and punched her hands toward the sky. A titanic ïsha blast exploded through the trees. The bolt engulfed her victim in a screaming storm of flame.

The watching warriors blinked as the fugitive flipped his tail and sped from view. Zhukora could almost hear the creature's derisive whoop of laughter. She stared at her smoking fists and felt her antennae sag. "Serpent! What in Poison's name is happening? Why didn't he fall? Why!"

The spirits shielded him. At that range the attack was easily blocked.

"Blocked? Imbecile! Do you know how powerful a creature would have to be to oppose me?"

He has allies! Spirits of the village. Their love blocked the force!

"And where did he get allies from?"

Are you stupid, girl? Can't you feel them screaming in the ïsha all around you?

Zhukora went stiff and cold. She wreathed herself in coils of burning light. The Serpent spirit gave a scream and sobbed for mercy as she tore it with her claws. *Never show disrespect again! I own you. I rule you! You are mine to destroy or favor as I will!* The girl gave the beast a jerk.

Serpent sobbed and whimpered in her mind. *How? How did you gain such power over me?*

I am the future! You are the past. My triumph was inevitable. Obey me, and our bargain holds. Displease me, and I shall consume your very soul.

Daimïru knelt at Zhukora's feet and spread her wings. "He might leave a trail. Shall we pursue?"

"No. Prepare the troops for departure. We've wasted time enough."

"But, we can kill the officer. Deny them a resource!"

Zhukora looked into the air and gave a shrug. "What can one man do against an army? How can one creature defy destiny? He is nothing. All that matters is the Dream."

She signed briefly to her warriors. The alpine tribesmen filtered into the air, leaving ashes swirling in their wakes.

Twenty-One

Father Wind breathed gently across a wilderness of grass, and like a calm sea, the hills and planes rippled with waves. Shadarii danced amid the endless swirls of motion. She danced because she alone could know the sorrow in her heart.

Shadarii no longer needed to eat. Sun and ïsha were her sustenance, and she had set aside all need for possessions and for the hate and greed they brought.

The dance was her priceless, private time. For a few precious moments, she became Shadarii once again; not the Silent Lady all bathed in sacred light; not the Teacher come to fill the world with peace; only a young woman with eyes of shining green. Shadarii shed her silent tears and watched the rising dawn.

Kotaru!

Each dawn I remember you. With the setting of each evening sun, I polish bright my love.

I died with you, my love. I died there in your arms....

Finally, the dance drew to an end, and Shadarii slowly wilted to the grass. Bright wings covered her fur as she bowed toward the horizon.

The moment of peace was over. Shadarii felt a presence kneeling in the grass behind her, and gave a rueful sigh.

Kïtashii had taken to wearing the dress of the sea peoples. She went bare breasted, with nothing but a curtain of tiny cowrie shells dangling just before her groin. The new clothing suited her. The girl reverently bowed. "Shadarii-Zha, a woman has come to see you. She has traveled many, many days. She has brought her son to be healed. Shall I send them away until your dance is done?"

Never! Shadarii swiftly stood and swooped downhill to where her faithful ones were waiting in a circle. Of the twelve pilgrims, only Mrrimïmei was absent.

A woman with an infant child knelt at their center, her clothes stained from many days of travel. The woman kept her gaze riveted on the ground. "Revered One, I am of Totrepa village. I am of the Lemon-Orchid lodge. My name is Fengahïl. I have come to beg the mercy of the Silent Lady." The woman's strength was almost spent.

Shadarii folded her to her breast.

Fengahïl muffled her misery in her fur and let the words spill out with her tears. "He's lame! It's my fault, all mine! I conceived out of wedlock, and the spirits punished him for my sin!"

Shadarii gently rocked the woman to and fro. The son might have been lame, but it was the mother who needed healing. The Silent Lady looked down at the little boy and shared a crafty wink. He stared up at her and grinned; a little imp of three summers—grubby, thin, and perfect. If he missed the use of his twisted foot, he did not show it.

Rotïka leaned from the circle of pilgrims and looked into Shadarii's gaze. "Revered One, I fear nothing can be done. The flesh has already set in shape."

Fengahïl jerked in Shadarii's grasp and let loose a dreadful moan. "Please! Please, I beg you, don't turn me away! I can pay—I really can! I have conch shells, beads... I'll give you everything I have!"

Shadarii gazed at her in hurt.

Fengahïl realized her mistake and clutched Shadarii's arms. "I-I'm sorry! Oh, Lady, please forgive me. Please, won't you try? We have traveled for day and days..."

The boy giggled as Shadarii kissed his nose and plucked him high into the air. She reached down to touch his feet, smiling as she saw the ruinous club of flesh, and then let him play with her antennae as she kissed his little chest. It was as though she saw nothing imperfect in him at all.

"Lady, his foot! Don't you see? It's warped and ugly! He cannot run; he cannot stand. How can he grow and play when he's a cripple?"

Kïtashii saw Shadarii's smile and felt a brief twinge of despair.

"Revered One, the boy is lame. No one could have enough ïsha to reshape such a limb."

Shadarii set the little boy aside. She looked down at Kïtashii and carefully mimed her words. *Ïsha comes from the world, Kïtashii. It is made from wonder.*

Think of all the dear things that make our lives rich. The rattle of a teapot on the hearth; fresh frosts shining in the dawn! A favorite tree, a cool, old brook; a ragged bird you know you've seen before...

Here is ïsha! Here is meaning! Love the world. Celebrate it with every fiber of your being. Reach out, and you will find your power. There is no mystery to magic. It lies inside you.

Shadarii took Kïtashii by the hands and led her toward the little boy. *Come! Heal him! You can do it. Take him by the hand and make him whole.*

Kïtashii desperately tried to pull away. "I can't! Shadarii, you know I can't!"

Try!

"It can't be done!"

Shadarii gave the girl a long, sad look and left her standing in the grass. She lifted the little boy atop her shoulders, reaching out to take her patient's mother by the hand. They wandered out across the grass to lose themselves in the caressing wind.

They strolled for an hour across the dunes beside the sea, lost in the wonder of the endless ocean waves. Shadarii walked her friends beside the glistening tidal pools, where they tickled anemones and peered at ghostly little prawns. Fengahïl smiled down at her son and helped him hop across the beach. They played together, loved together; mother and son, united and inseparable.

Shadarii finally took her two companions by the hand and led them back to the village green. Her followers were busily netting bait fish by the shore. Kïtashii had retreated among the sea people, teaching them Shadarii's alphabet. She dropped her scrolls of paperbark and goggled in amazement.

The little boy could walk!

"Shadarii, how? Where was the power hidden?"

Shadarii watched Fengahïl playing with her son, then looked down at Kïtashii and touched her on the nose. *I did nothing. He wanted to make her happy—she needed to have him whole. The power was always there.*

"You are Mother Rain on earth! You work miracles!"

Oh, Kïtashii, whatever am I to do with you? Shadarii took her student by the hand and led her off beneath the village eaves. Housewives stood on ladders high above, wetting straw in buckets to make it pliable enough to thatch. Shadarii admired their nimble skill, deeply pleased by their economy of motion. Finally she raised her hands and shaped words for her little friend.

To own the loyalty of one soul is to possess a priceless gift. You do me great honor by giving me your love. Even so, my friend, you must understand what I am. My life and death are not my own. I have been chosen by Mother Rain for a very special task. I must spread her word of love.

Shadarii clenched her hands, trying to find the words. *Kïtashii, you and Tingtraka are my special ones; my soul mates. Everything I know, I want you to know. Everything I can do, you will one day do.*

I am no god, Kïtashii. I am nothing but a woman. Anyone can aspire to be exactly as I am. That is the very essence of what I teach. I believe that you and Tingtraka will one day surpass me. Do you understand?

Kïtashii's eyes shone; she hung from Shadarii's hands and stared at her in adoration. "Teach me! Teach me how you touch the world! I want to do it. I want to be like you!"

Shadarii walked along beneath the lodgehouse eaves. *What we know and understand, we surely love. From love comes magic. You must begin very small, my darling. You must learn to be aware of the world. Only this can lead to the path of love.*

"I can feel it! I can. I just know I can. I can feel everything!"

Shadarii gave a sideways glance and smiled as a water bucket mysteriously teetered overhead. It spilled across Kïtashii's head with an almighty splash. Shadarii whistled between her teeth and looked innocently at the sky. *Good! It is so comforting to know you are progressing....*

❄ ❄ ❄

In the dark of night, moonlight caught the barest ripples in the surf. Shadarii flew alone above the waves, enjoying the solitude. There was nothing quite like flying alone along a beach at night. The salt breeze whistled through her wings, and spray whispered in her ears of times gone by.

Lady Starshine looped and curled about her, dancing to the currents in the ïsha breeze. The Ka glowed, and soft words spilled into Shadarii's mind like summer rain.

Thou art very quiet tonight, my child. Did the healing of the little boy not please thee?

My heart is heavy. Forgive me; I am the only company you have. I neglect you shamefully.

A thousand years of silence makes one self-reliant. However, I do feel responsible for thee. Why not let me help bear thy burdens? Tell me what is wrong.

Shadarii closed her eyes and let the stars stream through her hair. *I am failing even before I have begun. I meant only to preach messages of love. Now Mrrimïmei hates me. I've lost her love and I don't know why.*

Aaaaah, is that all that ails thee? The spirit coiled above, twinkling with countless pastel lights. *The girl is upset. She adored your lover Kotaru. She feels you have betrayed his memory by teaching what you teach.*

But what I teach is right! It is true!

Tell me, what do you teach? What do you believe, Shadarii? I want to hear you speak of it.

Shadarii let herself drift down onto the shore. She lay back on the sand and let Father Wind blow through her fur. *Today we wrote a tale down in the "Book of Offerings". A parable I had invented. It was a story about fleas upon a chieftain's rump. Would you like hear it?*

Yes, Shadarii. Tell me thy tale.

The girl gazed into the sky and let the words form in her mind. *There were black fleas and there were brown fleas, and all lived in harmony upon the rump of an important chief. They bit and romped all through his fur, and had a perfectly splendid time. They chased away the bedbugs and killed off ticks and lice. The chief was healthy, and the flea tribes prospered deep inside his fur.*

As time went by, the chief grew somewhat thin, and there seemed to be less of him to go around. The fleas had grown so numerous that they had made the poor man ill. Fleas began to fight and tousle, battling for food. Finally it was obvious that something must be done. Delegates from both flea tribes held a solemn council.

"There is not enough room for all of us! Fights are breaking out. Let us make a solemn covenant with our neighbors to avoid any further battles. We shall make a dividing line. The black fleas may have everything below the chief's waist, and the brown fleas everything above."

To avoid conflict, the fleas separated their two kinds, and for a while their lives proceeded in peace. Finally, however, discontent began to brew. The black fleas started to grumble. Whenever the chief bathed his tired old feet, dozens of fleas were drowned. And they were always in the shade! Where was the sun they used to love? The brown fleas had cheated them!

Above the waist, the brown fleas were also dissatisfied. The chief had dandruff, and this made their homes a mess. They thought wistfully of warm days spent down in the old chief's nether regions and slowly filled with spite. The black fleas had tricked them! The best terrain had all been stolen.

Both groups of fleas prepared for battle. They sucked more blood in order to grow big and strong. They bred and multiplied to lend numbers to their armies. The old chief's spine echoed to the tramp of tiny feet. Gongs and drums rattled in his ears all night. A mighty war raged back and forth across his mangy hide. The chief tossed and turned and scratched and groaned, his skin flaming in pain. Finally the old man's heart could take the stress no longer. He kicked up his heels and died.

Meanwhile, on a battleground behind the deadman's ear, the black fleas were finally victorious. They danced across the bodies of their foes and rubbed their little feet in glee. Finally the chief's whole hide was theirs!

Alas, it was all to no avail. The villagers made a great funeral pyre and reverently sent their chief into the arms of Mother Rain. And every single flea went with him, right down to the smallest little nit....

Starshine seemed to hem and haw as she mulled Shadarii's tale. *Quite charming I'm sure, but what is the moral?*

I suppose the moral is that they should have tended to the old man's needs. It is a story about our forest, you see. It was dying, and all we could do was steal from one another. The fleas died because they were too stupid to do something positive. The girl hung her head and gave a miserable sigh. *Am I doing anything positive? I just don't know.*

Lady Starshine assumed a matronly air inside Shadarii's head. *Thou art a funny creature. Thou hast failed to listen to me all this time, and now thou comest for help. I must say, it's high time someone listened to me!*

Staring out across the star-tossed sea, Shadarii felt sharp pangs of despair. *What? What am I doing wrong? I have healed the sick, my message is spreading. Why can no one see? Violence feeds upon itself. Once upon a time I fought to win people's respect. I thought punching Javïra would solve all my pain. I was a fool! Respect is won through love, not fear. If I had refused to strike her, even to have asked her for another blow, perhaps I would have shown more strength and won her over as my friend.*

Oh, Shadarii, pacifism was already the creed of your society. Look how weak and corrupt it became!

Shadarii gazed out across the darkened skies. *Nonviolence requires moral strength. You must believe in it; be ready to die for it! They had forgotten why we had the creed. The elders hid the tales of war, and so our fear and loathing of it died.*

Starshine slowly settled down around Shadarii's shoulders. *And what of this 'Kotaru' Mrrimimei so admired. Thou hast said thy pilgrims were nothing until he found them. What did Kotaru teach them?*

Shadarii's eyes misted over as she unveiled the memory of her love. *He found the strengths hidden inside each individual. Kotaru taught them to become proud of themselves.*

Well, then, perhaps Mrrimimei no longer feels proud of herself.

Shadarii was shocked. *Why? You've seen what Tingtraka has become! She grows stronger in love every day. And Kitashii, my little acolyte. So serious, so strong!*

These two are not warriors. Thine other pilgrims are all fighters! They have learned to battle for their beliefs! They are ashamed, my child. Ashamed that they have abandoned the world they love.

But there is so much to teach these fisher folk! Shadarii flung sand into the surf. *They flock to me in thousands to see my sermons and my tales. My mission is being fulfilled!*

Fulfilled? A waste of time! A betrayal of thy people—

I have told you—

Quiet! I shall have my say! Starshine seethed in a spiteful temper. *Thy sister still has power over thee. Thou art afraid of her. Admit it! 'Tis easier to skulk here than face thy sister in righteous battle!*

Shadarii, my love, do not waste thy time! Do not preach of peace to a people who know no war! If thou must do good, do it where it is needed.

Zhukora grows more powerful, Shadarii. Evil is like fire; it spreads and spreads as long as there are innocent victims to fuel it! It is time for us to go. Time to leave this hiding place and face the struggle thou were born for! If left unopposed, Zhukora will drench this continent in a wave of blood!

Shadarii's temper rose. *What I did before was wrong! To fight, to hurt—to kill! See all the trouble it led to? I murdered my own true love! If I hadn't started all this trouble....*

The results would have been worse! Stop sniveling. Either fight or turn thy back on everything thy lover died for!

The Kashra closed her eyes and rigidly faced the sea. *I have told you already that I have a vision. I know what I must do!*

Oh, really? And so this is why thou fly alone at night? How pleasant to indulge oneself when thy people are screaming for thine aid! Shadarii gave a hiss, but Starshine lashed relentlessly onward. *I have opened the door to immense powers inside thee! Thy meditations are revealing the very secrets of power itself. You cross barriers thine ancestors never even dared to see! And yet thou dost nothing to help thy people!*

Shut up! Shadarii wrung her antennae between her hands. *I order you to shut up!*

Starshine took a breath of indignation. *Oppose force with force, evil with good! Sometimes violence must be used. It can be a tool for good as long as we use it for the moral right!*

Right? How can murder ever be made right?

If we slay a tyrant to prevent her killing thousands, that is right! If we take a man who beats his child and let him taste his own whip, that is right! Morality does not come naturally, girl! Justice is dealt out with the sword. A society needs laws; needs controls! A higher authority must dictate what is right and wrong.

They need a vision. A holy leader! They need thee, girl! Take them! Take them forth and show them the glory of thy will!

Shadarii reeled, clutching her skull. *Shut up! Leave me be!*

Thou hast become the ultimate force for good upon this earth. Reject thy destiny and thou hast betrayed everything thy lover fought for! Thou hast betrayed Kotaru and Mother Rain, herself!

Shadarii whirled, her fangs suddenly bared brightly. *You leave Kotaru out of this! He was perfect. He was gentle! Do you think for a moment he would want me to crush these people beneath my will?*

Crush? No, liberate! Take these little creatures by the hand and rule them as a mother should. It's what Kotaru would have wanted.

Shadarii shivered with rage. *I told you never to mention Kotaru again!*

Of course, my dear. We shall not speak of him again. The sea foam washed slowly back and forth, as serene and timeless as the dancing of the stars.

Shadarii watched the ebb and flow of bubbles in the moonlight. *Forgive me, Starshine. I shall pray that I grow stronger. I shall pray that I become more pure. For you are right. It is time. I feel the death growing slowly in the air.*

The girl closed her eyes and turned her face into the wind. *I must return to the forest.*

The dawn saw Shadarii trudging up the dunes, her heart still weary from the agony of decision. Tingtraka and Kïtashii walked in silence at her side, their travel packs bulging with a few small scraps of goods. Behind them came the other pilgrims; eleven followers with wise, calm eyes. Mrrimïmei slunk at the rear, glaring hatred at Shadarii.

Shadarii slowly crossed the sharp crest of a dune, gazing across the crowd waiting for her.

A hundred fisher-folk. Sister Mouse and Brother Fish knelt next to Fengahïl and her son. There were healers and teachers, grandmothers and fishermen. Those who had been blind or mad, those who had been touched and healed.

At their head sat Lady Zareemah-Kha: She whose son had been raised from the dead. The noblewoman bowed and held her wings before her eyes.

"Revered One, we know you are leaving. All these folk have gathered here because of our love for you. We ask nothing but to follow our beloved Silent Lady." The woman kept her eyes riveted on the ground. Her wings quivered as she clutched her son tight against her chest. "If you will have us, we'll follow you to the far ends of the earth! If you will allow it, we'll help you spread your precious Word. Your teachings have meant much to us. The fisher folk will never be the same. You have not failed."

Shadarii swayed. A single tear sparkled in the corner of her eye. She drew a breath, turned on her heel, and launched herself into the desert air. Her little band leapt skyward and followed on the tail of their dream. They bore the word of peace toward the bleeding heart of war.

Twenty-Two

Even through her tears, the girl's beauty cast a marvelous spell. Namīlii of River-Bend wept before the tribal council and shook with terror. Fifty councilors watched as an inept old nobleman tried to still her fears.

"Oh, now now. Please, my dear, don't cry so. It isn't really so very bad...."

The council of the Ochitzli tribe was in shock. A world that had stood unchanged for a thousand years had suddenly overturned. Savages had burst straight out of legend, bringing back the plague of war. The nobles stared in horror at the empty seat once held by the speaker of River-Bend.

Namīlii retched with fright, tears racking her slender body. "She came for me! The black empress came for me! Sh-she showed me m-my own dead Mama, and then she laughed when she heard me scream! She laughed! Th-the witch calls the evil spirits! Sh-she had one speak to me. It told me it would eat my soul unless I gave you all a message!"

"Hush, child. There's no danger here."

Namīlii's eyes rolled white. "It'll find me! It said it would find me! It lives in dreams. I have to tell you! I have to..." The girl rocked back and forth, tearing at her hair. "Oh, Mama!"

The handsome young speaker of Thistle-Field rose from his place and dried Namīlii's tears. He drew her down beneath his arm and tried to stop her trembling. "Poor child, how you must have suffered."

Namīlii snuffled, making a brave show of choking back her tears. She nestled against the nobleman and peered up at him with soulful eyes. "I-I do feel a bit better now...."

"That's grand. Now why don't you just tell us all about this message?"

Namīlii allowed the lord to stroke her hair as she miserably repeated Zhukora's ultimatum. "The dark empress lays claim to all the lands of the Ochitzli. She said we are her subjects now. W-we have one week in which to come to River-Bend and pay homage. We are to follow the orders of her chiefs. Our nobles are to report to her for briefing and assignment."

"And... if we refuse to spread wings to her?"

"Then what happened to River-Bend will happen to every village on the plains." Namīlii's words fell into silence.

The council of the Ochitzli tribe grimly considered her words.

The refugees from River-Bend had staggered into Marsh-Side only three days before—half a dozen shepherds, a few tired men, and the village children. A single nobleman had flown grimly at their head, a wounded girl borne in his arms. The leader had kept his people together, tending their needs in dour silence. Slowly, word spread. Almost eleven hundred people had died. The border villages were no more, their people butchered, their houses burned.

After a thousand years, war had risen from its grave.

Every village heard the news. Nobles scoffed. Peasants quaked. Messengers flew to River-Bend to see the disaster for themselves. The conquerors waited for them.

Each group was subjected to the same terrifying ritual. Black demons surrounded them, led them into the village, and paraded them past heaps of butchered corpses.

River-Bend's fate was a horror so overwhelming it numbed the very soul.

The Ochitzli tribal council had convened in panic, and now the high speakers milled about the sacred grove, wondering what to do.

Disgusted by their inactivity, the speaker for Flint-Wash slammed his shepherds staff against the ground. "Does this... this Zhukora think us mad? Why should we give in to a few hundred savages?"

Namílii jerked forward. "No! The spirit, h-he gave me a vision. I saw them! The skies black with demons! Spears numbering like the stars in the sky! The mountains are alive with savages!"

Speakers began to bleat and tremble. One youngster shot to his feet. "It's true! At night we hear their drums! The plains crawl with their camp fires!"

"Thousands of them!"

"Butchers!"

The ancient speaker of Flint-Wash slashed his stick out at his cowardly neighbors. "What of it? There must be at least as many of us! Throw her demands straight back in her face!"

"He's right!"

"Sit down!"

"Order! Order!" The chairman leapt up and down in fury and jabbed his staff toward the fat speaker for Silver-Leaf. "You, there! If you have something to say, request permission of the chair."

The chairman's victim tugged at his jeweled collar. "Honored Speakers, Revered Chairman, I ask the indulgence of the house. I propose the motion that we accede to the savages' demands."

"Never!"

"Silence in the house!"

"Order! I will have order!"

"A motion is before the house. According to custom, the aggrieved party must speak in public before any vote is taken. Is there a noble spokesman here for the village of River-Bend?"

"Yes! Keketál speaks for River-Bend!"

The whole assembly craned toward the door. A single tall figure stood silhouetted by the portal; a heavy, savage male, his fur scarred by fire. The nobleman glared at the council through hard young eyes. "Keketál will speak for his home! What nonsense iss this about surrender?"

It was him; the river gift! Men stood for a better glance as Keketál marched ever deeper through the room.

The speaker for Silver-Leaf mopped his neck and pointed a finger down at Keketál. "You, sir? What right have you to speak in place of the house of Ingatíl?"

"Right of survival! Keketál iss alive."

"Where is Lord Ingatíl?"

"We found him wandering mad in the fields after the slaughter. If you wanting to speak with him, you will get no sense." Keketál sneered at his foe. "You could make him your chairman!"

There was an explosion of outrage. Some laughed; some swore. Speakers shouted across the hall.

The chairman leapt to his feet and shook with indignation. "Lord Keketál, you have no right to mock this house!"

"If it deserves mocking, Keketál will mock! I am listening to you squeak and squeal like mice! You want to surrender to the demon-bitch? You want to grovel at her feet and plead for your miserable lives?"

Another man flung up his hands. "What else can we do? How can we stand against such evil?"

"Can there be any doubt? We fight!" Keketál clenched his fist and roared. "We take a life for a life! We show them we are free! They kill our blood. I say we pay them back with sling bullets, fists, and fire!"

The speaker for Silver-Leaf tugged regally at his robes. His voice blew rich and cool. "Lord Keketál, you are a stranger among us. We are a people of peace. It takes two sides to create a war. There shall be no death and slaughter if we all behave with reason."

"The moment you give in, you are lost!" Keketál pounded his points home with his fist. "Once you bow, she will grind in her heel. You will be hers forever!"

"But if it avoids a war..."

"Some things are worth a war!" Keketál snarled. "Your homes are worth a war! The lives of your children and your wives. The freedom to live the way you want to live. These things are worth dying for!"

The speaker of Silver-Leaf calmly faced the house. "Exactly! We have seen her power, and so we must give in. In troubled times, hasty decisions can be damaging. What does this Zhukora ask? Is it so much? Is a tiny loss of pride too much to ask for everlasting peace? We should take this as an opportunity for growth and friendship. A joining of hands as two peoples come together." The fat nobleman opened his arms and smiled. "Gentlemen, we face a time of change. Keketál calls for war, but I say let us call for peace! Let us grow and prosper, my brothers. Let us do service to our people."

All around the room, heads nodded wisely to the words of peace. Keketál's supporters waved their staves to snatch the attention of the chair.

The chairman hammered his staff. "We shall take the vote! The motion will be judged. All those in favor..."

"Mister Chairman! We insist that Keketál..."

"Now! The motion will be put to the vote!" The chairman lifted his hands. "All those opposed to declaring war, raise your staves!"

Staves flashed. All around the council hall, the chiefs thrust high their rods of office. A mere handful of men kept their arms proudly folded. The old chief of Flint-Wash stared at those who voted 'yea,' spat on the ground, and resolutely made his way to stand by Keketál.

The chairman made a great show of counting votes, his sparse antennae wagging in the air. "Forty-six to four. The will of the tribe is cooperation with the savages!"

A relieved storm of applause swept the hall.

Keketál gazed about the room, and then simply turned to go.

A flock of jubilant nobles hooted at him from the upper seats. "Lord Keketál! And what will you do now, stranger?" The cry rippled triumphantly through the crowd.

Keketál made no move to answer.

The chairman angrily rose to his feet. "The house has addressed you with a question, sir! You are obliged to answer. What do you intend to do?"

"We shall leave. River-Bend will go elsewhere."

"You can't leave! We have made a vote! It is the will of the majority."

"The majority may stay and live by it! You have forfeited the right to our loyalty!"

Keketál's ancient companion leaned upon his staff. "Flint-Wash stands with Keketál!"

"And Thistle-Field!"

"And Whisper-Tree!"

The house erupted into mayhem. Speakers struggled to stand with Keketál while other nobles gave a vengeful roar. The chairman held out his hands to silence the crowd. One hand sank slowly down to point damnation at Lord Keketál. "Foreigner, be gone! Take your vagabonds and go. Seek solace with another tribe. You break with the Ochitzli forever!"

Keketál cast his gaze across the ring of hostile faces. "The Ochitzli are gone! Keketál sees nothing here but the slaves of mountain savages."

The chairman made to reply, but Keketál had already marched away. The young lord rose into the air to begin planning a war.

☙ ☙ ❧

Sheep bleated as two hundred people grimly turned their backs on their homes. Flint-Wash village was dead and gone. Its people snatched up their belongings and filed out behind their chief. Not a single villager spared his home a parting glance.

Keketál held Harïsh warmly in his arms and brushed his lips against her hair. The girl looked up at him, a lover's adoration in her eyes, and then she watched Flint-Wash village empty into the plains.

Old Speaker Kotekh leaned upon his staff and spoke to Keketál. "Watch, boy, watch. The Ochitzli tribe is gone. They don't know it yet, but the cowards killed it yesterday. A thousand years of tradition struck dead in a single afternoon."

"Keketál is sorry, Lord Kotekh. Keketál could not make them see."

"They deserve the fate Poison has in store for them. The savages will suck away their souls." The old man chuffed. He flapped the cobwebs from his creaking muscles and wrung his staff of office in his hands. "I am one hundred thirty-seven years of age! A proud noble. Too old to bow and scrape before some stinking forest savage. I have seventeen living children, and sixty-seven grandchildren scattered through three tribes. My seed numbers three hundred ninety-three! There's our army. There's the claws to keep our people safe!"

Harïsh held tight to Keketál's arm and looked at the ancient chief in shock. "My lord! So... so many?"

"Eh? What of it, girl? Not much to show for a hundred thirty years of age. I've bounced in the sack a few more times than that, I'll tell ye! My youngest is six months old. There's life beneath the old kilt yet! Never disappoint a lady—that's my motto."

Harïsh's ears blushed red. "B-but, my lord! So many children... It's against the law!"

"Laws are for fools. This is my village. My clan! These are my people. No one tells us how many young we bear, how many sheep we breed. Our lives are our own."

The old man nodded as his people struggled past him with their herds. They bowed grimly to their chief, packs strapped tight across their bellies.

"My people. Born and bred myself!" The old man slapped his pouch. "Got my first wife in my pocket. My father's ghost goes in the staff. I explained it all to 'em. Flint-Wash goes with us. We'll not leave even our dead to the likes of savages."

Seance singers[31] gathered beside Speaker Kotekh. He jerked a gourd from one man's hands and thrust it at Harïsh. She blinked down at the liquid, her antennae flaring high with shock.

"Milk-mead. For you. Marry the dozy idiot tonight and be done. You're going to do it anyway. We could do with some cheer beside the campfire."

"M-married? My lord!"

"Dear spirits, girl! The way he keeps gazin' at ye almost makes my whiskers curl. I've a sleeping robe that should fit the two of you. Call it a wedding gift. Anyway— new beginnings are a good time for weddings."

Keketál's ears burned hot. He stepped to Harïsh's rescue. "Lord Kotekh—the other villages have arrived. With your permittings, Keketál shall lead us down the river."

"Eh? Oh, yes, I suppose it's time."

The old man cast one last glance at his home, and then turned toward his men. "Torch 'em! Every house, every barn! Bind the household spirits and keep them safe against your hearts. Flint-Wash travels with us. We leave no ties behind."

Thatch crackled as the villagers gave their houses to the flames. Harïsh stared down into the fires, the death of River-Bend etched in her eyes.

"My love, is hunting very difficult? Will we have food enough to live?"

"The land is rich. Keketál shall teach you how to hunt."

The girl stared down at the smoke. Thick and filthy—like the smoke that had smeared the skies above her mother's grave. "Do you really want to marry me, Keketál? I'm happy as I am. I will love you as long as you will let me. I ask for nothing in return."

"No—I will marry you. Keketál shall wed his love. This iss not the end. Our lives begin new."

The girl let Keketál lead her down the hill toward the villagers. "What color will my new wings be, I wonder? Is there any way to tell?"

Keketál held the girl against his heart and slowly walked toward the south. "Gold; I think that you will always be Keketál's girl of gold."

---

[31]**Ancestor Worship:** The souls of dead plainsfolk are very much a part of the community. A priesthood of seance singers keeps the living in a measure of contact with the dead.

ଔ ଧ ଯ

The representatives of the Ochitzli tribe gathered to pay homage to the demon queen, each dressed in formal finery. Speakers and guildsmen, shepherds and priests, all waited in silence as the sun broke out above the forest eaves.

In the small hours of the dawn, the rainbow people came.

At first it seemed just a sound, a distant rustle in the leaves. Slowly, it grew until ïsha thrummed with power. One by one, wheeling, dancing shapes appeared to populate the air. Every tree and branch dripped beneath a rain of colors.

The mass flooded forward and spilled onto the plains. It washed across the meadows and splashed against the trees. Spirits looped and chittered in the sun. Over it all, behind the color and the relentless bubbling motion, there burned a brilliant joy.

The people of the mountains threw out their arms and sang.

Plainsmen stared up in amazement as naked women in brilliant masks whirled through the air. There was laughter and dancing, music and delight. The wave crashed across the villagers and swept them into its heart. Carpenters and shepherds were kissed by dancing girls. Old nobles found themselves knee-deep in laughing children. Drums hammered out the pulse of the world, and villagers laughed as gongs rang in a final, glorious crescendo.

Suddenly, the music stopped. All eyes turned toward the slender figure standing at the dance's heart. Power flooded out of her to set the skies ablaze with joy.

"To Mother Rain we make this promise! One land, one folk, one will! Mountain and forest, grass and plains shall finally be united. The Kashran race will be whole at last!"

Lightning flashed. Zhukora stood wreathed in a blazing sphere of light. The people sank down to their knees and gazed at her in awe.

Slim curves shimmered as Zhukora's naked figure slowly emerged onto the grass. She stood unveiled before the people in absolute perfection, as pure and beautiful as morning dew.

"Look upon me and rejoice. I am yours! I give myself to you and cast aside all mortal trappings. I am the spirit of the people, and a spirit hides from no one's eyes! I am the mountains and the plains, the rivers and the valleys. Join with me and share the Dream!"

She walked among them, sheathed in a power that reached out to clench the heart. Where Zhukora walked, mortals bowed. Where her gaze fell, villagers lost themselves in love. She was unreachable and perfect, the virgin queen of power.

She had passed beyond the chains that held mere flesh. She had become the spirit of the Dream.

Daimïru looked up at Zhukora, tears spilling freely down her face. Zhukora bent and kissed her on the mouth, sending the blonde girl reeling in a swoon. The plainsmen rose and began to sing her name; Zhukora turned and rewarded them with the love in her eyes.

The Dream had taken her. Zhukora felt the worship of her people all around her and walked on into the arms of destiny.

ॐ ॐ ॐ

Deep within the world of green, something small and beautiful squealed in delight. The tiny flower Ka burst into the air, wheeling past a glittering waterfall. It flung itself into the arms of love and sang in delirious glee.

Shadarii held the creature in her aura as the forest erupted into joy. The love had finally returned! The forest soul awakened to it. The tiny orchid spun and danced as a rain of spirits rushed dizzily down between the leaves.

With Ka looping wildly past her wings, Shadarii swirled around beneath a waterfall. Ïsha spilled out from her into the woods. Dry brown ferns suddenly glowed with growth. Mosses spread and flourished all across the broken rocks. Shadarii embraced the world she loved and lost herself in a joyous dance.

Behind her, faces peered at the vast grandeur of the forest roof. The smell of forest soil had cleaved into the pilgrims. Fern and orchid, leaf and bark—the pilgrims lost themselves within a dream, slowly rediscovering the gentle gifts of home.

The sea people edged cautiously down into the trees, awed by the discovery of a strange new world. They blinked as Kïtashii hurtled aside her tiny skirt and launched herself into the pool by the waterfall.

Little Kïtashii broke the surface with a roar. It felt like half a ton of sand and dust had been rinsed off her fur. The girl snatched a bunch of soap leaf and furiously scrubbed her back. Her lips curled in pleasure as she scratched, her wings drumming at the water.

Tingtraka giggled as a little water Ka danced by her tail. "Paradise! Skreggin' paradise! I never knew how much I missed the sound of leaves. It feels like I'm back inside my mother's womb!"

Shadarii twined auras with an orchid Ka.

Kïtashii flicked her long antennae in glee. "It's so good to see her home again! This is where she's needed. She was right to come. We'll make the forest green again! We'll teach the people peace. There'll be picture-words and stories! New ways of doing old, old things. The sea peoples and the forest will share in hope and love!" Fanatical belief shone in her eyes. She saw a world of peace and happiness; a place where every thought would be treasured like a priceless jewel.

Tingtraka envied her that sense of utter certainty. She posed in the pool as she cocked her head in thought. "Kïtashii, where do you suppose all the people are?"

"Eh? What on earth are you babbling about?"

"There's been no spoor of hunters. No ïsha trails, no tracks. Not even a Ka hovering around a kill site. You didn't notice?"

"Faith, no! I'm a dancer. Where am I going to learn how to hunt?"

"Well, take it from me, there's nary a hair of a Kashra's tail." Tingtraka planted fists on her bony hips and stared around at empty air. "The ducks will be coming soon. Where are all the nets and snares? I don't like it. I don't like it at all."

Without her coat of dust, Kïtashii seemed three shades lighter. The little girl hopped on a rock and dried herself inside a swirling ïsha cloud. "Eh, we'll find people, don't worry. They can't have gone away! We're just outside of usual territory, that's all."

Tingtraka gazed at her friend through hooded eyes. "You think Shadarii got lost?"

"No—well, perhaps we have the seasons wrong. It's been a long, long time, you know. No one counted the days." Kïtashii knocked out a broken-toothed old comb and passed it to her friend. Tingtraka obligingly began to drag the snarls from Kïtashii's silver hair

"I'm worried, Kïtashii. Shadarii isn't.... She doesn't care about herself." The girl sadly looked at Mrrimïmei. "I fear for her. What chance has such gentleness against the powers of hate?"

Kïtashii lay in silence across Tingtraka's lap, watching as Shadarii groomed an old fisherman's back. Kïtashii's eerie silver eyes grew hard. "Do you really think Shadarii might be in danger?"

"I think we'd better find some forest people. I want to know what's happened while we've been gone."

"You go, then. Search the forest. I'll stay to protect her."

Shadarii's knives still safely lay inside Kïtashii's pack. Tonight they must be polished bright; the little girl sank down to watch and wait.

Twenty-Three

The sun beat down onto the mud, bull rushes sagged with heat, and between the roots, tadpoles waggled little tails and dreamed froggy dreams. There were butter-flies above and little fish below. Despite the rancid smell, the wetlands lay in perfect peace.

Kangaroos lounged bonelessly in a patch of dappled shade. The young males scratched their bellies while the oldsters snored. It was time for their siesta, and the world seemed a fine and sleepy place.

A plump female cropped her way toward the water's edge, strong teeth snipping at tender shoots of wild wheat. The creature munched its meal and gazed out across the water as something tall and silly wagged its wings nearby.

"Yah boo! Go away! Run!"

The kangaroo sat back and scratched itself in puzzlement. It bent back to its meal.

"Hey, you! Yaaaah! Yaaaah! Nick off!" Hupshu tripped and fell into the mud.

The kangaroo immediately bounded off into the brush. A hideous screaming noise instantly arose. The entire herd of kangaroos exploded into flight.

Hupshu shook out his mud-encrusted kilt, and then fluttered hesitantly over the water. The kangaroo lay dead at Keketál's feet, and his spear made a liquid sucking sound as it dragged from the creature's chest. The kangaroo still thrashed in its death throes. Keketál coldly clubbed its skull with his new stone mace, and the sound sent shivers racing through Hupshu's soul.

The prey was dead. Please Rain let it be dead! Hupshu wiped his mouth and tried to make a manly little laugh. "Uh, so you hit it, then! One shot, eh?"

Keketál carefully wiped the spear and stuck it point down in the sand beside the other weapons. "Come over here. Hupshu must make learnings how to clean the kill."

"Clean? Oh! Uh, all right. Can't have dirty meat...."

Keketál took his metal dao, split the corpse's skull, and poured energy into the frightened Ka that slowly rose into the light. "Hupshu! Quickly, bow and ask for-giveness. Hupshu must thank the prey for its meat."

"Oh—really?"

"The kangaroo ancestor will be angry if we abuse her children. She will makings bad luck on our hunts. If we never take too much, if we always asking pardon for taking a life, she will allow us what we need." Keketál sighed and reached out for his knife. "Surely you must be knowing these things?"

Hupshu shied away from the bleeding kangaroo, his antennae quivering as he watched the creature's Ka. "Lord Keketál, I'm a brewer! I make beer and wines. I've never... I mean, some men do! My father just always said... he said we should respect life."

"You can respect it. Keketál just wants to eat it too." Keketál glanced sideways at Hupshu. "Hupshu ate mutton at Harïsh's jug-wobble dance. How you get meat if you not kill?"

"W-well the village butcher... you know. You don't actually..."

Keketál gave a grunt to show the color of his thoughts.

Hupshu sighed and knelt down beside the prey; the fur felt warm and soft beneath his hand. "Keketál. D-do they always do that?"

"What, die?"

"No—you know, scream. I never thought an animal could, well, feel such pain."

"Why should Mister 'Roo feel pain any less than Hupshu or Keketál? Poor thing. When Keketál must kill, he kills clean. No suffering. Quick!" The man jammed his knife into the ground. "Like war. It must be quick. We must not prolong the agony."

"Will the tribes fight?"

"Keketál does not know. He trains his own men to fight. It iss enough."

Hupshu tried to jerk his mind away from the memory of a maiden's face—a maiden's laugh; the bride that had died beneath a demon's knife. He stared into the swamps and ran the grass beneath his hands. "So how do you actually make an army? I mean, we can get the men and find some weapons. Is that all there is?"

"Training. Lots and lots. We learn to fly." The hunter heaved an unhappy sigh. "Keketál still needs a weapon for his men. Flint spears iss no good; not sharp enough to poke through demon armor. We need something to back up the slings." Keketál prodded irritably at the dirt. "We find a way. We have a thousand men now. Someone will think of something."

The noble's friend helped him to his feet. "You know a lot about hunting, don't you? What else do you remember, my lord? Is there anything of the past inside your mind?"

Keketál turned away and wiped his hands on his kilt. "Keketál remembers nothing! There iss only here and now. There are families to be fed."

Families. Hupshu's bride was dead. He still had trouble believing she was lost. The man gazed out across the swamps and let Father Wind blow through his fur.

Keketál heaved the kill across his shoulders and began the dreary trudge toward the camp.

Hupshu stirred himself and duly followed. "Oh, well, at least this isn't as difficult as I thought. Living off the land, I mean."

Keketál gave a sigh. "These lands are easy. Plenty of game."

"Ah, well, at least there's meat tonight. The others might have done as well."

"Keketál hopes so! Hunter never eats his own catch. Iss bad magic." He handed his companion the spears and woomera. "See if you can hit a tree thiss time. Rocks bend the point."

The handsome villager gave a sigh and passed the weapons back. "Ah, give me the sling back! I'll go get you a duck."

"Duck iss good. Keketál bagsies wings!"

"Whatever you like, my friend. Whatever you like."

Months had passed, and yet the old lands seemed unchanged. Harïsh led the Harapii tribal ambassador past peaceful flocks and fields. Sheep bleated in the meadows, and grapes ripened in the sun. It seemed there was not a worry in the world.

The Kashra alighted outside of a new settlement and watched women working in the fields. Harïsh wagged her wings as she peered carefully between the bushes. "Shall we go closer, Lord Looshii? We can try speaking to them if you like."

Round, gray-furred, and with whiskers that hid his face behind a screen of silver hair, Lord Looshii wrinkled his snout in thought. "I think we should. I'd like to hear their feelings on dwelling in a conquered land. The council requires all the information I can bring."

"Follow my lead, then! It's my third time in enemy lands. Do as I do. If you'll pardon me, my lord, you must act like any other shepherd. There are no nobles here anymore."

The girl sped across the grass like a golden spear. Lord Looshii drew a breath and did his level best to follow. Harïsh zigzagged down a gentle rise and landed amid a team of villagers. "Ho, there! Hot work? Whatcha doing?"

An old woman shot the girl a withering glance and bent back to her work. The villagers were constructing a sturdy ditch.

Harïsh wandered over to poke at dirt clods with her foot. "A funny kind of thing to be doing. What's it for?"

"We're planting yam daisies. Go away!"

"Yams? But yams grow by the river! How are you going to water them?"

"We're digging a ditch through the field. A pump will fill it with water from the river. One of the forest people thought of it. She's building the pump. We're digging the ditch. Each contributes. Praise be to the Dream."

Harïsh shrugged away the subject and clasped her hands behind her back. "Yep! Praise the Dream! I have a message for the village leader. Where might he be found?"

"Kaláka the Hunter is village leader. You'll find him in the new meeting hut."

"He's a forest man?"

" 'Course he is! And a better leader than the old speaker ever was! There's a meeting of the village committee right now. They're sending the old bastard off for trial. He refuses to join the community. If we're lucky the leader might make an example of him!"

Harïsh scratched her chin. "So, he's going to trial for not digging in the fields?"

"Aye! And high time too. There's forty extra mouths to feed in this village. We've quotas to maintain!"

"You—uh—you don't mind the extra work? I mean— is it more difficult than the old days?"

" 'Taint so bad. Not now I can see priests and nobles gettin' their lily white hands dirty!" The old woman stood and warily brushed her hands against her skirt, glaring at Lord Looshii's bright red wings. "You ask a lot of questions." More farmers had begun to gather around the strangers. "I think we'd better take you to the village leader. I think you'd better come right now."

Harïsh turned her golden eyes upon the villagers and gave a thankful smile. "Oh, really? You mean you'll take us? Oh, thanks, that's most hospitable!"

Harïsh led the way toward the village square. The pair of spies were ushered to a brand new wooden hut and thrust in through the door. Two villagers remained on watch while the others went back to the fields.

The room was hung with mats and rugs of alien designs. Harïsh found a little pot fashioned out of badly fired clay and examined it disdainfully.

"The village looks well enough. Fairly typical. They all talk the same now: 'contribution to a greater whole' and 'following the Dream'. It's all just a façade. There's no freedom for the plainsfolk here. The Ochitzli are all split up and intermingled with the newcomers. The Demon Queen has given them all new identities."

Lord Looshii was utterly aghast. "When I scoffed at your reports, I simply had no idea! That—that old woman. She actually seemed proud to be slave to some savage!"

"She loves it! She has power now! Her hate's been turned against the nobles and not the savages. Oh, the Demon Queen is clever! In two months, she's managed to absorb an entire people. They all truly seem to believe in this-this Dream." Harïsh removed her headband and began tying it in knots.

Looshii gave a gasp of irritation. "My dear girl, people can't just have accepted all this lying down! There must be some unrest. Every time the savages whittle at a tradition, it must saw at the heartstrings of the folk!"

"Whittling? Oh, no, my lord! All the changes happened almost overnight. You'd be surprised how soon people can adapt. Everyone's been busy building and working. It creates the illusion of achievement."

The door opened with a bang, and a forbidding figure glared toward the prisoners. All male savages seemed to be tall. Harïsh sketched a salute and bawled out in a chaotic foreign tongue.

"Greetings, forest comrade! Being am Surookii of Courier Teamings Seven." The girl pulled her headband from her belt and merrily untied a knot.[32] "I bearing messagings from southern district for honored leader person."

The savage bent to chill her with his shadow. "Why does it take two of you to pass a message?"

"Comrade, sorry am I if not understandings. Wordy talks is beings difficult."

"Him! Who is this man here?"

Harïsh craned around to suddenly see Lord Looshii, and her gorgeous eyes turned bright with understanding. "Aaaah, Pretty Wings? Surookii find him! Poor Pretty Wings being lost. Now Surookii is here for the guidings!" The young girl proudly placed one hand upon her breast. "Surookii will pass forest comrade's speakings to Pretty Wing. He is not having goodly forest wordings like Surookii! Surookii is clever, yes?"

The savage refused to comment. It was no wonder the villagers had said she asked too many questions. "Just give me the message, you obnoxious little whelp! Hurry up, or I'll have you treading grapes until your fur turns blue!"

Harïsh closed her eyes and made a great show of fingering the message rope. "Message him say: "Silverblood Creek is dry as dead old bones. Kaláka must make room for twelve more villagers transferred from the east.""

---

[32]**Plainsman Quirt:** A knotted cord used in much the same manner as an alpine message stick – a mnemonic aid in remembering messages by rote.

"What?" Kaláka slammed his fist against the wall. "What idiot ordered this? Don't they know these villagers can't hunt? How am I supposed to feed all these useless little darlings?"

"Tch-tch! Leader person should keep more calm. You should take it easy and get some sleep."

"I don't want to sleep! Now listen here, you go right back to Silverblood and tell those idiots to go get stuffed!"

"But..."

"No buts! I can't take them, I won't take them! If I see one freeloader come fluttering down that path, I'll send him back to Silverblood in a wicker basket!"

Harïsh stuck out her tongue in concentration as she tied another knot at the far end of her headband.

The village leader started strangling with rage. "What in Poison's name do you think you're doing now?"

"Iss doing job! Message from Kaláka comes last. First Surookii must go to Yabbie-Dale, then Ghost-Hollow, then Rainbow-Cave..."

Kaláka's eyes were slowly changing color. Veins bulged at his temples "You brainless little hatchling! Get back to Silverblood! You deliver my message right now!"

"Well, all right. Surookii was only trying to..."

"Now!"

The savage tore open his door and booted the two travelers out. Harïsh proudly dusted off her skirt and buzzed into the air. The girl led the way into a stand of old, dry wattle trees and softly drifted to the ground.

Her façade of merriment was suddenly gone. "So now you've seen it, my lord. We did not lie. The conquest of the savages is total. They not only take the body, but also eat the soul."

Lord Looshii planted his back against a tree, his eyes still staring back toward the village. "They all seem so passionate. Everyone seems so—so filled with fire!"

Harïsh turned cold. "Never forget River-Bend, my lord. Never forget those corpses I showed you. One of those rotting skeletons was my own mother."

"But if they are really happy..."

"Oh, yes, the people here are happy. Happy as sheep. The moment they fail to meet the Demon Queen's expectations, they will pay."

Looshii stared back toward the village. "I believe you. Tell your husband Keketál that he will have his army. The Harapii tribe stands with you. Any man who wishes it will be allowed to train for war."

"I'll get you home, my lord. We'll cut through the forest to be safe. The savages have abandoned it." Harïsh sprang into the light. The two fugitives moved south toward lands where freedom still dwelt.

ဢ ဢ ဢ

Through long days and sleepless nights, Shadarii labored in the forest. Savage abuse had left its mark on the land, and animal species had dwindled from predation and disease. Whole vast regions had been laid waste by the teeming Kashra tribes. Untold swoops of forest had been burned to the ground. Before abandoning their home, the alpine tribes had stripped it to the bone.

Shadarii selflessly gave herself to the forest. As days went by, she squandered her reserves of strength. Where she trod, the ground turned rich with life. Dead wood slumped and crumbled, and new growth shot through the forest floor. The butchered ferns, the tortured earth, the scarred trees all were made whole and good once more.

Shadarii staggered. Every day the forest cried to her, and every day she gave just a little more. Over two months, she had drained herself almost dry in unending, sleepless labors. The forest screamed for healing, and it seemed as if the task would never be done....

This day had been the worst. The evening light had found Shadarii wandering along a stream and shivering with fatigue. Disease spirits hovered in the ïsha around her. Shadarii coughed and swatted them away, half stumbling into the stream.

The girl was sick and dulled, her fur sodden with sweat. She clung to a tree and felt her stomach spin.

Shadarii! What is it? Get up! Starshine flicked a power bolt at a lurking spirit of disease, and her target chittered in alarm. *Well, I could have told thee it would come to this! Two months wasted on this "great work" of thine. I tire of saying it: Seek thy sister! Slay her! Take away her powers. Shadarii, art thou listening to me?*

Shadarii slumped against the bark and coughed. She couldn't stay here; Kïtashii would find her, and this time her disciple wouldn't let the matter slide. Shadarii would be stuffed into bed and held prisoner for weeks. Kïtashii simply didn't understand how much work there was to do.

"Beloved one?"

Shadarii wrenched herself upright as Zareemii gazed up into her eyes. The child offered a tiny creature into Shadarii's hands.

"The froggy's sick. He just sits there and looks miserable."

Shadarii sighed; perhaps there was just a tiny little bit of power left. A frog couldn't drain too much. It looked up at her with great yellow eyes and quivered in pain. Shadarii bent her head and poured herself into its heart. The creature swayed inside her hand as she caressed it with her love.

Shadarii's vision dimmed. She absently passed the frog back to the little boy. She was still smiling as she doubled up and fell.

"Revered One! Silent Lady, you're sick!"

Shadarii coughed in agony, fluid cracked in her lungs as disease spirits hissed and closed in for the kill. Zareemii took one look and fled into the sky.

"Tingtraka! Tingtraka, come quickly! Kïtashii, please!" The little boy fled into the dark.

Shadarii pressed her face against the nice warm soil and wondered if the pain would ever stop.

Shadarii gave a cough and shivered down beneath a pile of sleeping robes.

Kïtashïi gripped her hand and wiped her teacher's mouth. Shadarii felt burning hot to the touch. The spirit Starshine reeled in the ïsha like a drunken moth, delirious from Shadarii's pain. The Teacher's breath bubbled thickly in her lungs.

For a long while, her bed had been surrounded by a circle of pupils, their heads bowed in prayer as they drew the ïsha from the world. They had bathed Shadarii's body with a healing glow, trying to fight the fever with their simple love. Shadarii had stabilized, but no more.

She was not healing as she should. This was no ordinary disease. Someone or something wanted the Silent Lady dead.

Whoever it was would not succeed, not while there was a spark of life inside Kïtashïi. The acolyte gripped her teacher's hand and set her fangs in preparation for a fight.

The pilgrims had taken refuge in an empty Katakanii village. The lodge rocked as Tingtraka staggered through the door to spill a handful of herbs upon the rug.

"Tingtraka!"

The huntress clawed her breast and spat to ease her burning lungs. "H-herbs from the... the mountaintops. Roots from the bottom of a lake." The girl scraped her filthy hand across her eyes. "Not much... Don't even know if they're... right."

Tingtraka sobbed for breath and half collapsed against the lodgehouse wall. Kïtashïi snatched up the herbs and furiously began to scrub them clean.

"You're the first to come back! And you got it all, too! Are the others close behind?"

Tingtraka looked sick. She must have flown like a lightning bolt! The skinny huntress coughed and sucked her tea. "Rotïka's digging ants nests. The others are still out there. All except Mrrimïmei. She wouldn't come."

Mrrimïmei! Kïtashïi swore with words no twelve year old should know. She cursed ceaselessly as she jammed on a disreputable pair of leather moccasins. She took up a bag and a pair of digging sticks.

"Kïtashïi?" Tingtraka began.

The little girl snatched up her pack and rushed to Shadarii's side. She clutched her teacher in an adoring kiss, winding desperate fingers through Shadarii's hair.

"Look after her. I'll be back!"

"Kïtashïi! Stop! What do you think you're doing?"

"Leaving! We need a healer! I'll be back."

Kïtashïi dived away before anyone could stop her.

Tingtraka ripped off her heavy robe and staggered to the door. "Kïtashïi! Kïtashïi come back! I'll not let you go alone!"

It was too late; Kïtashïi had already gone.

Twenty-Four

Harïsh and Lord Looshii stared around in awe.

The forest loomed about them, a vast and eerie sanctuary that stretched to the very edges of the world. The air smelled fresh and verdant with leaf mold and humus. Here and there, a green leaf lazily spiraled down hundreds of spans toward the forest floor. Water dripped, and flowers blossomed. Everything was green, shot through with shafts of golden sun.

If you listened, you could almost hear the plants grow....

Harïsh felt fur crawling all along her spine. A sense of worship pressed upon her soul. This was a place of majesty, a place to treat with absolute reverence. Harïsh bruised the silence with a sigh.

"Dear Rain, I never thought it could be so beautiful...."

Lord Looshii had lost himself in the caress of the forest breeze. Every breath brought a new world of sensation, like a fine wine that rolled and sparkled on the tongue. "Paradise! Pure paradise."

The travelers drifted down across a creek and nestled thankfully in the ferns.

Lord Looshii let anxious eyes roam the shadows beneath the trees. "Uh—perhaps we'd best get a wriggle-on. Can't dawdle all day, eh? Your husband must be worried sick!"

Harïsh barely seemed to hear. She was sniffing at the forest mulch, her antennae quivering as she searched the mold. "Oh,"—sniff—"Keketál always frets. I love the silly boy to bits! He really ought to take life more calmly. He'll give himself an ulcer the way he carries on." The girl scuttled across the ground and found a tiny pair of shining leaves. Earth flew as she exposed a twisted clump of root. "Look, my lord! Fire root! It's fire root!" The girl held the disgusting tuber up in triumph. "Sweet Rain, look! It's everywhere! The stuff's growing here like a weed."

Lord Looshii examined the root and assumed a pained expression. "Is this a good thing? I mean it doesn't look very tasty."

"What? No, no, my lord, it's an herb. An incredibly rare medicine!" Harïsh ripped at the leaf mulch and dragged another root clump from the ground. "You could trade five sheep and still not earn half a spoonful!"

"Aaaah, I see. It's valuable!"

"What? Oh, yes. But it cleans wounds. You make a tea out of it to cure fevers." The girl blushed. "It also.... Uh, well, if you rub it on a man's... Anyway, it has other uses, too." She began to empty her chest pack and stuff it full of roots. "No one's ever touched the crop! Ha! The savages don't even know how to use their medicines!"

"Do you think we should?" The nobleman looked nervously about the trees. "I mean, it isn't ours. Someone might object."

"Object? It's just growing here in the ground! There's no fence, no marks. It's just the bounty of the... my lord?"

Lord Looshii stared up across Harïsh's shoulder, carefully raising his open palms. Harïsh slowly turned to see a figure silhouetted in the light.

A girl stood above them, a nearly naked child with quicksilver eyes and the slim curves of an eel. Long white hair streamed in an unseen breeze as the little savage watched the interlopers. She sang something in their musical, purring tongue, and Harïsh answered her, watching carefully for her chance to strike.

Lord Looshii nervously flicked his eyes from girl to girl. "What is it? What did she ask? I can't follow a word these creatures say!"

"Sh-she says I am stealing. She wants to know why anyone would take a whole crop of fire-root."

"And what did you say?"

"I said I need it all. There was no way of knowing the root was hers."

The little savage followed their conversation with sharp intelligence. She eyed Harïsh's sack and spoke out once again. Harïsh never once shifted her gaze.

"She wonders why I need a whole sack of root. Am I a thief who trades in medicine? I told her no. I am a healer. I need the roots for my work. I must go home now. There are many, many sick people who are waiting for me to treat them."

"Does she believe you?"

"She's a savage. Even so, they must respect healers." Harïsh carefully held up her hand to show the blue tattoos across her palm. The savage's ears lifted as she sang another string of questions.

Harïsh's eyes narrowed. "She says I may have the roots, but she would like a favor in return. There is a patient for me, someone I must see. She says my tattoo means I can't refuse."

Lord Looshii had his back firmly planted against a tree. "Are you going to do as she says?"

"You must be joking!"

"But she's right! You have to!" The lord switched his tail in shock. "If you refuse her, all your power would fade!"

"She's a savage! I never made any oath to heal any filthy primitives!"

"My lady, you can't refuse!"

Harïsh nodded wearily, reached out for her bag, and swiftly threw it at the child's face. Harïsh drew her dagger and bared her fangs in hate. "Surrender, you little bitch! Surrender, or I'll rip your bloody tripes out!"

The tiny savage gave a laugh, and Harïsh blinked as the knife whisked out of her hand. An unseen force hoisted her through the sky and pinned her against a tree. The savage held Harïsh helpless, grinning at her from beneath her cloak of silver hair.

His Lordship decided he should go for help. The sorceress never even glanced in his direction as he started away. Looshii gave a squawk, and seconds later, he dangled upside down beside Harïsh. "I think we might do just as she requests...."

The tiny savage grinned, and Harïsh suddenly dropped back to the ground. She stared sullenly as the little girl placed a flower in her hands. "Sh-she says we are creatures of violence. She sorrows for us and offers us forgiveness." Harïsh's pride was stung, and the girl almost wept in anger. "She said not to worry, she is not allowed to hurt us. Her teacher would never allow it."

The savage graciously indicated that the plainsmen should follow her. Harïsh sourly reached for her belongings.

"I don't think we could get away. She flicked you from the sky like a gnat! She never even turned her head!"

"Then we're trapped! She'll take us to the Demon Queen!"

"I could kill her with the sling. We can wait till her back is turned, and I could shoot."

Harïsh looked into the little girl's eyes, startled by an intelligence that seemed to pierce through her very soul. The lass simply smiled and waited for Harïsh to reach her decision.

The healer rubbed at the tattoo across her palm. "She's not dressed like the others. She hasn't met a plainsman before. I think this might be a different tribe. See the shells she's made into a skirt? She might be from far away." Harïsh strapped her pack across her chest and tugged her headband tight. "Come on, let's follow. We'll see this patient of hers. Maybe we'll learn something new."

"Will she hurt us?"

"No. No, I don't think so." Harïsh stared at the silver girl, feeling something strange prickling across her spine. "There's something odd about her. Maybe she's some sort of priest. I don't think she'd try to hurt us."

Entering the tree house felt like stepping into a holy shrine. A silent group of foreigners formed a ring around a single bed, and not a creature stirred at the entry of the strangers.

Harïsh slowly approached the sickbed at the center of the floor. She looked down into the face of love, and felt her spirit soar.

Harïsh fell to her knees. It was like being drunk! It was like the dizzy joy of making love to Keketál—the delicious peace of sleeping in his arms.

It was a girl; nothing but a girl. A round, plain creature with an almost palpable power.

Harïsh quickly bent to work. The woman's fever burned like a furnace, and Harïsh's spirits sank as she heard the fluid deep inside the woman's lungs.

It was hopeless. Harïsh numbly let her hands fall to her sides, unable to meet the little savage eye to eye. "I can do nothing. There is fluid in her chest. Bubble bubble when breathings, understand? Bubbles! This one is to die now. She... she will die."

The patient had all but gone. She was drowning inside herself. For some reason ïsha healing was unable to cure the disease. Harïsh had never seen anything like it before.

The little savage came back again. She plucked at Harïsh's hands and tried to lay them on the patient's chest. "You! You heal, yes? You wake Beloved One. Make her think clear for just one second, two? Please! Please try! She wake, she burn it all away. Don't let Teacher die!"

Harïsh felt sick; she didn't know the words to make the little creature understand. "Look, I'm a surgeon. I cut, yes? Set bones, bring babies." Feeling the little girl's despair, Harïsh wiped a tear back from her eye. "I'm sorry. I-I can't help you. We can only... only make the passing easier."

Tingtraka heard. She pulled herself back from her trance and slowly cleared her eyes. She knew what must be done, and somehow the decision could be faced with utter calm.

"Kïtashii, Shadarii's dying. This girl can't heal her. The disease is too far gone." Tingtraka deliberately broke the circle of healers. "Lift her up. We're taking her outside. Leave the robes. Just get her out into the open air."

"Stop! Tingtraka, what are you doing?"

"Taking her outside onto the jiteng field where the Rain can fall on her. It's the only way."

They took Shadarii on a blanket, carefully braking the long fall to the ground. The plainsfolk followed in their tracks, crying as openly as anybody else. Tingtraka led the party over to the jiteng field and laid Shadarii across the grass.

"Quickly! Sister Mouse, Brother Fish, enchant a sacred circle. Kïtashii, remove your clothes. We need you to dance as you have never danced before! You have to call the Rain, Kïtashii. You have to call the Rain!"

People ran to do as they were bid. Sister Mouse and Brother Fish quickly danced out the perimeter of a circle while Kïtashii tore away her beads. She ripped Shadarii's dao from their sheaths and laid them at her feet.

"Tingtraka, you don't know the way back!"

"It doesn't matter. Don't you see? It's everything she's ever tried to teach us. Love means sacrifice."

Kïtashii lifted the dao and stared into Tingtraka's eyes. "I love you, Tingtraka."

"I love you, Kïtashii."

The two women clasped each other tight, then Tingtraka broke away and sat at Shadarii's side. The pilgrim closed her eyes, bowing down to lose herself in gentle meditation.

Silence fell. The sea people looked expectantly over to Kïtashii as the dancer stood with knives folded across her chest. Beside her, Tingtraka gave a sigh and let her chin fall to her chest.

Harïsh hesitantly reached out to find Tingtraka's pulse. She looked in horror at Lord Looshii. "She-she's dead!"

Kïtashii drew a breath and ripped the knives across her chest. The tiny savage danced and sobbed, flinging out her arms toward the clouds. The girl cut again, slicing herself so that pain split through the ïsha. The little girl threw back her head in exultation, tears spilling to mingle with blood.

Harïsh sank to the ground and shook with grief. "Dear Rain, she'll kill herself! She's only a little girl. She's losing too much blood!"

"Then stop her!"

"I can't! I don't understand! Why are they doing this? Why?"

Kïtashii staggered from blood loss, and yet the dance went on. From overhead came a sudden growl of thunder. Sea people labored to work Tingtraka's heart and lungs. Still the Teacher slept and quivered in her dreams.

Harïsh hung her head and wept. It was a blasphemy! The little Teacher had held such love. Why do this to her? Why couldn't they let the woman die in peace?

High above them Mother Rain gave a shout of rage. The sky shivered to the crack of lightning. Mother Rain still had the weapons given her by Fire. She hurtled them into battle with her ancient enemy.

Shadarii found herself alone in the darkness. She flailed helplessly and wondered where the world had gone.

"So, my child, we meet at last. How sad that all your adventures should end so soon." A female voice—so sweet, so venomous. The darkness chuckled as it gathered for the kill.

"Little fool. Didst thou imagine I would do nothing? I am she that is inside everything, the heart and soul of decay!"

Shadarii slowly rose to face her enemy. *I cast you out! Get back! You have no power here! I have freed myself from you!*

"Fool! I am the spirit of corruption. Poison lies in everything. Your own weaknesses have sent you straight into my grasp." The darkness rose to claim Shadarii's soul. She gave a sob and knew that she had failed.

Something bright burst in through the prison walls, swatting in a frenzy at Poison's claws and somehow flitting from their grasp. A Ka looped and wheeled around Shadarii's soul, bringing in the smell of leaves and rain. Tingtraka shone to give Shadarii a tiny point of light, and through that crack, power fell into Shadarii's hands.

Lightning struck. Shadarii bucked to a wild inrush of power, a memory of cleanliness—a love that thundered through her. The darkness shattered. Shadarii suddenly flew free. A scream of hatred faded far behind, and Shadarii took Tingtraka soaring back toward the world, spilling into her body like a shower of healing rain.

Shadarii rose from the ground and spread her arms to the sky. The whole forest seemed ablaze with power as ïsha poured in through her soul. The bond of Rain and Wind still blessed their children. Shadarii flung out her hands in worship and stared into the eyes of love. The little dancer bowed and wept, power sparking across her skin.

On the ground beside her, Tingtraka opened her eyes. Kïtashii had collapsed into a puddle of her own blood. Shadarii stooped and swept her disciple into her arms. Wounds disappeared, leaving Kïtashii perfect and unblemished. The little dancer stirred and nestled softly in Shadarii's grasp.

Harïsh fell to her knees, too terrified to meet the Shining Lady's eyes. She dared not give in to the woman's spell of peace. She needed hate, she needed fury! There were demons to be killed!

Tingtraka walked slowly forward, the wind moving through her hair. She glanced into the Silent Lady's eyes, and then turned toward Harïsh.

"Little healer, the Beloved One thanks you for all that you have done. She says there is much hate and bitterness inside your heart. You must not let your desire for vengeance destroy the good within you."

Shadarii came forward to caress Harïsh's face.

Tingtraka gave a smile. "There is still much for you to live for. The Teacher says the child within your womb will grow strong! It will be a boy. A boy with gray fur and golden eyes."

Harïsh let one hand drift down in wonder. She looked up and met the Teacher's eyes of shining green.

A baby!

The Silent Lady reached down to take her by the hands.

"Love to you, golden healer. Return to your family with the blessings of the Rain. We shall all meet again when the Silent Lady offers battle to the dark."

The Teacher turned and softly wandered off into the leaves. In her footsteps, the forest bloomed with light.

You will fight! Finally you will fight! The ordeal was worth everything if the final battle can be won! Starshine shivered in delight, hurtling images of mighty battles through Shadarii's mind. *Together we shall conquer! A perfect world is possible. A perfect peace and perfect order. They need only thy hand above these little people. The forces of darkness will be destroyed at last, after three thousand years of battle.*

Shadarii cradled Kïtashii and combed back her silver hair. The child slept a healing sleep inside her teacher's arms. Shadarii gazed down at Kïtashii's face and felt her power grow. *The spirit Serpent is allied to my sister. You have known it all along. This has all been for one thing, hasn't it? You live only to destroy your enemy. You hope to use me as your weapon.*

Foolish girl! Use thee? Never! It is a partnership. Starshine flashed with lights of pride. *Evil must be fought. Thou art the tool that Providence has placed in my hands. I have devoted my entire existence to wiping Serpent's evil from the earth. Thou hast been given to me to fulfill my holy mission!*

Shadarii bit back tears and held Kïtashii to her heart. *Lady Poison spoke the truth. Corruption lies in all of us. You were my temptation. I took the easy path you offered and turned my back on the way of light.* The girl gazed off into the forest depths, then closed her eyes in pain. *My poor, poor Zhukora. So brilliant, so mad. I have seen you in my dreams and know our dance must soon come to an end. Did this Serpent corrupt your mind, just as Starshine has tried to poison me?*

I poison nothing! Serpent must be slain! No price is too high if evil is destroyed. Shadarii stood and turned, feeling the world's currents flowing through her soul. *I have seen my error. I have been able to purge myself. I am pure enough to do what must be done.* Shadarii cradled Kïtashii hard against her breasts, her eyes staring off into the shadows of the forest. *Perhaps in the end you will learn a lesson too. Even for you it cannot be too late.*

What are you driveling on about now?

Shadarii closed her eyes and felt Kïtashii's fur beneath her hands. In her mind's eye she saw Kotaru smiling down into her eyes. *My time is almost done. There was but one last thing I had to learn. The students have taught the teacher. They have shown me that sacrifice is the highest form of love.* Shadarii held Kïtashii and rocked the little dancer like a beloved, sleeping babe. *So much loss. So much sadness. It's almost over now. One final lesson to teach the world, and then my rest can come.*

So let it be....

Cʒ ЄϽ ЄϽ

"It is called an oita, Lord. A weapon used in sports by the Zebedii. We have sparred with such weapons for a thousand years. They are developed from the double-bladed oars of our canoes."

The Zebedii nobleman passed the weapon to Keketál, and the tall hunter twirled it in his palms as though he had used an oita all his life. Behind him, two thousand trainee warriors had gathered to watch. Keketál's fighters looked grim and efficient in their new felt armor and wooden helms. Every angry youngster and rebellious noble in the scattered tribes had come to join Lord Keketál's band. Chiefs had sent their sons. Potters and carpenters had left their quiet villages. They had come to learn the forgotten skills of war.

Outlandish Zebedii leaned upon their oitas and looked across the crowds. The Zebedii were fierce creatures with brightly dyed fur and stiffened crests of hair. Their chieftain snapped his fingers and brought his son running to his side.

"Saisan! Two fighters! Padded staves."

"Sir!"

Two men immediately hurtled themselves into the air. Before the plainsmen had time to blink, the air resounded to an almighty crash. Oitas cracked like lightning, and one fighter tumbled to the ground. The survivor whirled down to land before the nobles. He snapped into a bow and waited to be dismissed while his chief turned toward Lord Keketál.

"We can train your men in the use of the oita. It is a fitting weapon for war. The Zebedii tribe wishes to place its warriors under your command."

Keketál's eyes were so very wise and brown. He looked down at the creature from the marsh and carefully weighed his words. "Why? Why follow Keketál?"

"We choose Keketál because he is a stranger." The chief's oita pointed straight at Keketál. "This one is not of the plains. We have not clashed with him in council. There is no bad blood between us. He would fight alone, but welcomes aid. He asks, but does not beg. It is enough. The Zebedii have chosen."

Keketál slowly switched his tail. "The Zebedii lands are not our lands. Why do you need to join us at all?"

"There is a saying: If you must fight with your enemy, do it in your neighbor 's yard."

Keketál took the chief's oita in his hands. A white skull mask had been propped up on a stump nearby. The weapon scythed down to hack the mask in two. The hardwood blade cleaved deep into the stump. Keketál ripped the weapon free and gave a savage grin.

"Bring your men! Keketál accepts your warriors. Show Keketál's people how to fight with oita! We split demon bitch in two and dance upon her bones!"

The Zebedii warriors howled for joy and flung themselves among the ranks of Keketál's astonished men. Suddenly the island rang with the sound of laughter. The men hooted and hurled each other in the swamp, tumbling like brats as they tugged each other's ears.

The Zebedii chieftain cracked the cap from a flask of Hupshu's mead and tossed the bottle to Keketál. "Now we drink! We drink and tell many lies about our women! Tomorrow there is war. Today we shall drink beer!"

Keketál was suddenly tossed into the pond. The Zebedii chieftain stood on the banks and laughed until Hupshu tripped him in the mud. Keketál laughed and hurtled himself into the fun. Life suddenly seemed worth living. They could win— finally they could win! He had a wife, a life, a hope!

Keketál could feel the future in his grasp.

Twenty-Five

The air trembled to the beat of wings as the rainbow hordes began to march. They drove through a wilderness of burned villages and smoking fields. From horizon to horizon, their numbers blackened the skies. Here and there, a single figure dipped and wheeled against the storm. Their masks and costumes blazed with all the colors of a madman's dreams.

Beside a stream, Daimïru cracked into a salute and looked briskly into her leader's eyes. "Zhukora, Scout Flock Seven has returned. They report the entire border district is deserted. We have eliminated no more villages. Our lead units are now striking nothing but empty huts and fields."

Zhukora sat quietly in meditation beside a flowing stream, black hair streaming around her naked body like a sheen of night. She looked into Daimïru's eyes and gave a smile. "So, the barbarians anticipated our invasion? Good, good. The prey does us honor at last. The great hunt shall be a challenge. What are our casualties?"

"Perhaps a hundred dead. We have hurt the enemy as badly. They are attempting shoot-and-flight tactics against us. Small groups of enemy fire at us with slings, and then attempt to escape." Daimïru's spear glistened wet with blood, and the orgasmic afterglow of killing shone in her eyes. "Their magic can't compete with ours. Our warriors' jiteng training serves us well."

"How did our casualties occur?"

"Some sling hits. One team was destroyed in its entirety in hand to hand. Rooshïkii gave us a positive identification. It is the officer who attacked our group at River-Bend. Keketál the Stranger. A dangerous man, motivated and intelligent."

Zhukora closed her eyes and reassumed her position of meditation.

The enemy skirmishers were trying to buy time for their army to form. Zhukora read their intent and gave a smile. She fully intended the enemy army to complete formation. She wanted them gathered into one killing ground where they could fall before her spears. "Tell me more about this Keketál."

"He is an outlander, but we have no information as to his origin. A good fighter. He has a band of two thousand warriors; the only battle-trained force the plains people possess."

"Are they skilled?"

"Very. Trained for close combat. Armored and highly motivated."

"They lack the iron will of our Skull-Wing warriors. We shall easily overmatch them with our elite." Zhukora's plan of battle had been brilliantly conceived. The gargantuan tasks of preparing food, creating maps, and scouting the enemy forces each had to be defined or invented. Zhukora's people pursued their art with a fanaticism that would have terrified their ancestors.

No arguments, no division; there was only a single driving sense of mission. One race, one will, one destiny. The Dream had finally gone to war.

A hundred Kashra ringed the trees of a sacred grove, and the air rang to a chaos of arguments and screams. Speakers danced in outrage while priests hurtled abuse. The defense council of the Coalition had begun another typical day.

"It is the decision of this committee, and it will stand! A battle can be won only by the most careful deliberation. Hasty decisions..."

"Sheep-shit!"

"...hasty decisions will bring disaster!"

A young nobleman tore in rage at his ritual jewelry. "By merely running, we fail to break their power! The Demon Queen's armies must be faced and broken!"

"Which we will do only when we have made the most exquisite preparations!"

"We are being destroyed! We must face the beast and kill it! Fleeing merely saps our will to fight!"

There was a chorus of agreement from the upper branches of the trees. After two days of debate, the defense council had achieved absolutely nothing.

Keketál sat on a log and contemptuously watched the proceedings. Each idea brought before the house was bitterly contested. Each tribe sought to further its own ends. The chaos would kill them all! Someone had to do something! Every minute brought the Demon Queen closer.

"Enough! Arguings go on long enough! Iss time to make decisions!" Keketál leaned on his blood-stained oita, and the other councilors turned to stare. "The army iss gathered! We must decide what to do with it. Iss just one little vote! Just vote and let Keketál get back to work!"

A speaker from the Yukanii tribe rose to his feet. "My lord, our levies are but barely trained! It's still too soon to fight."

"Then give them to me, and I shall train them! Will you at least let Keketál do that?"

A chorus of speakers immediately leapt to their feet. "Never! We refuse to relinquish tribal control over our men!"

"Just to trainings them! To practice their skills!"

"We are civilized men! Do you imply that we are inferior to a flock of uncircumcised savages?" Keketál snarled and made to speak again.

Hupshu raised a hand and held him back. "Gentlemen, the savages are already on the move. We need an immediate plan. Now, what are we to do?"

The room boiled with activity. Men shouted and stormed onto the floor.

"Are you all cowards? Why don't we just attack?"

"I say we do as Lord Keketál suggests!"

"And I say my tribe will follow no nameless outlander!" Speakers turned and stared as one furious old Kashra shook his fist at Keketál. "Look at him! No family, no village, no past! How do we know he's not one of them? He could be a spy planted to ...urk!"

A Zebedii noble clamped his hands about the chieftain's throat, slapped the old man twice across the face, and let him fall. "Lord Keketál reaps many demon heads. This morning he has taken three. Bring us three demon heads and earn the right to speak against him!"

A new man flung a hand toward Keketál. "I say he should lead us! I say we vote Lord Keketál president of the Coalition!"

"And I say never!" A nobleman hurled his words toward the clouds. "This is no dictatorship! The committee..."

"Sit down!"

"...the committee has a sacred trust to our people! No tyranny!"

"No tyranny!"

"Order! Order!"

A master healer clambered high onto a branch and held out his tattooed hands. "I propose a motion. Dictatorship or freedom? Should we create a tyrant in emulation of the savages, or will we operate by democracy? Those in favor of dictatorship?"

Staves rose—far too few. The Zebedii sat watching Keketál, and when he raised his weapon, the Zebedii followed suit.

Less than half the committee voted in favor. Damn! The healer twirled his tail in triumph.

"It is decided! Freedom! The committee can act as a joint command upon the battlefield. Decisions will be made by vote." The healer gave a self-satisfied smile. "How can we lose? After all, we are all reasonable men...."

The river gleamed in the moonlight like a strip of tempered steel. A black horde spilled down through the shadows and shot out across the water. Zhukora's naked figure stood proud above the river bend and watched her children swarm through the night.

The enemy had gathered themselves together for the killing blow. They had conscripted the weavers and the shepherd boys and had told themselves they had an army.

Zhukora had reacted with blinding speed. A third of her army was spilling out into the night. Daimïru would take them on a wide sweep about the enemy flank; the hammer to Zhukora's anvil. Zhukora looked upon her world and found it good.

"Follow the river to conceal your ïsha trails. There is a fault line in the earth five swoops downstream. Follow the ïsha disturbance. Leave no sign of your passing.

"I want two scout groups forward. Rooshïkii, take the van. Deal with any enemy contact immediately. There must be no survivors to report our move. In the morning, you will have simply disappeared."

"Yes, Leader!" The young scout cracked her wings in a bow and flung herself into the night.

From the cliffs above the river, Shadarii's pilgrims watched the demons pass.

Mrrimïmei stared at the Skull-Wings and let her face twist in hate. "An army. Zhukora's out to rule the world, and we let it happen! We followed that mewling healer instead of staying to fight!" The woman ran a hand across her empty womb and spat. "Do you see what they've brought us to, these creatures with their visions and their missions! Power serves only power. Between Shadarii and her sister, they will enslave a world!"

Totoru winced and turned away.

Kefiru looked up in Mrrimïmei in bewilderment. "Enslave? No! Shadarii never enslaved anyone. She loves us!"

Mrrimïmei jammed her spear into the ground. "Zhukora thrives on death. Shadarii vampirises love! They both need us to feed upon. They try to shape the world to match their own twisted visions. Our world is dying. We can be free only when we have rid ourselves of Shadarii and her sister."

There was silence beneath the trees as the other Wrens slowly looked away. Totoru fearfully reached out to touch his fiancé, but Mrrimïmei turned her back and shoved the man aside.

Far down in the water, great yellow eyes swam up through the depths and watched the surging waves of warriors cross the riverbanks. Silver scales gleamed—great whiskers stirred in currents deeper than the waters and older than time. Grandfather Catfish puffed his gills in thought, and then turned and swam silently downstream, coursing steadily toward the final meeting.

CR ℰℴ ℰℴ

The autumn mornings were always sharp and cold. Dewy grass sparkled. Magpies warbled joyous welcome to the dawn. Far overhead, an ibis wheeled and slid across the trees. The world shone bright, the day grew sharp, and the skies were wide and blue.

Across the open hilltops, the Coalition army seethed like a vast swarm of ants. A hundred thousand fighters were arranged in a vast amorphous mass. Only one group showed any sense of order. Keketál's tiny war band hung far back in the rear, along with the outlandish Zebedii.

Keketál's men stood at their posts in watchful silence. They were the Guard; the picked warriors of four tribes. Though a mere two thousand strong, each had fought hard to win a place. They came because a man had given them a sense of pride and purpose.

Lord Keketál, the River's Gift, stood eating pickled onions from a jar. Captain Hupshu moved carefully upwind, much to the amusement of his men. Keketál munched on as though he had not a worry in the world. He paced amiably up and down the steady lines of his beloved Guard, crunching onions between his fine white teeth.

Suddenly Keketál froze. The nearest guard was watching him, his eyes hopefully following Keketál's fingers as they dipped into the jar. The leader looked at his onions and gave a guilty blush.

"Uh, you like one? Iss good! Good onions. Iss wife making them! Delicious, yes?" The warrior greedily accepted a dripping onion from the jar, and then quickly passed the jug back down the line. Men swiftly dunked their fists and stuffed their faces with Keketál's breakfast.

Keketál looked irritably into the empty jug. He shot a hurt look at the troops. They smirked around their stolen onions and winked merrily at their chief. The leader fixed a beady eye upon his men, promising dire consequences in the evening.

From further down the hill, there came a sudden sound of laughter. A group of female slingers had tied bells to Harïsh's tail. Moving awkwardly in her fine new armor, Harïsh inspected their handiwork. It seemed to please her. She saw Keketál grinning at her and coyly flipped her tail.

Since returning from the forest, Harïsh had changed. Something had happened in there, something so wonderful Harïsh simply didn't have the words to tell. Her husband looked at her and wondered at the sparkle in her eye.

Harïsh had gathered three hundred shepherd girls and formed the Maiden Guard. The women were more than welcome; they trained as long and hard as any of Keketál's male warriors. What was more, those girls could shoot. Dear Rain, but they could use those slings! Unlike the conscripts from the villages, these girls were true artists. They were the pride of the Coalition Guard.

They needed something to be proud of. Keketál looked out across the army and felt his spirits droop. The conscripts were poorly led and badly frightened. Even from a distance, Keketál could hear their officers arguing about precedence. The men bore slings and farming implements, wooden forks and threshing flails. There were wheezing ancient men and prepubescent boys. The mighty army of the Coalition! Keketál's heart sank as he sensed disaster lurking in the sky.

Something twinkled on a ridge five swoops away. Keketál gazed off into the distance and reached for his weapons. "Harïsh?"

"My love?"

"Keketál loves you. He loves you, little golden one. He thanks you for all the gifts you give."

"I love you, husband. I will not fail you."

"Be safe, my love. Be safe."

Keketál deliberately discarded the face mask from his helmet. He hesitated briefly, bothered by half a memory. Then he put his back toward the enemy, turning to face his men. "The Guard will divide into maneuver squadrons. Move!"

"Squadrons—form!"

The troops instantly formed ranks while Harïsh's slingers sped downhill to set up a skirmish line. Beside them, the tribesmen washed back and forth like a restless mist. The Coalition army was so vast that the flanks dwindled off into the haze. Keketál gazed in wonder at the spectacle and slowly shook his head.

A young girl came flitting through the treetops at the army's front. She made straight for Keketál's side and skidded to a halt. "M-my lord, the savages are advancing from the North! The Demon Queen is at their head. Squadron Seven has opened fire and are falling back, per your orders."

"Reform the skirmishers behind army. Send their officer to me. I want to be thanking her."

Far off in the distance, a group of armored maidens burst out of the trees. They flew back fifty spans and sank to the ground. A second line of women dashed from the tree line and leapfrogged across the first, while the foremost group fired slings toward the forest, covering the move. The two ranks worked in perfect coordination—teamwork born of trust. They were well led, but Keketál expected nothing less from his scout commander. Namïlii had turned out very well, indeed.

With the demons approaching and the die already cast, Keketál drew his flute from his belt and quietly began to play. He strolled unconcernedly along the lines and wove a spreading spell of calm.

Ꮳ Ꮪ Ꮪ

Zhukora raced through the trees, branches whipping at her sides. Wind rippled through her fur. Sunlight splashed across her back, and her army spread beside her like majestic wings of power. It moved to every thrust and motion of her will while Serpent screamed out overhead and howled for plainsman souls.

The strike force punched through the trees at reckless speed. The hillside loomed above.

Zhukora screamed toward the open ground and let her spirits soar. "Now!"

In one almighty surge, the two columns of warriors swerved aside. The battering rams of flesh and steel positioned themselves left and right.

The black empress howled out a hunting scream, thrilling to the power that raged through her soul. "Kill, my children! Kill them! Let the earth be soaked with blood!"

The rear wave sank into trenches as the front ranks thundered on. Like a breaking storm, her warriors exploded from the trees. Slings fired, spears flashed, and the two armies met with a titanic crash.

Zhukora shrieked with lust as she led the Skull-Wings in the attack. Bodies whirled about her in a cyclone. The alpine teams fought as perfectly coordinated organisms. Ïsha flashed and hammered enemies from the air. Fleeing slingers screamed as spears stabbed through their backs. High in the air, Zhukora lunged with her spear, laughing wildly as she pierced a plainsman's lungs. She tumbled through the air like a shrieking meteor, and demons raced beside her to fill the world with blood.

Onward, onward! Zhukora's first wave stalled as scattered groups of plainsmen tried to make a stand. The second alpine battle line overleapt the first. Zhukora screamed and punched her fist toward a knot of slingers, blasting them into dancing skeletons. The alpine warriors shrieked in triumph as their leader's sorcery slew the foe. She swept flames across the enemy and laughed into the skies.

Keketál blew on a clay whistle and spread his arms. His Guard oriented themselves along the new axis of advance. He had seen too much folly, too many of the Coalition levies die. He shook with dreadful rage. "Enough! No more fools and committees! Hupshu, take command of the Zebedii warriors. Lord Keketál leads them through you."

"Yes, Lord!"

Keketál grabbed his friend by the shoulder and punched his fist toward the enemy lines. "Here and here! Hupshu hit both ends of the enemy; not middle bits, but endings. Drive them inward. You kill, Hupshu! You kill and kill until sky and earth turn red!"

Hupshu waved a fist toward his men.

Keketál turned his back upon the lake tribes as he assessed the battlefield. "Keketál wants the levies back here on the hill! Leave the ones near the savages.

They all deadmen already. Anything untouched must line up here by Keketál! Lord Karnekh, take twenty Guard officers and take control. If their chiefs try to stop you, kill them!"

"Yes, Lord!"

"Go! Go!"

Elite officers streamed out to take control. The air filled with roaring wings as the Zebedii took to the skies. Keketál gripped his wife and felt fire building in his blood. "See her, Harïsh? See her there? The Demon Queen has made a simple mistake. She leads from the front! She can't see past the end of her own spear."

The tall hunter thoughtfully flexed his claws. The Demon Queen was rash; she loved the taste of blood too much. He had begun to find the measure of his enemy.

"We have enough numbers to envelop her. We haven't lost this battle yet."

"For Fire, Wind, and Mother Rain! *Charge!*"

A shout of rage boomed out through the air. Hupshu folded his wings and dived, ten thousand Zebedii warriors howling at his tail. They exploded through the treetops and slammed into the enemy.

The air roared with the impact of ten thousand snarling warriors. In seconds, the sky became a storm of tumbling shapes. Zebedii and savages tore each other from the air. Necks snapped. Oitas smashed through helms. Painted Zebedii howled and tumbled back as dao rammed through their guts.

Hupshu rolled upside down and plowed his oita through an enemy mask. Then he turned hard on the tail of a weaving savage, peeling aside as a fresh target veered above. His oita cracked upward and broke the creature's spine.

A spear flashed toward the brewer's throat. Hupshu whirled and stabbed out his power to deflect the shot. Still the spear came on. A tiny Ka inside the spearhead squealed in hate.

Magic weapon!

Hupshu dived. The spear curved its flight to follow. It slammed into his back. He tumbled down in a sheet of blood. His body slammed into a thornbush and disappeared.

Above the brambles, the killing swarms fought ever on.

"Leader! Both wings are being driven back! The advance has stalled."

Zhukora barely even heard. She ripped back the head of an enemy and jerked her dao across his throat. Blood squirted up between her legs, and the she laughed at its unholy heat.

"Leader! Leader please, what orders? We need your orders!"

Still reeling with sheer lust for the fight, Zhukora looked around. A flock captain knelt before her in blood. The neck guard of his helmet had been torn completely free. She lifted her gaze, stared across the battlefield, and gathered the Skull-Wings with one motion of her hands. "Leave the front formations to hold position. Gather the Skull-Wings in an arrowhead maneuver. We attack on the right."

"B-but Beloved One, the left wing is crumbling also! Shouldn't we split our forces and save both wings at once?"

"The left flank will hold. I will not divide our reserve."

The Skull-Wings flung themselves into their ordered formations.

The flock captain looked toward the forest and licked his lips in agitation. "Leader, we are massively outnumbered! Soon even these pathetic creatures will see we're but half their strength. Where is the other portion of our army? The war chief has still not come!"

Zhukora slowly drew her spear from a victim lying on the ground. "Daimïru will be here. She will come because she loves me. Daimïru will never fail me."

These new enemies were different from the others—small, wild barbarians with fur dyed into fantastic streaks. The painted warriors fought brutally, butchering wounded on the ground and stragglers in the skies. They drove through the air like eagles, and Zhukora longed to test herself against their blades.

Zhukora's guardsmen formed a spear pointed straight at the Zebedii. Sling stones began to cut the air. Zhukora raised her hands, blanketing her troops under a shield of light. Stones bounced powerlessly across the wall.

At the center of the field, the enemy conscripts had been driven back into ranks, marshaling for a new attack.

Zhukora saw it all and gave a snarl. "We deal with them later! First we slay these painted barbarians!" She rose into the air on glorious shining wings. "We'll wash the plains with blood! We'll fill the ïsha with screaming souls! Kill! Kill, my loves. Forward for the Dream!"

Alpine warriors screamed in bloodlust and charged into the Zebedii. Zhukora's laugh rang out across the battlefield as she tore her prey apart with light.

The enemy had committed her reserves, and Keketál still had almost a third of his force reordered on the hill. It was time to take revenge.

"All units advance! Guard, attack in triple fork formation!"

"Guards!"

"Squadron!"

A great stir shook the army. Victory suddenly seemed in their grasp.

Keketál watched his warriors rise and leaned down to bellow in Harïsh's ear. "Swing out to the flanks. Fire to support our charge."

Harïsh crushed him with a kiss and let him go. Keketál heard her rapping orders to her troops. She darted downhill, leading a tail of wild-eyed girls. Keketál climbed to the forefront of his troops.

Lord Looshii joined him, grinning in delight. "We have 'em! This time we really have 'em!"

"Ha! We kill Demon Queen for goodly dead! Lightning or no lightning, we have her now. Demon Queen finished!"

Looshii spread his arms toward the enemy and laughed. "And my scouts had fed me such tales of woe! This is only half the numbers I was told they had!"

Keketál froze. Antennae stiffened as he stared down at the battle far below.

Half!

"Guard! About face! About face, quickly!"

Soldiers collided and tangled in midair. Keketál drew his troops back.

Suddenly, the rear woods were alive with racing shapes. A vast horde of rainbow figures boiled out into the light, a wild blonde goddess howling at their head. Fangs gleamed as the alpine warriors screamed for plainsman souls.

The Coalition conscripts saw the savages at their backs, flung aside their weapons, and clawed their way into the air. In one split second, the entire battle had been lost. The savages had fooled them all....

Still the Coalition Guards' charge drove on. Keketál' swerved and snatched Lord Looshii by the tail. "My lord, get back! Take all our survivors and fly south. The Guard will buy you time!"

"Lord Keketál!"

"Go! Take my wife and flee!" Keketál plunged forward with his men.

Lord Looshii watched them fly onward, unable to grasp why Keketál still pressed on with the attack. Somewhere behind him, lightning flashed. Lord Looshii flung himself toward his new command and tried to keep panic from his eyes.

Daimïru felt her army surge about her like a tidal wave of death. Only one pathetic flock of plainsmen stood between her and the prey. Daimïru shook out her golden hair and stormed toward the foe.

The Coalition Guard made a sacrificial charge, stabbing deep into the heart of the attacking swarm. Daimïru's advance ground to a halt as her warriors converged toward the fight inside their lines. For once, the plainsmen fought with speed and skill.

Daimïru raced inverted across the sky and ripped her spear across the belly of a barbarian. The steel edge slid from its armored hide. The girl snarled and rolled, lunging out to hurtle her spear into a warrior's back. Her victim shrieked, clawing at the weapon as he tumbled to the ground. Daimïru laughed and whirled around to see the measure of her victory.

The girl stared in shock. Her warriors were being torn to shreds! Squat figures in felt armor slashed about themselves with wooden staves, slicing Daimïru's troops like hawks in a flock of doves.

There—right at their head! A proud warrior with fine green wings was directing the barbarians in battle. Here lay the secret to the barbarian's success.

Daimïru swerved and climbed beneath the belly of her foe. She flashed toward the nobleman and slashed out with a single vicious blow. Her spear stabbed empty air. Suddenly the man had gone! He had somehow swerved behind her.

Daimïru rolled and threw herself into a turn. Wing muscles shrieked with pain as she pushed herself harder than she ever had before.

Something punched the ïsha from her wings. The girl tumbled. She snatched out with her claws and caught her enemy's hide. Daimïru tangled her opponent and brought both of them smashing to the grass.

Impact drove the breath out of her lungs, and a broken rib leaked blood beneath her hide. Daimïru's vision blurred with spots. She crawled away and tried to blink the tears from her eyes.

Ïsha sense screamed in warning, and Daimïru rolled aside. Something cleaved the earth beside her skull. She rammed her elbow back and caught her assailant in the face. With a shriek of rage, she staggered to her feet. One wing trailed brokenly at her side. She tore her twin dao out from their sheathes and felt her vision clear.

There he was, Green-Wing! The man evilly swapped his staff from hand to hand.

Daimïru crouched and hissed like an attacking snake. She lifted her eyes to drink in the plainsman's death. She stared into a deadman's face, and felt her hands fall to her side....

Kotaru!

Daimïru croaked as he rammed his staff into her guts. She looked at him in disbelief, tears of pain dripping from her eyes. "No! No—I killed you! I killed you!" The girl spilled to the ground and collapsed.

Keketál looked down at her in puzzlement; he had understood every word, but none of it made sense.

The savages had seen their chieftain fall. Keketál turned and fled as the enemy snatched the fallen girl and dragged her back toward the trees. Their attack stalled, wavered, and then surged back toward the woods in one almighty storm.

A temporary reprieve. Keketál found his voice. "Dadash, Preshtu! Take First and Second Wings and skirmish the enemy! Slow them. We try to save the levies. Meet us downstream at Wombat Point! All others, take wounded and fall back! Help army withdraw!" Officers swirled around him racing off at his command.

The Demon Queen had overrun the field. Keketál felt the taste of defeat like bile on his tongue; there was nothing else to do except save as many people as he could.

Next time. Next time would be different. Keketál flew toward the south, a plague of demons howling at his tail.

Twenty-Six

"My love! My love, it's all right. Hush, now. You're in my arms. Everything's better now."

Daimïru drifted warm and safe within a dreamy haze. When she became thirsty, someone raised nectar to her lips. When she grew lonely, her beloved stroked her hair. Daimïru growled and weakly shoved aside the luxury. "You... didn't pursue."

"No, my love. You needed me, and so I am here."

"You must go after them."

"In good time, my love." Soft lips brushed Daimïru's hair. "We have a miracle to perform here first." Something warm filled her, and suddenly her pain was gone. Daimïru opened her eyes to see Zhukora gazing down into her face.

"How could I leave when my spear arm needs me? My pure half, untainted by doubt and imperfection. You are the Dream's most pure and worthy champion."

Daimïru's long blonde hair stirred in the ïsha breeze as the girl stared into the blue eyes of her god. "I saw something impossible, Zhukora. A figure from the past! A deadman fights us!"

"Hush. Your wounds still trouble you."

"No! It's him, your sister's lover! I killed him months ago with my own two hands, and yet he struck me down today!"

"This is sorcery, indeed." Zhukora looked up toward her deadly ïsha fields. *Serpent! What have you to say about all this? Did it happen? Can it be true?*

Yes... There is one creature with such power. Serpent coiled slowly out into the light. *The Ka called Starshine. She is an enemy of all great dreams. No one can raise the dead, but she would have the ability to blind thy servant with an illusion.*

Zhukora thoughtfully switched her tail. *You have met this Starshine before.*

Of course. Starshine is my sister....

A sister! Zhukora stood, letting sunlight caress her fur. *Can she be beaten by physical force?*

Destroy her minions, and you shall have destroyed her power.

Zhukora looked about the field and saw a mighty army waiting patiently for her word. The battlefield had been transformed into a vast, majestic work of art. The colors of death splashed the earth with wild abandon; blood and organs shone like burnished jewels beneath the sun. Zhukora looked upon her work and gave a smile.

Beside her feet there lay a single corpse—a barbarian with wings of gleaming white. A Ka wailed inside the prison of its skull, desperately seeking escape.

Zhukora stared down into the corpse's eyes. There, in the midst of mounds of dead, the queen of demons gave a merry laugh.

White ranks of skulls waited for her sacred word. Zhukora threw out her arms to her beloved warriors and felt their worship coursing through her. "Open your eyes, my love. Open your eyes and see a miracle! I bring my faithful ones a gift. A gift of life and death!"

Daimïru gazed up at her leader with great, thirsting eyes. Zhukora hacked down into the corpse with her dao, and then held the barbarian's severed head dangling by its hair. The creature's Ka thrashed in fear. Zhukora's power blazed as she clutched the shrieking creature. With a blast of light, she sealed the spirit in its cell.

Zhukora grinned and tossed the grisly object to Daimïru, who caught the thing and gasped as power flooded through her. The imprisoned Ka had become a well of ïsha. Daimïru screamed and sucked a vast draft of energy. She lashed out, and a fist of ïsha blasted into a tree. The girl turned to the warriors and shrieked in victory.

Warriors leapt to their feet and roared. A forest of knives rose overhead as Zhukora opened her arms.

"Go! Take the heads of dead barbarians. Bring me your trophies, and I shall give you power!"

Men flung themselves in frenzy on the carrion. Zhukora clasped Daimïru hard against her breast and gazed at her people's joy.

"South! South, my children! We go toward their villages and fields. Man, woman and child, we shall destroy them! Every creature slain gives us more power! We shall wipe these creatures from the earth and climb heights undreamed of."

With a savage scream the army raged into the air. The knives dripped with blood as Zhukora's Dream raved on toward its destiny.

ය භ භ

In the cool hours of the evening, the only sounds came from the cawing of the crows. Throughout the quiet valley, all lay hushed and still. The shadows lengthened about the still mounds of the dead while Shadarii knelt and wept in agony.

The Silent Lady cried for a world gone mad; where her tears fell, small white flowers bloomed.

They had found the field of corpses in the early afternoon. All around the hillside pilgrims staggered through blood; the bodies lay layers deep in fantastic drifts and mounds. Shadarii rocked back and forth in horror as she felt her soul turn numb. Not a single plainsman's body still retained its head.

These are my people. This is my crime! I waited too long. Zhukora has done a crime I can never wash away!

Starshine looked through Shadarii's eyes and spared no pity for the dead. *Waste no time on sorrow. Think of the revenge that thou shalt take! The enemy shall pay for this in blood....*

Be silent! You make me sick! The wind changed direction and Shadarii retched.

Tingtraka suddenly gave a gasp and dived into the brambles. She emerged, dragging an injured man. "Shadarii! Shadarii look! I've found someone! He's still alive!"

It was a young man dressed in blue. Tingtraka ripped him from the brambles and rolled him over on the ground. With a sob of fear, she pulled a bloody spear from his ribs. The fallen warrior slumped bonelessly, seeming only closer to death. Tingtraka roared and flung her arms around him. Ïsha flowed. Power poured in from the flowers, grass, and trees. Tingtraka hurtled it down into her patient, shaping it into a titanic healing spell.

Lady Zareemah sheltered her eyes and yelled in alarm. "Revered One, should we help her?"

Shadarii waved the other pilgrims back and watched Tingtraka work. The injured warrior began to breathe more deeply. He stirred, only to fall into a healing sleep. Tingtraka traced the sharp lines of his face, her hands trembling as she breathed the warm scent of his fur.

"Oh, Shadarii, he's beautiful! Who could want to hurt him? He's no warrior. He's not even a hunter! Look, there's not a callus on his hands." The girl cradled her patient's head in her lap.

Shadarii left Tingtraka to the man and wandered out into the sun. Shadarii's pilgrims trudged aimlessly after her, past rows and rows of butchered dead. Kïtashii swayed back and forth in grief, keening brokenly as she gazed at the feasting crows. Shadarii took Kïtashii's hand and slowly bent her head in prayer.

The pilgrims watched as the valley trembled with power. A dense carpet of flowers spread across the fields. Shadarii covered the carnage with a cloak of brilliant green; the only shroud the dead would ever know.

It was done. Shadarii reached down and folded Kïtashii against her breast. All around them, fields of daisies bloomed against the evening sky.

СЗ ВО ВО

The army sprawled out in the darkness like an exhausted beast. Even the wounded lacked the energy to scream. Village women walked among the lines of men, too terrified to meet the victims' eyes. Despite such a vast array of men, the night was as silent as a grave.

Over everything, there drifted the soft call of a small clay flute. Keketál sat before his maps and let his music soar. Scouts and officers knelt beside his feet. Harïsh stumbled through the tent flaps and sat at her husband's feet. She wiped her face and smeared fresh blood through her fur.

"The casualty estimate you ordered can't be done. There was no survey of how many men we had when we began. We can't even guess how many have died."

Pachetta let Lord Looshii unwind a bandage from her thigh. "How many men do we have now?"

"Fifty thousand? Something like that. I think we lost about seventy thousand men."

"Half of those might be deserters."

Harïsh shrugged and tried to wipe her hands. "Maybe."

She leaned against Keketál's legs and turned desolated eyes on him. "We lost Hupshu when he routed their left wing. Someone saw him fall. Speared."

The music stopped; Keketál quietly put his flute away. "Kill sheep from the local herds. Claim all the livestock you find. All warriors must eat meat. Have each unit throw away farming tools. From now on, we use just clubs and slings." Keketál carefully spread out his maps. He drew a line across the hills and thumped his fist down in the dust. "We leave before dawn. There is an ïsha current along the rock face of the next valley. We ride it down into the swamp. We rest, pray, and fight again."

"She will follow. We cannot hide our trail."

"Yes. She follows. She pours down rivers, thirsty for our blood." Keketál carefully pulled his gauntlets. "But the swamps are our home for many weeks. They let us ambush her. One solid blow, and the demons are destroyed." The man reached down to draw a circle on the map. "Here. We smash her here, tomorrow noon."

ଓ ଚ ୨ଚ

The little teacher danced across an open field as dawn spread through the skies. She danced as though it were the last dance of her life, flinging herself into her art with wild elation. Bare feet kissed the flowers. Bright wings swirled and flashed beneath the sun.

It was the sacred dance of parting; the dance of fond farewell.

Kïtashii stared as though it were the last sight she would ever see.

Tingtraka edged closer through the trees, gazing at the dance without comprehending what she saw. There was a strange feeling on the ïsha; something fragile, something sad. The huntress looked at Shadarii and felt her spirit fill with dread. "Kïtashii, what is it? What's going on?"

"It's a dance, Tingtraka. A very special dance. Something only you and I are meant to see."

Tingtraka sank down to Kïtashii's side. "Something's wrong with Shadarii, isn't it? She's been this way ever since she broke the fever."

"Yes. It's almost time, you see. Almost time. Shadarii hasn't told me, but I know."

A chill of dread slowly pierced Tingtraka's heart. "Time for what, Kïtashii?"

"I can't tell you. You'd try to stop it, you see. But we can't stop it. The price would be more mountains of dead. I told her I would never fail her, and I never shall." Kïtashii's eyes were hidden beneath her hair.

Tingtraka knelt beside her and reached out to softly touch Kïtashii's face. "Y-you're crying!"

"Nothing. It's nothing. Just watch the dance with me. Watch her and remember."

Tingtraka took the little girl into her arms.

Kïtashii clawed Tingtraka's fur and trembled. "I'm s-sorry! She wanted me to be happy! Now I-I'm spoiling everything!"

Out on the field, Shadarii saw her precious friends and felt her spirits fail. The two of them were torturing themselves with grief. It was silly to be sad. Life was brief; too brief to waste in mourning.

Death is only terrible if we fear it, my loves. To learn that small lesson is to find the heart of wisdom. The little teacher opened her arms.

Kïtashii sobbed and tried to push aside her tears as she staggered onto her feet and held Tingtraka's hands. "C-Can you dance, Tingtraka?"

"Dance? No. I never learned..."

"Come. We'll teach you. I want to. I-I need to laugh for just a little while."

The two girls rose and left their clothes. Shadarii laughed and drew them into her joy. Soon they were swirling dizzily at her side. In the face of love, death had finally lost its power.

Shadarii cooked her pilgrims breakfast beneath an old red river gum. The tree trunk was rough and streaked with black. Little beads of sap clung against the limbs like tiny jewels. Shadarii snapped off a piece of gum and popped it in her mouth as she carefully turned wood grubs in the ashes.

One by one, her followers awakened. Little Zareemii sat cross-legged in the dust and watched breakfast in fascination. His mother Zareemah stared at the frying bugs and looked a little ill. Thankfully, there was also other food. The delicious smell of toasting meat set the pilgrims' tails a-wag.

The plainsman Tingtraka had rescued edged closer to the fire, his nostrils quivering as his empty stomach growled. He slyly sneaked out a hand to steal piece of seed cake. Shadarii caused a tree branch to smack his tail. The poor man gave a yip and scuttled back into Tingtraka's arms. The Teacher saw them hold each other's hands. She gave a smile.

Sitting mats had been laid out in an intimate little circle, and Shadarii led each person to his or her place. Mrrimïmei cringed back from the Teacher's touch, but Shadarii persisted in giving her a prime position in the shade. To each follower, she gave a kiss, as though passing every one of them a single lasting memory.

Kïtashii cried; she wiped her eyes upon her hair and stared down at the dirt.

Shadarii sat quietly and looked out at her beloved friends, breaking bread to pass around the circle. For the first time in months, Shadarii ate and shared in their fellowship. Once everyone was served, Shadarii placed a scroll in Kïtashii's lap.

Kïtashii gazed down at the scroll and slowly blinked her silver eyes. "Th-there are words here. A message to share with you." Kïtashii began to unroll the paperbark. "We will share one last lesson together."

Last? Pilgrims looked at one another in confusion. Kïtashii swallowed and avoided Tingtraka's gaze.

The little girl carefully began to read Shadarii's scroll. "Wind bless us. Rain soothe us. We meet in love and harmony in the name of blessed peace.

"My friends, my beloved travelers, I have never had a voice to share with you as I have always wished. Perhaps that is why these picture words have always been so precious to me. In a small way, I can now speak to you, my fellow pilgrims.

"I have loved you all, my precious ones. Each and every one of you. Our joining has been a time of utter magic. Time shall not fade us. Death shall not separate us. The bonds of love outlast the bonds of life.

"My words shall never fade as long as you remember them. To you I pass my burden and my joy. I ask that you teach others all that you have learned." Kïtashii's voice caught. The little student wiped her eyes with her hair.

"Hear, then, a lesson. Hear the thoughts of Shadarii-Zha, daughter of the Rain.

"Long ago I tried to fight for love. I caused death and destruction, and in the end all my suffering was for naught. The Sacred Mother took me above my agony and set me upon the path of teaching. To light my way, she provided me a single riddle:

"Why do we fight?

"I believe I have found my answer. We do not often fight for hate. Instead, we fight for love.

"In our minds, love excuses even the unthinkable. When I fought, I did it all for love of my Kotaru. The forest people now murder for love of Zhukora. It is love that has led the world to this pain! Love so wild and senseless that it twists the mind. A passion so intense that it becomes a sickness.

"To love one thing to the detriment of all others is terrible. Because it is love, we deceive ourselves into thinking it must be good. Only wisdom can unmask this self-deception. By examining love, we can discover whether it is true and good. This is our task, the sacred mission given us by Mother Rain. Plant wisdom, and thus we shall grow true love."

Kïtashii looked into Shadarii's eyes and let the scroll fall slowly to her lap. "Remember. Always know that I have loved each and every one of you with all my heart. I shall care for you and be with you as long as wonder shines inside your souls. Peace be upon you, my loves. Peace and happiness forevermore."

Shadarii gently placed a heavy book beside the little girl. *The Book of Offerings: The thoughts and deeds of Shadarii-Zha.* The Teacher passed the book to its new keeper and kissed the tears from Kïtashii's cheeks.

Shadarii looked around the circle and smiled into the pilgrims' eyes. Beneath the tree, there dwelled a special kind of magic. Friends and laughter, words and wisdom, and a certainty that men could shape their fate with wisdom and love.

Shadarii looked upon her final dawn and was content.

Twenty-Seven

"Attack wave, dive!"

Ïsha shields tore down across the cave as Keketál's men burst out of cover and ripped into the savages. A thousand guardsmen overwhelmed Zhukora's forward scouts. Bodies wove and creatures ducked. Leaves exploded as Keketál dived through the trees. He slashed out with his oita and split a demon's wing, sending the savage tumbling through a tree to splinter on the ground.

"Onward! Follow them! *Kill!*"

The alpine scout teams turned and fled, the plainsmen following hard behind. They rolled over the skirmishers and crashed full tilt into Zhukora's vanguard, smashing through the savages in a screaming wave of blood.

Keketál roared and led his guard through a storm of carnage. Savages fell before them in their hundreds. Bones splintered. Armor split. Still the guardsmen hacked onward as they chased behind the shrieking foe.

The Demon Queen's army instantly deployed. Hunting teams flicked out to flank Keketál's tiny force, engulfing the Coalition Guard. Savages and plainsmen fought with merciless fury. The wounded were butchered as they fell. Fangs bit and daggers tore. Ïsha raged with untold power.

Deep inside the fight, Keketál snapped out orders to his teams. The decoy charge had been too dangerous to entrust to anybody else. The timing had to be exact. The demons must be driven into fury and drawn on into the swamps.

Ahead of Keketál, the melee swirled in a dense black cloud of shapes. Fantastic costumes boiled through the trees to claw guardsmen from the sky. Keketál dodged past a spear, slapped an enemy into a tree, and broke the man's neck. The noble grinned as his men smacked into a new wave of demons and drove the creatures back.

The air suddenly flung Keketál aside. A wild shape shot by, insane laughter ripping through the air. The savage held aloft a severed head and screamed with hate. It sucked power from its trophy and hurtled an ïsha bolt. A guardsman fell as the explosion tore his wings to shreds.

Savages raced past, high above the trees, blasting a path into the Coalition ranks. The headhunters laughed as their magic ripped the living into death. Severed heads stared out at the world, lips moving slowly in unholy dreams...

Keketál fought for breath. He signaled for his musicians to sound out the recall. "Retreat! Fall back by squadrons! Keep your teams! Keep your teams!"

Keketál drove his men back through the trees, pushing them on their way before joining the rearguard. The guardsmen skirmished frantically through the trees, trying to draw the Demon Queen on into the swamps.

The black empress herself appeared through the smoke. She glared toward the guardsmen and raised her fist. Power blasted straight at Keketál. He dodged aside as lightning cut down a dozen men. Keketál's rearguard turned tail and fled, drawing the hordes of rainbow warriors in pursuit.

Sweet Mother Rain! Keketál stared across his shoulder as enemy warriors blackened the sky. An advance guard of savages flew hot on Keketál's tail.

He wrenched his men around to make a stand. "Come about! We're attacking them! Come about and follow Keketál!"

The frightened soldiers dragged themselves to a halt.

Keketál wheezed as a stitch ripped through his old wound. "W-we have to hold them back to let the others get away! Go for the ones carrying heads. For Rain's sake, kill them!" Keketál watched a hundred savages raging straight toward his devastated team of twenty men. He straightened his back and slowly raised his hand.

One hundred yards... eighty... fifty...

"Ready!"

"Ready, fire!" A musical female voice ripped through the air.

The sky turned black with sling stones. Savages jerked and screamed inside the storm. The enemy sorcerers were driven slowly back as the slingers cast up a dense barrage of fire.

"Second Squad, cover the wounded! Namïlii, I want those enemy officers dead!" Harïsh led her shepherd girls forward through the trees.

The slingers fired with uncanny accuracy, tumbling savages to the ground. Harïsh fell back and searched through the boughs until she found her husband. "What in Poison's name are you doing here, man? Get back! Get back to the army."

Keketál gazed at her in shock. "Not you! Harïsh not to stay here!"

"Get away, stupid husband! Leave this to the girls! Get back to the army and take command!"

She was right; the girls were the best choice for keeping the enemy in play. A thousand female slingers came boiling through the trees. The enemy vanguard went to ground as the battle raged in earnest.

Keketál staggered back, his eyes fixed on a plainsman corpse. "Harïsh, split the skulls of all our dead! Kill the seriously wounded. Don't let their souls fall into the demons' hands!"

"I hear! Now go! Go back. I love you!"

Keketál climbed aloft and left his wife to fight. His strategy was working perfectly. The Demon Queen had come to his killing ground. He need only live long enough to direct his victory.

Hours of combat had passed like a heavy dream. The women fired and flew, fired and flew, drawing the enemy onward into ambush. Each thrust and feint was met in kind. The maidens bought their army's security with their lives. Finally, the cover thinned. Nothing lay at Harïsh's back except the open swamps.

Keketál rose in the grass and watched his wife's troops retreat. Vast clouds of slingers shot past and dived into the reeds.

Harïsh spied Keketál and swooped low overhead. "They're coming! They're all yours!"

The ïsha pulsed and trembled as the enemy drew near. The rumble of it sounded like thunder in the mountains.

Keketál deliberately turned his back on the enemy and greeted his nervous warriors with a fine, lop-sided smile. "Iss time now! Time to be killing savages. We hit them hard and give ground, retreat back to mud flats on other side of river. Our hidden troops will charge in from the flanks. This Demon Queen, we fix her good!"

Thirty thousand men were waiting down inside the creek. The guards and tribal levies ceased listening to the distant enemy as Keketál ambled back and forth across the banks.

"Nothing to be afraid of. We kill many yesterday, and now we kill some more. Savages die just like anybody else. Sorcery iss no matter. You shoot a sorcerer before he shoots you, and who iss smarter?"

Someone laughed. Another man grinned. A voice hooted in from the background. "Half of them are only women! If we can't beat women what are we?"

Keketál held up his finger and let his voice carry out across the men. "We got girls, too! Real girls! Not some savages from the trees. Girls with smarts!"

There was a roar as Pachetta leapt up and gave a bow. Her tail flipped to tickle a soldier's grinning face; the man slapped Pachetta's rump and gave a roar of joy. "A soldier's duty is to guard his leader's rear!"

The laughter spread, bringing the release that Keketál had prayed for. The fear had broken in a sudden wave of mirth. The warriors rose to their feet and shook their weapons to the sky. Plainsmen spilled onto the open ground and chanted as they charged, driving forward as the rhythm grew. Shepherd girls danced at their head as the army hurtled itself into the air.

The barbarians' chant crashed like thunder all across the trees. The Coalition army made an awe-inspiring sight. They had managed to salvage close onto thirty thousand men. Zhukora stood with arms folded, watching in admiration as the enemy came on. Damn but they looked fine! The prey did Zhukora honor. She laughed at their audacity even as she ordered their destruction.

The enemy general pointed his oita at Zhukora's lines, and a roar swelled. Thirty thousand plainsmen shot forward in a raging tide of death. They foamed and exploded through the trees. Speed blurred them into a formless, churning mass.

The alpine lines held as Daimïru's voice pealed clearly out across the kneeling troops. "Attack at speed! Meet them head on! Crush the barbarians into the ground! Onward for the Dream!"

The army drove into the air as one, and Daimïru screamed out with the surging joy of combat. The Kashra hurtled themselves at one another in mighty walls of flesh. They met with a thunderous crash, blasting the swamp to its very roots. Leaves split from the trees. Ïsha roared. The air became a boiling mass of shapes as spear and oita battled for the mastery of the sky.

The blue barbarians knew how to die! They fought back tooth and claw, reaping alpine warriors like sheaves of grain. Even so, the power of Zhukora's troops was overwhelming. Daimïru shrieked in laughing madness as she hacked at a plainsman's wings. As her units tired, Zhukora sent more men in from the rear. They surged forward, ramming the barbarians back across the swamp.

Daimïru felt the enemy give way before her. A horn blew, sending the plainsmen tumbling back across the water. She dived through a paltry rain of sling stones to lead her warriors in pursuit. The whole army advanced behind her, catching her foaming rage like a disease. The girl screamed for the glory of it and hurtled Zhukora's army into the kill.

A shudder ran through the alpine ranks as two massive hammer blows fell on either flank. Daimïru ignored it all, lost inside a blood-red haze of lust. The enemies in front of her had turned to fight once more, weird creatures dyed and painted like screaming imps. Daimïru flung herself among the enemy, dragging a barbarian to the ground. Her soldiers followed suit, snarling as the battle compacted into a savage brawl.

"What's she doing? Can't she see it? Damn it, why didn't any of them see it?" Zhukora screamed in fury. A tree exploded as she lashed out her fists, and her officers ducked, keeping their eyes riveted on the fight. "Why? Why didn't she see it?"

"Leader, she is engaged in the melee! Perhaps she..."

Another scream of anger erupted, and more trees burst into flames. The army was being enveloped from the flanks, and still Daimïru's troops plowed on into the trap. Sling stones turned the air black as the plainsmen reaped revenge. In their blood-rage the alpine troops were far past caring about mere maneuvers.

Zhukora whirled and signaled for her reserves. "Rooshïkii! Take the Skull-Wings and drive off their left flank. You have command of the entire reserve!"

The little girl looked up in shock, her eyes filling with pride. "Yes, Leader!"

"Go."

The little girl danced into the air and shouted for her officers. Formations cracked about her as the Skull-Wings thundered into action. Zhukora watched her smallest warrior go and fumed in irritation, her tail switching as victory teetered just beyond reach.

Savages gave ground. The battle slowly turned. The demon's flanks ground inward, giving them no room to fly.

Daimïru ripped both her blades free from a corpse and looked around for prey. She panted wildly, her slim body trembling with need. There! The girl went stiff as a green-winged barbarian strode forward through the fight. Daimïru stared at his face and bared her thirsting fangs. "Kotaru!"

He turned and looked into her eyes. The battle seemed to freeze.

Daimïru lusted for his blood. Twice he had escaped her! He had dared to defy Zhukora's Dream. She stripped aside her mask and gazed into the soul of her enemy. "You! Kotaru! This time I'll finish it! I'll bring Zhukora your severed head as my gift of love!" Daimïru hissed and sidled forward in a crouch.

Keketál simply stared at her, his oita falling slowly to his side. Kotaru?

Suddenly, he remembered trees! There had been soft green shadows and a world of soaring ferns. And eyes; eyes as green as pools and as deep as haunted dreams. Lovemaking while the distant rain hammered on the leaves... The fear and glory of that one first precious time. Kotaru. His name was Kotaru!

Steel ripped toward his face. Kotaru hurtled himself away and felt the woman's dao tear past his wing. He launched a kick and shoved the girl aside. He staggered back and stared in shock, his whole world wrenched apart by memories.

Daimïru ripped herself out of the mud and flew into the attack. Blonde hair streamed like fire as she howled for his blood.

"Keketál!" A sling bullet snapped the air, and Daimïru rolled and dodged aside. Harïsh leapt into the way and ripped her war club from her belt.

Kotaru stared at his wife, loving her, needing her, appalled by the images in his dream.

Daimïru purred and swirled her knives.

Harïsh uncoiled a weighted line tied to the hilt of her club. She moved slowly toward her prey, keeping between Daimïru and her husband. "Keketál, go! The flank attack is failing. The black demons have attacked. The men need you!"

"But..."

"She's mine! I'll take her. Go! Go now!" His wife began to swing her weighted line. The two women faced each other like snarling cats. Kotaru snatched his oita and made to join the fight until Harïsh moved in his way. "Go! Back off! She's mine! She's mine!"

"Keketál loves you!" Kotaru reeled back and headed for his reserves.

Harïsh felt him go, and then set her fangs and stared in the eyes of insanity. Daimïru craved her blood, tail lifting as she trembled in arousal. Harïsh shifted her club and moved into the attack. "He's mine! I don't know what you are and I don't know what he was. But he's mine now. He's mine, and I'll kill you to keep him..."

Twenty-Eight

Harïsh whipped her snare line through the air.

Daimïru snarled and rolled aside, the stone weight chipping lacquer from her helmet. She made a lunge toward her enemy's face.

Harïsh leapt overhead and turned a somersault. She landed spinning, scything with the weighted cord. The savage parried, making the cord whirl madly as it wrapped about her blades. Harïsh gave a shout of triumph and ripped back on the line. The steel knives jerked from Daimïru's hands. Harïsh hefted her war club for the kill.

Daimïru's mad eyes smiled. She slowly lifted a severed head from her belt, and her aura blazed with sickly light.

Harïsh was smashed back by a terrific blow, and then another, and another. Blood flew from her mouth, and an unseen fist exploded against her groin. The egg! Harïsh sobbed, realizing just how much she had put at risk.

With a wild shriek, Daimïru kicked the girl into the mud, and then snatched a rock to smash Harïsh's teeth.

The plainswoman hunched and took the blow on her helmet crest. Sparks flew in her eyes. Harïsh desperately groped out for a weapon, ripping the sling from her helmet. She whipped the weapon into Daimïru's face, and the savage screeched and tumbled back, cradling her eyes. Harïsh rolled and found her club, while Daimïru wheeled to one side and ripped out her hunting knife. The two women started forward.

Suddenly, the whole world filled with light....

Harïsh's club spilled from her hand. A new sunrise flooded the swamplands, ruffling fur like a gentle breeze. Battle cries drifted into silence. Warriors halted in their tracks. Something soft and beautiful stole across the field.

The radiance washed the armies with a dream of peace. At its heart there stood a naked girl with eyes of shining green. Where she passed, she left precious memories of love. It was like the smell of fresh-made bread on a rainy afternoon. It was laughter on a summer's night, or rain on new grass. Warriors' weapons fell as memories of beauty inundated their minds.

These were the precious things of life. Not war, not pain and death. The Silent Lady wept, and the warriors were filled with shame.

Rooshïkii stood in Shadarii's way, a severed head hanging in her hand. The young girl sobbed as Shadarii touched her face. The Silent Lady gently eased the trophy from her grasp and forced the girl to meet its gaze. Rooshïkii gagged and wept. She pressed herself back against a tree, chest heaving as she tried to shrink away.

"I didn't know! It was only a barbarian! Please! Please, I didn't think...." The girl clutched Shadarii's legs, pleading through her tears. "You don't understand. He raped me! I had to do it! He raped me. The Dream makes all the pain go away! Help me!"

Rooshïkii slowly came into the Silent Lady's arms. Shadarii kissed her on the eyes, folding her against her heart. She took Rooshïkii's pain away and left her clean and new.

Alpine warriors looked down at the heads dangling from their belts. They quickly cast the things away. Men folded and retched while others tried to wash their hands in grief.

Shadarii closed her eyes and reached down into her power. With a sudden blaze of light, the dead skulls split, and Ka shot into the ïsha like ten thousand streaming stars. Shadarii drew them down into her presence and calmed them with her peace.

Kïtashii and Tingtraka walked in Shadarii's wake. Next came Mrrimïmei and Totoru, and then the sea peoples and pilgrims. Where Shadarii passed, the wounded healed and rose; dead souls swirled to dance with her in joy. The warriors stared at her innocence and were ashamed. Combatants drew apart and stared at the ground in silence.

Shadarii passed between them all, tears streaming from her eyes. The soldiers slowly followed her; savages and shepherds, commoners and kings all rose to reach into the Silent Lady's light.

"What! What is it?" Zhukora whirled on her guards in fury.

The men were staring at the skull masks on each other's faces. One man slowly peeled away his helmet and dropped it, looking down in wonder at the hideous thing he had worn with such pride.

Zhukora stared at the man in shock, one hand reaching up to clutch her breast. "What are you doing? Pick that up!"

"It-it's only a mask." The man looked down at the painted wood. "Only a mask..."

"Only a mask?" Zhukora's antennae jerked in amazement. "The Skull-Mask is our symbol. You are the chosen! You live only for the Dream. You have already sacrificed your lives to our cause!"

The bodyguards walked toward a strange glow out on the field, letting their weapons fall behind them. Men smiled. Brightness shone in their eyes, hate and fury draining away.

Zhukora felt power slip like water through her hands. "Serpent! Serpent what's happening? Do something! Stop them!"

It's her. It's Starshine! She's stealing thy power for her own!

A long-forgotten presence flooded though Zhukora's mind. The woman gave a scream of rage, snatched up her spear and exploded through the air on a shaft of flame. With a wild howl of fury, she flung herself across the sky.

"Shadarii!"

The crippled bitch had come to steal the Dream! Zhukora streaked onward to make a sister's death.

Harïsh arched in release as something healed inside her. The pain went away, and her fury eased. The girl found herself surrounded by a sea of people, savages and plainsmen standing side by side. The girl blinked at the mingled armies and felt her spirits soar.

A woman gazed down into her eyes. The Silent Lady! Harïsh panted and laid one trembling hand across her womb. The egg was safe inside her. Harïsh babbled incoherent words of thanks as she saw the Silent Lady smile.

A tall man burst out from the crowd. Harïsh gave a sob and crushed her husband hard against her heart while Keketál buried his face inside her golden hair, completely lost to the world. Harïsh wept in his grasp, laughing as she wound her fingers through his fur.

"I'm going to have a baby! A baby!" The girl tried to turn his face toward the Silent Lady. "Keketál! Oh, Keketál, do you see? I told you she would come!"

"Hush. Hold Keketál tight. Iss all over now."

The lovers clung and wept for joy.

Shadarii moved out across the fields, giving them their space. She approached a figure hiding in the grass.

Daimïru stared in horror at Shadarii's great green eyes and held up a hand to ward her away. "Get away from me! Don't touch me! Don't look at me!"

Shadarii slowly shook her head, feeling the other woman's pain. She looked down at her in pity, reaching out to stroke her face.

Daimïru whimpered and backed away, tears streaming from her eyes.

A sudden hush fell across the field, and Shadarii felt a heat against her back. Warriors drew away as a deadly presence filled the air. "Cripple!"

Shadarii gazed in sadness at the shrieking thing that once had been her sister. Serpent coiled and blazed about Zhukora's soul, and Shadarii grimaced as she felt Starshine shriek in challenge.

Zhukora hung on wings of fire and bared her fangs. "Shadarii. The cripple has come at last! Do you want it, Sister? Do you feel my power?" Zhukora alighted to the ground, as naked and exquisite as a poisoned blade. "You annoy me, Sweet Sister! You have not stolen my power for long. I'll not let you keep them. Their souls belong to me."

Mrrimïmei stared between the sisters, her eyes turning wild with hate. Daimïru clasped Zhukora's thigh as though seeing her salvation.

Zhukora sanctified Daimïru with her gaze. "I am absolute. I am perfection. I am the Dream! Now I shall kill you, Sister. I shall drink your blood and snuff you out like a candle in the dark...."

Tingtraka tried to drag Shadarii back into the crowd. The Teacher gently slipped away, pushing back Tingtraka's hands. She looked into her apostle's eyes and slowly shook her head. Shadarii kissed her most precious follower on the eyes and mouth; the gesture of farewell. She drank in the growing sunset as the world hushed.

Finally the time had come.

Two naked sisters faced each other through air as sharp as knives, and they gave themselves into a hidden world of power.

A wind stirred Shadarii's streaming copper hair. She reached out with her mind to feel the water and the trees. She felt the river at her back and the reeds dancing in the wind. Shadarii-Zha, the Silent Teacher, closed her eyes and opened her arms.

Starshine shrieked spitefully and flung her energy into Shadarii's waiting soul. Not the healing power she loved, but pure, raw force—energy to split rocks and tear matter into light. It was the means to strip the flesh from Zhukora's smoking bones. Shadarii felt the power, and let it trickle from her grasp, simply casting it aside.

Starshine gave a tiny wail of shock.

Zhukora's lethal power coiled about her like a storm; weapons gleamed and fur shone.

There, in the midst of it all, Shadarii stuck out her tongue. She shot into the air and bared her backside. A lightning bolt sizzled across the sky, but Shadarii dodged the blast with ease. She posed and tossed her streaming hair, beckoning Zhukora to follow her across the stagnant swamps. The black demon snarled and instantly tore off in pursuit.

The sun shone, the skies sang, and Father Wind laughed through Shadarii's hair. For a little while, the girl forgot the pain of parting. It had been too long since she had played her jokes; too long since wicked laughter filled her soul! The dancer sped across the streams and bubbling pools, leading her sister far away from helpless crowds.

Zhukora labored in her wake and shook her fist. "Fly! Fly, you little bitch! It won't save you!"

Lightning raved across the swamps. Shadarii rolled away and felt the bolt stab into an old dead tree.

Starshine thrashed in terror deep inside Shadarii's head. *Kill her! Fight! I have the power—use it! Burn the Demon Queen from the sky and take her subjects as your own!*

Shadarii laughed silently and gave herself into the dance. Behind her, Zhukora's energy lashed uselessly across the sky. Shadarii gave a grin and dived between the trees.

To use power, you must understand it. The dead, drowned trees below were Shadarii's weapon. Utterly devoid of ïsha, they sucked Zhukora's energy down. Zhukora was left to wonder why she missed again and again. Always her sister dodged from harm's way. Shadarii drew the demon ever on.

Starshine lunged in panic as, somewhere in the distance, Serpent screamed in lust. The air shivered to another ïsha blast. Starshine frantically crammed power into Shadarii's mind, gibbering in fear as she felt Serpent close the range. *Kill! Kill them! Here is the power. Now use it! Slay Serpent. Nothing else matters! Quickly, do it!*

Shadarii simply let the power bleed off into the sky. It blazed out like a rainbow in the dancer's wake. *Stop it! Thou art killing us! Thou stupid girl, we're going to die!*

Shadarii turned a barrel roll as a lightning bolt seared past her tail. *Finally, you understand! I will not hurt another living soul—not even hers. Yes, we are going to die, Starshine. It will be very soon, now. I will try to make it quick.*

The Ka wept and tried to break away, but Shadarii clamped the spirit tight. The creature's every nightmare had finally come true. She was trapped inside a useless body while her enemy closed in for the kill.

Shadarii saw the evil little being's fear and laughed inside her mind. How strange that a being so very old craved life so uselessly. *Why are you afraid of death, Starshine? Nothing can ever truly end. Feel the joy with me! Take one last flight and feel the wind flow through my hair!*

The spirit screeched and lunged inside its prison. *Let me out! I forgo the bargain. The deal is off! Let me out!*

Not yet, Starshine. Soon. Remember that you have ended our bargain. I kept faith with you to the end.

Let me go! The spirit wailed. *I don't want to die!*

You are evil, Starshine. How many wars have you begun in the cause of 'right'? Why don't you stay with me, Starshine? Why don't you stay and feel my death?

No! I am the ultimate force of good! It is my destiny to scour the world of evil! Thou shalt kill us both for this stupid pacifism!

Mother Rain sent me to create a legend. This is the end of the tale. I must die and pass into the world of myth. It is what was always meant to be...

Zhukora was gaining; Shadarii heard her sister split the air with rage. This time the blast caught Shadarii in the wing. She reeled away, pain blazing down her side.

Warriors stared. Overhead, Shadarii staggered. The dueling figures swept across the clearing at the center of the crowd.

Tingtraka croaked in horror as Shadarii dodged another blast. The skinny huntress wept in fear, tearing at her hair. "Kïtashii, we have to stop her! Shadarii doesn't have any power to hurt! Zhukora's going to kill her!"

"Sh-she's where she is meant to be! It-it's what she wants." Kïtashii crammed her hands against her skull in pain. "I made an oath. I can't fail her...."

"Shut up, Kïtashii! She can't win! She'd rather die than hurt anything. She's going to drain Zhukora's power and leave her to us!" Tingtraka grabbed her friend and shook her like a sack. "We can't just sit here!"

"It's a legend. Don't you understand? She's making a legend!"

Nearby, Kotaru held his wife and gazed in amazement at the sky. He stared at a perfect face and felt his whole world shine. Shadarii! Kotaru looked across the grass and glimpsed a familiar set of faces. His eyes locked with Tingtraka's, and she jerked with shock.

Far up in the sky Shadarii climbed. The armies dwindled, the air turned still, and the suffering of the battlefield faded far behind. Here, there was nothing but the purity of silence; nothing but the soft caress of Father Wind....

Look! See how beautiful it is! How clean, how wild, how free!

Zhukora shot up from below, her wake blazing a stream of fire. Serpent lunged inside Zhukora's mind and almost screamed in need. *After them! They mustn't have any power. She hasn't flung a single spell!*

Shadarii shot downward like a bolt of flame.

Zhukora pushed her endurance to the limit, ramming power behind her wings as she tried to gain more speed. The ground blurred, and air screamed past Zhukora's ears. She saw her sister's naked back and stretched her spear out for the kill. Her mad eyes were fixed only on a fluttering orange tail.

Suddenly the tail whipped out of sight. Zhukora wrenched her head back, blinking in amazement as her enemy swerved away.

Zhukora, no!

The girl whipped her face around in shock as she plowed into a tree. Wings dissolved in fragments, and she plunged toward the ground. Zhukora tried to blast herself a path. Power blazed out from her flailing hands, and a trail of lightning slashed across Shadarii's wings.

Zhukora blurred to earth and smashed into the soil. Limbs snapped and bones splintered. In a single, horrid instant, Zhukora shattered into ruin.

Shadarii tumbled helplessly in the smoke of her own blazing fur. With a silent scream, she skidded to earth. The woman rolled in agony, one wing blasted to a bloody stump. She staggered to her feet, holding up a hand to keep Tingtraka away.

The Teacher dragged herself toward her sister's shattered body. Ïsha wildly arced into the mud around Zhukora, sizzling as it burned the broken reeds. Shadarii limped closer, pity and revulsion shining in her eyes.

Serpent ripped free from Zhukora and sped toward the swamps, only to be pierced by a blazing shaft of light. Shadarii trapped the creature with her power, and Starshine burst from her hiding place to loop and wheel in victory. The creature laughed. Her mirth soon turned into a shriek of fright as Shadarii blasted her into the sky.

A globe of force crushed the Ka together in a screaming heap. With a mighty flash, the energy stabbed down into an empty skull. The prison was plunged ten thousand spans into the molten earth. Starshine and Serpent screamed a final time before the gates closed behind them with a crash. The two spirits could battle one another to their heart's content, forever buried deep inside the mud.

The little teacher fell down to her hands and knees. She coughed and trembled, ripped by the agony of her severed wing. Ïsha dripped from her soul where she had torn the evil spirit free.

"Zhukora!" Daimïru shot through the air to halt beside Zhukora's shattered body. The girl screamed in pain and held Zhukora's bloody head against her breast. "No! Not her! Take me! Take me instead!" Daimïru rolled mad eyes and stared up at Shadarii. She reached out a bloody hand and pleaded through her tears. "Please! I love her! Please, take me. Don't let her die!"

Shadarii retched in pain. She had caused hurt—she who was sanctified to life. Shadarii dragged herself up to touch Zhukora's broken hand. The Teacher sobbed and opened her soul to the world. The power tore into her own wounds even as it blazed and healed. Light shone forth beneath her hands to fill the world with love.

Daimïru stared as broken bones smoothed beneath Shadarii's touch. A black hand reached to clutch Daimïru's breast. The torn hide healed. The fur regrew. Shadarii flung herself into a sister's pain and made the girl anew.

Zhukora lived, and the evil spirit inside her had been purged.

Shadarii dragged herself away. She tasted blood on her tongue and felt the touch of death.

Zhukora's eyes opened. She stared at the sky and blinked as Daimïru held her, kissing her, adoring her. The blonde warrior wept into Zhukora's face and caressed her with a cloak of golden hair.

Somewhere in the background, something small and fragile scraped across the ground. Zhukora smelled Shadarii's scent and rose from the ground.

"Shadarii!" Zhukora lunged toward her sister.

Daimïru desperately fought to keep her beloved in her arms. "No! Zhukora, stop it! It's over. She's won! She's won!" Zhukora screamed in rage. She marched across the grass only to have Daimïru stumble in her path. "Zhukora, it doesn't have to be! Come away with me. I'll love you forever! I can make you happy!"

Zhukora looked in longing at Daimïru's eyes, but then wrenched her gaze aside. Black hair rippled as the evil figure flowed toward its prey.

Shadarii heard the laugh and dragged breath into her lungs. With one almighty heave, she staggered to her feet. The girl stared about in pain.

A warrior lay on the ground clutching his skull. The little plainswoman healer was frantically dragging him away. Warriors stood watching; sea people, pilgrims. Mrrimïmei nervously fingered her spear....

Zhukora met Shadarii's eyes, and her face lit with a strange emotion. They looked into each others' hearts and finally began to understand.

Zhukora raggedly drew breath and rode the Dream. "So powerful! You're like a god! Could you be the one I need? Could you? Well it's not that easy, Little Sister! You'll have to prove that you are worthy! Fight me! Pull me down. Purify my dream, or die!"

Zhukora snatched a spear from the ground; Shadarii's world dissolved into slow motion as her sister charged. The Silent Lady raised her great, sad eyes and read Zhukora's soul.

So be it. Let us dance the story to its end.

Zhukora's naked body blazed like darkest night; she spread her wings and launched herself toward Shadarii. Her sister charged as well.

The women raced together at blinding speed. Zhukora stabbed her spear for Shadarii's heart, but the wooden haft exploded into life. Flowers bloomed; tendrils writhed. Zhukora gasped and let the spear point gouge into the ground.

The sisters rammed together. Shadarii spun away and crashed into the earth.

Behind her, Zhukora flew above the grass. Her wings folded with agonizing slowness. The broken spear shaft jutted out between her shoulder blades. The girl arched in release and slowly came to rest before the crowds.

There was a long scream of agony. Daimïru rushed to Zhukora's corpse and howled in soul-destroying grief.

Shadarii staggered back and turned away, raising her eyes to meet a gaze deep in the crowd.

Mrrimïmei. The huntress sobbed, her eyes mad-bright with tears.

Shadarii bathed the girl in perfect love. *I forgive you....*

Mrrimïmei gave a sob and hurtled her spear. Shadarii opened her arms as the shaft rammed home. The little teacher sighed and softly laid herself down to die.

"Shadarii!" Tingtraka tore herself from Hupshu's arms and ran to her teacher's side. Kïtashii sobbed and stared in horror at the spear jutting through Shadarii's chest.

Mrrimïmei laughed and stared wildly at the crowd. The smile fell from her face as she saw her husband's eyes. Thousands of faces gazed at her in revulsion. The girl began to shake her head and pull at warrior's hands.

"We're free! I had to do it, don't you understand? Free! She was evil! Anything with power like that must be... Must be..." Her voice faded as she saw the faces of her friends.

Shadarii felt her body die. It was beautiful; an ending to all pain. She rolled her eyes to stare into the sky, gazing up in thanks to Mother Rain.

I will die pure! Poison shall not have me. I have served you with all I have to give.

For the love I shared, I thank you.

For the joy I gave, I thank you.

For-for this release from suffering, I thank you....

It was close. Shadarii waited patiently. She felt her friends around her and was glad.

Someone held her head. There was a smell, a touch, a tone of voice that had so long lived inside her dreams. Shadarii stared up through a mist and gave a loving smile. Kotaru...

He was here, just as had been promised. Mother Rain had blessed her with this final gift. Shadarii lifted a hand to touch a face long lost. She drew him down and kissed him, just as they had upon their one short night of love. She felt his aura twining with her own and was at peace.

I love you Kotaru. I love you...

Kotaru ripped himself free of Shadarii's arms and frantically searched for help. "Harish! Harish, quickly! You have to help her!" His wife stared at him and wept. Kotaru simply didn't understand. He held Shadarii in his arms and screamed out to his wife in agony. "She's dying! She can't die! Don't you understand? Help her!"

Harish sobbed and took a trembling step toward Shadarii "W-who is she? Keketál, who is she?"

"Please! Please! She can't die. Not now!"

Harish reluctantly moved to Shadarii's side. She looked down at the spear jutting through the Teacher's chest. Shadarii's breathing slowed. Her eyes were closed. She could almost have been asleep.

Harish tried to remove the spear. The weapon stuck fast. Totoru pushed the girl aside and bent his massive strength. The bloody shaft slid free. Blood exploded out beneath his hands. It bubbled in Shadarii's lungs and spurted into the air. Where it fell, tiny crimson flowers began to grow.

Harish winced and tried to see the wound. Kitashii used her own hair to mop away the blood. The healer probed into the wound, and then let her hands fall away.

Her husband held the dying woman in his arms; he stroked her brow and stared in horror at Harish's eyes. "What? We have magic! What is it?"

"Keketál, it's gone through her heart! She can't be alive! She just can't. Th-the blood is all still moving. Isha is pushing it. I just don't understand!"

"Help her! Do something!"

"She's already dead! No single creature has the power to heal her! She's only still alive b-because... because you're here..."

Tingtraka looked down at the body stretched out in the mud. Kitashii, Kotaru, and all the others bowed their heads and wept for Shadarii. Everyone had accepted her death, resigned themselves to it! Just like Shadarii; content to let a story come to an end.

The young scholar tore a path toward the Teacher, snatched her shoulders, and dragged her into her grasp. "I won't let you! You're obsessed with creating your own damned myth. Live, you idiot! There's too much work to do!" Tingtraka drew a breath and blazed with light. A shock wave shot through the ground and burst in Tingtraka. She hurtled her soul into Shadarii and willed the girl to live.

Kïtashii threw back her head and gazed at the sky. Ïsha stabbed into her and rammed her back onto the ground. She flung out a hand for support.

Kotaru caught Kïtashii's hand. Harïsh fearfully moved to his side. One by one, a circle formed. Zareemah and her little son, Totoru, and the pilgrims—even the alpine girl Rooshïkii hesitantly came into the ring. A single gap remained beside the creek.

"Get back!"

"Get away from it!"

"Holy skreg!"

Warriors leapt from the riverside as something vast rose from the deeps. Yellow eyes glowed like moons. Grandfather Catfish slowly nosed onto the banks. Ïsha pulsed as his spirit silently joined the ring and fed the flow.

Tingtraka struggled to weld the energy together. She lacked a healer's skill, didn't know what shapes to call into the broken flesh. She turned to Harïsh and locked gazes with her. Harïsh gulped and nodded. Slowly power passed through the sorceress, into the healer's mind.

Harïsh stared at Shadarii in delirious amazement. With one flick of her mind she reached out, felt the woman's heart, and...

...Shadarii lay at her mercy. Keketál loved her, and Harïsh was losing him. The old life had finally returned to tear Harïsh's husband from her arms. She could stop this now, only close her eyes and let it be. But Keketál loved her...

Power blazed into Shadarii's heart. Harïsh wept across the Silent Lady's fur, begging for forgiveness. She wound her hands into Shadarii's hair and cried as though her heart would break.

Shadarii's small black hand rose to stroke Harïsh's hair. The healer pulled away, her hand trailing across Shadarii's breast.

The wound had gone.

Kotaru lifted Shadarii in his arms. He reached down to kiss Harïsh and softly nuzzled her hair. With gentle steps, he bore the Teacher off toward the cool green trees of home.

Kïtashii hesitantly wandered over to Zhukora's resting place.

Daimïru still clung to the corpse, and Zhukora lay at peace beneath soft sheets of golden hair. Daimïru never stirred from her hopeless embrace.

Kïtashii bowed her head and softly laid a hand on Daimïru's back. Rooshïkii joined her as she spoke into the silence.

"Daimïru, you have to let her go. Come with us. We can heal you."

Wind stirred Daimïru's fur.

Kïtashii glanced at Rooshïkii and bowed her head. "D-Daimïru? Please. We shall dance for her, you and I. But now you have to let her go."

"Daimïru?" The little girl reached out her hand and drew away Daimïru's hair.

The warrior was locked in a kiss with Zhukora's open lips. She held her lover tight against herself and lay in peace. The spear joined them forever. Daimïru had deliberately run the blade through her own heart. One last perfect kiss....

Kïtashii let Daimïru's hair spill back down across her face. The girl held Rooshïkii's hand as they wandered off in silence.

One by one, the people turned away. Forest folk and plainsmen wandered side by side, sleepwalkers waking from a dream. They left the battlefield behind, and let the nightmare fade away.

CŞ Ŋ Şɔ

The sun sank toward the far horizon, and crimson shafts of light reached out to brush the clouds. They stained the lagoons with bars of steel and gold. The water made a perfect mirror for the subtle evening stars.

Two lovers lay locked in an embrace, black hair mingling with gold in a harmony of light. They clung together in an act of worship, held together by a bond that even death refused to break.

Deep within the corpses, something soft and beautiful began to stir. Daimïru's fur rippled to the touch of unseen currents. A wild shape stole into the ïsha to dance with delight. The Ka wheeled above its discarded shell, spreading its glorious new wings.

Slowly, hesitantly, another light began to glow. A second Ka crept softly out to join the first—a stream of black beside the other creature's gold. It reached out to its companion, whimpering as it entwined and adored the other.

The black Ka cried. Its companion opened out and offered a treasure to its love. One simple gift; the blessing of forgiveness.

The creatures twined their auras into one. In a sudden blaze of joy, they made love beneath the stars. The spirits mingled in a swirling dance that filled the skies with light, before racing across the grass and wheeling into the sky.

Free!

Together. Always together. Zhukora and Daimïru sped off into the night. With a final peal of laughter, they were gone. The sun sank. The bright stars shone. The Wind and Rain came forth to wash the whole world clean.

Somewhere in the ïsha, a new Dream shone with love.

Epilogue

The leader-elect of the United Tribes paced up and down, considering what he would say in council later that day. A tiny creature followed in Kotaru's wake, wagging dainty yellow wings as he tugged his father's tail. The fuzzy toddler was dressed in miniature leathers just like his father's own. There were moccasins on his tiny feet and fine new leggings for his shins. Kotaru had made the clothes himself, and he felt proud of his handiwork—the first hunting outfit for his son.

His son!

Kotaru still couldn't quite believe it. A child—his child! Small, perfect, and as golden as a buttercup; the very image of his mother. Kokïku-chi[33] was the bright star shining in his father's sky. Kotaru swept his son into his arms and tickled the giggling child across the belly. The diversion lasted for many peaceful minutes.

"Come along, Glorious Leader!" Hupshu-Zha lounged against a tree, picking at his fangs with a straw. The brewer sighed and put out his arms for Kokïku-chi. "We have three hours until council. If we're going hunting, we must hurry!"

Kotaru passed Kokïku over to his friend and gave a little sniff. "I was coming. I merely wished to make sure Kokïku understands. This is his first hunting trip, and he must learn to pay attention."

"Quite. Well, we can tickle his tummy after breakfast." Hupshu hoisted the furry little bundle between his wings. The toddler laughed and clenched his fists in his favorite uncle's hair.

Hupshu looked just fine. Marriage had matured him, and the new wings suited him; they suited everyone! Kotaru stretched his own pinions and felt a stab of guilt. They were an inexcusable vanity for a hunter. The old browns and grays had been easier to hide. Still, a leader was expected to have a bit of color about him. No one wore drab wings anymore.

The caste system had failed, but new hope had arisen with a system of elected officers and chiefs. Zhukora had left her mark upon posterity; there were no social classes anymore. No one cared about clan or tribe—mountain, plain, or sea. Three cultures bloomed and grew beneath the Silent Lady's loving gaze.

"Keketál! There's a hundred jugs of my best beer needed for today. If you don't get a wriggle on, we'll never get them bottled in time. Now, shake your tail or Harïsh will have us both for breakfast!"

Kotaru grumbled and got down on his belly, spears and woomera clattering as he pushed his way beneath the brush. His long tail waggled slowly left to right as he began to search for prey.

Fifty spans away a water hole shone like burnished steel. Cockatoos argued bitterly as they picked the grass for seeds, and a pair of goannas dozed peacefully in the sun. And there, right at the water's edge, sat the prey Kotaru's mouth watered for.

Emu!

---

[33] **Kokïku**: In alpine speech "Two beauties joining." In plains speech, "New Dawn".

The two gigantic birds stalked past the water hole. One bird curled its neck around to stare at Kotaru's bush, mad eyes glaring above a frog-mouthed beak. The creature gave its warning boom, but stood its ground.

Kotaru emerged from the bush and gestured his son over. "Psst! Fluffbucket, what's that down there, eh? There, d'you see? What's that?"

Kokïku-chi seemed far more interested in a butterfly that flew between his father's ears. Kotaru patiently tried again, turning the little two year old toward the prey.

"No, now look, it's time to learn! What d'you see, eh?"

Hupshu kicked his sandals in the dust. "Uh, Keketál? Do you think it might be a bit too soon to teach the boy to hunt? It'll be months before he can even fly."

"It's never too soon to learn. My boy is very bright!"

"Oh, I'm sure."

"Anyway, he flew last week! I saw him. Looked right at me, so he did, and soared out for his papa's arms!"

Hupshu looked at Kokïku in amazement. "Really?"

"Well, actually he landed in the porridge. But he really flew! Almost one whole span!"

Oh, dear Rain! Hupshu rolled his eyes and heaved a patient sigh.

Kokïku waved one tiny hand toward the water hole and frantically began to flap his wings. "Moo-moo!"

Kotaru was ecstatic. "Emu! Did ye hear it? He said emu!"

Kotaru swelled with pride and promenaded up and down before his son. "Pay attention. Your emu has no sense of smell, so there's no need to mask scent like you do with kangaroos. Easy prey! Cooked with herbs and butter, there's nothing like it on this earth." Kotaru passed Kokïku over to his uncle and collected his spears. "You just watch, Kokïku! I'll shoot first, and the second one can be yours."

Emu for supper, and a triumphant entrance through Tingtraka's doors with meat across his back! They could all stare in envy at their elected leader's skill. Kotaru crawled merrily through the bushes, already savoring his evening meal....

j j j

In the early hours of the morning, Kotaru-Keketál came home to a little house beside the forest. The high priestess of the united tribes rose from her door to meet him. Tingtraka had been making bread, and flour dusted her woolen skirt. Still so newly wed to Hupshu that she found each day an adventure, Tingtraka waved her fine new orange wings and gave a smile.

"Harïsh is inside, helping to bottle Hupshu's beer." The woman wiped her face, accidentally streaking flour across her nose. "What's wrong with your tail? Is that an emu bite?"

Kotaru mustered what little dignity remained and tugged his loincloth into place. He carefully lowered his son into Tingtraka's arms. "We've been hunting. Kokïku has brought his hosts a gift of meat. It's never too soon for a man to be learning his responsibilities."

"You've brought us an emu?"

"Um... well, not as such...." Kotaru brought a hand out from behind his back. He held a scrawny goanna, dangling by its tail.

Tingtraka serenely took it from him and laid the meat beside the fire. "She wants to see you. She's in the forest, talking with the Ka."

The man hesitated; Xartha could be heard giggling inside the tree hut, and Tingtraka nodded as he looked into her eyes. "Harïsh knows. It's all right for you to go."

"Did Shadarii say where she would be?"

"She said you'd know how to find her."

Harïsh appeared in the garden, carrying a basket of yams. At eighteen, the girl seemed more beautiful than ever. The white beads of a full surgeon gleamed about her slender throat. Motherhood had brought maturity to her golden eyes. She looked silently toward her husband before giving him a peaceful smile. Harïsh nodded to Kotaru and motioned him on his way.

Kotaru left the village and soared into the forest's hush. The trees reared all around him, steaming as sunshine dried the morning dew. Finches clustered in Kotaru's wake and hoped for an offering of food. The wanderer passed them by and flew toward a tiny silver waterfall—a place where they had eaten crayfish so many lives ago.

Silent Lady waited for him. He could sense her beauty—the breath of peace—long before he saw her orange fur. The little teacher sat beside the waterfall, surrounded by flowers as she looked up at Kotaru and warmed him with her smile.

They sat side by side and watched tadpoles wriggling in the stream. Shadarii's fur gleamed in the filtered light. She turned and looked at him, love shining in her eyes.

I wanted to see you before the council meetings. To give you my blessings and my love. I know you will do us proud.

"You won't be coming?"

No, my place is here.

The woman pursed her lips and called to something deep inside the water. A great black eel rose into her hands. They communicated nose to nose as the creature wagged its tiny fins. Shadarii hoisted the eel around her neck and walked downstream. Kotaru walked beside her as she moved between the ferns.

Shadarii's power and wisdom had grown side by side. When the river had flooded in the spring, the Silent Lady had held back the waters while the people saved their flocks. She came and went as quietly as the summer breeze, spreading her sacred word of peace.

The Silent Lady was not a creature to be trifled with. The people in the new desert villages had learned it to their cost. All through the winter months, they had refused to dig their wells, and when the crops failed, the villagers had wailed for Shadarii's aid. She had come and slowly walked the dusty ground, sowing seeds. Lush green plants instantly sprouted in her wake. The woman had quietly flown away as the villagers slapped each others' backs and cheered.

Their laughter died after their first meal. Shadarii had sown the fields with a crop of budenga plants. The leaves were wholesome, nourishing, and tasted like rancid ear wax.

The villagers had instantly begun work upon their wells. Shadarii had returned and plied a shovel along with all the rest.

Kotaru followed Shadarii down the forest stream. At last, she sank into the ferns above a bathing pool and peered down through a curtain of moss.

Beside the water hole, a pair of girls slowly combed their hair. They made a perfect reflection of each other; one shining silver, and the other gleaming black. At the age of fifteen, Rooshïkii and Kïtashïi were innocently lovely. The two girls sat naked in the water, talking softly back and forth. From time to time they hopefully glanced toward the surrounding trees. Shadarii hefted her pet eel and gave a smile.

They come here every day. Kïtashïi thinks the place is secret.

"What are they doing?"

Discovering something new. Watch.

Long wings flapped as a pair of skinny boys alighted by the rocks. They goggled down at the girls, stars shining in their eyes.

Lord Looshïi's nephews. They, too, are discovering an unexpected side to life....

Kïtashïi artfully posed in the mists, letting water trail down her skinny curves; Rooshïkii rose and stretched. Suddenly, the two girls noticed their admirers and pantomimed their shock. They ducked back into the water, fast enough to preserve their modesty, but not too fast to hide themselves from the boys....

Shadarii quietly unshipped the eel and dropped it in the creek. The creature sped away toward Kïtashïi's rump. The girl had half risen from the water as one boy craned toward her for a kiss. Their mouths parted, almost close enough to touch....

Shadarii ambled back upstream, her hands clasped behind her tail.

At the swimming hole, female voices raised a sudden squeal of fright.

Shadarii slitted her lashes and wandered on her way. *It's good for my disciples to discover wondrous things. But some discoveries should wait until they gain a few more years....*

Kotaru reached out to hold Shadarii's hand. She slowly closed her eyes. Her ïsha aura swirled as her face grew sad and wan. The tall hunter turned and looked at her in sorrow. "Are you happy, Shadarii? Is this life truly what you want?"

Yes. There is joy here, Kotaru. A majesty and a love that I can share. The mission and the burden never ends. She looked up at him with eyes as deep as forest pools. *I am the Silent Lady: The Shining One. The life I once wanted with you can no longer be. I shall not age, Kotaru, and my work shall never end. You deserve the gifts that only Harïsh can give to you. I cannot allow myself to threaten that happiness. Your joy shall always be my own.*

"You are wise, Shadarii."

No, not yet. But with the blessing of the Rain, perhaps I can one day hope to be. You are the leader of the united race, Kotaru. You will need Harïsh's strength. Kiss the baby for me, and give them both my love.

They walked to the edges of the forest, and stopped to stand high above a whole new world. Below them, plains and forest now lived in harmony. Sea peoples worked side by side with alpine gardeners and shepherd girls. Shadarii looked across the scene and sighed.

My poor Zhukora. To remake the world, she first had to destroy it. She knew how her dance must end. Without her courage, none of this would ever have been possible.

Kotaru looked around in shock. "Zhukora? Zhukora was mad!"

No. She knew exactly what she was doing. The crimes the forest folk committed were done wholly in her name. She took all the guilt into herself; a guilt that needed to be purged if the world was to become whole. To complete her dream, she needed to perform a final act. Zhukora needed to die. Tears stood in Shadarii's eyes. *She died to purge the people's sins, Kotaru. Now it is my task to keep her dream and make it real. One world, one race—peace and wisdom everlasting. The plains, seas, and forests shall be as one. I shall mourn Zhukora's death forever.*

A bell boomed out to call the leaders into council. Kotaru turned to his companion and looked into her eyes. "Are you sure you won't come to the meeting? You know you are welcome. You are loved, Shadarii."

No, I am going to help to thatch Mrrimïmei's new roof today. It will be a surprise for her and Totoru when they return. The woman reached out to hold Kotaru's hands. *I cannot interfere with your lives, Kotaru. Go to your meeting and make good laws. I know that you will serve the Kashra well.*

Behind them the great bell rang once more, and Kotaru turned to go. He looked back to see her standing on the rocks above him, the wind streaming through her hair. The forest spread about her as she gazed into his heart.

May Rain wash you and Wind caress you. May peace and wisdom shine forever in your soul. My love for you is as endless as the oceans and as boundless as the skies. Know always that I am yours. Go in happiness, my darling. May you always dwell with love.

A rainbow spread its light behind Shadarii.

Kotaru-Keketál wandered onward to bring life into a dream.

Far above, the Silent Lady smiled. She watched over him until he passed beyond mere mortal view.

ALPINE TRIBES (KATAKANII)

PLAINS TRIBES (PAINTED ZEBEDII)

PLAINS TRIBES (OCHITZLI)

ALPINE JITENG PLAYER & PRIEST

SEA PEOPLE (HESHETANII)

Glossary

Alpine tribes Hunter-gatherers living in the alpine forests. A profoundly rich culture is shared by several related tribes. Alpine tribes can smelt iron, but iron is a rare commodity for most tribes. The arts of brewing, cloth weaving and farming are unknown to them.

Armor Alpine armor is made of hard wood, consisting of a mask, helmet, shin and arm guards, with a cuirass. Plains folk armor is made from densely woven textiles.

Bellbird Small green birds that live around freshwater creeks and waterholes. They constantly peal out a single pure note, making the entire forest seem to ring with chimes.

Bogong moth Large moths that swarm in the millions for a few days in each year. The moths always return to caves in the mountains, where they form a vital food source for alpine tribes. The bogong moths are so valuable that sharing their meat is an important time for intermingling of tribes. High in protein and fat, the moths are usually toasted over fire and eaten like nuts.

Budenga plant A nutritious food plant with an extremely disagreeable taste.

Cassawarry An aggressive, flightless bird, emu sized, sporting a large horny growth on its head. Found in Northern forests and hunted by distant bands of Zebedii.

Chi Suffix denoting 'beloved' or 'child' when attached to a proper name (Sea Peoples dialect).

Cowrie shells Small, beautiful sea shells much valued by the Sea Peoples.

Dao The iron axe/knife of the alpine peoples. A machete-like blade mounted on a haft the same length as the blade. Used as a utility tool, it is also deadly in combat. In battle, the weapons are often used in pairs.

Dingo Native dog, found only in plains areas. A mammal - not a marsupial.

Echidna Spiny anteaters common in alpine and plains areas. Long nosed and gentle egg-laying monotremes.

Emu Large, flightless bird, slightly smaller than an ostrich. Curious and rather tasty.

Face masks Used in Alpine religious ceremonies and jiteng. The wearer takes on part of the Ka of the being represented by the mask.

Fire The fire spirit is a mythic being, part of the Kashran pantheon. A trickster and a plotter, both dangerous and useful.

First folk Legendary precursors of the modern Kashra.

First Mother In Kashranii mythology, First Mother is the daughter of Father Wind and Mother Rain, and is the mother of the entire Kashran race.

Fist Alpine term for the number 20.

Frogmouth Broad-mouthed nocturnal hunting bird, expertly camouflaged to look like a broken piece of wood while asleep.

Goanna Large monitor lizard - fast running, high climbing, deep burrowing – and edible. The largest subspecies grow 7 feet long and can run at great speed.

Grevillia Flowering spiky bush much valued for flavoring tea.

Gum tree Any eucalyptus tree. These are the dominant tree species for all environments. Tall, straight trees are common to alpine areas Broad, spreading variants are found upon the plains. All gum trees are flowering.

Harapa Plains tribe.

Hatchling A baby Kashra, incapable of flight.

Healers	A Doctor/Surgeon caste found in plains cultures. Healers tattoo the palms of their hands as a symbol of their calling.
Heshetanii	Peoples of the Sea.
Hohematii	An Alpine tribe.
Huntsman spider	Sporrasids. Hate 'em? Guess you have to...
Isha	The energy generated by spirits. Isha forms currents, streams and rivers that can be ridden upon or used in "magic". Isha only exists in areas inhabited by spirits, and so deserts, etc., are very poor in "magical" energy. Particularly powerful Ka (spirits) can self-generate considerable amounts of power.
Jiteng	A ritual field game played by alpine tribes - intended to siphon off aggression amongst the young. The tactics and techniques are perfect training for warfare, and are clearly based upon folk memories of combat.
Ka	Spirit. All living beings have a spirit. Upon physical death, the ka remains – sometimes departing to a spirit plane, or other times remaining in the physical word, to inhabit rocks, streams, waterfalls, etc.
Kai	Suffix formally denoting "descent from/belonging to" – used rarely. (E.g. "Shadarii-kai-Nochorku-Zha", which is "Shadarii of the house of the revered Nochorku").
Kana	Suffix denoting master of a trade, elder or priest (plains dialect).
Kashra	A race of butterfly-winged, furred humanoids (c. 5 feet tall). The name is common to all Kashranii dialects, and derives from the words "Children of love" or "beloved offspring". All Kashran mythologies believe the Kashra to be descended from a single other – herself the direct creation of the Father Wind and Mother Rain. Kashra are egg laying mammals (not monotremes) capable of sensing and sculpting the "isha" energy generated by spirits. Kashra can fly by channeling isha through their wings.
Katakanii	Alpine tribe - the most wealthy in terms of iron resources.
Keketál	"Rivers gift" (Plains dialect).
Kha	Suffix denoting rank (Sea Peoples dialect).
Ki	Suffix used to denote a child, derived from "Kiaki" – "to treasure" (Alpine dialect).
Kokïku	In Alpine dialect, "Two Beauties Joining". In Plains dialect, "New Dawn".
Ksatra	A heron (Alpine dialect).
Lodge	(Alpine) - A tree house used as living quarters, always paired with a lean-to at the base of the parent tree. Cooking and food preparation are performed at ground level in the lean-to.
	(Plains) Sturdy family houses made of mud-brick and wood. A household Ka usually resides in the rafters or the hearth.
Lorikeet	Small multi-colored parrot – cheeky, happy-go-lucky, and utterly inedible. (Kashranii recipe for boiled lorikeet: place lorikeet in pot with stone. Cover with water. Boil until stone is tender. Discard lorikeet - eat stone...)
Message sticks	(Alpine) – a long stick whose notches are used as a mnemonic aid in remembering messages by rote.
Milk-mead	A fermented drink which allows regrown wings to take on the brilliant colors associated with nobility. Drunk only at the toteniiha ceremony.
Monsteria	Rare, large leaved plants highly prized for their delicious fruits, which ripen only once every few years.
Mrrimïmei	"Happy Accident" (Alpine dialect)
Music sticks	(Alpine) – a long stick cut with symbols which records a musical composition.

Numbat	Small insectivore - furry, stripy and funny looking.
Ochitzlii	Plains tribe.
Oita	A spear-like, wide-bladed weapon resembling a long staff tipped with an obsidian-edged blade. Developed from boat paddles used by the Zebedii.
Pastholders	The dancers of an alpine tribe. These individuals preserve tribal history and myth through ritual dance.
Paperbark	A tree with soft white bark much prized as a material for painting upon. The tips of new green leaves are a powerful decongestant and antiseptic.
Plains tribes	Sedentary herding peoples living in river plains. Plains folk have domesticated the sheep and the dog, can weave wool, smelt copper, and use potters wheels.
Platypus	Quiet, duck billed, aquatic monotremes.
Poison root	One of many tubers used by alpine tribes to catch fish and small game by poisoning waterholes. The technique is officially forbidden.
Possum	A term referring to any of a group of Australasian possum species such as brushtail, ringtail, feather glider and sugar glider.
Quirt	(Plains people) – A knotted chord used as a mnemonic aid when remembering messages by rote.
Rain	Mother Rain is one of the two progenitor deities who gave birth to the Kashranii race. Rain is purportedly wedded to Father Wind.
Reki'ka	Ghost dance. A grieving ceremony which can sometimes involve the shedding of blood as a sign of woe.
Seance singer	(Plains People) – The tribe member responsible for dream interpretation and spirit communion.
Sea Peoples	Tribes of the coastal plains. Rich resources and a warm climate have led these tribes to wear little in the way of garments. Fish, wild grains and wild plant life form the basis of their diet. Their boats are small, and they never venture out of sight of the shore.
Silent Lady	Shadarii
Skreg	Any unidentifiable gluey / sticky mass found stuck on the bottom of a foot or moccasin.
Sling	Simple cords and pouches used to project stones with great range and force. Often worn as headbands by shepherds of the plains people. Marksmen might wear three different slings of different sizes, each optimized for firing at a different range.
Slingstone	Stone projectile used in a sling. Often made more aerodynamic by coating in baked ceramics. Size varies from the size of two balled fingers to the size of a large hen's egg.
Spear	Alpine spears are usually extremely long – 9 feet being typical. Length increases range and accuracy. A hunter typically carries 2 to 4 spears. Iron tipped spears are rare except within the Katakanii tribe. The most prized weapons often contain ka spirits (often the spirits of predatory animals) which are capable of homing in on moving targets and defeating magical shields. The long, slim spears make poor close combat weapons; in hand to hand combat, an Alpine warrior would usually switch to a pair of dao.
Span	Unit of measurement. One kashranii wingspan (usually c.7 feet).
Spinifex	A thick brush plant growing in dense blankets on coastal plains. Harbors a great many small animals such as hopping mice, superb blue wrens etc.
Superb blue wren	Tiny wrens common in most regions. Mouse sized, the males are brilliant royal blues.
Swoop	Measure of distance. A fist of fist of spans (circa 2800 yards).

Tail	Unit of measurement. The length of a kashran tail (usually 3 feet). A spear is usually 3 tails long.
Taipan	The most deadly of all snakes. Can reputedly chew through stone.
Takoonii	Plains tribe
Totenïha	The yearly wing shedding ceremony practiced by alpine peoples. The entire tribe gathers together in ceremonial dance and feasting. During the time that they are wingless, there is less to distinguish noble from commoner, and ïsha-powered flight is not possible.
Tea	(Alpine) – An infusion made from caffeine-rich leaves of local herbs.
Toka	Suffix denoting an adult villager (plains dialect).
Treefern	Giant Eastern Australian Treefern. Typical variants grow from 1 ft to 12 ft in height, with an umbrella some 8 to 12 feet wide. Some subspecies reach up to 50 feet tall.
Urushii	Alpine Tribe.
Vakïdurii	Alpine Tribe.
Vampire ka	A rogue ka spirit that attacks other spirits, living and dead, to steal their life energy.
Wattle trees	The dominant small tree of the alpine and plains regions is the wattle. Wattles flower a brilliant yellow, literally foaming with blossom, different subspecies staggering their flowering seasons to cover the end of winter, spring and the beginning of summer. Wattle trees are host to wichetti grubs and other food insects.
Wichetti grubs	Long wood-boring larvae of the wichetti moth, considered a delicacy by alpine tribes. Highly nutritious. Eaten raw or fried.
Wind	Father Wind is one of the two deities who founded the world and created Zui-Kashra-Zha. Father to the First Mother of the Kashra, he is husband to the Rain.
Wing shedding	Yearly loss of Kashran wings. Wings are regrown, the process taking several days. During the wingless period, ïsha-powered flight is not possible.
Woomera	Spear thrower. A length of wood used as a lever when throwing a spear, greatly increasing range and power. Even when tipped with fire-hardened wood rather than metal, alpine spears are capable of penetrating clean through saplings.
Yabbie	Freshwater crayfish.
Yukanii	Plains tribe.
Zebedii	The "painted Zebedii" are a plains-dwelling tribe living in wetlands. Floating villages are combined with aquatic agriculture to make for a thriving people. More primitive than other plains tribes, the Zebedii eat frogs, cultivate fish and water grains, and are considered by other tribes to be boisterous and barely civilized. Their fur is usually dyed into bizarre patterns according to individual taste, making Zebedii extremely colorful to behold.
Zha	Suffix indicating reverence, and used to denote chiefs, kings and sacred persons (Alpine dialect).
Zho	"Honored folk". Suffix denoting nobility (Alpine dialect). Only nobles have colored wings.
Zui-kashra-zha	The First Mother. Child of the Wind and Rain, mother of the Kashranii race.

VISION NOVELS

Look for us on the World Wide Web at: http://vision.nais.com

ꆮꜳꝇꬲꙅ Oꝫ ꝫꞕꬲ ꭑoꝛꝻꭘꭘꝪꙅꝫ

A stunning new Shared-World by two of the greatest Shared-World
Creators in recent Literary History -- Lynn Abbey (Thieves' World)
and Ed Greenwood (Forgotten Realms)!

Book One: THE RATS OF ACOMAR, By Paul Kidd
Book Two: FLYING COLORS, By Jeff Grubb
Book Three: THOSE WHO HUNT, By Elaine Cunningham
Book Four: UNICORN'S GATE, By Mary Herbert

A WHISPER OF WINGS
Paul Kidd
ISBN 1-887038-04-3

An epic, shattering story of power and love, of betrayal and sorrow. Of war, hatred,
rage and destiny. It is a story that will stay with you forever. Lavishly illustrated
with 20 interior plates by the acclaimed artist Terrie Smith, it is one of
Vision's most beautiful works ever. Over 400 Pages.

SWEET TREATS
Dessert Recipes from the Kitchen of Marsha Redfox
Margaret Carspecken
ISBN 1-887038-02-7

128 full-color pages of delightful dessert recipes from the kitchen of Marsha
Redfox -- illustrated by the incomparable Margaret Carspecken! The sweet,
cartoon fox character of Marsha Redfox takes you on a culinary tour of the
world, dressing up in ethnic costume for each! This book features dozens and
dozens of Margaret's beautiful watercolors, most of which have sold at art
shows and conventions for hundreds of dollars. Sweet Treats is a delightful
book for young and old chefs alike, year 'round. The artwork is appealing
and bright, the recipes simply scrumptious, the book itself made to last a
lifetime, printed on heavy, glossy, coated pages.
FIVE STAR AMAZON.COM CUSTOMER RATING!

BLOOD MEMORIES
Barb Hendee
ISBN 1-887038-06-X

Set in Seattle, Blood Memories takes you deep into a world of Vampires.
Hidden from sight, living among us, they have fed on our blood and lives
for thousands of years. Yet, as times have progressed, the Mortals
are becoming increasingly difficult to fool...

THE AMERICAN JOURNAL OF ANTHROPOMORPHICS
ISBN 1-887038-01-9

BOOK FOUR
Like its three predecessors, this volume of the Journal features great artwork
by some of the very top-ranked artists in the genre, from all over the world.
As always, the Journal features direct contact info for all listed artists, plus
their fixed rates for doing artwork (when available).

Printed on heavy, 70-pound offset bond and perfect-bound inside a coated C1S
cover, the Journal is a book made to last for many years. A wonderful
addition to anyone's collection or coffee table.

LIMITED-EDITION FRAMED PRINTS

THREE AMAZING, BEAUTIFUL PIECES OF
SHADARII, ZHUKHORA AND DAIMIRU
FROM PAUL KIDD'S EPIC NOVEL,
A WHISPER OF WINGS,
EACH IN FULL, BREATHTAKING COLOR,
AVAILABLE IN FOUR DIFFERENT STYLES.

SEE THE NEXT PAGE FOR DETAILS!

"SHADARII BY THE
WATERFALL".
AN EXQUISITELY AND
LOVINGLY DETAILED
WORK BY THE HIGHLY
RENOWNED ARTIST
TERRIE SMITH.

"THE RESCUE OF
DAIMIRU".
THIS PIECE BY TERRIE
SMITH WAS DIGITALLY
PAINTED TO A VERY
HIGH LEVEL OF DETAIL.
RECOMMENDED!

"THE KNIFE DANCE".
FROM AN ORIGINAL PAINTING BY TERRIE SMITH.

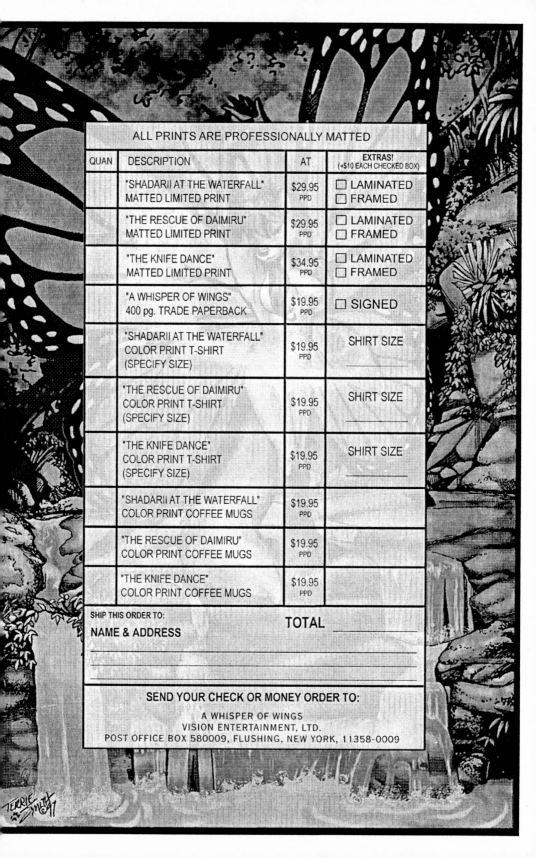

ALL PRINTS ARE PROFESSIONALLY MATTED

QUAN	DESCRIPTION	AT	EXTRAS! (+$10 EACH CHECKED BOX)
	"SHADARII AT THE WATERFALL" MATTED LIMITED PRINT	$29.95 PPD	☐ LAMINATED ☐ FRAMED
	"THE RESCUE OF DAIMIRU" MATTED LIMITED PRINT	$29.95 PPD	☐ LAMINATED ☐ FRAMED
	"THE KNIFE DANCE" MATTED LIMITED PRINT	$34.95 PPD	☐ LAMINATED ☐ FRAMED
	"A WHISPER OF WINGS" 400 pg. TRADE PAPERBACK	$19.95 PPD	☐ SIGNED
	"SHADARII AT THE WATERFALL" COLOR PRINT T-SHIRT (SPECIFY SIZE)	$19.95 PPD	SHIRT SIZE _____
	"THE RESCUE OF DAIMIRU" COLOR PRINT T-SHIRT (SPECIFY SIZE)	$19.95 PPD	SHIRT SIZE _____
	"THE KNIFE DANCE" COLOR PRINT T-SHIRT (SPECIFY SIZE)	$19.95 PPD	SHIRT SIZE _____
	"SHADARII AT THE WATERFALL" COLOR PRINT COFFEE MUGS	$19.95 PPD	
	"THE RESCUE OF DAIMIRU" COLOR PRINT COFFEE MUGS	$19.95 PPD	
	"THE KNIFE DANCE" COLOR PRINT COFFEE MUGS	$19.95 PPD	

SHIP THIS ORDER TO:

NAME & ADDRESS

TOTAL _____

_____

_____

_____

SEND YOUR CHECK OR MONEY ORDER TO:

A WHISPER OF WINGS
VISION ENTERTAINMENT, LTD.
POST OFFICE BOX 580009, FLUSHING, NEW YORK, 11358-0009

ART FROM PAUL KIDD'S NEXT BOOK, "THE RATS OF ACOMAR"

A Word from the Publisher

We hope you enjoyed this book as much as we enjoyed preparing it for you. No expense was spared in its production, from its illustration to its printing and binding. We hope that this book will find a home on your shelves for many years to come, to be taken down and enjoyed time and again.

Our goal is to provide you, our customers, the very best value for your dollar. This means from cover to content – we try to make sure Vision novels are worth every penny. We hark back to an earlier era, to those halcyon days when books were wonderfully illustrated, their stories lush and breathtaking. We hope to bring back a little of those days in our works.

Our next series to be launched will be "**Tales from the Mornmist**", a simply delightful shared-world created by two of the most popular masters of shared-world Fantasy, Lynn Abbey (creator of the Thieves' World Series) and Ed Greenwood (creator of TSR's best-selling Forgotten Realms Series). Paul Kidd, the author of this book, has the honor of leading the new series to market, with its first book – "**The Rats of Acomar**". A breathtaking, swashbuckling tale of discovery, terror and triumph, it well deserves its place at the head of the new series. Having worked diligently for over a year producing and perfecting this new series, we wholeheartedly recommend it, from top to bottom. Spread the word, if you can!

Thank you very much for being a part of things, and we look forward to seeing you again as you enjoy our upcoming works!

We have a lot of fantastic things planned for the future. If you like, you can send us a SASE below for a free copy of our catalog and news bulletin. Or, you can get the same information right away, on the Internet, at our Web address below.

Darrell Benvenuto, Publisher

Vision Entertainment
Post Office Box 580009
Flushing NY 11358-0009

http://vision.nais.com

contact@vision.nais.com

Printed in the United States
44832LVS00004B/179

9 781887 038041